Praise for *The*

"**What a feast** Woody Woodb
very special Table of tables. Fu .... and
turns, I had to strap myself into my chair! What a tale, **what a treasure**, what a time!"

—TAVIS SMILEY, broadcaster and author

"*The Butterfly Tree* will keep you engaged from the first page to the very last. **It's an emotional must-read** you won't want to put down."

—RHIANNON POTKEY, journalist

"Woody Woodburn is one of the great observers of life. Besides his **powerful prose and profound insights,** Mr. Woodburn reaches deep into the heart and soul of his readers. His positive outlook on the human experience is contagious and **fills the heart with an enduring love for life!**"

—BARRY KIBRICK, PBS "Between the Lines" host

"The **page-turning storytelling** takes the reader on a journey through life's joys and the tribulations faced along the way, from one generation to the next. *The Butterfly Tree* **will remind you what's most important in life.**"

—JEFFREY DRANSFELDT, journalist

"**Masterfully woven,** this epic novel is **a literary triumph!** At its heart lies a seemingly ordinary Table, yet through each generation, it becomes not only a silent witness to **the complex tapestry of human connections**, but serves as the cornerstone that binds us across time."

—CONNIE HALPERN, Mrs. Figs' Bookworm

The Butterfly Tree

An Extraordinary Saga of Seven Generations

a novel

The Butterfly Tree

An Extraordinary Saga of Seven Generations

a novel

WOODY WOODBURN

Published by

BarkingBoxer Press

The Future of Sports Fiction

The Butterfly Tree / by Woody Woodburn — 1 ed.
Published in the USA by BarkingBoxer Press LLC
Sheridan, Wyoming

© 2024 by Woody Woodburn
Cover Design © 2024 by BarkingBoxer Press LLC
Graphic Design Artist © 2024 by Bianca Blasquez
Interior Design © 2024 by BarkingBoxer Press LLC
Author Photograph by Scott Soens
First Printing, 2024

Issued in print and electronic formats
ISBN 978-3-9822801-8-9 (pbk)
ISBN 978-3-9822801-9-6 (ebook)

FIC008000   FICTION / Sagas
FIC038000   FICTION / Sports
FIC045020   FICTION / Family Life / Siblings

This story is dedicated to trees lovelier than poems——
——and to my family and friends lovelier than trees

*"We delight in the beauty of the butterfly but rarely admit
the changes it has gone through to achieve that beauty."*

—Maya Angelou

——and to everyone going through their own beautiful
metamorphosis towards a higher calling.

"There are times when wisdom cannot be found in the chambers of parliament or the halls of academia but at the unpretentious setting of the kitchen table."

—E.A. Bucchianeri, American author

"In every deliberation, we must consider the impact on the seventh generation...even if it requires having skin as thick as the bark of a pine."

—Indigenous American Iroquois wisdom

If a person desires a wish to come true, it is wise to capture— and gently so—a butterfly and then whisper the wish as one would a prayer. This wish will remain secret, for the butterfly can make no sound to reveal it to anyone. After making the wish, the wisher must release the butterfly unharmed. In gratitude for giving this beautiful creature of flight its freedom, The Great Spirit will grant the wish. At a wedding, it is wise to release many butterflies in order that the wishes made by those in attendance for the happy couple will be flown heavenwards to The Great Spirit and all will be granted.

—Native Peoples Butterfly Legend

STEAL AWAY

Steal away, steal away,
Oh, Lord, oh
Steal away to Jesus!
Steal away, steal away home,
I ain't got long to stay here.

Steal away, steal away,
Hallelujah,
Steal away to Jesus!
My Lord, my Lord calls me,
He calls me by Thunder!
The trumpet sounds within my soul,
I ain't got long to stay here.

Green trees are bending,
Poor sinners stand a trembling.
The trumpet sounds within my soul,
I ain't got long to stay here.
My Lord, my Lord calls me,
He calls me with Lightning!
The trumpet sounds within my soul,
I ain't got long to stay here.
Steal away!

—Slave spiritual communicating in song that a person was planning to escape on The Underground Railroad

Things Turn Dicey

Ka-BOOM!

Thunder exploded, its volume deafening, its lightning flash brilliant as the Biblical bolt that blinded Saul, shooting down from the heavens with the earthshaking power of a million hatchet blows. The blade of electricity cleaved The Black Walnut Tree as effortlessly as a honed hunting knife slicing a stalk of celery.

A life of 231 years ended in a split-second.

The regal tree was sliced cleanly in two, from leafy crown to grassy ground, the splayed halves as identical as a left and right hand. The newly exposed surfaces seemed as if a master cabinetmaker had spent endless hours sanding, varnishing, buffing.

In death The Black Walnut Tree had been a lifesaver, shielding a clan of Roma migrants from being lanced by the thunderbolt. The ensemble, encamped along the riverbank in March 1852, had sought shelter beneath the tree's colossus canopy—most importantly, Aisha Beswick, who was in labor with her first child. Huddled alongside Tamás, the expectant father, was Dika, Aisha's mother and a revered fortuneteller.

Half an hour before the fateful lighting strike, as moody clouds roiled ominously darker, darker, closer, closer, Dika bemoaned, on the edge of weeping: "The peril is great for Aisha and the baby. We must fetch a doctor or they shall both die, this I know."

Without hesitation, Hanzi volunteered for the emergency errand. The teenager, as if a descendant of the wing-footed Greek messenger god Hermes, raced two miles to town with such swiftness that the falling raindrops seemed to miss him. At the first house he came upon with a lighted window, panting for breath, he rapped on the front door.

"Where does"—*breathe*—"a doctor"—*breathe*—"live?" Hanzi asked. "It's"—*breathe*—"an emer"—*breathe*—"gency!"

Anyone in Bellaire could have offered directions, because everyone knew "Doc" Lemuel Jamison—the only physician in town.

"One block straight ahead, then right three blocks," Hanzi was told. "You'll know it's Doc's house by the ugliest front door you've ever set eyes upon."

Hanzi found the street quickly and identified the house easily, for the top edge of Doc's door was so uneven that light seeped out, eerily illuminating spider-web-cracked paint and a bronze lion's head doorknocker dangling askew.

In one soaring stride Hanzi vaulted all four stairsteps onto the porch, then pounded on the eyesore entry—*Bam!-Bam!!-Bam!!!*—with such adrenaline-fueled force he bruised the heel of his hand.

~~~

Aisha's contractions became more frequent, more fierce, more worrisome.

The apocalyptic sky was having its own contractions, three-hundred-million-volt flashes of lightning followed by deafening whipcracks.

"Oh, Lord, please watch over my child," Dika said softly, head bowed, "and keep safe my precious grandbaby."

Dika's prayers seemed suddenly answered with Doc's hasty arrival, but just as he set down his medical bag—

—*Ka-BOOM!*

The fateful thunderbolt smote The Black Walnut Tree like a mighty swing of Paul Bunyan's giant axe. Miraculously, no one was killed by the lightning strike, nor injured by the falling twin timbers. All, however, were dumbstruck with fright. All, except Doc.

"Gentlemen, I need you to hold a blanket overhead—like a tent," Doc calmly directed the gathering. "We want to keep our expectant mother here as dry and comfortable as possible."

As this was being done, Doc removed his raincoat and favorite derby hat, dropped to one knee, went to work.

Another wave of contractions washed over Aisha and she wailed loud as a thunderclap.

"Omen bad," Dika sobbed, staring at the felled tree halves. "Two sunrises this poor child will not live to see."

Not a believer in prophecies, Doc was deeply concerned nonetheless. His heart raced like Hanzi's feet had for this was the first baby—the very first—Dr. Lemuel Jamison would endeavor to deliver *all by himself.*

Only two weeks earlier, Doc had completed a nine-month obstetrics internship at Cincinnati's Commercial Hospital that was affiliated with The Medical College of Ohio from which he graduated top of his class.

During his internship, Doc delivered countless babies. Always, however, there had been an experienced obstetrician by his side, ready to help—or take over fully—if things turned dicey.

Things were dicey now. And about to turn dicier.

A Vision

The day arrived when Lemuel crafted the most beautiful Table imaginable.

To consummate the task, whistle-humming softly as was his habit when deeply lost in woodworking concentration, he applied two parts beeswax, one part linseed oil, and three measures of elbow grease—just as his father Tamás had taught him.

Like a glassy pond reflecting luminous moonbeams and starlight, the Table's surface shone. The wood's tight grain reminded Lem of a master artist's brushstrokes as he dragged his fingertips softly across the godly wooden canvas. His touch lingered to admire, and trace, a lovely butterfly-shaped knot at the Table's center.

Fatigue from his labor took hold and Lemuel gently rested his forehead on The Butterfly Table. Into daydream he drifted, slipped into sleep, then fell down a rabbit hole. In this wonderland Lem was greeted by visions of the future—a few years ahead, perhaps many generations, he was unsure.

Lem did not recognize these visitants, yet strongly felt them to be family. Some scenes seemed like his own foggy memories that had not yet happened.

To begin, he saw a chestnut-haired girl seated at a table—at *this* Table—writing. She looked sad. No, it was beyond that—Lem could *feel* she planned to take her own life. At once, he tried to speak, talk sense to her, but no words exited. Urgently, he screamed—*Stop! Please don't kill yourself! Nothing is that bad!*—but Lem's voice remained muted even as his lips moved.

Despite his breathless silence, the girl suddenly looked up as if she heard him. She stood and, a hint of a close-lipped smile escaping, walked away. A wave of hopeful relief washed over Lem.

His gladness was short-lived, however, for no sooner had the girl disappeared when a teenaged boy materialized. As with the dream girl, Lem sensed a whirlpool sucking the boy down down down into emotional darkness.

"I can't—go on—living," he sobbed, gasping sharply for air between short bursts of words. "I'm like scissors—missing one of—the blades—with my twin brother—"

His heaving breaths came rapidly now, jerkily, four or five in a row, like a reverse stutter, like gunfire.

"—dead."

The tearful boy climbed atop the Table, raised on tiptoe, knotted a rope around an overhead beam, and next fashioned a noose. As with the dream girl, Lem shouted to the boy. As before, his tongue was muted.

At that very moment, a moment that would change every moment to follow, a gentle voice came. But it was not Lem's. Impossibly, it was The Butterfly Table that spoke: *Keep trying, Lemuel. You mustn't give up. Speak to the troubled boy. Calm him—save him.*

But it was no use. No matter how loudly he tried to yell, Lem remained as voiceless as a shadow.

Standing on the Table, the boy took a moment, a moment, a moment reliving cherished memories. Images of parents and friends, and a twin brother, flashed before the boy's—and Lemuel's—eyes.

More images rolled by, the Table appearing in each and all: people eating, talking, laughing; Thanksgivings and Christmases and other occasions of birdsong in the heart; a woman sewing a quilt, a young man studying textbooks, a tiger—a real, roaring, full-grown tiger!—leaping onto the Table; two lovers, a baby's birth, the death of an old man.

The parade of memories dissolved like incense smoke in a wind gust, replaced by the boy coming back into focus standing on the Table. Again Lemuel tried to speak. Again he was mute as a tombstone, the Table collapsing into an abyss, the boy vanishing into vapor.

Lem witnessed one final scene. A young man, alone in a cemetery, stooped to pick up a small stone—shiny and flat and round as a silver dollar, albeit thicker—and resumed walking. Arriving at his destination, the man reverently balanced the earthly coin atop a modest headstone.

Lemuel squinted, trying to make out the name on the grave marker, but it was shrouded by thick frost. Just as the man began to brush the engraved letters and date clear, Lem awakened with a chilling shudder.

He feared the headstone was his—or Jamis's.

Against All Odds

In early autumn of 1620, as the twenty-ninth sunrise of September yawned itself awake, a fox squirrel scooped up a fallen black walnut, paused nervously scanning the landscape for imminent danger, then skittered off.

Nearby, a buckeye tree grew a stone's throw—by a strong and able arm—from the western bank of the Ohio River. Before reaching the safe haven of its den inside the buckeye's trunk, the fox squirrel was mugged by a raccoon. Despite being the largest species of tree squirrel native to North America, the two-pound fox squirrel was little match for the ring-tailed bandit outweighing it nearly tenfold. During the brief scuffle the fox squirrel lost a few tufts of orangish-grey fur—

—and the black walnut.

Nearly three thousand miles east, a merchant ship with three masts tall as treetops had set sail for The New World from the Port of Southampton on the south coast of England. Midway into its long and hazardous voyage, at the very moment the black walnut slipped from the fox squirrel's grasp, passenger John Howland slipped overboard as the Mayflower was pounded by a ferocious storm and tossed about by enraged waves.

Black walnut is one of the most beautiful hardwoods in all of nature, valued especially for furniture, gunstocks, and canoe paddles. English White Oak, however, is superior for shipbuilding. Also known as Royal Oak, these grandiose trees can grow a towering 150 feet tall, even surpassing this under ideal conditions, with trunks exceeding thirty feet in circumference. Of such Royal timbers was the noble Mayflower built.

Measuring roughly one hundred feet long and twenty-five feet wide, the Mayflower had 102 English Puritan passengers shoehorned within its dank cargo hold, plus thirty crewmen aboard deck. The sixty-six days at sea en route to arriving at Plymouth Rock on December 21 were as perilous as they were cramped. Midway, seeking respite from the claustrophobic conditions below, John Howland ventured up to the outdoor deck.

It is remarkable how far the concentric ripples made by one single cast stone—or by one individual person—can travel. Howland's ripples extended out out out throughout American history. In fact, future world events hung on the lone strand of rope that, against all hope and impossible odds, he managed to grab hold of after falling overboard.

Ripples. Howland, a twenty-eight-year-old indentured servant who would one day become a freeman, was thus rescued from the frigid Atlantic waters and completed the consequential journey to America; was in turn one of only fifty-one Pilgrims to survive the first winter of illness and starvation; and ultimately had more descendants than any of his fellow passengers. This is no insignificant ripple because today, four centuries thereafter, it is estimated more than thirty million people have Mayflower roots.

John Howland's linear descendants include United States presidents Franklin Delano Roosevelt, George Herbert Walker Bush, and George Walker Bush. Literature's Henry Wadsworth Longfellow and Ralph

Waldo Emerson also shared Howland's genealogy. None of these famous figures, and more, would have been born had the young Howland perished before snatching that divinely dangling towline.

The far-reaching lineage of a single black walnut—or individual acorn or pinecone, for that matter—is equally profound. If a seed does not grow into a tree, how many nesting birds will need a different home; how many squirrels; how many ants and caterpillars and butterflies? How would the landscape be altered without the tree's roots stabilizing the soil and thus thwarting erosion?

Similarly, how many human homes and church pews, violins and guitars, and, yes, kitchen tables—and conversations and love and life shared around them— would never exist if a particular tree did not first rise heavenward from the soil? On and on and on the ripples go, expanding endlessly out out outward.

The odds of life are delivered in grand lightning strikes and microscopic cancer cells, in automobile accidents and stray bullets, in miracles and coincidences, in blind luck and blind curves and blind dates. And, also, in a fox squirrel being attacked by a raccoon and in the skirmish dropping a black walnut directly on top of a half-eaten fish carcass decaying in the muddy paw print of a black bear.

Fertility And Flame

Tisquantum, commonly known as Squanto in modern history books, was the Indigenous American who befriended the English Separatists, now referred to as Pilgrims, upon their arrival at Plimouth, now universally spelled *Plymouth*, in the winter of 1620.

A member of the Patuxet tribe, Squanto served as interpreter and guide to the Pilgrims. Also, he taught them the "Three Sisters" method of agriculture whereby corn, squash, and beans were planted closely together— and buried shallowly, along with a small dead fish as natural fertilizer to provide extra nutrients and maximize the odds of life sprouting.

The black walnut, about the size of a modern baseball with matching hardness, that was dropped by the fox squirrel faced extreme odds against germinating; against becoming a sapling; and against surviving into a mature tree. Yet this black walnut was lucky, even truly blessed, in a good number of ways.

To begin, the fox squirrel had hungrily chewed away part of the protective green husk. Also, the floodplain's rich topsoil featured an ideal near-neutral pH of 6.0. Moreover, the silty loam subsoil was free of hard clay a full four feet down and unobstructed by gravel for an additional two feet, making it a haven for roots to reach deep and wide and grip securely. Additionally, the topography was of a gentle slope, providing perfect drainage. And, not insignificantly, mature trees that might shade a sapling from photosynthesis-nurturing sunlight above, and steal water from below, were spaced forgivingly apart.

In other words, the black walnut set anchor in a spot that could not have been more promising.

One final beatific ingredient to this magic elixir of life was demanded—and received: Old Man Winter saw to it that the black walnut fruit remained moist until the arrival of Lady Spring.

In the course of time, the black walnut beat the odds and overcame all hardships. It germinated and sprouted, avoided choking weeds and strangling vines, grew from seedling to sapling to tree. Spring after winter, until the laps of God's blue marble around the sun added up to well past one hundred, this native Eastern Black Walnut tree—also known simply as American Walnut—grew and flourished, thicker and wider, taller and higher, until its top branches seemed to brush the clouds.

Too, The Black Walnut Tree's roots grew deeper and stronger, reaching down four feet until grabbing clay, then descending another two feet, and well beyond, into gravel that further strengthened its foothold. All the while the roots spread wider, radiating outward fifty, sixty, eighty feet, making its foundation so solid that to topple it would be no easier than tipping over a great Egyptian pyramid. Indeed, powerful tornadoes thrice failed to cause The Black Walnut Tree serious harm.

Through summer rains, The Black Walnut Tree experienced growth spurts—much like a human teenager—sometimes rising three or four *feet* in a single year. Through seasons of drought, it climbed skyward much more slowly, even stalling briefly. But by and by, and by Nature's grace, reliably it grew.

Like pencil markings on the back of a door measuring a child's growth, The Black Walnut Tree's history was recorded in its growth rings—thick during years when sunlight and rain were plentiful from early spring to late fall; thin when the growing season was drier. One ring was particularly skinny, resembling the razor-thin black line of a sharpened pencil. This was the result of a lightning strike that ignited a fire which engulfed The Black Walnut Tree in 1732—the very year George Washington was born, some three hundred miles away as the eagle flies at the convergence of the Potomac River and Popes Creek, at a British colony site that would eventually become Westmoreland County, Virginia.

The odds of life-and-death come in such lightning strikes—also in a fire-dousing cloudburst so voluminous it seemed to have been poured from The Big Dipper. Fully mature at 111 years age in 1732, The Black Walnut Tree survived the blaze, although its growth that summer was stunted due to its scorched bark.

As if to prove its vigor was not also scarred, the following year The Black Walnut Tree gained an astonishing twelve feet in height.

Childbirth Perfect Storm

 Doc was in the middle of nowhere, in the middle of the night, in the middle of a thunderstorm.

And in the middle of a childbirth perfect storm.

The baby was arriving a month prematurely, in haste, with a precarious brow presentation. And Doc had rushed out of the house without forceps in his medical bag.

Why didn't I take time to grab forceps, Doc scolded himself internally. Outwardly, his palms dampened. *They'd be a godsend right now—possibly the difference between life and tragedy. Next time, I mustn't forget what Pops always told me: "Be quick, son, but don't hurry."*

The urgency at hand precluded Doc from chastising himself further. Without delay, but without hurry, he rolled up his shirtsleeves and asked Tamás for some whiskey.

"Whiskey?" Tamás replied, worried the young doctor needed a stiff drink to calm his nerves.

"Moonshine'll do," Doc allowed, his tone reassuring. "Any spirits you've got—I need it to sterilize my hands."

As the rain poured down on the navy-and-red wool blanket held taut overhead, Tamás poured *pálinka*—Hungarian brandy—into Doc's cupped palms. The expectant father trembled as he tilted the bottle, but Doc's hands were steady as granite. As he scrubbed in, Doc mouthed a silent prayer.

Prayer was a fine idea because a brow presentation, even under the best of circumstances, is troublesome. Huddled from rain beneath a blanket-turned-tent, with another soggy blanket on the ground serving as a delivery bed, and working by the dim light of two kerosene lanterns, the dicey-ness was multiplied.

Adding further distress, Doc could feel all eyes focused on him—and they did not strike him as overly friendly. Roma itinerants were known for being convivial, and deservedly so, but they also had a cutthroat reputation that was equally merited. If this delivery went south, Tamás might seek vengeance by showing Doc his own surgical skills with a sharp blade.

With twin kerosene lamps casting a mere dull glow, Doc relied on his hands more than his eyes. His fingertips, possessing their own 20/20 vision, told him the fetus's head was tilted slightly backward. At this odd angle, Doc well knew, the skull's diameter was too large to pass through the cervix. Moreover, risk of spinal injury loomed if Aisha pushed and forced the baby's neck to hyperextend further.

"Don't push," Doc cooed. "Just breathe. *Innnnn* and out-out-out. That's good, Aisha. *Innnnn* and out-out-out. Don't push yet."

Doc then did what he told Aisha not to do: he pushed, ever so gently, ever so expertly. With his two cupped palms and nine fingers—Doc was born missing an entire right index finger—cradling the baby's skullcap as protectively as a chrysalis around a fragile butterfly, he maneuvered the head backwards an inch; then a fraction further; slightly more still.

Doc had an idiosyncrasy of which he was unaware—he whistled, soft as a lover's whisper, when concentrating deeply. The tone was actually more of a pleasant hum and always had a soothing effect on his patients. He began administering this audible anesthetic.

Storm gusts could have extinguished the two lanterns and it would not have mattered now for behind his glasses Doc's steel-blue eyes were squinted shut in total concentration. His hands provided his sight, allowing him to envision the birth canal perfectly, know the position of the fetus's head precisely.

Suddenly, like a safecracker successfully dialing the tumbler into place, Doc's nine fingers froze. *Open sesame.* He stopped pushing and instead tenderly *pulled* to adjust the baby's forehead downward into the proper angle.

Aisha, now fully engulfed in childbirth's "ring of fire" pain, wailed.

"You're doing great," Doc praised. "Now—gently—I want you to push."

Aisha did as told while Doc, with a precise blending of finesse and firmness, guided the head through the cervix. Time seemed to hold still, a river of blood did not. Abruptly, Doc's whistle-humming stopped—

—replaced by a newborn's healthy cries.

Doc lovingly laid the son on Aisha's chest and congratulated Tamás. The other gathered Roma all exhaled as one and applauded and cheered. But the peril was not over. Doc quickly went back to work, his whistle-humming filling the stormy night air once more.

Majestic Masterpiece

The annual growth ring of a tree is not singular, but rather like twins.

The inner part of each ring is comprised of "earlywood" which grows during spring and is slightly lighter of color. The outer "latewood" portion of the ring is created at summer's end, when the growth of cambium cells slows to a crawl, and in the process becomes more dense and deeper in color.

Furthermore, rings are broadest near a tree's center because the early stage of life is when a sapling grows most rapidly. Moving outward, the rings progressively become more narrow because trees grow more moderately in diameter—as well as in height—as they mature. Growth almost ceases during a tree's old age.

Just as different colored and textured strands of wool yarn are woven together to form a beautiful tapestry, varied growth rings—of earlywood and latewood; of early life and later life; of prime growing conditions and poor seasons; of attacks from summer locusts and harsh winter freezes—combine to create Nature's own artwork. To appreciative eyes, the rings of a tree—its wood grain—comes into focus like a beautiful rainbow of earth tones.

In a black walnut rainbow, the bands of color range from light caramel to dark chocolate to coffee black, with occasional hints of cherry and plum. Added to this visual loveliness is a steely hardness, making black walnut wood highly prized by cabinetmakers.

Summer 1770 marked The Black Walnut Tree's sesquicentennial. It towered more than one hundred feet, with a glorious leafy crown—a Monet of autumn's reds, oranges, and golds—equaling that grand measure in width. Its trunk was likewise so massive three men touching fingertips could not reach around it.

To be sure, it was the most breathtaking tree—and cherished landmark—in this bucolic paradise along the banks of the Ohio River. The location was also a prized spot for rest and rendezvous. One warm summer day, despite heated tension between their tribes, an Iroquois warrior and a Shawnee woman made forbidden love beneath The Black Walnut Tree as its leaves sang in the breeze. In the near future, westward settlers would take pleasure from its shade.

It was therefore not surprising that a frontier surveyor marking plots of land with "tomahawk improvements"—these being hatchet marks cut into tree trunks to serve as identification for legal claim—in October 1770, took sharp aim at The Black Walnut Tree. If you had examined the growth rings in the wedge that fell to the ground, you would have learned that the surveyor cut exactly thirty-eight years deep—back to 1732, the year a fire tried to kill The Black Walnut Tree, and also the birth year of the hatchet-wielding surveyor.

George Washington's tomahawk improvement aside, The Black Walnut Tree dodged all lumbermen's axes and saw blades—as well as potentially deadly attacks from insects and disease. Heavenward it continued to grow, straight and strong, early fall after midsummer after late spring, year after decade after century, ultimately rising like a God-made skyscraper measuring 140 feet tall. Black walnut trees today, in the twenty-first century, rarely reach half that height due to overharvesting and growth retardation caused by air pollution.

It is fair to state that the likes of The Black Walnut Tree will never again be seen. To be sure, words fail in fully describing what a true masterpiece it was, but the poem "Trees" penned by Joyce Kilmer in 1913—nearly three centuries after a fox squirrel inadvertently, and serendipitously, planted a black walnut husk in a muddy pawprint left by a bear—perhaps comes nearest:

I think that I shall never see
A poem lovely as a tree.

A tree whose hungry mouth is prest
Against the earth's sweet flowing breast;

A tree that looks at God all day,
And lifts her leafy arms to pray;

A tree that may in summer wear
A nest of robins in her hair;

Upon whose bosom snow has lain;
Who intimately lives with rain.

Poems are made by fools like me,
But only God can make a tree.

God made one of His loveliest in The Black Walnut Tree.

Suddenly, A Snag

 Twins.

A second baby followed, facing an even more difficult arrival. It was jumping into the world feetfirst—a breech delivery.

The odds of naturally conceived identical twins are roughly 1-in-300. The odds of a breech birth, meanwhile, are about three percent—of which fewer than ten percent are "complete breech" with the fetus in a cannonball position. Young Doc was facing a once-in-a-medical-career delivery straight out of the gate.

"We're not done yet," Doc told Aisha, a warm timbre masking concern. "You have another beautiful baby on the way. Just like the first time, don't push 'til I tell you to."

Dika, a grandmother—*nagyanya* in Hungarian—as of a minute ago, swaddled and then cradled the firstborn twin in one arm while nervously rubbing a silver crucifix necklace with her other hand. Tamás sought less churchly comfort, anxiously drinking shot after shot after shot of *pálinka* until he finished all that remained in the bottle after Doc's handwashing.

Doc, who only attended church on Easter and Christmas Eve and for weddings and funerals, whispered his second prayer of the night. It was a brief offering, but heartfelt, and this time aloud: *Lord, please guide my hands as though they are your own.* Without further delay, he resumed answering his life's calling—being a doctor.

Doc's hands made a careful diagnosis. He had never before seen a complete breech fetus, much less delivered one, but he knew what he must do: unfold the legs, grasp the feet, and extract the baby by pulling. That was the simple one-two-three. In reality, it would be infinitely complex.

The rain softened, then ceased, but Doc did not notice. His whistle-humming also slowed, then stopped, so absolute was his concentration. The entire universe was presently at the ends of his nine fingertips. He located one leg, and the other, and skillfully unfolded them.

Next, Doc grasped the left foot—his hands so gifted, his fingertips so filled with magic and fully in tune with his mind, he could actually tell it was the *left* foot by the curvature of the arch—and then took hold of the right foot.

Be quick, Lem— he thought, remaining unshakable.

Gently and deliberately, but not tentatively, Doc began the extraction.

—but don't hurry.

In less time than it took Grandma Dika to recite three Hail Marys, the baby's feet peeked out into the night air, then the knees, and thighs.

At this point, the obstetrical calculus focused on the angle of the baby's hips and shoulders, tilt of the head, location of the umbilical cord. Once more, Doc closed his eyes to see more fully.

"You're doing wonderfully, Aisha," Doc encouraged as his enchanted hands pivoted the baby's pelvis a few degrees. Out came the newborn's hips. Doc breathed easier and resumed whistle-humming. The abdomen followed smoothly.

Suddenly, an alarming snag.

Doc did not panic, not for a single heartbeat. Supporting the lower torso with his left hand and forearm, he artfully slid his four-fingered right hand higher up the baby's anatomy. Here Doc's birth anomaly proved an advantage for it had the effect of giving his right hand a pinch more room to maneuver—and a pinch was as good as a mile.

Doc's whistle-humming grew fainter, his eyes shut tighter, as he listened to his fingertips. They told him the baby's left arm had been pushed awkwardly upward and become wrapped around the neck—"nuchal arm" is the medical term. It was a complicated maneuver and yet, astonishingly, Doc remedied the predicament in one nimble motion.

Beginner's luck, he laughed inwardly, followed by a more serious reflection: *Maybe my Creator truly is helping guide my hands.*

Time compressed further, thirty seconds now passing as but one. With trained and knowing hands, with the masterly fingers of an artist, and with God's guidance perhaps, Doc rotated the shoulders minutely. The shift was nearly imperceptible, yet also sublime. Without dislocating either fragile ball-and-socket joint, or fracturing one of the clavicles, Doc had the shoulders out free and clear.

The problematic birth had been solved faultlessly thus far. The next instant, the tide of good fortune reversed. Trouble that Doc could not possibly see, impossibly he felt.

Graveyard Silence

 Doc's movements instantly petrified.

The umbilical cord is wrapped around the neck, he reasoned.

Seconds became precious as gold. Aisha's breathing turned shallow, her pulse a rapid drum solo.

Think, Lemuel, think.

Once more, Doc's hands held the answer. His first impulse had been wrong. The resistance he felt was too firm to be caused by the umbilical cord acting as a lasso. Rather, the baby's head was surely tilted upward in the "star-gazing position." This impeded passage and also caused the neck to hyperextend—a potentially perilous situation that could result in spinal injury or oxygen deprivation, or both.

Like a musical virtuoso performing a sophisticated composition for the first time, *by ear*, Doc instinctively knew what notes to play and did so in perfect rhythm. With a minuscule shift of his baby-cradling left forearm and hand, he retreated the delivery an inch backward into the birth canal; delicately adjusted the head's angle with his right middle finger; then, with calm assurance, instructed: "It's time, Aisha—time to push."

Wearily, Aisha bravely answered the call, her moans escalating into a howl until, for the second time, the birthing was done.

Night turned quiet as a falling feather.

Time stretched.

Graveyard silence.

"What's wrong?" Aisha whispered, her hoarse voice laced with anguish.

"Why no cries?" Grandma Dika demanded. "A curse! I knew this baby will see no sunrise."

Tamás, squeezing his wife's hand, looked to Doc for reassurance.

But Doc did not see Tamás's pleading eyes, nor hear Dika's weeping despair. He was too intent auditing God's newest creation. Out of habit, despite the urgency, he counted the fingers—*one, two, three . . . nine*—all ten, and smiled. Quickly, he focused on what worried him: skin color. A bluish hue would mean the "star-gazing" neck had compromised the baby's oxygen supply.

Doc tilted his cradle-hands so the two lanterns could shine better light upon the baby—

—rosy pink, and born smiling!

Doc slapped the newborn's bottom and a healthy cry lovelier than Mozart's *Eine Kleine Nachtmusick*—"A Little Night Music"—filled the air. He tenderly placed the second infant on Aisha's chest and Grandma Dika did likewise with the eleven-minutes-older firstborn.

Twin boys.

Doc whistle-hummed with joy. And relief. He was safe from a "Texas toothpick"—a hunting knife—wielded in vengeance by Tamás. To the contrary, the exuberant new father insisted Doc stay for a late-night dinner as payment for medical services rendered.

The rain clouds auspiciously parted, like drapes drawn open, and under a new sky of shimmering crystal shards, Tamás, over an open fire, cooked a feast of burgers and beans. Until his final breath on the face of the Earth, Doc would claim it was the best hamburger he ever tasted.

The *pálinka*, used to wash Doc's hands and pacify Tamás's fears, was gone, so out came two jugs of hard cider. Out also came a violin, seemingly as old and bedraggled as its grey-goateed owner, Emilian, who made the homely fiddle sing beautifully. Dancing began, drinking continued, rhythmic clapping swelled. Tamás joined in with a clarinet.

One half of The Black Walnut Tree lay in front of the campfire, its flat surface facing up, making it a perfect bench. Doc took a seat and was eventually joined by Tamás.

"A clarinet?" Doc observed, surprised by Tamás's instrument choice.

"Because my arms are too short for the trombone," Tamás said with good humor.

Doc laughed: "Maybe I shall take up the drum because I don't have enough fingers for the guitar."

Tamás smiled, then turned earnest.

"*Köszönöm*," he said in his native tongue; in his eyes, tears. "That means 'thank you.' Three times *köszönöm*—for my wife and my two sons."

"You're quite welcome," Doc replied, humbly. Raising his glass: "May the storm clouds be in your sons' past and rainbows in their future."

Tamás drank to the toast and rejoined: "There's one more thing—I have a gift for you."

"No, no, Tamás. That's not necessary."

"Yes it is, Doctor Lemuel Jamison," Tamás said, formally. "I've named my sons Jamis and Lemuel."

Overcome by the honor, Doc whistle-hummed while regaining his composure. At last, he spoke: "*Köszönöm*. Two times, *köszönöm*."

Tree Soliloquy

 Sitting in the orbit of the campfire's crackling glow, side by side with Tamás on the split Black Walnut Tree, enjoying the radiating warmth of both flame and new friendship, Doc's right palm rested on the wings-like knot resembling one side of a butterfly.

And so it was that the felled majestic timber spoke to Doc, the vibrations of its silent timbre delivering the soliloquy to his subconscious.

Please, yes, sit here in your weariness and rest for a while, dear Doctor—your labors tonight were glorious and deserving.

While I never imagined this destiny, it is a rewarding feeling. To be a bench may seem a humble thing, but it is also a good thing, I think, for helping another living being in any way is a holy thing.

I have known you but a short time, Doctor, not even a blink in my long long long lifetime, yet already you remind me of a tree—and I can think of no higher compliment. You help others, providing warm comfort instead of cooling shade, and care for them when they are ill. Trees do this as well.

It is true—trees are social and caring creatures that communicate with each other and help one another. Perhaps one day your scientists will discover and confirm this, but for now please take my word for it.

You see, we trees are linked to our neighbor trees by an underground network of fungi—imagine telegraph wires strung between neighboring towns. When one of us becomes infected by disease for example, or infested by insects, we send a warning to our neighbors, who in turn warn their neighbors, and so on, out out outward in an expanding ripple. The alerted trees then produce extra enzymes to protect themselves and, equally importantly, selflessly send doses of these enzymes back to the trees already under attack. It is our version of a firefighting bucket brigade.

Furthermore, larger healthy trees assist ailing trees, and also vulnerable young seedlings and saplings, by passing along lifesaving carbon and, of course, water, for a grand old tree's siphoning roots can reach deep deep deeper than immature trees can. This is not so unlike a wet nurse breastfeeding another mother's infant, is it, Doctor?

Do you see that lovely family of birch just across the way? It was my responsibility to assist them during a severe drought when they were half their current height. And that gorgeous cluster of buckeyes behind you—I gave them medicine when violent leaf blotch threatened their lives. I say "medicine" because we trees have inestimable curative properties within our bark and sap and leaves and roots. The Indigenous Peoples have long known this.

During my lifetime on God's green Earth, I hope in these ways I made a difference in this corner of the forest. I believe a similar destiny lies ahead of you, Doctor, in your town.

As I have helped, so have I been helped. Many many many summers ago, when I was set ablaze by a lightning strike, my bark was scorched so terribly that I surely would have perished if my neighbors—pine and birch and buckeye, and twenty species more, tall and small alike—had not rallied together with the communal spirit of a barn raising to give me lifesaving nutrients. They also encouraged me, even soothed me with song, much like you whistle-hummed while delivering two beautiful babies this night.

Poets through the ages have been inspired by trees, yet the reverse is also true. Here is one of my poems, A Tree's Life:

The tall tree dies, but its wood lives on
In a home, violin, grandfather clock
Ticking the minutes of Earthly lives away
For a family, a musician—tick-tock

My wood may become a chair or a table
Baby crib, sailboat, a book or piano
Benevolent shade gone, nutrients linger
Nourishing new trees—strong and tall now to grow

Tonight, beneath the rain-scrubbed sky, spangled with diamond stars, I shall savor being a welcoming bench while also wondering what my future holds. Too, I wish you a good life, Doctor, rising tall to your purpose and eventually leaving a proud and enduring legacy.

Straddling The Equinox

 Doc had been so intently focused during the deliveries, and so relieved directly afterward, he overlooked part of his medical training: noting the time of birth.

Learning the twins' names reminded Doc to check his gold pocket watch: 11:55.

Not yet midnight—still Saturday, he thought with glad recognition. *March 20 is a special date to be born.*

Allowing for the hamburger dinner and impromptu Hungarian folk songs concert, Doc estimated Jamis had been born an hour previously. He would record 10:55 p.m. on the birth certificate.

Lemuel followed about fifteen minutes thereafter, Doc figured, so his time of birth was 11:10 p.m. Like a grocer weighing a melon by feel, Doc's determination was five and a half pounds for Jamis, five-even for Lem.

The clock hands in Doc's mind wound backward to breakfast. According to *The Old Farmer's Almanac,* which he dutifully checked each morning, this year summer officially arrived today at 11:05 p.m.

Doc smiled, realizing the infant brothers came into the world straddling the vernal equinox: Jamis born just as winter bid "goodbye" and Lemuel arriving as spring was saying "hello." This struck Doc as being serendipitous, portending uniqueness despite their identicalness.

Another pretty thought embraced Doc—Constance! He hoped she would forgive him for spoiling her special day, *their* special day.

Only eight hours earlier, at four o'clock in the afternoon, Lemuel Jamison had married his grammar-school sweetheart, Constance Figs. Connie well understood the new life she was taking on, that her country doctor husband would be beckoned away at all hours of the night, all days of the week, in all weathers. But she failed to anticipate this might include her bridal night.

Following a private ceremony at City Hall, a small reception was held at Doc's home. During their first dance as wife and husband, Connie gave Doc a memory he would cherish the remainder of his life. With her soft lips touching his ear, she cooed: "I can't wait to have your babies."

"How many do you want, my dear?" Doc replied, playfully.

"Oh, let's start with two right away!" she blurted, her voice as bubbly as the wedding champagne.

Their dance-floor pillow talk was interrupted by loud banging on the front door and Hanzi breathlessly saying a doctor was urgently needed.

"Be careful," the new bride told her groom, adding a kiss and goodbye words sweet as song: "Know that I will be thinking of you until I see you again."

"You know it as well," Doc echoed lovingly.

It was now the far side of midnight and Doc knew Constance would be worried about him. He also knew he must remain with his new patients until morning. Nearly all that could go wrong, had. And yet everything also went perfectly right: twin sons, both healthy, and mother doing well. Nonetheless, Doc was concerned the good fortune might take a bad turn. Connie would understand his delay in coming home.

Between visits checking on Aisha and the babies, Doc listened to the music—Hanzi had joined in with a harmonica—and watched the free-spirited dancing, its rising zeal fed by dwindling cider. It was not the type of music and dancing Doc had expected on his wedding day, but life brings surprises. *Things turn out best for those who make the best of the way things turn out*, he reminded himself, hearing his father's voice in his mind, and relished this welcoming kinship and festivities.

During a break from playing the woodwind, Tamás again joined Doc on the fallen-tree-turned-bench in front of the roaring campfire. Glowing sparks drifted skyward like dancing fireflies melding into the starlight shining down. It was enchanting.

"Aisha and I fled Hungary during The Revolution of Forty-eight," Tamás shared. "I was twenty, barely more than a boy really. Aisha was not yet nineteen."

Doc listened with earnestness.

"We were in love, in fear, and in such a desperate hurry we did not dare take time to get married until we safely reached the shores of America," Tamás continued. "In New York, our second day, we were wed. That was the fourth of September almost four years ago."

"You've been married *far longer* than I have," Doc grinned.

Knives Come Out

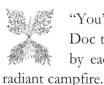 "You've been married *far longer* than I have," Doc teased Tamás, the two men now warmed by each other's company as surely as by the radiant campfire.

"No, no," Tamás said. "Me and Aisha have been married for only three years."

"I've been married only ten *hours*," Doc replied.

Tamás tilted his head in bewilderment: "*Tonight* is your wedding night?"

Doc nodded.

"You are an angel without wings," Tamás said. "*Köszönöm.* You must go to your wife straight away."

"My Constance, she's the angel—and she'd want me to stay through the night to look after your wife and babies. We can celebrate our wedding tomorrow."

"You mean *today*," Tamás corrected, realizing the wee hour. "It's already *tomorrow*."

Tamás stood, raised a tin cup, and addressed the gathering: "*Felköszönt vkit!* To Doc and his new bride and to their happiness. We will sing of this night for as long as trees grow."

More toasts—*Felköszönt vkit!*—followed, to Jamis, to Lemuel, to Aisha. The wine and cider flowed and the congregation drank like victorious Vikings and the dancing and music began anew. Amid this merriment, out came the Texas toothpicks for a knife-throwing contest.

Doc put up no protest when his favorite moss-green derby was nailed to a tree as the target. Four blazing torches made with kerosene-soaked rags provided illumination. Each competitor would get five throws from ten paces.

Doc watched with admiration as Emilian stuck the hat with three throws out of five. After two men each hit the target once, Hanzi, despite his bruised throwing hand, scored a pair of bull's-eyes.

Last up was the new father. Wiry thin of average height, Tamás's erect posture and square shoulders and blacksmith-like forearms proclaimed power. He toed the stick on the ground marking the foul line, calibrated the knife's weight and balance as he gently pinched its blade between his index and middle fingertips and thumb, and took aim.

Effortlessly, the knife leapt from his hand at blurring speed, torchlight flickering off its spinning blade. *Thwack!* Steel pierced wool—barely—at the target's top edge. His second throw also struck the hat's brim, again by a slim margin, near the bottom.

Two lucky throws, Doc thought. *An inch higher, an inch lower, and Tamás would be oh-for-two.*

His third effort was a tad right, stabbing the derby's brim at the three o'clock position. Throw number four chimed in at nine o'clock.

Tamás isn't lucky at all, Doc realized. *He's putting on a circus show!*

The fifth-and-final flying toothpick—*Thwack!*— pinned Doc's rain-soaked hat dead center.

Cheers erupted and Doc, with astonishment, proclaimed: "Tamás, you could bring a knife to a gunfight and triumph."

Emilian grinned wryly: "Doctor, you should see Tamás with a gun. He can shoot a squirrel in the eye. Ain't that so, Tamás?"

"Oh, I don't know," the marksman answered modestly. "From how far away?"

"Fifty paces," Emilian suggested.

"Fifty?" Tamás rejoined. "From that close, do you want me to shoot the squirrel in the *left* eye or the *right* eye?"

Laughter all around. And so it continued until sunrise, no one sleeping a wink, except for Aisha and the twins as, thankfully, no childbirth complications had arisen. As consolation for missing Constance dearly, Doc felt grateful for a wedding night to treasure, if uniquely so.

Upon morning's arrival something that had been invisible in night's darkness caught Grandma Dika's eye. Inspecting one of the split-open halves of The Black Walnut Tree, she noticed an oddly shaped knot. Roughly the size of a man's hand with fingers splayed, the ebony-colored knot was marbled with burnt orange. It did not require big-sky imagination to see it as the left forewing and hindwing of a Monarch butterfly.

She walked over to the opposite half of the fallen tree and found a mirror image knot—right wings of a Monarch.

"It's an omen," Grandma Dika said, tracing her fingers over the second knot. "Identical twins."

"Yes," Doc said, amusement in his voice at this after-the-fact prescience. "Your daughter gave birth to twins *last night.*"

"No, Doctor," the fortuneteller said, cradling the baby catcher's cheeks in her palms, looking him in the eye: "The omen is of *your* future."

Lincoln Beswick Jamison

 Halley's Comet arrived in springtime 1986.

Two new Jamison generations had also arrived during the seventy-six years since Doc's passing that coincided with the famous comet's previous Earthly flyby.

Sans a telescope, the celestial ball of ice and space dust was but a fuzzy green blip in the night sky. Nonetheless, seventeen-year-old Lincoln Beswick Jamison squinted heavenwards, bringing the comet's tail into focus through imagination as much as his eyes.

In an oral history passed through generations, Lincoln knew much about his surrogate great-great-great-grandfather Lemuel "Doc" Jamison. Two other things had been passed down from Doc—on behalf of Tamás and Aisha—to identical twin Lem; to Lemuel Tamás; to Samuel; to Flynn; and lastly to Lincoln: an heirloom Hungarian Opal ring and The Butterfly Table.

Linc no longer was in possession of either.

The Butterfly Table now served as an oversized reading desk in Bellaire's Matthew Murphy Memorial Library. Linc had donated it seven years prior, when he was ten, before he and his mother, Vanessa, fled to Cleveland's North Coast bordering Lake Erie.

~~~

Lincoln arrived on Earth on July 20, 1969, precisely as American astronaut Neil Armstrong was making history as the first human to set foot on the moon at 10:56 p.m. Eastern Daylight Time.

Weeks later in mid-August, on the heels of Armstrong's famous "one small step for man—" proclamation, Flynn Jamison, with long dry-beach-colored sideburns and longer hair hued like wet sand, hitchhiked from Ohio to the Woodstock Festival in upstate New York. He never returned home to his wife and newborn son. Vanessa blamed a surplus of drugs, not lack of love, for the abandonment.

Vanessa soldiered on, providing her son a safe place to lay his head at night, gave him love in enough abundance for two parents, and somehow managed to earn a nursing degree by the time Linc started first grade.

Vanessa's new job as an RN was a godsend—at first.

The tempest began when she slipped and fell on a wet tile floor in the hospital. After her injured hip healed, she continued taking painkillers. Slowly at first, then with increasing speed, she spiraled downward. Surreptitiously, she swapped over-the-counter pills when giving patients their medications; stole narcotics from locked cabinets accessible only by nurses; even—twice—forged physicians' prescriptions.

When a sealed box of Vicodin went missing, suspicions at the hospital zeroed in on Vanessa. Terrified of losing her son, she fled—as Flynn had done. Linc, then ten, begged his mom to rent a U-Haul so they could take all their possessions, or at least more than would fit in their tiny three-owner-old Pinto—and, most importantly, take The Butterfly Table.

"We have to at least put the Table in a storage unit," Linc pressed on.

"No," Vanessa snapped. "We're never comin' back here."

"Please, Ma," pleaded Linc, his heart in weightless freefall. "Can't we ask someone to keep it for us? I bet the Millers would—for sure Aunt Veronica would."

"I'm sorry, honey," Vanessa said, her tone softening. "We've gotta leave right away."

Despite being an antique of 124 years, The Butterfly Table looked newly made only months ago. Its surface, hardened by the cauterizing thunderbolt, retained a mirror-like buffed luster. More than a century of accidents and incidents—from silverware handled carelessly to, unbelievably, a circus tiger's razor-like claws—had left neither scar nor mar.

Linc's brown eyes pooled at the thought of losing this beautiful Table; this piece of his family's history; this piece of him, really. While hastily packing, a canny idea occurred to the boy. In careful cursive, and trying to sound as lawyerly as a fourth-grader possibly can, he wrote a note and taped it to his beloved Butterfly Table left abandoned in the apartment:

My name is Lincoln Beswick Jamison and this cool table that belonged to my many-greats-grandfather is now mine. I, being of a sound mind, wish to lend it to The Bellaire Library as a giant homework desk until sometime in the future when I can come back to reclaim it.

Thank you,

Linc

P.S. Please take good care of it for me!

The fate of the Hungarian Opal ring was far more woebegone.

Everything To Lose

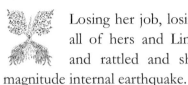Losing her job, losing her home, losing nearly all of hers and Lincoln's possessions rocked and rattled and shook Vanessa like a 7.0-magnitude internal earthquake.

With fear in her soul, with tears pooling in her hazel eyes, with Bellaire and most of her worldly possessions in her rearview mirror, Vanessa had an epiphany: *I haven't lost anything important.*

Glancing at Linc in the front passenger seat, leaning sideways and sleeping, his sandy-haired head resting against the vibrating window at sixty miles-per-hour, she further realized clearly: *I still have EVERYTHING to lose.*

In the next instant, Vanessa knew a third thing: she was on the precipice, with toes hanging over, of doing exactly that.

Fear is a forceful motivator, love even more so. Vanessa was pushed forward by both. Instead of running from her troubles, she ran into the arms of salvation, in Cleveland of all places, by checking herself into a substance abuse clinic.

~~~

Vanessa emerged from rehab a changed person. Not only was her body cleansed of pharmaceuticals, she jettisoned a victim mentality that had burdened her ever since

Flynn's abandonment. Too, she accepted responsibility for her addiction and the turmoil it caused Linc.

Worried her thieving past would catch up to her if she applied for a Registered Nurse opening, Vanessa enrolled in a one-year License Practitioner Nurse night program under her maiden name, Morgan. Thanks to her RN training, she aced test after test and in the process regained some self-esteem. After graduation, she had no difficulty finding work in home hospice care.

Lincoln missed his friends back home in Bellaire, and dearly so. Nonetheless, he adapted quickly and thrived in Cleveland Heights. Despite being a latchkey kid, he sailed through middle school with minimal teenage angst and high school began no differently. He attracted friends freely, earned high grades easily, and breezed onto the varsity football team as a freshman wide receiver.

Evading a drug relapse is far more difficult than dodging would-be tacklers. Vanessa would have been wise to run away from the entire field of nursing—away from any occupation affording access to prescription medications—with the same urgency she fled Bellaire.

In truth, home hospice care proved even more perilously seductive than working in a hospital. True, Vanessa no longer swapped over-the-counter pills for prescription drugs. Nor did she resort to stealing narcotics from under lock and key. Forging prescriptions was also a risk she stopped taking.

Instead, Vanessa safely snooped a little inside the homes of her hospice patients. Most people, and particularly the elderly, rarely throw away unused prescription medications. They regularly save half-empty bottles and vials of pills believing they might be needed in the future. When new prescriptions are filled, the old and expired ones get pushed to the back of the medicine cabinet; stored in the far reaches beneath the bathroom sink; shoved and forgotten behind vitamins and teabags and baking soda in kitchen cupboards.

One of the first duties when a hospice nurse comes into a new client's home is to dispose of all medications that have either expired or are no longer required under doctor's orders. It is not unusual for the nurse to collect a bucketful of such partially filled pill bottles and vials.

For three years and the better part of a fourth, Vanessa proved stronger than these temptations. Then, on a Friday afternoon during an exceptionally stressful week, she weakened and pocketed two Percocet pills. *Just to take the edge off and get me to the weekend,* she reasoned.

Saturday morning, Vanessa groggily awoke wishing she had kept a few more Percocet. At dinner with Linc come Sunday evening, however, she was relieved and proud of her two-pill restraint. She steadfastly vowed the Percocet slip-up would be her last: *I'm an addict. No more dancing with the Devil. I must be strong—for Linc.*

Only weeks thereafter, grieving the death of Sharlene, a lovely client and young single mother who had fought breast cancer valiantly, Vanessa broke her pledge. Instead of tossing out the potent opiate pain relievers that had aided Sharlene through her malignant nightmare, Vanessa pilfered a jumbled cache of OxyContin and Percodan.

As Vanessa danced, the Devil smiled.

Rock Bottom

Vanessa spiraled like a handful of Vicodin pills flushed down the toilet.

She began arriving late for hospice work. Her tardiness grew more frequent, grew more pronounced, ten minutes becoming twenty, then an hour. When she altogether failed to show up one day without alerting her supervisor, Vanessa was fired.

Without access to household medicine cabinets, she resorted to buying painkillers from shady sources. In short time, opioid addiction broke her financially; worse, it broke her spirit. But she did one prudent thing during her terrifying freefall. In a rare moment of sobriety and clarity, she gave Lincoln the Hungarian Opal ring for safekeeping.

"Hide this and no matter what I say, don't give it back," Vanessa emphatically instructed Linc, now a junior in high school. "Even if I scream and swear and tell you I've changed my mind, don't give in. We both know I'll just sell it. This ring has been in the family for generations, so don't let me lose it now."

"I'll hide it real good," Linc vowed.

Vanessa's mood swings, sleeping binges, and extended absences became the new normal. Linc, always good at taking care of himself, now cared for two by doing the grocery shopping, cooking, laundry. Fortunately, Vanessa had frugally pirated away some savings and thus far the electricity had remained on and Linc had gone hungry only occasionally. But the rainy day fund was drying up quick as dew in July sunshine.

Linc successfully hid his home strife. In the classroom, his grades did not suffer. On the football field, he channeled his private pain into delivering hits far more savage than those he received.

"Where's the ring?" Vanessa greeted her son the moment he walked through the front door after Cleveland Peak High's season-opening football game. Even though she had been a no-show in the stands, she did not ask if the Cougars won or if Linc had seen playing time. The question, Linc knew, was in truth a demand to give the ring to her.

"I hid it—like you told me," he said, defiantly.

"I know, honey, but I need it," Vanessa said with false sweetness, trying to mask her irritation and desperation. "We'll be evicted if I don't come up with the rent money for last month *and* this month."

"You told me not to give it to you even if—"

Vanessa abruptly cut him off, her voice turning sharp and cold and loud: "If I don't have the money by Monday, we'll be tossed out and sleeping on the streets. Is that what you want?!"

Linc replied with a brooding headshake, but no words.

"The ring is our only option," Vanessa said, conciliatorily now. "I need to pawn it, just temporarily. Don't worry, we'll buy it back—you know, the way Tamás sold it to get his start in America and then got it back later. We'll pay the rent, and buy some food, and then after I go back to work we'll buy the ring back—I promise."

"You keep sayin' you're gonna get a job, but you never do," Linc said, his tone filled with venom. "I'm not giving you the ring. It's mine! Dad would have wanted me, a *true* Jamison, to have it."

Vanessa collapsed inwardly, then flipped out. *Jamison* to her meant *Flynn* and *Flynn* was responsible for all of her problems. She exploded: "I said give me the god! damn! ring!"

"Nooooo!" Lincoln shouted, one syllable stretched into three. "I'd rather lose our apartment than lose *my* ring. I hid it where you'll never find it—ever!"

Speedier than he could run a fifteen-yard slant route, Linc was out the front door with an angry *Slam!* in his wake.

Vanessa turned her son's bedroom upside down and inside out. Nothing. Linc had indeed hidden the ring well—but not as furtively as Tamás did on his voyage across the Atlantic Ocean from Hungary to America. In a flash of intuition, Vanessa focused on the ring's lore. Recalling Tamás's anatomical hiding cavity, she suddenly knew where to look.

Inside the toilet tank, inside a zip-lock sandwich bag secured to the porcelain base with duct tape, Vanessa found her rock bottom.

Rebirth

 A thunderbolt can split rock, but in The Black Walnut Tree it created stone.

The lightning's voltage and heat—at fifty thousand degrees Fahrenheit, the strike was five times hotter than the surface of the sun—altered the molecular structure of the split tree's exposed surface, creating a granite-like veneer.

Tamás had a good many talents besides throwing a knife with William Tell-like accuracy. One was as a woodworker. Beholding the two butterfly halves, Tamás felt an artistic calling to marry them side by side.

To begin, he cut two raw planks from either half of the fallen tree. Each measured a thumb's width beyond seven feet long, by two feet wide, and approximately three inches in thickness. This task normally should have required only a couple hours of muscle grease and sweaty toil, yet it took Tamás a full three days and into a fourth.

The hardship was literally the wood's newfound hardness. Tamás dulled six steel sawblades, and broke a seventh, in harvesting the two boards. He furthermore half-ruined a chisel while creating a three-inch round hole to accommodate a doorknob, for his vision was to craft a one-of-a-kind entry door with an exquisite butterfly as its centerpiece.

The butterfly would be rich with symbolism.

Firstly, as Grandma Dika had interpreted, the identical knots forming two sides of a butterfly—which in

Hungary represents the soul—symbolized twin souls. Specifically, of course, Jamis and Lemuel.

The butterfly had a further spiritual element as well, inspired by the time Tamás crossed paths with a group of Iroquois. When a Monarch flitted by, one of them explained that in their culture a butterfly was holy for it represented rebirth. Bending over his work now, Tamás felt The Black Walnut Tree was undergoing its own metamorphosis, being reborn as a door.

This reincarnation was higher than as a mere door, however—it was to be a belated wedding gift for Constance and Doc.

Tamás could not have selected a finer canvas for his masterpiece. Black walnut is prized for its denseness and strength; its straight, tight grain; its delicious chocolate hues. All of these qualities the two boards had to the highest degree.

Tamás took exacting care to unerringly match up the butterfly halves when he wedded the planks. As he had learned to do in Hungary, and coincidentally the same method local Ohio Quaker craftsmen used in making their highly esteemed furniture, Tamás joined the boards without nails.

With a surplus of skill making up for his shortage of hand tools, Tamás cut a narrow groove nearly the length of the joining edge in each board. Next, he wedged a thin strip of wood—called a "spline"—into the groove of the first board and then connected the second board onto the exposed spline. The door's backside was reinforced with two horizontal batten boards—one near the top, the other at the bottom—secured with hardwood pegs.

This door will last a hundred years, Tamás thought with genuine satisfaction as he hand-rubbed the surfaces with his secret concoction: two parts beeswax, one part linseed oil, three measures elbow grease. *No, even longer than a century—it'll last seven generations, as the Iroquois spoke of. I must remember to tell this to Doc.*

For a fortnight Tamás labored. On the fifteenth day, he and Hanzi delivered the handsome door. They did so in stealth, waiting until Doc and Constance were both out.

As was commonplace in Bellaire, the front door at Number 210 Frederick Street had been left unlocked, making it no problem for Tamás and his teenage helper to remove it from its hinges and attach the replacement. Tamás disassembled the doorknob hardware from the old door and, with a little adjusting, installed it into the new one.

When Doc and Constance arrived home that evening, the paint-chipped eyesore door was no more. For a full moment they half-thought they had lost their minds and were at the wrong house. A note on the unexpected gift, affixed with a dab of beeswax just above the butterfly, cleared all confusion:

For Dr. and Mrs. Jamison—
May your love grow with each sunrise and be as beautiful as a summer sunset.

Fangs Flashing, Claws Extended

Tamás shut the door on his nomadic life.

At the very site where The Black Walnut Tree had been uprooted, the new father planted roots for his young family. When the Roma clan moved onward in midsummer of 1852, the Beswicks—Tamás and Aisha, Jamis and Lemuel, and Grandma Dika—remained, for this was a fine place to live, work, raise a family.

The village of Bellaire was founded in 1834, consisting of a mere six acres at the outset. Located within what was originally called Washington County, in honor of its famous first surveyor, the expanse was later renamed Belmont County meaning "beautiful mountain" in French. With the Cumberland National Road passing through, it was also known as "The Gateway to the West."

So alluring was this frontier portal that westward settlers, in bountiful numbers, abruptly halted their journeys here. By 1852, Bellaire's population had topped one thousand, making it an idyllic locale for a talented cabinetmaker to ply his trade.

Tamás's craftsmanship was already revered for his chairs and tables, but the wedding gift to Constance and Doc created a newfound demand: front doors of art. In short time, word of mouth spread about the "Rembrandt of Wood" and a rush of new customers were literally knocking on Tamás's door.

The Black Walnut Tree not only provided Tamás with premier wood, it helped him command a premier price. No tree he cut down ever afterwards yielded wood half so attractive.

Just as a wedding gift established a market for Tamás's doors, a birthday gift a decade later generated desire for a new signature product. Actually, *two* birthday gifts were jointly responsible—one each for Jamis and Lem.

When they turned ten, as was the prevailing rite of passage for boys reaching double-digits, the twins were given .22-caliber hunting rifles. Theirs, however, had custom-made black walnut gunstocks.

The two gunstocks—highly polished, naturally, with linseed oil, beeswax, and elbow grease—mirrored Doc's front door in beauty. Not only were they born from cherished pieces of The Black Walnut Tree that Tamás had squirreled away, but Jamis's stock contained a left half-butterfly knot and Lem's had the mirror-image right wings.

Once men in town laid eyes on either gem, they too wanted a Tamás-made gunstock. Business boomed.

Both boys, having inherited their father's marksmanship gene, were natural deadeyes. While Jamis regularly brought home small game—cottontail rabbits, gray squirrels, fox squirrels, mostly; a few wild turkey; and, once, a white-tailed deer—Lemuel refused to take a life. Possessing a passionate tenderness for animals, which they seemed to sense and reciprocate, Lem instead focused his shooting skills on plunking pinecones and acorns off tree branches.

One autumn morning when they were eleven, the twins ventured deep into the woods hunting—Jamis for rabbits and squirrels; Lemuel for Chanterelle and Slipper Jack mushrooms. The boys were following a narrow path, one still occasionally used by indigenous Iroquois, Shawnee, and Delaware who still populated the territory. Lem trailed a few steps behind Jamis so as not to spook any animals—or dangerously be in his brother's line of fire.

With muted careful footfalls, the boys stalked their individually desired prey. Jamis, not noticing that Lemuel had stopped at a cluster of wild mushrooms, proceeded alone up the pathway. Chanterelles are easy to spot because of their orange-yellow caps, but there are look-alike poisonous species to avoid. Bending down on one knee allowed Lem to examine the telltale underside gills, but also made him look smaller and weak.

This vulnerability triggered the attack instinct of a bobcat lurking in the fall foliage. Adult male bobcats typically weigh between twenty and forty pounds; this wildcat was a brute, a truly colossus cat, nearly equaling the boy's seventy pounds.

Lem had no warning to flee or try to appear menacing by standing tall and shouting with waving arms at the ferocious feline. He did not see the predator, brown and white with black markings, creeping forward in a stealthy crouch. He did not see it bolt into swift attack from twenty yards away.

And he did not see the killer carnivore spring airborne, fearsome fangs flashing, scalpel-sharp claws extended, as it soared towards him.

High Stakes Poker

 Shortly after the wildcat attack, Tamás found himself in a murderous encounter with an evil-tempered human bobcat named Marcus Murphy.

Stancliff Davidson, owner of The Hotel Bellaire, hired Tamás to repair the oak bar that had been badly damaged in a recent gunfight. Tamás finished the job, flawlessly matching new wood with the older portion, and was enjoying an ale "on the house" when he was invited to join a poker game.

"Thanks," Tamás said, setting down his empty stein. "But I gotta be goin'."

"What's your hurry?" Marcus said with quiet hostility, knowing full well the woodworker had fresh money in his pocket from Stancliff. "Play a few hands."

The other four players echoed the plea.

"All right," Tamás relented, taking the vacant chair directly across from Marcus. "Once 'round the table—six hands."

Tamás had a unique ability to look at a rising tree, or fallen log, and size up the quality of wood. He did this with people, too, and immediately appraised his poker opponents. Marcus made Tamás's neck hairs jump.

On the sixth hand—five-card draw, dealt by Marcus—Tamás picked up his cards and, on a backside corner of the ace of hearts, noticed a nearly imperceptible indentation made by a sharp fingernail. Tamás folded on the first go-round of betting, but before tossing in his cards he furtively put matching tiny crimp marks on the other four—king of diamonds, ten of clubs, deuce and four of spades.

Marcus won the hand, a meager pot, and when he gathered the cards for the next dealer his cheeks blanched. He saw the new indentations. Tamás's message had been received loud and clear: *I'm on to you.*

"That makes a full round," Marcus abruptly announced. "Guess you need to be going, Tamás."

"Reckon I can stay a bit longer," Tamás replied, his tone carrying a chilly undercurrent of confrontation.

The ensuing hand found the two adversaries locked eye-to-narrowed-eye in a high-stakes showdown after the other four men folded. To stay for the draw, Tamás emptied his billfold, including wages for repairing the bar.

Tamás took one card.

"I'll play these," Marcus said, swagger in his inflection.

His bet to open, Tamás checked. Marcus pounced, scribbling out an I.O.U. promissory deed for four acres of his massive land holdings.

"I'm already all-in," Tamás protested stoically.

"Too bad," Marcus declared. "You call or you lose."

Tamás peeked at his cards, held close to his chest, and while doing so glimpsed Marcus's right hand sliding off the table to his lap. Instantly, curtly: "How 'bout keeping both hands in plain sight, Marcus—

"—and how 'bout I call your bet with my clarinet?"

"What hell use I got for some fancy flute?" Marcus growled. He ran his hand through his hair, shark-grey like his predatory eyes, then pressed his hat back on. "Toss in your gold ring. It'll do just fine."

Marcus did not notice Tamás's temples twitch. While it was just a simple gold band, he could not risk losing his wedding ring. And yet, how could he fold now?

Poker is a game of seeing all possibilities. Tamás was wearing two rings, one on each hand. The second ring had a stunning Hungarian Opal, a large translucent stone of midnight blue swirling with fire—reds, oranges, yellows—and a personal history even more priceless than the gemstone.

The fare for voyage from Port of Rijeka in Croatia to New York City varied from passenger to passenger as unscrupulous crews demanded everything of value before allowing embarkation. Anticipating this shakedown, Tamás had sewn five silver coins, and a sixth one of gold, inside the back waistband of his trousers.

Alas, the ploy did not fool the crewmen working the gangplank of the creaky vessel *New Hope*. Not all was lost, however, for the deception had also been a contingency bluff shielding a greater treasure.

And so it was that Tamás successfully smuggled the Hungarian Opal ring, hidden safely beyond detection inside the uncomfortable human darkness just south of the discovered coins. After being washed clean, the heirloom, given to Tamás by his mother on her deathbed, provided him and Aisha with a hopeful landing in The New World.

Perilous Voyage

The voyage across the Atlantic Ocean from Port of Rijeka to New York Harbor, in late summertime 1848, in cramped steerage quarters for three weeks and a day, had been anything but comfortable.

And anything but safe.

The journey was plagued by deteriorating weather, and by men of deteriorated character. Daily, and nightly, raven-haired Aisha experienced unwanted advances emboldened by alcohol, its overconsumption fueled by boredom. Time and again, Tamás diffused matters before they escalated.

One run-in did escalate—quickly, greatly, perilously.

Like John Howland, just before falling overboard two centuries earlier, Aisha ventured from the below-deck squalor seeking some fresh sea-spray air. Tamás eventually went looking for his nineteen-year-old fiancé.

Rounding a corner at ship's aft, Tamás saw a deckhand grab Aisha to steal a kiss. Instead of the sweet taste of her rosy lips, Aisha gave the assailant a violent elbow to the Adam's apple and nimbly escaped his inebriated clutches.

Tamás by nature was a portrait of goodwill. The square jaw and sharp angles of his face, including a nose twice broken, combined in a handsome way. A toothy smile he did not ration, warm topaz-brown eyes, and a shock of wavy dark hair too thick to run a comb through, all softened his rugged countenance. He was a practiced fighter, yet chose to be peaceable if possible.

Now, Tamás turned cold-eyed and seemed to grow three inches in height as he strode forward with swiftness, with purpose, with fists balled.

In a flash, from a pocket in his peacoat the deckhand pulled out a rigging knife, the blade's edge gleaming as if freshly sharpened on a whetstone. Tamás balked and retreated a half-step.

"Figured as much," the thug sneered, adding a malignant grin. "Coward."

Tamás's myriad gifts included measuring a man, measuring a situation, and keeping his cool under duress. He at once relied on all three powers, the first two performed quickly, then with deliberate strides closed the distance between them.

"You'd best hold that toothpick tight," Tamás warned, with placid assurance that was unnerving, "'cause I'm gonna take it from you—and use it."

The words landed like a champion prizefighter's solid hook. The thug's lungs went breathless, his face blanched, his legs fled.

Lying in Tamás's arms that night, on her side, two spoons in the middle bunk of a three-high stack, Aisha wept. The shipboard confrontation had shaken her far more than the rough seas ever could. The couple spoke in midnight whispers, in their native Hungarian tongue, in distress.

"What troubles you, my lovebird?" Tamás soothed.

"I'm scared, Tamás—scared we were fools to leave Hungary."

"No, no," Tamás sympathized. "With me at your side you have nothing to fear—this is my promise."

"What if America is even worse than this awful voyage?" Aisha sobbed.

"America is good," Tamás reassured. "It's the land of golden dreams."

"But we know no one there—not a single person."

"You know me and you know your mother," Tamás corrected, tightening his embrace. "You are not alone. I'm here."

"I fear we never should have left home."

"Our homeland was no longer the home it once was," Tamás countered. "The Revolution changed that. It's more dangerous to stay than leave."

"You're right, Tamás. I know you are. But my fear for what our future holds is great."

"Fear and excitement are neighbors on opposite sides of the same fence," Tamás said, the braveness in his voice as comforting as ol' Emilian's string music. "I know this much about our future in America—we will get married and make it our home. The rest will fall in place, in time, you will see. Have faith in me, my lovebird—"

Using his shirtsleeve, Tamás wiped away the salty emotion rolling down Aisha's face. Her cheekbones were as soft and angelic as his were hard and chiseled.

"—have faith in *us*."

Snuggling against *New Hope*'s damp chill, together against the cold world, Aisha and Tamás drifted into golden dreamland.

Dika, eavesdropping on the pillow-less pillow talk, closed her eyes in the berth below and smiled. No longer did she harbor any doubts that her daughter had fallen in love with a good man.

Treasures And Trouble

Their second day in New York City, the first thing Tamás did was visit a string of pawn shops.

The nicer a shop appeared outside, the worse Tamás was treated within. Pitiless owners saw an opportunity to swindle another fresh immigrant.

With limited English skills, with morale as blistered as his feet, Tamás trudged past "Laszlo's Pawn Treasures." Rundown even for a hole-in-the-wall, it seemed hardly worth the effort of crossing the street. He walked on.

A block later, intuition—or Destiny—shook Tamás by the shoulders. He went back. A brass bell above the door—*ding-ding!*—announced his entrance and the proprietor greeted him with a gap-toothed grin.

Serendipity smiled also. Laszlo was a fellow Hungarian immigrant, a half-century on Lady Liberty's shores. Along with an honest loan price and fair interest rate, the stoop-postured man promised not to sell the Opal ring for six months. This would give Tamás a long-shot chance at buying it back.

"*Köszönöm*," said Tamás, sincerely.

"*Nincs mit*," Laszlo replied: *You're welcome—'tis nothing.*

To Tamás, it was everything. He exited Laszlo's Pawn Treasures with rent money for a tiny slum room, as well as some overused-but-serviceable carpentry tools, and two unadorned gold wedding bands. That afternoon, alone except for a priest, the young loverbirds were wed.

The six months passed, and two more, before Tamás finally saved enough money as a journeyman carpenter to buy back the Hungarian Opal ring. He ran to the pawnshop, hoping he was not too late.

"I never lose faith I again see you," greeted Laszlo, almost singing. "So I hold on to your *gyönyörű*!"—beautiful—"ring."

The old man's eyes embraced Tamás: "You remind me of my son. He gone many years now—scarlet fever."

"*Sajnálom*," Tamás said, softly, heartfelt—*I'm sorry*.

Sorrow on one side of the fence, joyous surprise on the other. Laszlo would accept only the amount of the original loan, explaining: "The money you saved for interest is my gift to you and your *gyönyörű* bride to build a blessed life in America."

"Are you serious?" said Tamás, overwhelmed, his English greatly improved.

Laszlo nodded.

"But why? You don't even know me."

"Some day, when you are old like me, you do same for a young stranger—*igen*?"

"*Igen, igen*"—yes, yes—"I promise. *Köszönöm*!" Tamás said, sealing the transaction with a hug before slipping the heirloom Opal ring on his finger and—*ding-ding!*—slipping out the door.

~~~

Tamás slipped off the Hungarian Opal ring, a decade later, and pushed it to the middle of the poker table.

It was nearly imperceptible, yet Tamás saw it clear as a summer night sky: Marcus's temples tightened, his upper lip moistened. Marcus had miscalculated—his greedy eyes had been focused on the plain gold band.

A banker, and a cunning one, Marcus was ignorant of the fact that in Hungary, as in much of Europe, wedding bands are traditionally worn on the *right* ring finger. Hence, when Tamás removed the Opal ring from his *left* hand, the consequences were threefold:

First, Marcus thought it was Tamás's wedding ring.

Second, Marcus knew that only a man who was confident as hell would risk such a thing.

Third, quick as a rattlesnake strike, Marcus knocked back his chair while springing to his feet.

"Whoa! Don't want no trouble," Tamás said, rising, cautiously, open palms held out in a take-it-easy gesture.

"Oh, you've got trouble, gypsy," Marcus said, blackly. "Nobody cheats Marcus Murphy."

"Me, a cheat?" Tamás gibed. "Then how come *you* have a card sticking out of your belt?"

Marcus, without taking his snake-slit eyes off Tamás, used his right hand to see if the purloined card was indeed visible. His thumb brushed an exposed edge, pushed it back down.

While Marcus was performing this sleight of hand, Tamás—in a flash!—plucked a beer bottle off the poker table and, gripping it by the neck, whacked the bottom half on the table's edge.

Marcus laughed and, from behind his back, pulled out a revolver. Emboldened with the upper hand in this gun-versus-glass-knife fight, he repeated: "You got big trouble, cheater!"

Deliberately, Marcus took dead aim.

Courage of Different Kinds

He squeezed the trigger, gunpowder exploded, a bullet flew towards its destiny.

Jamis, sensing Lemuel was no longer close behind, had turned around just in time to see the brute-sized bobcat in a predatory charge. Reflexively, in one seamless motion, Jamis raised his rifle took aim fired.

A .22-caliber bullet is not the ammunition of choice for hunting bobcat, more likely to wound than kill, and a wounded animal is the most dangerous.

Jamis's shot did not wound. His aim was fast and true, striking the brawny beast in mid-pounce, in midair, in the heart. The bobcat was lifeless before it landed atop Lem.

Bowled over and bewildered, Lem was blessedly unharmed. Jamis, realizing how close to death his brother had come, began to quiver, then shook uncontrollably as he tried to hold back his tears and failed.

Lem cried also, for an altogether different reason. After crawling out from beneath the dead bobcat, he studied the creature and was overcome by its beauty; overcome by its bloodstained fur; overcome by its glassy lifeless eyes. He did not blame Jamis for killing it, but neither did he wholly comprehend that his brother had saved him from death.

There were many things Lemuel did not understand—*could not* understand. As the identical twins grew older, a consequential difference emerged: Lem was regarded by most, including his teachers, as less than bright—"slow-witted" and "a little simple" and "soft in the head" being among their cruel labels.

Lem's difficult breech birth had played no role, of this Doc was most certain, for oxygen had never been deprived. Aisha and Tamás, ever grateful for Doc's heroics that stormy night, blamed him not at all.

Jamis, on the other hand, blamed Doc fully. His bitterness festered as his twin fell further and further behind in intellect, in school, in life.

Although only a few minutes older than Lem, Jamis took to feeling like he was the big brother by many years. Over time, he became powerfully protective—often with punches. Born on winter's side of the vernal equinox, a cold and angry and growing wind began swirling in Jamis's soul.

Lemuel's personality, contrarily, mimicked the spring side of the equinox marking his birth. His warm and gentle soul was exemplified by the way he related to animals. Not only did Lem refuse to hunt game, he would bring injured wildlife home and nurse the animals to health before releasing the rescues back into the woods.

Jamis readily accepted Lem's softness for animals, but he bristled when his brother showed no fight when someone called him "stupid" or "village idiot" or worse.

Jamis's disapproval hurt Lem far more than the taunts. Once, when the twins were nine, Lem brooded for days after being teased by a schoolboy because he felt he let Jamis down by turning the other cheek.

To lift his mood, Tamás asked Lemuel to help him with a project in the workshop. Unlike Jamis, Lem showed considerable interest in woodworking. He showed a great natural talent as well.

While he easily lost focus on schoolwork, Lem could concentrate hours on end sanding a door or chair or gunstock. Whereas Tamás generally toiled in focused silence, Lem had a lovely habit of faintly whistle-humming while woodworking. It was an auditory birthmark affected by the first sound he heard as he exited his mother's womb.

"Son," Tamás began as the two sanded a chair together. "Don't let Jamis get you down. My father—your Grandpa Viktor, you never met him—taught me an old proverb."

"What's a proverb?" Lem interjected.

"A piece of wisdom," Tamás answered. "Like this lesson from my dad: *If a man kicks you down, get back up, extend your hand and call him 'brother,' for the surest way to destroy an enemy is to make him your friend.*"

Tamás blew on the chair seat, a concentrated short puff as if extinguishing birthday cake candles, sending a small cloud of sawdust floating away, then continued: "There's courage of different kinds, Lem. Jamis always gets up swinging, but it's a rarer bravery to offer a friendly hand instead of a clenched fist—the way you do."

Lemuel, whistle-humming through a proud grin, returned to his woodworking task.

Something Glorious

Lincoln questioned his mother's love.

Following their fight over the hidden Opal ring, Linc spent the night at his friend Keven's house, in a borrowed sleeping bag, on a hardwood floor. He replayed the drama with his mom over and again. What little sleep he got was tortured.

Linc's waking nightmare was just beginning.

There was no football practice Saturday following the Cleveland Peak High Cougars' 14-13 season-opening victory, only a brief morning team meeting. Afterward, despite the lingering celebratory atmosphere, Linc trudged home with spirits deflated. A big part of him hoped his mom had already left, but a forgiving measure wanted her to still be home and—hope over expectation—in a good mood. Maybe she would like to hear all about Friday night's game, especially his one-handed catch in the end zone for the game-winning two-point conversion.

All three of Linc's wishes came true: Vanessa was initially gone, but shortly returned home in a happy state of mind.

"Where were you last night?" she asked, her tone surprisingly pleasant, not accusatory.

"I slept at Kev's."

"That's what I figured," Vanessa said, peaceably. "I wish you'd call next time, though, so I don't worry."

"I wish you'd go back to rehab," Linc said, not tersely but as a sincere plea filled with concern.

"Everything's going to be okay, honey," Vanessa replied. "Don't worry. We won't get evicted, I promise. I got the money we needed so I can pay rent Monday. Look, I even bought groceries—there's Pop Tarts in here somewhere!"

Linc wondered where the money came from for two full bags of food, much less two months' back rent. The dog-eared Pinto was parked out front, so at least she hadn't sold it. Suddenly, he shivered as if an icy Gatorade shower had cascaded down his back.

There's no way she found the ring, Linc thought. *It's not possible—is it?*

He raced out of the kitchen to the bathroom, slammed and locked the door. With heavy foreboding, he lifted the clunky porcelain lid off the toilet tank, looked in, looked longer, kept looking for something that obviously was not there. It was like the time in middle school when his ten-speed bicycle was stolen and he frantically searched every row of bike racks—once, twice, three times—convinced that his purple Schwinn Varsity had to be there, somewhere, and he was simply blind to it.

In disbelief, in denial, in desperation, Linc reached into the cool water and felt all around the flapper and fill valve tube. The cold truth made him shudder once more, his neck hairs stood at attention. The zip-lock plastic bag truly was not there. The ring, *his* ring, was gone.

Linc slumped to his knees on the linoleum floor, cold and piss-stained, ran his wet fingers through his thick hair that was always neatly tousled, then did something he had not done when his mom dragged him away from his friends and classmates and happy life in Bellaire; had not done when he was lonely and afraid while she had been away at rehab; had not even done when she lapsed back into addiction. He cried.

Vanessa knocked.

Silence.

She knocked louder: "Open the door."

"Go away."

"Let me in."

"I said, go! away!"

"Oh, Linc-y, please don't be mad," Vanessa pleaded, her voice weighted with defeat. "I had no choice. I couldn't let us be homeless."

Angry silence.

"It's only temporary. I'll get the ring back—trust me."

Funeral silence.

"I'm giving you some of the money—two hundred dollars, how's that? So you can buy those football cleats you've been begging for. And a Walkman, too."

Unbearable silence.

"I know you hate me right now," Vanessa said in surrender. "I'll leave the extra money on your dresser—"

She swallowed a rising sob.

"—I love you."

Linc doubted he would ever again see the heirloom Opal ring.

He doubted his mom would get sober and clean.

He doubted he could feel smaller, hurt worse, be more lost.

Despite these crushing doubts, despite his anger, despite the depths of his forlornness, Lincoln did something glorious.

"I love you, too," he called out from behind the locked door.

Heartache, Hardship, Hardiness

 Monday is a marathon away from Friday if you are battling substance addiction.

Vanessa did not even make it through Saturday clean.

When Tamás pawned the Hungarian Opal ring upon his arrival in New York City in 1850, he made the shop owner promise to wait six months before selling it. This gave Tamás a puncher's chance to buy the heirloom back.

Vanessa bargained for no assurance beyond *Top Dollar! Pawn Shop*'s standard thirty-day grace period. Nor did she bargain for top dollar. The owner tendered a price of fifteen hundred dollars, surely expecting a counteroffer double that, but Vanessa hastily accepted. It was inequitable, even by greedy pawnbroker standards, as the antique ring's market value was easily tenfold the loan.

Still, fifteen hundred dollars would have covered residency in a substance-abuse facility. Lincoln would have happily slept on Keven's bedroom floor while his mom received such life-saving treatment. Indeed, he asked God for her rehab.

But the Devil's grip on Vanessa was vise-like. Saturday evening, while Linc was at the movies with friends, she searched his room and found the Walkman-and-cleats apology money poorly hidden in his underwear drawer. It wasn't nearly enough for the rent, but it was more than enough for some black-market OxyContin.

As his eleven o'clock weekend curfew ticked near, Linc phoned his mom. After six rings it went to voicemail and he left a brief message: *Hi Ma, it's me. Guess you're already asleep. Anyway, I'm spending the night at Kev's. See ya tomorrow.*

Sunday morning, Linc came home to an empty apartment. Vanessa did not return until mid-afternoon and without so much as a hello went straight to her room, passed out on the bed with her shoes on, and was still sleeping off her jag when dinnertime arrived. Linc ordered a pizza and went to get money from his top dresser drawer to pay the delivery driver.

Unlike with his stolen purple Schwinn and the midnight-blue-and-sunset-hues Opal ring missing from the toilet tank, this time Linc did not search in disbelief for what was not there. He knew rummaging through his underwear and socks was pointless. He knew his mom took the money.

Nor did he have any uncertainty how she spent it, that she had traded away his future football cleats and Walkman for drugs. That she had traded away *their* future.

Monday, when Linc came home from football practice, the apartment was empty once more. The sin of the father had become the sin of the mother. And for the second time in Linc's young life, this sin visited upon the son.

Unlike when Flynn bolted, Vanessa left a goodbye note:

Dear Lincy-Linc,

I'm sorry for everything. I need to leave for a while before I hurt you worse than I already have. I didn't pay the rent so eviction happens Friday. I'm so sorry. Take the Greyhound to Bellaire and go see Aunt Veronica. I know she'll take you in. Please forgive me. Please don't hate me forever.

Love,
Ma
xoxo

Resting atop the note was a thin stack of bills—ninety-seven bucks—for bus fare and food. It was half of all that remained from the pawn money after Vanessa's latest self-destructive binge.

Linc had heard the family lore of Tamás leaving his wife and twin sons. Notably, that his departure had been noble—Tamás ran *towards* the noble cause of fighting for the Union in The Civil War. Linc's father, and now his mother, ignobly ran *away* to chase their next drug highs.

All the same, remarkably, Linc did not hate his mom. As Vanessa had done when Flynn fled, Linc blamed addiction for putting a deathly chokehold on love.

When heartache and hardship apply a stranglehold, there are two possible reactions: sink into despair, or rise to the challenge. Linc chose the latter. He did not teeter towards self-pity, not even for a heartbeat.

He had a football season to play.

He had a school year to finish.

He had new friends in Cleveland Heights.

Unlike his mom and dad, Linc refused to run from his troubles. He chose to stand tall and face them head-on, even if it meant being homeless.

And it did.

Hospital Pass

The crowd's chant was deafening: *Two! Points! Two! Points!*

The scoreboard: *Home 20, Visitor 21.*

The game clock, with four bulbs burned out: *0:00.*

Cougars Beat Dawgs! cheered a banner painted in gold and black. Another: *Tavis For President!*

The visiting Chillicothe High Bulldogs' blue-jerseyed defense waited at the three-yard line. A Cougar player raced from the home sideline to the offensive huddle, bringing the play call from Coach Harry McFadden: "Red Rocket, Twenty-Eight Pitch, Right."

"Again?" groused quarterback Tavis Jordan. "Rhett got knocked on his ass the last three sweeps."

"Hey, man, just telling you what Coach called."

Tavis, his eyes darting around the huddle, barked brashly: "This is for the state championship! Let's show some guts!"

"No, Tav," Rhett pleaded. "Don't change the play."

"Okay, fine," Tavis relented, reluctantly, after hurried consideration. "Red Rocket, Twenty-Eight Pitch, Right, on two—and block your asses off. This is our chance to become legends."

Breaking the huddle, Tavis seized Rhett's facemask: "You aren't gonna *run* the ball—you're gonna *throw* it."

"Throw it? To who?"

Tavis grinned cocksure: "To me, buddy! Eleven Bulldogs will be chasing you and I'll be scratching my ass all alone in the end zone."

"Coach will kill us if—"

"Don't worry, Rhett. Just chuck me the ball and I promise I won't let go of it."

Tavis spat into his palms, rubbed them together, crouched under center. Defenders dug in their cleats. The stadium roared with one voice, loud as Niagara Falls.

Hut! Hut!

Tavis took the snap, spun clockwise, pitched the pigskin to Rhett. Led by a tidal wave of pulling blockers, the speedy tailback glided towards the right sideline.

Meanwhile, Tavis curled left out of the backfield, as ignored as the homeless, and headed for the end zone.

A gap of daylight opened and Rhett dismissed Tavis's private audible. He would run for glory.

One stride later, before Rhett could turn up field, the hole closed tight. Coach McFadden spit out an obscenity and slammed his clipboard to the ground. Red Rocket was doomed.

Quick as finger snap, Rhett slammed on the brakes, planted his right foot, pivoted left, flung the football across the field.

Tavis was wide open.

But the pass arced too high, seemingly floating in slow motion, giving defensive back Bobby Bautista time to recover in a mad dash. A "hospital pass" is what receivers call such a throw because it leaves them stretched out and exposed to injury.

Fearlessly, Tavis leapt high and reached higher.

The nanosecond his hands touched the spiraling football the defender delivered a hit that sounded as horrific as a car crash. Tavis, limp as a ragdoll, landed flat on his back with a sickening *Thump!*

Bautista, his back turned to the fallen foe, celebrated his game-saving blow. He did not see Tavis laying motionless in the end zone, his flexed arms folded lifeless across his chest like the deceased in an open casket—

—but still wrapped around the football!

The referee raised his arms to signal the successful—and game-winning—two-point conversion: *Home 22, Visitor 21.*

Bautista spun and could not believe his eyes, thinking as he stood over Tavis: *How the hell?! No one could catch the ball after that hit. I should be the hero, not you.*

Bautista's disbelief and anger at once turned to worry and prayer: "Move, dude. Come on, move! Wake up! For the love of Jesus, open your eyes—*pleeease.*"

Paramedics rushed in.

Four thousand people fell hushed as a single held breath.

Tavis, unconscious, was strapped on a stretcher and loaded into an ambulance. Coach McFadden and Rhett rode along to the hospital.

"Pulse strong, pupils responsive," one EMT reported.

"Un-bloody-believable," replied his partner. "Kid gets knocked out cold and still holds on to the ball."

"Of course he did," Rhett bristled. "Never bet against Tav."

"This boy's tougher than any man I know," added Coach McFadden.

Tavis, still clutching the football to his chest, at last opened his eyes: "Did we win?"

"Yes, son," Coach McFadden answered. "*You* won it."

Flashing an impish grin, Tavis winked at Rhett: "So whose house is the victory party at?"

Entrance To Escapees' Haven

 The party rolled on for Tavis Jordan.

He received a full-ride football scholarship to the University of Michigan, surprisingly as a wide receiver, not quarterback. It was a homecoming of sorts, for while Tavis was born and raised in Cleveland, his family roots reached deep into Detroit's fertile river basin soil. Ann Arbor, home to U of M, is only thirty miles from Detroit proper.

Tavis's great-great-great-grandfather, Sawney, was a slave on a large Virginia tobacco plantation. Gambling his life for a chance at freedom, he escaped north on the Underground Railroad through West Virginia, Ohio, and Michigan before reaching Canada.

The Underground Railroad's code name for the Detroit River was "Jordan," a biblical reference to the river that led to The Promised Land. Before his attempted border crossing to a land that promised freedom in Windsor, Ontario, Sawney's final stop was The Second Baptist Church on Monroe Avenue in the Detroit neighborhood of Greektown.

At the top of a stairway leading down to the church basement hung a carved wooden plaque announcing: *Entrance to Escapees' Haven.* Sawney, like nearly all of the estimated six thousand fleeing slaves who passed through Second Baptist, could not read the sign.

Thirteen wooden steps, precariously steep and narrow, descended into the unlit unknown, each blind footfall creaking under the weight of both fear and hope. At the bottom was "Croghan Street Station," the Underground's code name for the *Haven* dream. Here the air was dank, smelling like decomposing leaves, like death, yet within two miles of a new life. It might as well have been one hundred miles, for this final leg was fraught with swirling river currents—and a maelstrom of greedy, heartless, resolute bounty patrollers.

Before departing Croghan Street Station, Sawney, who never knew his birth surname, nor knew his given name meant "defender of mankind," was inspired to choose one: Jordan.

~~~

Five generations forward, Tavis Jordan was chasing his own dream.

As a Michigan Wolverine, he was a lightning-in-a-bottle punt returner. His uncatchable legs, even more than his Velcro-like pass-catching hands, made Tavis a two-time All-America Team selection. As a senior, he garnered a handful of Heisman Trophy votes.

On the field, Tavis was a success story; off it, a cautionary tale. Like too many college athletes, he foresaw a future of fame and riches in the pros and thus did not take his studies seriously. His declared major was History, but in truth Tav studied only Football. After four years, he had not earned his diploma.

No matter. Tavis's charmed life continued with another homecoming when the Cleveland Browns selected him in the sixth round of the 1980 NFL Draft.

He shined so brightly in training camp as a rookie that he earned a spot in the starting lineup.

In the Browns' regular season opener against the Kansas City Chiefs, Tavis ran a slant route across the middle of the field. The spiral from quarterback Brian Sipe sailed "hospital pass" high. As on the final play of Tav's high school career, a linebacker delivered a sledgehammer-like blow.

Again, Tavis miraculously held possession of the football. Again, he was taken off the field on a stretcher and to the hospital in an ambulance. This time, however, he suffered a spinal injury—two ruptured discs in his neck. Despite "successful" fusion surgery of vertebrae C-4 and C-5, nerve damage resulted in permanent numbness and diminished motor skills in his left thumb, index and middle fingers.

Tavis's first catch in the NFL had also been his last. His playing career was over almost before it began.

When a figurative boulder rolls over you, there are two possible responses: slump into self-pity and despair, or rise to the challenge. Tavis chose the latter. He re-enrolled at U of M and completed his undergraduate studies. Pursuing a new dream of becoming a high school teacher—and coach—he further earned a Masters in Education.

On the Underground Railroad "dawn" was code for journey's end and the beginning of freedom. Tavis made an oath to himself to always teach his students, and most forcefully his athletes, that "education" was the code word—and secret ingredient—for a life journey filled with dawn's sunshine.

Be Quick, Don't Panic

Marcus Murphy's wooden armchair tumbled backwards as he thrust himself away from the dining-turned-poker table and vaulted to his feet.

Tamás, having been accused of cheating, guardedly rose out of his chair.

Both men's five playing cards lay facedown on the tabletop, but Marcus had the upper hand that mattered at that instant: he held a .31-cailber Colt Pocket Percussion single-action revolver, pearl-handled, in his right hand, a handgun of choice by officers in the ongoing Civil War. Tamás was armed with a broken-off bottleneck in his left fist.

Tamás raised the makeshift weapon away from his body, ever so cautiously, causing Marcus's villainous squint—and the pistol barrel—to instinctively track the jagged glass bottle. This miniscule misdirection divided Marcus's attention by half, but that was enough. In the span between two heartbeats, Tamás—

thrum-bump

—flicked his right hand down and forward and, without taking his eyes off Marcus, blindly plucked a steak knife off the tabletop;

—pulled his right hand back up, and behind his ear, while simultaneously dancing his fingertips from the stag-horn handle down to the four-inch steel blade; at the same time, he mentally gauged the knife's heft and appraised its balance; and also calculated the distance, and knife-blade rotations, across the poker table;

—the instant his arm reached the cocked position, Tamás snapped his elbow straight and flicked his wrist with power and sent the knife whirling like a propeller towards its target.

thrum-bump

The whirling blade flew fast and it flew true and it skewered the derby, grey as Ahab's sea, just above the front brim, dead center. A crimson bull's-eye appeared instantaneously. Marcus, a steak knife protruding from his forehead, never squeezed off a single shot.

The bull's-eye seeped larger as Marcus remained standing, motionless as a stone sentinel. The crimson grew, his face blanched, his soulless eyes glazed over, he swayed slightly, like a cattail in a breeze, then his legs gave way.

Tamás, fleet as a spooked deer in flight, was out the front door of The Hotel Bellaire before Marcus hit the floor, but in his haste left the heirloom Hungarian Opal ring on the poker table.

Tamás had never killed a man. He had been in his share of fights, but always the weapons had been fists. Never bullets. Win or lose—most often it was the former for Tamás—he wound up sharing a drink with his foe. The thought of taking a life agitated a cloud of wasps in his stomach.

Be quick, don't hurry, Tamás told himself while walking briskly through town, trying not to attract undue attention. Trying to reign in his galloping heart, he revised Doc's maxim: *Be quick, don't panic.*

Tamás knew he had acted in self-defense, knew Marcus was mean as a wolverine, but he did not know if judge and jury would see it that way. He could not risk it.

The majority of citizenry in Bellaire had warmly accepted the Beswicks. All the same, even after living in town for a decade and more, Tamás had never entirely escaped the frosty stares that every foreigner, every minority, every outsider who is different in some way, experiences most everywhere.

As a Hungarian immigrant, and a former hobo at that, Tamás reasoned he would be considered guilty until proven innocent. Stancliff Davidson might testify on his behalf—unless, that is, Marcus's bank held Stan's mortgage note on The Hotel Bellaire. That kind of leverage could fog an eyewitness's account. Moreover, the other four players were friends of Marcus and would surely lie on his behalf.

Poker is a game of chance and calculation—as is a fight. Tamás had weighed the odds of the five cards Marcus held, but failed to calculate into the equation the chance of killing Marcus before flinging the steak knife. It was a costly oversight.

Tamás now sized up his odds as being best if he vanished for a while—a good long while. The idea of leaving Aisha squeezed his heart; to abandon Jamis and Lemuel nearly stopped it between beats.

No matter. Tamás was certain running away was a far better verdict than his wife and twin sons seeing him hanged for murder.

Full House No More

Regret seized Tamás in a choking stranglehold as he fled The Hotel Bellaire:

Why didn't I leave right after I finished repairing the bar?

I shouldn't have played poker.

With each getaway step his self-reproach intensified:

Why, oh why, did I bullheadedly stay for one extra hand?

If only I'd aimed for Marcus's shooting shoulder.

Not a praying man, Tamás did now:

Lord, forgive me for killing a man.

Please, dear Lord—please forgive me for leaving my family.

Tamás resolved that taking Aishia and the twins, and Grandma Dika as well, away with him was both pointless and perilous. A family in tow, slowing him down, would guarantee apprehension by the law. Soul-wrenching as it was, he had no choice but to leave them behind.

Tamás's heavyheartedness was buoyed, in small measure, in knowing his loved ones would be in good hands with one another. Aisha and Dika would naturally watch over Jamis and Lemuel—not that the boys needed much taking care of anymore as they proved with their recent bobcat encounter. Indeed, when need be, Aisha and Dika could lean on the eleven-year-old twins.

Tamás found further reassurance in telling himself he was not abandoning his family, merely taking a long trip. He vowed to one day, some day, return.

By autumn 1863, the American Civil War was into its third year of unholy bloodshed. The Union continued to recruit heavily—and anti-slavery Ohio continued to answer the Blue's call robustly. By war's end, more than three hundred thousand Ohioans would serve.

Tamás reasoned, and hoped and prayed, that if he went away to fight for President Lincoln, upon returning to Bellaire his military service would be rewarded with leniency from Judge Cullen Graham. As for the war's perils, Tamás decided a Confederate's bullet would be a nobler ending than a noose. At least then his death would bring no shame upon Aisha and the twins.

All this, and more, raced through Tamás's mind as he hustled home on foot. His spur-of-the-moment plan was to enlist for a one-year hitch in Union blue, maybe stay until victory was won, then return from exile before Jamis and Lem had turned into teenagers.

Bellaire held strategic significance during "The War Between the States." Its location on the Ohio River made it the vanguard between "The Buckeye State," which was pro-Union, and the "Old Dominion" slave-holding state of Virginia, which had voted to secede. Railroads on either side of the border river added to the military importance. For these reasons, Camp Jefferson was established on the outskirts of Bellaire as a Union training outpost.

But Tamás reckoned he would be readily found at Camp Jefferson. Instead, he decided to head 260 miles east as the raven flies for Camp Dennison—seventeen miles north of Cincinnati—to join the Ohio Volunteer Infantry.

First, goodbyes needed saying.

"Jamis and Lem—listen closely," Tamás began, gently placing his strong, oversized hands on one shoulder of each twin. "I've gotta go away for a spell. A man kicked me down, and instead of getting back up and extending my hand to him and calling him 'brother,' I retaliated and hurt him."

A lump materialized in the father's throat. He swallowed with difficulty, breathed deeply, and at last continued: "No, that's not true—I *killed* him. I didn't mean to, but I did so all the same. That's why I must leave for a while. I'll be back, that is a promise, but I'm not sure when. Sons, while I'm gone you are the men of the house. You take good care of Ma and Grandma, understand?"

The twins nodded, battling to be brave and tearless, and Tamás squeezed their shoulders in benediction—like a king bestowing knighthood by ceremoniously tapping a sword on a soldier's epaulets. Next, he turned to Aisha. He kissed her tenderly, hugged her tightly, and whispered these departing words into her ear: "Keep faith in me— keep faith in *us*."

It was ironic: a full house—kings over sevens— resulted in a house no longer full. Less than an hour after a poker game ended with a knife-throwing contest, Tamás departed to join the biggest gunfight in American history.

Duel With A Devil

Tamás need not have fled Bellaire.

He had never before put a man in a grave—and had not still. The thrown steak knife lacked enough mass to fatally penetrate a man's skull. Pain and shock had caused the banker to faint.

Doc made a house call to The Hotel Bellaire. While he was suturing the unconscious patient's wounded forehead, owner Stancliff Davidson described the poker showdown: "I've never seen a richer pot, Doc, not in all my years. Tamás bet that flashy ring—his wedding ring, by God!—to call Marcus's IOU for some land."

It was not just *some* land. The wagered plot was precisely where The Black Walnut Tree once proudly stood; where Jamis and Lemuel were born; where Tamás long dreamed of building a home. But the plot had never been for sale.

That is not to say the land had never changed hands. Just a year earlier, ownership did so *three* times in an hour.

First, Matthew Murphy, Marcus' younger bother, wagered one prime acre in a horse race of two hundred yards. Living up to its name, Marcus's Pegasus beat Matty's Blackjack handily by five yards.

The loser demanded a "double-or-nothing" rematch. Marcus, as a sporting gesture, boastfully offered to race on foot—himself—against Blackjack at a distance of forty yards. Matty eagerly accepted, ignorant that this handicapping proposition was shrewdly cunning.

Marcus well knew it takes a horse a good twenty yards to reach top speed—perhaps thirty yards with Matthew's burly weight in the saddle. A quicker-starting human would have an edge straight out off the gate. What is more, Blackjack would still be winded from the first race.

Further stacking the odds, Marcus *allowed* Matty to fire the starter's pistol. Cagey again, Marcus anticipated the gunshot from astride Blackjack would spook the horse, even if only slightly, adding extra distance to his own head start.

True to plan, by the time Blackjack was at full throttle it was too late. Marcus had established an early lead and held on to win by a man's full stride. Matty, now owing two acres, furiously demanded a re-rematch—this time a duel with pistols, double-or-nothing, four acres or none.

Marcus declined, Matty challenged his big brother's manhood, and so it came to pass. The brothers stood back-to-back, marched ten paces each on Matty's verbal count, whirled around—

—*Ka-Pow!*

Matty fired first, too hurriedly, and missed.

Marcus raised his pistol barrel, squinted his left eye shut, took careful aim—

"No!" Matty begged. "You can have six acres if you don't shoot."

"Make it eight."

"Yes, yes. Of course. Eight acres."

Marcus, grinning like Satan himself, sneered soullessly: "I think four acres is all I need."

Ka-Pow!

For the rest of his years, Matthew needed a cane because of the .31-caliber slug lodged in his left femur.

That is the kind of human devil Tamás thought he had killed. Truth be told, Tamás was more likely to have been given a parade than jail time.

After tying the final catgut suture in Marcus's forehead, Doc eyed the poker table. Two five-card hands remained facedown. Doc flipped one over and fanned the cards: king of clubs, king of spades, king of diamonds, seven of clubs, seven of spades—a powerful full house.

"Whose hand?" Doc asked.

"Tamás's," answered Stancliff.

Doc reached across the table and, one by one, rolled Marcus's cards.

Ten of hearts.

Jack of hearts.

Queen of hearts.

King of hearts.

Doc hesitated, then revealed the decisive card—

—six of clubs.

"He was bluffing," Doc declared. "Busted straight flush."

"Check under his belt buckle," Stancliff advised.

Doc returned to Marcus, conscious now but groggy, and found the purloined card.

"Ace of hearts," Doc announced acerbically. "The winning card—had you pulled off the cheating switch."

Doc scooped up the final pot, including the Hungarian Opal ring and IOU, and commanded evenly: "You be sure to give the official deed to Tamás."

"Whatchya gonna do if I don't," Marcus spat out sourly. "Tell Sheriff Garman?"

"Just do right," Doc gibed, displaying the bloodied steak knife. "Or I'll take those stitches out with this."

River of Tears

 Doc went directly to deliver the Hungarian Opal ring and poker winnings to Tamás, but arrived too late.

"He's gone," Aisha sniffed, crimson-eyed.

"Where to?" Doc asked.

"You'll keep the secret?"

"On my honor, Aisha. You know you can trust me."

"He went to join the war," Aisha shared, her voice low, spirits lower. "He had to leave 'cause he killed a man"—s*niffle*—"said it was self-defense"—s*niffle*—"but that people might not believe him. *Sniffle.* If he comes home as a Union hero, maybe then he won't have to go to prison."

With the mention of prison, Aisha's fragile composure cracked and the floodwaters rushed forth. Doc embraced her, whistle-humming tenderly. Sometimes the best medicine is a caring shoulder to lean on, and he administered a long dose. When the heaving sobs subsided, Doc said, barely above a whisper: "Listen to me, Aisha."

Then, looking her in the eye, louder, firmer: "Tamás didn't kill anyone."

"But he said—"

"I just finished stitching Marcus up," Doc explained. "He bled quite a bit, as head wounds are apt to do, but it wasn't anything at all serious. It'll heal up fine—although I'm not so sure about his wounded pride."

This good news was instantly overshadowed by a grave voice coming from the kitchen.

"I see a storm coming," Grandma Dika foretold loudly. "I see death and I see Jamis and Lemuel crying. Tamás must not join the Union army. He *must not* fight in The Great War."

"You've got nothing to be worried about," Doc called out, trying to quell both women's well-founded fears. "I'll go find Tamás before he enlists and bring him home."

Doc turned to Aisha: "Is he at Camp Jefferson?"

"No," she answered, assuredly. "He said they'd find him there."

"How 'bout Camp Dennison?" Doc asked.

Aisha shrugged her burdened shoulders.

"Camp Dennison—in Cincinnati?" Doc tried again, hoping perhaps Tamás had mentioned the camp's city.

Again, only uncertainty from Aisha.

"Camp Chase in Columbus, maybe?" Doc persisted. "Or Cleveland's Camp Taylor?"

Aisha quizzically shook her head to both: "I'm sorry, Doc. I have no idea. Tamás didn't say where he was going. He just told me to have faith in him and that he would return to us as soon as it was safe."

Doc applied a salve of reassurance: "I've never met anyone more capable of taking care of himself in a dangerous situation than Tamás. He's a good man, your husband. He'll keep his word and come home. In the meanwhile, Aisha, let me know if you and your mother and the twins need anything, anything at all. Promise me you will."

Aisha nodded weakly.

"Tamás left this behind," Doc continued, giving Aisha the Hungarian Opal ring along with a stack of cash. For safety's sake, he held onto the IOU.

"One more thing," Doc said. "When Tamás comes back he's going to build you a house on that lovely spot of land where Jamis and Lem were born. Y'all own that now."

Incomprehension washed over Aisha's face.

"That's right, it's yours," Doc reiterated. "Something bad happened today—but something good is going to come from it. Stay strong and keep the faith."

Aisha embraced Doc, hugged him tightly, longly, her slumping morale and hopes lifting as surely as her posture grew taller.

"Remember, let me know if you need anything," Doc said in his tender bedside-manner voice. He tapped his heart twice. "While Tamás is away, I feel responsible for my two namesakes."

"Thank you, Doctor."

The house call finished, Aisha watched from the front doorway as Doc walked away down the street. Before he was out of earshot, she called out a parting sentiment: "Doctor Jamison—"

He stopped and turned.

"—you've been our hero since the night we met you. We love you like family."

Doc removed his favored derby, green as Ireland's hills and scarred with near-invisible knife-blade punctures, held it over his heart and smiled. His joy was pure and deep.

He had no way of knowing the river of tears ahead, had no way of knowing those sweet words—*We love you like family*—would be the last he heard from Aisha's lips.

Pulling In, Acting Out

 For the second time within a month, Doc arrived at the Beswick's house too late.

Aisha already lay unconscious when word reached her family's hero. Doc rushed to the rescue but was powerless to save her. On a dreary November night in 1863, with Doc and Grandma Dika and the twins at her bedside, cholera, a heartless and virulent disease with no cure then, stole the thirty-four-year-young life of Aisha Rózsa Beswick.

Multiplying anguish with cruel irony, Aisha died on Thanksgiving Day. Jamis and Lemuel, now age eleven, had little to be thankful for. Their father was gone, serving in the Union army—if he was not already one of the soldiers who "gave their lives, that the nation might live" in President Abraham Lincoln's words during the Gettysburg Address one week earlier—and now they were motherless as well.

Grandma Dika, bless her grieving heart, provided motherly love to the twins. Filling the role of a fatherly disciplinarian, however, she was impotent. Love without the counterbalance of discipline left Jamis and Lem like a row of books with only one bookend: they toppled over.

Lem pulled in emotionally, becoming absorbed in woodworking as if nothing else existed. He completed a chair his father had left unfinished and next created a chair of his own design.

Jamis, conversely, lashed out. He already blamed Doc for Lem's mental challenges. Now he also held Doc accountable for allowing his mother to die.

A black walnut tree produces a toxic chemical called *juglone*. This natural herbicide, released through the tree's roots as well as from its decaying leaves and nuts after they fall to the ground, prevents other plants from growing nearby. Scientists call this territorial protective mechanism *allelopathy*.

Jamis developed the human equivalent of allelopathy and began excreting his own form of juglone. His disposition grew more and more toxic, preventing people from being close to him. Heretofore unimaginable, Jamis even began to push Lem away.

From the moment Doc first placed Lemuel alongside his minutes-older brother on Aisha's chest, the twins had displayed a sacred bond. As infants, Aisha would put the boys down at nighttime with their heads at opposite ends of their shared crib. Each morning, she would find them sleeping face-to-identical-face.

After they outgrew the crib, Aisha would tuck each twin into his own separate bed. Come morning, they would be snuggled together in one or the other's bed. Tamás eventually pushed the two mattresses together, believing it would not be long until the toddler boys asked him to move them back apart. At age eleven, Jamis and Lem still had their mattresses paired as one.

Being orphaned, as the twins were for all intents, made Jamis's juglone even more pernicious. After Tamás left for the war and Aisha left for heaven, Jamis left Lem's side to sleep alone, pushing his twin away by pulling their two mattresses apart.

Lem responded by isolating himself further in his woodworking. Jamis, in turn, acted out more aggressively than ever. He got into fights almost daily at school—and not only when someone bullied Lem. Jamis was metamorphosing into a bully himself.

~~~

One autumn afternoon, as the one-year anniversary of their mother's death approached, Jamis went hunting and Lem tagged along to pick mushrooms.

Instead of going deep into the woods as usual, Jamis circled around to town. In pursuit of a rabbit, the boys found themselves on a knoll overlooking Doc's house. The very-long-eared quarry hid in the bushes on the right edge of the front yard. The twins waited silently and patiently waited some more. Time moved forward in inches and eventually the rabbit hopped forward out into the open.

Jamis lifted the .22-rifle to his shoulder, clicked off the safety, and in this same instant Lemuel spotted Doc nearing home from their left.

"Don't shoot," Lem warned under his breath, gently pushing the gun barrel towards the ground. "Doc's comin'."

Jamis retook aim.

"Don't!" Lem whisper-shouted, sternly now, and again pushed the gun's aim downward. "It's too dangerous."

"I hope it does scare him," Jamis snarled. "Doc deserves it."

Once more Jamis raised the barrel and, before Lem could react a third time, squeezed the trigger.

Fortune Favors The Bold

 "People talk about love at first sight," Doc shared one afternoon in January 1864.

"But I think I fell in love with Constance—my dear Connie—before we were even born. I just had to wait until I met her to make it official. I didn't have to wait all that long, either. We met in first grade if you can you believe it. Who meets the love of his life when he's six years old? Well, this lucky fool did.

"She was the first girl I ever kissed and—oh, boy!—I never wanted to kiss anyone else afterward. I'll never forget that first kiss. We were in sixth grade and Danny, my best friend, dared me during recess to kiss Connie. Well, anyone who knows me knows I don't easily back down from a dare. Danny could have challenged me to eat a live cricket and I wouldn't have chickened out. Come to think of it, he did make that exact dare once.

"Kissing Connie was far sweeter than eating that crunchy cricket, let me tell you. I was nervous as a cat inside a kennel of dogs. So here's what I did—I imagined myself as a brave medieval knight. I held my head high, puffed out my chest, and marched straight across the playground. By the time I reached Connie every kid in the schoolyard was watching, but I just pretended their stares were arrows bouncing off my steel armor. Up close, face-to-face, I winked at her and whispered, *Danny dared me, so don't get mad*, and kissed her.

Did she get mad? you might wonder. Nope—she winked back before pretending to be embarrassed and skipped away to her friends.

"Danny, naturally, was the best man at our wedding so before I kissed Connie for the first time as husband and wife, I teased her at the alter: *Danny dared me, so don't get mad.*

"Without missing a beat, she whispered back with a wink: *Well, Danny dared me to marry you—so I guess we'd better kiss and win both dares.*

"With laughter on our lips, we kissed long enough to fulfill a dozen dares from Danny, and it was wonderful.

"That first dare kiss on the playground was just a quick peck, but I replayed it in my mind a million times afterward. And it changed my life, truly. You see, it made me realize at the early age of twelve that *Fortune favors the bold* as the Roman poet Virgil observed. Emily Dickinson put it this way: *Fortune befriends the bold.* I'm partial to that phrasing because Connie was my best friend.

"Ever since, whenever I was afraid to do something—including going to medical school—I remembered how bold and brave I had pretended to be when I first kissed Connie, and that has always given me an extra dose of courage.

"But mostly that childhood kiss changed my life simply because it was with Connie. I've always been deeply indebted to Danny for that dare—and he never lets me forget it.

"I didn't get my second kiss from Connie until we were freshmen in high school. I walked her home from a school dance and, transformed into a medieval knight once more, I boldly kissed her at the front doorstep—and this time she kissed me back.

"I didn't have to wait nearly as long for a third kiss, it came the very next weekend at a hayride, and from then on we went steady all through high school.

"After graduation, we both worked for two years to earn tuition money before heading off to Oberlin College—she to become a schoolteacher and I, of course, to become a doctor. Oberlin was nearby and it was also highly regarded. It was actually the very first college in America to accept women, back in 1833, when it was still called Oberlin College Institute.

"Following our graduations from Oberlin, Connie returned home to Bellaire to teach primary grades while I went off to Cincinnati to study medicine. Those two long-distance years were difficult, but we wrote plenty of letters and never had a minute's doubt we would get married."

Storybook Love

"Maybe not in sixth grade or ninth grade," Doc continued with his love story, "but by the time we were high school seniors, and certainly in college, Connie and I knew we would one day get married.

"And we did—March 20, 1852. The grandest day of my life and the most exciting night, too"—a half-laugh and full wink—"not in the way you imagine a wedding night to be, however.

"You see, a few hours after exchanging our vows I delivered my very first baby solo—and ten minutes later, a second baby as well! Those twins were Jamis and Lemuel Beswick, and their deliveries were a bit dicey so I was gone from nightfall until morning. But it all worked out.

"My marriage to Connie sure worked out. Ours was a storybook love that began, as I mentioned, in first grade and lasted the next thirty-three years until tuberculosis took her from us. She'd have turned forty on May twenty-sixth.

"Thirty-nine is too soon to die—but so is forty-nine or seventy-nine. Our Maker gives us each a certain number of years, of special days and magical moments really, and the trick is to make the most of them. Connie did that better than anyone I've ever known. She lived a masterpiece life, truly she did.

"Regrets are normal, but the only regret I have is that I didn't marry Connie sooner—during medical school or even in college. Heck, I wish Danny had dared me to marry her in grade school.

"Actually, I have one true regret—that we never had children."

Winter sunlight glinted off Doc's spectacles, or perhaps the reflection was from his moist eyes: "One stillborn and three miscarriages broke our hearts.

"Yet the truth is, Connie considered her students her children. I feel the same way about every baby I deliver. By that measure, Connie and I were blessed with a wonderfully large family indeed.

"Connie believed in doing all the good you can, for all the people you can, in all the ways you can. She lived this tenet faithfully, which made some people think of her as an angel. I know better. Don't get me wrong, she was filled with goodness and kindness and most every other fine virtue—but she also possessed a pinch of mischief.

"Once, just like Danny had done, Connie dared me to eat a cricket. She cooked a delicious brook trout a patient had given me, and as garnish she placed a dead cricket—on a fishing hook—next to the fish's mouth. When I caught my breath from laughing, she dared me to try the bait—minus the fishhook, naturally. Yes, indeed, my Connie had a puckish sense of humor.

"In jest, I told Connie I wouldn't want to be married to an angel anyway because her wings would get in the way. She liked that. I don't believe any angel could have a more divine smile than hers, though. Oh, how I miss it—and her laugh, sweet as a songbird's melody.

"She'd always use that honey-sweet smile when she playfully *dared* me to take out the trash or *dared* me to take her on a picnic. Or, just like Danny did so long ago, when she often *dared* me to kiss her. That was her favorite dare to make—and mine to accept."

Doc drifted into private thought, many seconds crawling by as he removed his spectacles, blotted welling tears with a handkerchief, returned his glasses and secured his composure and resumed: "Now she really is an angel and I can't say much more or I'll start bawling like a baby. Connie was my world. Thank you all for coming."

The moving eulogy finished, Doc strode, regal and brave as a sixth-grade knight across a playground, over to his true love, one final time. Resting his forehead on the maple casket, his lips brushed the closed lid as he whispered:

"My dear Connie, I miss you beyond all measure. Surely you look lovely in your new wings, even if they get in your way. Know that I love you and will be thinking of you, always, until we are together again."

Eviction Notice

 Dawn arrived Monday, a week removed from his mother's addiction-fueled abandonment, and Lincoln awoke to a harsh reality.

He was homeless.

Three nights earlier, after the season's second football game, the high school junior came home to find a bright yellow *EVICTION NOTICE* form taped to the dingy brown door of the apartment. At the bottom, handwritten in the scolding red ink favored by English teachers, were instructions from the landlord about when they could retrieve their possessions because the lock had already been changed.

Linc's spirits, snake-belly low already after dropping two passes in the Cougars' loss, plunged further. He flung the useless door key onto a neighboring roof; before it landed, Linc made a decision: he would keep his dire circumstances secret. With one exception—

—Keven.

On his first day of school in Cleveland Heights, in fifth grade, Linc got into heated fisticuffs during a recess basketball game. He and Keven got slapped with detention and had been best friends ever since. Now, with Vanessa sucked back into a whirlpool of substance abuse, Kev was Linc's life buoy in the swirling waters.

After Game 2, with only the clothes he was wearing and a team duffle bag stuffed with a soiled football uniform, Linc trudged across town to the Baxter's house.

It was the far side of midnight, so Linc slipped around back. In a husky whisper he called up to a darkened window:

"Kev."

He pinged a pebble off the glass pane.

"Hey, Kev. It's me."

Linc was prepared if Keven's parents awoke. He would say he lost his key and was locked out at home because his mom was visiting her sister in Bellaire, a fabrication he had used often.

Keven, quiet as a burglar, padded downstairs and let his best friend in, no questions asked as always. As always, Linc crashed on the bedroom floor using Kev's sleeping bag.

Come morning, Linc confided his crisis.

Come Saturday night, Linc again slept in the borrowed sleeping bag—but not on the floor. Instead, he shared the mattress with Kev, who insisted: "We both sleep on the comfy bed or we both suffer on the hard floor."

Keven, with his older brother off to college, would have welcomed a roommate indefinitely. But both teens knew anything more than a weekend sleepover would jeopardize Linc's secret. Sunday night, he would need to sleep elsewhere.

Kev knew the perfect homeless hideaway: a ramshackle storage shed next to the school's football practice field. Supplanted by a shiny aluminum outbuilding, the forest-green wooden shed, paint peeling and listing off-balance with the posture of a drunk, had so little of value inside—rusty blocking sled, decommissioned tackling dummies, forsaken tractor tires once used for high-stepping drills—that Coach

Jordan never bothered to replace the broken combination padlock.

Sunday late, in the orphaned shed, Linc unrolled Keven's sleeping bag on the concrete floor, hard and cold as skating rink ice, and spent his first night effectively parentless—and truly homeless. Staring at the ceiling, he rationalized gamely: *On the plus side, I can sleep an extra half-hour in the morning because I'm already at school.*

The school bell jolted Linc awake like an alarm clock. Despite being a two-minute walk from his first-period class, he was tardy Monday morning.

Coach Jordan requested teachers inform him whenever a football player was tardy—or, worse, cut class—so Linc knew he would be running punishment laps at practice. He also knew he needed to retrieve his meager belongings from the apartment. The landlord's hard-boiled eviction note said to come by at two o'clock—but football practice started at two-thirty *sharp*.

Linc weighed his options during lunch break while eating an extra sandwich Keven packed for him. He could be late to practice and, combined with his morning tardiness, face a double-dose of wrath from Coach; or he could wait to get his stuff another day and risk having the landlord toss it all out.

Running laps, even until puking, seemed the lesser of two evils. Linc skipped his fourth-period class and jogged to the apartment at one o'clock. If by good fortune the landlord showed up early, Linc could make it back to practice on time.

Three Boxes, One Basket

Lincoln waited for the landlord.

One o'clock ticked to one-thirty, then to two, and three, and still no Mr. Nelson. *In for a dime, in for a dollar*, Linc reasoned and continued to wait, his impatience swelling like a badly sprained ankle.

Mr. Nelson remained a no-show.

At six o'clock, Linc finally gave up and headed heavy-footed to Duke's Burger Shack. From the payphone outside he called the landlord to make new arrangements. Mr. Nelson unapologetically said he was busy on evenings and weekends.

"Look, I'm already in deep shit with my coach because of today," Linc explained, suppressing his ire only half-successfully. "I can't cut school or miss practice again to come by in the afternoon. Just leave my stuff outside and I'll pick it up tomorrow night."

Mr. Nelson, perhaps out of vindictiveness for Vanessa skipping town while in arrears with the rent, said he couldn't clear out the belongings until Wednesday. For two more school days Linc would have to wear the same clothes he had worn since Friday.

Linc's mood was bitter as poison as he washed down a double-cheeseburger and large order of fries with an oversized "suicide soda" concoction of Mountain Dew mixed with Dr Pepper, Sprite, Pepsi, and Orange Crush. He got a free to-go refill and sulked back to the storage shed—*Linc's Homeless Shack*, he thought.

Entering the shack, its velvet-black darkness broken only by a shaft of streetlight stabbing through the open sliding door, Linc could hold back his tears no longer—not from despondency, but because laid out on the sleeping bag was a pillow, blanket, and stack of neatly folded clothes: a plaid flannel shirt, a few familiar-looking concert T-shirts, and Keven's favorite navy-and-gold *Notre Dame Fighting Irish* hooded sweatshirt. Linc instantly felt his own fighting mettle surge back.

Kev also left a grocery bag overflowing with Oreos, Goldfish Crackers, Pop-Tarts, M&Ms, Mountain Dew and bottled water, a new toothbrush and toothpaste, and a battery-powered camping lantern. And just like that, Linc stopped feeling family-less—he had a brother.

Coach Jordan turned Linc's restored smile into an anguished grimace at practice Tuesday *and* Wednesday.

Monday morning's school tardiness, plus two skipped classes, earned Linc a punishment of running four laps around the field, in full pads and helmet, before he could join Tuesday's workout.

Wednesday's discipline, for having missed practice on Monday, was more severe: five laps after practice followed by ten 100-yard wind sprints. Linc got a side cramp during the third lap; he dry-heaved after the seventh sprint; on the ninth sprint, his leaden legs gave out and he literally crawled the final twenty yards.

Fueled by his seething anger at Coach Jordan, combined with a son's-like need to impress, Linc willed himself to run the entire tenth-and-final length of the field with the full-out effort of an Olympic champion.

Then, he full-out puked.

"No more cutting classes or missing practice, understood?" Coach Jordan said, firmly, while gently patting Linc on the back.

Bent over, hands on knees, chin on chest, gasping like a trout on land, Linc nodded weakly in reply. Stooped as he was, with sweat stinging his eyes, he failed to see the luminous pride on Coach's face.

Linc could not rest fully just yet. Bone-tired, he hiked to the apartment to retrieve his belongings and, on the dark doorstep of 17B, was greeted by three stacked boxes alongside a filled laundry basket.

That's everything I own? The realization seized his chest, squeezing hard, like he had just run an eleventh wind sprint.

Making four trips back and forth to the football field would take a marathoner's stamina. Moreover, keeping all of it inside *Linc's Homeless Shack* would increase the risk of being discovered. He had managed to hide the sleeping bag, blanket, pillow, and food inside the hollow padding of the three-man blocking sled, but no room remained for the contents of the laundry basket and three boxes.

Maybe Kev can keep it in his garage, Linc considered.

Upon further quick consideration: *I'm too beaten for more than one trip. I'll keep only what I need that can fit in the laundry basket.*

What Linc really needed was a new beginning.

Smoldering Embers Take Flame

 The sun sank towards dusk and the rabbit in Doc's front yard was in Jamis's deadeye aim.

The boy squeezed the trigger.

The odds of what transpired next were longer than of identical twins being born on opposite sides of the vernal equinox, one by a rare brow delivery and the other by an even more rare total breech, and both brought healthily into the world by a young doctor missing one finger.

The bullet tore clean through the rabbit's shoulder, ricocheted off an axe head-sized block of flint, Ohio's official gemstone, struck The Butterfly Door and, without leaving so much as a nick on the hard-as-tempered-steel wooden surface, was redirected a second time, unimaginably, on a beeline for Doc, who was just arriving home on foot.

The bullet struck Doc in the left thigh and not, blessedly, higher in the lungs or heart or head. Adding to luck's grace, or the grace of God, the .22-caliber lead slug had flattened out greatly and lost much of its velocity after two caroms, and thus penetrated not deeply—only two stitches would be required to close the wound.

Doc initially thought he had been stung, but checking for a wasp or yellowjacket still attached to his upper thigh instead discovered a silver dollar-size splotch of blood on his grey wool trousers. In the next instant, in his peripheral vision, he glimpsed movement on the knoll, pivoted, and peered upward. Having been spotted, the twins stood rooted in place, in dread.

Doc, flinching from the white-hot pain with every other step, climbed the gentle slope.

"That was foolish and dangerous," Doc scolded Jamis, his birthday rifle in hand. Sternly, yet without raising his voice, he went on: "That bullet could've killed someone—could've killed me. I might expect your brother to do something so stupid, but not you, Jamis."

Doc regretted the last sentence the instant the words cleared his lips. It was an uncommon display of thoughtlessness from him and landed with cold, stinging force. Surprisingly, it was not Lem who recoiled, but rather Jamis. Had this been on the schoolyard, and Doc still a boy, Jamis would have decked him.

Instead, Jamis mutely absorbed the scolding. For the rest of the day his swallowed fury festered.

That night, Jamis pushed his bed back beside Lem's. Sharing conjoined mattresses again, Lem happily drifted to sleep like old times. Jamis, meanwhile, lay awake with poisonous thoughts seeping through his conscience like a black walnut tree's toxic juglone permeating the soil.

It's Doc's fault Lem's slowish.

If Doc had rushed to our house sooner, he could've stopped Dad from leaving us.

It's Doc's fault Mom died.

Doc never should've called Lem stupid today.

I'm gonna teach Doc a lesson.

The insult of Lem was the final wind gust that toppled a mighty tree, the flint spark that lights a fuse. When Jamis was certain his brother was soundly sleeping, he slipped out of bed; sleuthed down the hallway and out of the house without waking Grandma Dika; ducked briefly into the workshop; and under moonlight threaded his way through the woods bordering town.

Blinded by rage, Jamis had decided to punish Doc by destroying his beloved Butterfly Door.

Noiselessly, Jamis crept onto the front porch at 210 Frederick Street. From his front pocket he pulled out a handful of wood shavings. Kneeling, he pressed the paper-thin maple curls into a small pile against the base of the beautiful front door.

On the fourth strike, Jamis successfully lit a fickle phosphorus match and held it to the dry kindling. The flame's citrus-colored glow reflected in the blackness of the boy's smoldering eyes; the mirrors to his soul revealing anger and anguish. He blew gently, one slow prolonged exhale followed by three similar, until the infant fire took full hold.

Breathless from running home, Jamis removed his boots and padded down the hallway with the light steps of a burglar. Grandma Dika did not stir awake.

Lemuel, however, merely feigned sleep. As Jamis eased back into bed, Lem sensed a foreboding chill in the night air—and in his brother.

Meanwhile, a mile away, Doc was upstairs in deep slumber as his porch blazed.

False Confession, True Love

Fire consumed the front porch at 210 Frederick Street, quickly and fully, spread to the dining room, kitchen next, then the tiger-orange roaring flames stalked up the carpeted stairway with increasing pace and wrath on a path towards Doc's bedroom.

In the kitchen, in the cupboard, on the highest shelf, Doc stored a spare bottle of ether from which to refill a vial he kept in his black satchel. When the blaze overwhelmed the cupboard, the ether exploded with the thunderclap of a dynamite blast.

This proved the most serendipitous of ironies: liquid anesthesia Doc employed to put patients to sleep—in order to set a bone fracture, suture a laceration, amputate a limb—roused him awake before poisonous carbon dioxide could painlessly claim his life.

Instinctively, as if summoned for an emergency midnight house call, Doc grabbed his eyeglasses off the bedside nightstand and medical bag by the door. At the top of the stairs his escape was blocked by crackling flames and smoke thick as chowder and intense heat, forcing a retreat back to the bedroom. With no other route to flee, Doc started to climb out the second-story window.

Suddenly, he doubled back inside, coughing violently as the smoke grew thicker by the second. Acting with quickness, but without panic, Doc dropped to his hands and knees on the hardwood floor and retrieved something from beneath the bed. With a hatbox in hand, he exited the window and jumped. The hard landing popped both gunshot stitches in his left thigh, causing him to grimace and moan and collapse. Resting on the ground beside him was the medical bag—and the round hatbox decorated with flowers that he had gambled his life to rescue.

There was no rescuing Doc's home. It was wholly razed in an hour, except for one more irony: The Butterfly Door—Jamis's intended casualty—remained unscathed, standing upright among the smoldering ruins like a loyal sentinel. The lightning strike that split The Black Walnut Tree had not only hardened the wood so as to be bulletproof, too it had rendered it fireproof.

Doc's intuition told him, screamed to him, that arson—Jamis!—was to blame.

Even before the ruinous flames finished burning, Doc's smoldering fury was extinguished by empathy. Still reeling from Connie's death, he was intensely sensitive to what Jamis and Lem were going through after losing their mother and missing their father.

Listening to his heart, which understood that only an unbearable amount of emotional pain could drive a boy to lash out so violently, Doc decided not to share his suspicion with Fire Chief Gus Harris.

Come morning, Doc went to the Beswick's home and asked to speak privately with the boys.

"Did you hear about my house burning down?" he asked, looking for the true answer on their faces not in their words.

Lem would always struggle in the classroom, but he sagely connected these real-world dots: *Doc yelled at Jamis yesterday for shooting the rabbit and Jamis sneaked out of bed last night.*

Furthermore, Lem logically reasoned:

Grandma's been gettin' feebler with each passing month since Ma died.

Jamis could take better care of Grandma without my help than I could without him.

Jamis has been gettin' into lots of trouble at school lately, so this might be the last straw.

What if they send Jamis away?

The name Lemuel, in Hebrew, means "devoted to God." For perhaps the very first time in his life, and out of devotion to his twin brother, Lemuel lied in the eyes of God.

"Ididthebadthing," Lem blurted out to Doc. Then, with more composure: "Jamis didn't do it—it was me that started the fire."

Not for two wags of a puppy's tail did Doc believe Lem, for he had never witnessed a hint of unkindness or ill temper from the boy. *Bless his heart*, Doc was certain, *Lem is protecting Jamis.*

As a broken bone can mend, so too can a fractured soul. Lem's false confession, and the selfless love behind it, was a wondrous elixir. Like one tick of a clock moving the calendar from winter to spring, in one heartbeat's time Jamis crossed the equinox from fractured to mending.

Poison And Polaris

Doc's heart needed mending.

Outwardly, he was fit as the fiddle Emilian had played around the campfire the night Jamis and Lemuel were born. Within, however, a cancer grew. Doc's grief was malignant, dividing in two, growing and dividing, over and again, multiplying faster faster endlessly.

Doc had saved countless lives during his career, but the single life above all others he wished to rescue—Constance's—he was helpless to heal. Now Connie was gone, and with her died Doc's own will to live. His days were difficult, his long nights of solitude unbearable.

Healing others proved the best medicine for Doc's own suffering, but it was merely a salve masking symptoms. It was no antidote, no cure. Moment by minute, hour by day, and week by month, it became ever more difficult to push through a pain that seemed beyond endurance. Night after grief-filled night, the emotional cancer further metastasized.

Doc sought a small measure of comfort from the flowered hatbox. Inside, tied neatly with a royal blue ribbon, were love letters from Connie written during his medical training. Secured in the ribbon's bowknot was the most cherished keepsake of all: her wedding ring.

We mourn at the depth of our love; Doc's drowning grief rivaled the ocean's Marina Trench. As days turned into seasons, his depression spiraled downward and downward until this man who had dedicated his life to saving lives wished to no longer breathe.

Any number of medications, at a poisonous dosage, will put me to sleep and that would be that, Doc thought, putting the lid back on the hatbox. *My suffering will finally end and I'll be reunited with my dear Connie.*

Doc wrestled nightly with this grim demon, and nightly he prevailed, but each night's bout was fiercer than the previous until the night came when the unrelenting beast proved unconquerable. Only hours after delivering a beautiful baby girl into the world, Doc made preparations to leave it. He filled a dozen capsules with ipecacuanha powder—the remedy for whooping cough would be his antidote for chronic grief.

In the darkest of times, a man's true character bears light. Doc's moral compass had always pointed due North, and so it did now. He had sacredly pledged the Hippocratic Oath—which includes the promises "First, do no harm" and "Above all, I must not play at God"—and he was a man of his word.

Just as he could do no harm to a patient, Doc resolved anew to not harm himself. He must not play God. Fortitude supplanting tears, he went outside for fresh air. Taking in the heavenly stars, he located Polaris—the North Star—before resolutely tossing the deadly pills down the sitting hole in the outhouse.

The demon returned the following night, and the next, and ten more, and as February's "Maple Moon" waned so did Doc's resolve. His mettle, once unbendable, finally broke under the weight of his emotional suffering. Darkness had relentlessly succeeded in extinguishing his inner light.

Doc, this time, considered soaking a towel in ether, wrapping it over his nose and mouth, and lying down on his bed to go to sleep forevermore. But he worried survival instinct would kick in before unconsciousness took full hold and he would unwittingly remove the towel. He chose, instead, laudanum as his hemlock. An amalgam of powdered opium, morphine, and codeine in alcohol, it was widely prescribed as a cough suppressant and cold remedy—

—and for insomnia.

Insomnia, how ironic, Doc thought, perversely, further so because the reddish-brown liquid narcotic had one more key use—heart ailments. *Yes, laudanum seems the perfect prescription for my terminally broken heart.*

Outside, woolen clouds blocked all starlight and moonlight, the night black and forsaken. Inside, Doc, unshaven, unshowered, unconsolable, poured a generous overdose of laudanum into a cut-glass tumbler, added some Jameson Irish Whiskey, his favorite, to mask the medicinal bitterness. He knocked it back and, to ensure never awakening, refilled and swallowed a second lethal cocktail.

For the first time since Constance died, Doc lay down on her left side of their marriage bed. As he drifted off, Dr. Lemuel Jamison whistled-hummed a hymn, "Forgive Our Sins as We Forgive."

Our Little Secret?

The Hippocratic Oath states: "If I do not violate this oath, may I enjoy life and art, respected while I live and remembered with affection thereafter."

The esteemed Dr. Lemuel Jamison would be remembered with affection long after his death.

But the time for his eulogy and remembrance thereafter had not yet arrived. Dr. Jamison had decades remaining to be respected while alive. Doc had art still to enjoy.

Shortly after Doc had reclined in funerary repose on Connie's side of the bed, before the laudanum overdose could work its deathly evil, a bottle of ether *EXPLODED!* downstairs in the kitchen. Jamis had intended to hurt Doc emotionally by setting fire to his treasured Butterfly Door—instead, the anguished boy literally saved the suicidal doctor's life.

Jolted awake, Doc's survival instinct roared out of hibernation. Rushing towards the staircase, eyeglasses quickly on and medical bag in hand, he was met by hot flames and suffocating smoke, and at once retreated back to his bedroom. Thinking clearly, he retrieved the hatbox containing Connie's keepsakes, escaped out the second-story window, on the ground stuck a finger down his throat and vomited the lethal cocktail.

Two days later, having visited Jamis and Lemuel and deciding his mentorship, rather than punishment from the authorities, was the best prescription for what ailed the twins, Doc received a drop-in visitor at his medical office threatening this magnanimous plan.

"Real sorry 'bout your house, Doc," Fire Chief Gus Harris, a round man, said in greeting. "Quite a scare. We're all just thankful you got out safely."

"Thank you, Gus. It was a terrible accident. I was lucky not to be asleep yet."

"Yeah, about the *accident*," Gus resumed, removing his hat and running his hand through his snowy hair, wispy but not sparse, before continuing. "I just got back from your house—making sure all the embers were extinguished. Anyway, I found something curious."

"Do tell," said Doc, head tilting.

"That fire was no accident," Gus declared. "It was arson. I found a charred matchstick by the front door—how that door survived the blaze, I'll never know. I also discovered a small pile of unusual ashes with the match. Sure as a sunrise, someone used wood shavings as tinder to start that fire."

"That's preposterous," Doc disputed. "Who'd want to burn down my house?"

"Well—" Gus began, but Doc cut him off.

"I don't have any enemies. I have to scold ol' Willie now and again, but he's harmless. And half the town has had their own run-ins with Marcus. Besides, you'd think Marcus was my new best friend thanks to my day-and-nightly house calls when he had pneumonia. No, Gus, you're mistaken. I've got no enemies. No one wants to do me harm. The fire was a tragic accident, plain and simple."

"I agree it wasn't Marcus or Drunk Willie," Gus acknowledged. "You ain't gonna like this, Doc—I think

Lem done it. That boy's a bit simple, we all know that. Sure, he's always been a nice kid. But with his Ma dead and his Pa gone to fight in the war, he's more withdrawn than ever. Like I said, the boy is different. Who knows what he's capable of doing when he's depressed?"

"Lem didn't—" Doc began defensively, but this time it was Gus who jumped in.

"There's more, Doc. Lem's a gifted woodworker, just like his Pa. That pile of wood shavings—long, curled shavings, from planing—is like a bank robber leaving his own gun at the crime scene. Lemuel done it, I'm sure of it."

Doc's response required no contemplation: "Even if he did—and I'm dead set you're wrong, Gus—I don't want to press charges. Like you said, those two boys already lost their mother. And who knows if their dad isn't in a pine box, too, but word from the warfront just hasn't reached here yet. How 'bout we let your suspicions be our little secret?"

"Sorry, Doc," Gus said, putting on his hat. "That boy's a hazard to us all. I already told Sheriff Garman what I found and what I think. He wants to see you and Lem at the jailhouse straightaway."

Judge Weighs In

 Sheriff Clint Garman, bearded and stern-faced and already with company, was seated behind his stately, but messy, desk when Doc arrived.

Lemuel sat in the middle of three wooden armchairs lined against the wall opposite the door. Jamis, refusing to allow his brother to come alone, sat beside Lem.

A fourth person was also present: Judge Cullen Graham, flanking the desk in a banker's swivel chair that complained beneath his impressive girth.

"Come in, Doc. Good to see you," Sheriff Garman greeted with practiced amiability. "Terrible about your house, just terrible. Thank the good Lord you escaped safe and sound. And thank you for making time to be here."

"Gus said you needed me to make a house call, so to speak, so I hurried right on over," Doc replied, still standing. "What's on your mind?"

"As you can see, I've asked the Judge to join us and help sort out this troublesome affair," Sheriff Garman allowed.

Doc stepped forward and shook hands with Judge Graham: "Always a pleasure, Judge."

"You the same, Doc," Judge Graham said. "Sorry about your house. On a more pleasant note, thanks again for looking in on Louise awhile back. She's doing real fine now."

"Glad to hear it." Doc smiled. "Tell her I send my best and remind her to drink buttermilk if her ulcer acts up."

Before taking a seat across the tigerwood-veneered desktop from Sheriff Garman, Doc turned to the twins.

"Hello Lem, hello Jamis," he said, his tone resonating reassurance. Momentarily sideways to Sheriff Garman and Judge Graham, Doc winked intimately at the twins, adding: "Now don't you worry, boys. Everything's going to be fine here today, just fine."

Jamis and Lem managed weak smiles that failed to mask their grim worries.

"I'm afraid everything isn't fine, Doc," Sheriff Garman said, his voice chilly as a lakeside wind in November. "Gus tells me your house fire was no accident."

Then colder, snowy December: "Says it was arson—"

Finally, January icy: "—and he's dead certain Lem's responsible."

"Hold on there, Clint. I don't want to go stepping on our friend Gus's toes," Doc began, trying to keep things neighborly rather than official. "It's no more my place to tell him how to do his job than I'd want him questioning how I treat my patients. With that said, and no disrespect intended to Gus, I think he's mistaken."

"How so?" Judge Graham asked.

"I've known Lemuel from his very first breath taken and he wouldn't try to hurt me—or anyone else, for that matter," Doc asserted "Believe me, he didn't do it. Isn't that right, Lem?"

Doc looked to Lem and nodded gently, encouraging the boy to confirm this steadfast defense.

Lem straightened tall in his chair, pulled his shoulders back, then spoke politely but firmly: "Dr. Jamison, sir, I already told you I done it."

The admission—perjury, Doc knew in his heart—shocked Sheriff Garman and Judge Graham for its ease in attaining, and also because it meant Doc had tired to deceive them.

"You *knew* he did it, Doc?" Sheriff Garman growled, his temples furrowing with disapproval.

"That's not quite accurate, Clint," Doc contended. "Yes, it's true Lem told me he was responsible. But I didn't believe the boy then—and I don't now."

"That doesn't make any sense," said Sheriff Garman, his umbrage undiminished.

Judge Graham sat rigid, wordless, listening contemplatively, his fingertips rising into a steeple against pursed lips.

"It's like this," Doc explained. "Sometimes a patient has symptoms suggesting a certain ailment. The medical books confirm the diagnosis and a physician's training clearly tells him what treatment is called for. And yet—sometimes—the physician will just *know* the obvious diagnosis is wrong. That's why Socrates believed Medicine is an Art as well as a Science. It's the same in this instance—I just *know* Lem is innocent."

"That may be well and good in *Medicine*," Sheriff Garman snorted, "but in *Law,* we give overwhelming weight to a confession."

Judge Graham removed his wire-rimmed glasses, massaged the bridge of his nose, and weighed in: "Sheriff's right, Doc. Lem confessed his guilt and needs to go to a refuge house for juvenile delinquents."

Judge Solomon

"Idoneit!" Jamis blurted, three words coming as one.

Sheriff Clint Garman and Judge Cullen Graham recoiled at the startling assertion that belied Lemuel's guilt.

Lem slumped at the exposed truth.

Doc loosed a faint whistle-hum.

And Jamis, brave as a shining knight, rose from his chair and slayed his brother's previous private confession: "Lem lied to save me. He's innocent. I started the fire."

Jamis, without punctuation's pause, rambled forth: "I was mad at Doc for calling Lem stupid when I shot the rabbit and for not saving Ma from dying and because he didn't stop Pa from leaving so I wanted to hurt Doc back real bad by destroying his beautiful door."

The boy knight bit his quivering lower lip, jousting with tears, swallowed hard, and resumed more deliberately: "I'm sorry Dr. Jamison, really I am. I'm the one who should be locked up in jail or sent away—not Lem."

Sheriff Garman and Judge Graham sat thunderstruck. Doc nodded at Jamis, conveying a message to the boy that he was proud of his honesty and courage. Before the three adults could fully digest this sudden turn of the table, Lem muddied the waters further.

"Jamis is the liar!" Lem demanded emphatically. "I'm the one that burned Doc's house down. Leave Jamis be and punish me."

Sheriff Garman looked at Judge Graham, the Judge looked at Doc, Doc looked at the Sheriff. Each seemed more befuddled than the other as a suffocating hush hung in the room as palpable as the fog of smoke from Clint's cigar.

At last, Doc cleared the air with a forceful exhale—

—of laughter.

"Are you off your hinges?" Judge Graham protested, his face hot and temper warming. "What's so damn amusing?"

"You of all people, Judge, should see what's happening," Doc allowed. "What we've got here is a King Solomon situation. Instead of two women claiming to be the mother of the same child, we've got two boys—"

Judge Graham cut in, eagerly, not rudely: "I've shared that story—1 Kings 3:16-28, Solomon Makes a Difficult Decision—in my courtroom a number of times."

The Judge closed his eyes and proceeded to recite from the Bible:

One day two women came to King Solomon, and one of them said:

"Your Majesty, this woman and I live in the same house. Not long ago my baby was born at home, and three days later her baby boy was born. Nobody else was there with us.

"One night while we were all asleep, she rolled over on her baby, and he died. Then while I was still asleep, she got up and took my son out of my bed. She put him in her bed, then she put her dead baby next to me.

"In the morning when I got up to feed my son, I saw that he was dead. But when I looked at him in the light, I knew he wasn't my son."

"No!" the other woman shouted. "He was your son. My baby is alive!"

"The dead baby is yours," the first woman yelled. "Mine is alive!"

They argued back and forth in front of Solomon until finally he said, "Both of you say this live baby is yours. Someone bring me a sword."

A knight's sword was brought and Solomon ordered, "Cut the living baby in half! That way each of you can have part of him."

The second woman shouted, "Go ahead and cut him in half. Then neither of us will have the baby."

"Please don't kill my son," the first woman beseeched. "Your Majesty, I love him very much, but give him to her. Just don't kill him."

Solomon declared, "Don't kill the baby." He pointed to the first woman: "She is his real mother. Give the baby to her."

Judge Graham opened his eyes, grinning with no small self-conceit at his displayed prowess of memorization.

"How does this help us?" Sheriff Garman huffed. "There's no baby here for the Judge to threaten to slice in half."

Jamis remained standing, Lem sitting, both uneasily awaiting the verdict.

"Clint, if you and Cullen don't mind," Doc interjected, "I'd like to offer my own King Solomon-like judgment here."

Judicious Justice

 "Set your sheriff's badge aside for a moment—" Doc began.

Turning to Judge Graham, "—and let's all keep in mind this isn't an official courtroom."

"Go on," Judge Graham said, Sheriff Garman nodding his agreement.

"Jamis and Lem came into this world under difficult circumstances," Doc continued. "In fact, they remain the two most difficult deliveries I've yet encountered. As we know, these boys have faced more difficulties of late with their dear mother passing away and their father gone as well, fighting in The Great Rebellion after mistakenly thinking he killed Marcus.

"Under the circumstances, instead of focusing on the terrible misfortune one of these boys caused last night—and we still don't know which one actually set the fire—I believe we should commend them for their unwavering loyalty."

Doc looked at the twins, smiled with closed lips and twinkling eyes, then completed his thought: "Loyalty's a rare thing in our world today. Each boy is looking out for the other at his own expense—that's something special and worth celebrating, not punishing."

Ignoring Sheriff Garman's muddled grumbling, Doc continued with his oration: "I felt in my bones these boys were special the night I delivered them. For starters, it was like a heavenly sign that they were born on both sides of the equinox as winter eased into spring. Aisha and Tamás said I saved their sons' lives, but I honestly felt like divine intervention was guiding my two inexperienced hands.

"Here's an important thing not many folks know," Doc went on, his now-greatly experienced hands clasped soberly before him. "Most people think if you save someone's life, the saved person owes a lifelong debt to the lifesaver. But that's wrong—the opposite is actually true. When you save a person's life, *you* are the one now forever responsible for that saved person.

"If Aisha and Tamás's praise of me is at all warranted, then that makes me still responsible for Jamis and Lem. I read a profound quote from our President, which I think is pertinent here. Mr. Lincoln said, *I have always found that mercy bears richer fruits than strict justice.*

"With that wise sentiment in mind, Clint, I ask you to mercifully look the other way and let my house fire be officially determined an accident—a fortunate accident, in fact, because our Creator works in mysterious ways.

"And Cullen, in your capacity as our town's esteemed judge, I humbly request that you make me the legal guardian of Jamis and Lemuel until Tamás returns from serving the Union. I'll look after the boys and the three of us together can help care for Dika."

The twins' hearts revved.

Seconds slowly paraded into a full minute of authoritative contemplation.

"I'm fine with it," Sheriff Garman at last announced. "Judge, what do you think?"

Judge Graham cleared his throat before offering a verdict: "In all my years, not just thirty-two years on the bench—but my sixty-one years on this planet—I don't believe I've ever met a finer man than you, Doc. I mean that from the depths of my heart. This is a mighty selfless thing you're proposing. Assuming it's all right with Jamis and Lem—"

The Judge glanced to the twins, who both nodded their wide-eyed approval.

"—so be it," Judge Graham declared, thumping his fist gavel-like, once with authority, on the Sheriff's desktop. "Dr. Lemuel Jamison, with the powers vested in me by the great State of Ohio, I hereby grant you legal guardianship of Jamis and Lemuel Beswick. Congratulations to the three of you. I'll take care of the formal paperwork at the courthouse."

With that, Doc and his two namesakes—the children he and Constance had wished for, but never been blessed with—floated out of Sheriff Garman's office.

"Köszönöm," said Doc's two new sons, using the Hungarian word Tamás had extended the indelible night they were born.

"No, boys, thank you," Doc replied, wrapping an arm around a shoulder of each twin. "Köszönöm for giving me a new purpose. Now you are both responsible for my life for the rest of my days."

Köszönöm, Connie, Doc thought, his heart drumming a happy waltz.

Tavis Time

In their United States History class, Lincoln and his classmates were studying the American Civil War with the present focus on the Underground Railroad.

Linc's assigned written report was on escaped slave and famed abolitionist Harriet Tubman. Learning about her life story filled Linc with awe; it also haunted him, for he related in small measure to how she was lashed and beaten in childhood by her various masters. Growing up, Linc had suffered corporal punishment at the hands—most often, the cowardly right fist—of Uncle Roy, husband of Aunt Veronica, Vanessa's older sister.

In Linc's imagination now, the abandoned football shed seemed like an underground "station" or "safe house" along his own secret journey.

Moreover, Tubman, when she was young, had been struck on the head by a heavy metal weight thrown by an enraged slavemaster. The injury caused emotional trauma, spells of dizziness and severe insomnia, and strange visions throughout her life. These afflictions reminded Linc of the suffering his mom experienced when drug dependency slammed down upon her with full clout.

One Tubman quote in particular, with which Linc opened his report, moved him so deeply he wrote it in black Sharpie inside the door of his school locker: *Lord, I'm goin' to hold steady on to You, an' You've got to see me through.*

Football was the only thing Linc had left "to hold steady on to." Regrettably, like the touchdown pass he dropped in the previous game, this lifeline was in danger of slipping through his grasp.

"You're late, Jamison!" Coach Tavis Jordan barked as Linc jogged onto the practice field Thursday afternoon. All week the team had been sloppy and lethargic, and now Coach released his pent-up steam at the kid wearing jersey number eleven; at the kid without a mother for the time being, and without a father forever; at the kid suddenly without a home.

Unaware of these misfortunes, Coach Jordan sarcastically singled out the seventeen-year-old boy who was just trying *to hold steady on* until he could *see his way through*: "Can't you read a clock? Most of us learn to tell time in kindergarten."

Coach Jordan, who still appeared to be in NFL playing shape, focused his intimidating stare on Linc—but his anger was in truth aimed at the entire team: "If I say practice is at two-thirty, you get out here by two-twenty-five. If you aren't five minutes early, you're late—understand?"

Linc nodded, eyes downcast on the chalk-lined grass, as Coach railed on: "But being merely *on time* five minutes early is for Average Joes—champions are an *extra* five minutes early, so I expect you to be here at two-twenty instead of two-thirty! If I say practice is at six a.m., you get here when the moon's still out. From now on you're on *Tavis Time*—understood?"

"Yes, sir," Linc said, rallying his poise.

"I'm talking to all of you," Coach growled, scanning the assemblage of tense pimpled faces. "Understood?"

"Yes, sir," sang the full chorus.

"And another thing, men," Coach rebuked. "No more being tardy or cutting classes. No poor grades. No D's or F's. Heck, I don't even want C's. I want you getting A's—but I'll settle for B's."

He cocked his head and crossed his arms: "Jamison! Is that an earring?"

The diamond stud in Linc's left ear had glinted in the sunlight, catching Coach's eye—and his growing wrath. It was not an expensive gem, yet was of great sentimental value to Linc. It reminded him of the heirloom Hungarian Opal ring; at least his mom had not pawned this, too.

Coach Jordan, with the sternness of a Marine drill sergeant, strode up to Linc.

"You know the rules—no earrings on the field," Coach reproached, extending his hand, palm up. "You'll get it back after practice."

In his rush getting padded up, Linc had simply forgotten to remove it. He did so now and, feeling a pang of helplessness, handed it over.

Coach squeezed his fist around the tiny contraband before addressing everyone: "You're *all* gonna start following *all* the rules. No tardiness, no cutting classes, no poor grades—

"—and no more losses. Let's get to work!"

Late Again, And Again . . .

Following a league victory that saw the Cougars' season record improve to two wins against one loss, the players were waiting on the practice field Monday afternoon at two-twenty when Coach Tavis Jordan arrived.

He smiled, pleased that his dressing-down had sunk in, and commanded buoyantly: "Baxter! Jamison! Lead calisthenics, please."

"Coach," Keven reported, reluctantly, "Linc's still getting dressed." Thinking quickly, he fabricated an alibi: "Mrs. Stewart asked him to stay after in History."

"Then lead by yourself."

With warm-ups already well underway, Linc sprinted onto the field.

"Nice of you to make it, Jamison," Coach greeted, acerbically.

"It's just two-thirty now," Linc said defensively.

"That makes you ten minutes late. We're on *Tavis Time*, remember? Give me ten 100s—one for each tardy minute. And no dogging it."

~~~

Tuesday.

Again, Linc was the last player to show up.

Coach Jordan glanced at his watch: 2:26.

"Jamison, you're six minutes late. You owe me six 100s—get going."

Linc, remaining poker-faced without a syllable of protest, took off running.

~~~

Wednesday.

Four players raced hell-bent onto the field as if competing for a track-and-field blue ribbon, two minutes late by "Tavis Time," but Coach Jordan did not even blink at their tardiness.

A minute more, along came Linc, dead last yet again.

"You're doing better," Coach said, more bemused than irritated. "Only three minutes late today—"

Linc sprinted off to begin three 100s before Coach could spit out the prescribed punishment.

~~~

Thursday.

Linc, true to form, was the last to arrive on the field.

"What's with you lately, Jamison?" Coach Jordan grumbled sharply, his mood turning sour as spoiled milk. "Is your girlfriend making you late for practice?"

"No, sir."

"Can't read a clock, is that it—you can't tell time?"

"No, sir."

"Maybe you need someone to tie your shoelaces for you?"

"No, sir—how many?"

"How many?" Coach parroted, arching an eyebrow quizzically.

"Punishment hundreds, sir. How many do I need to run?"

Coach Jordan checked his watch. Mild surprise, which he tried to mask, replaced his annoyance—Linc was actually on time by *Tavis Time*.

"Give me one full lap and be quick about it. We're working on a trick play today and need to get started aye-ess-aye-pee."

The Cougars' best practice of the young season ensued, brimming with enthusiasm and sharply executed. Nonetheless, in the locker room afterward Keven confronted his best friend.

"Seriously, Linc, what the hell?" Keven griped. "I know you're going through a lot, but how come you're late—every—single—damn—day?"

"I just am."

"Don't you think it's bad for the team?" Keven persisted.

Passing through the locker room on the way to his office, Coach Jordan, unnoticed two rows of lockers away, stopped and eavesdropped.

"Don't you think you're hurting the team?" Keven repeated when no answer came.

"Kev," Linc said, unapologetically. "I'm doing it *for* the team."

Keven rolled his eyes.

"It's like when I spent part of the summer with my cousins," Linc explained, his emotional spigot turning open. "Whenever one of us was late to dinner, Uncle Roy—he's mean as cancer, I swear—would dish out a serious lickin'. It hurt, but I could take it. What I couldn't take was seeing little Murray and Jimmy get cuffed."

Keven listened, aghast.

"Here's the thing, Kev—if I was always the last one to the table, my younger cousins were safe. See, Uncle Roy was so busy watching and waiting for me, he didn't notice if Jimmy and Murray were late."

The disclosure struck Coach Jordan like a bare-knuckle punch that knocks the wind out of you. Flush with remorse for having ridiculed Linc, Coach also overflowed with new respect for this high school kid who suddenly came into focus as a young man of rare fortitude guided by a bright inner-polestar.

"That's horrible. I'm so sorry," said Kev, softly, sincerely. "But Coach isn't goin' to use his belt on any of us for being late. Don't you get tired of running?"

A goofy grin washed over Linc. He peeled off his sweaty No. 11 jersey, hung it in his locker, then gibed: "Nah—I'd rather run 100s than do jackass jumping jacks."

Peaks, Valleys, Prophecy

 Life is filled with peaks and valleys and the ever-changing terrain runs unbroken.

Indeed, it is impossible to go through life from one peak to the next without traveling through a valley between. While the depth of each valley varies, as do the heights of each peak, the valleys are always there to be navigated.

The day before becoming legal guardian of Lemuel and Jamis, Doc had been lost and stranded in the nethermost valley of his life. Only the embrace of death, he felt, would parole him from his valley of despair and prison of grief.

One day changed everything—Doc now found himself standing on a lofty mountain peak. Certainly, he did not miss Constance any less, but suddenly he had much to live for. He had two sons, even if only temporarily, to love and to raise. He vowed to make Connie proud by doing the task well.

Doc was freshly reminded of something all physicians know: Life and death—like triumph and tragedy, peaks and valleys—are two sides of the same coin. *Like opposite wings on one butterfly*, Doc thought, picturing his cherished front door. *The butterfly cannot flit and flutter without both sets of wings working in unison.*

The twins and he made a whole butterfly, Doc realized. By rescuing them, he too was being saved. Fortified by this insight, his mourning-filled despondency evaporated like summer dew under the morning's warming sun.

Being the legal guardian and acting father of Jamis and Lem came with a dilemma, however, which reared its head mere minutes after the trio left the meeting with Sheriff Clint Garman and Judge Cullen Graham.

"Dr. Jamison, where are we going?" asked Lem.

"Yeah, Dr. Jamison, sir—where're we gonna live?" Jamis echoed. " 'cause of me, you've got no house."

Doc stopped short, as abruptly as if a rattlesnake had slithered into his path two footsteps ahead, freezing in thought. Where he and the boys were going to live was important, but a second pressing question also needed answering.

"Boys, I'm not *Doctor Jamison* to you anymore," he said, his voice pleasant as poetry. "I'm your friend and guardian—that means I'm your substitute father, sort of, just until your daddy gets back from the war. So we need a suitable name for you to call me. Something less formal than *Doctor Jamison*. Something family-like."

"Like what?" Lemuel asked.

"Well, what do you call your father?" Doc replied.

"Dad," Jamis and Lem answered in characteristic unison.

"Then *Dad* won't do for me at all," Doc allowed. "Tamás will always be *Dad* to you. We need to come up with another name."

Whistle-humming, Doc mulled over a few possibilities—*Uncle Lem* perhaps or simply *Unc* or *Doc*—before offering: "How 'bout you call me *Pops*? That's what I called my dad. What do you boys think of that—*Pops*?"

"PopsPops," Jamis and Lem said, their trial runs riding piggyback.

"That sounds pretty good," Lem said without hesitation.

"Yep, I like it," Jamis agreed.

"*Pops* it is, then," Doc said, pleased with the choice himself.

"Pops?" Lem asked. "Where—"

"Where're we going live?" Doc interjected, anticipating where Lem was heading. "When the sun came up this morning, I figured I'd just make do in my office until my house gets rebuilt. But that would be mighty cramped for all three of us, wouldn't it? Plus, who'd take care of your dear grandmother? No, my office is not going to work in light of today's happy development."

"I've got an idea, Dr. Jam—" Jamis said.

"*Pops*, remember," Doc intoned kindly, adding a smile and a wink.

"Pops," Jamis began anew. "I've got an idea. Why don't you come live with me and Lem and Grandma in our house? Our parents' room is empty so there's an extra bed for you."

"Now that's a fine thought," Doc said. "Naturally, we'd have to ask your grandma."

"She'll say *yes!*" Lem blurted, fairly shouting in excitement.

A dozen years earlier, Grandma Dika had studied The Black Walnut Tree's split-open matching knot images of orange-and-black butterfly wings and delivered a prophecy. Now it had been fulfilled: *Doctor Lemuel Jamison, your future holds identical twins.*

With Many Tears

 Grandma Dika's distant foretelling of twins being in Doc's future had come to pass, but what about her more recent foreboding vision for Tamás?

"I see death and I see Jamis and Lem crying," Dika had said the day Tamás skipped town after flinging a steak knife into Marcus Murphy's forehead. "Tamás must not join the Union army. He *must not* fight in The Great War."

Would this prophecy also prove on target?

Had it already been deadly accurate?

Doc originally hoped Tamás signed on for the minimum enlistment of one hundred days. When that span passed, and stretched twice over, Doc rationalized: *Tamás wouldn't have considered six months a long enough absence to allow the smoke here to clear. More likely, my friend is serving a full one-year hitch trying to atone for the murder he falsely thinks he committed.*

Of one thing Doc was fully certain: nothing shy of death would prevent Tamás from eventually returning home to Jamis and Lemuel—and, of course, to Aisha, as he had no way of knowing his dear wife had fallen gravely ill and taken her final breath.

In March 1865, the twins turned thirteen.

In April, Confederate General Robert E. Lee surrendered to Union General Ulysses S. Grant at Appomattox Court House in Virginia, bringing to an end The Great Rebellion.

May arrived and summer departed and still Tamás was not among the multitude of homecoming soldiers.

Belmont County, which included Bellaire, had sent upwards of four thousand patriotic men to fight for the Union. Additionally, hundreds of county sons with Southern heritage joined the Confederate's 1st and 2nd Virginia Cavalry, as well as Battery D. West Virginia Light Artillery. It was all the more heartbreaking to see these "former enemies" safely return home while Tamás remained missing.

As autumn's colors turned vibrant, hope for Tamás's reappearance further faded.

When winter's biting winds swept the dead leaves off the trees, Doc and the twins and Grandma Dika all sorrowfully, finally, accepted that Tamás had been killed on a far-off battlefield. Likely, his body could not be identified, making it impossible for official word to be sent to kinfolk.

Doc, understanding there could be no closure without a proper memorial service in Bellaire, ordered a headstone. For the epitaph he chose a quote from Harriet Beecher Stowe's recent groundbreaking novel *Uncle Tom's Cabin:*

Tamás Bruno Beswick
Born: 1828—Died: 1865
Loving Husband, Caring Father, Valued Friend, Brave Man
"There are in this world blessed souls, whose sorrows all spring up into joys for others; whose earthly hopes, laid in the grave with many tears, are the seed from which spring healing flowers and balm for the desolate and the distressed."

The modest headstone of polished marble was positioned on the riverfront land Tamás won in the tragically fateful poker game. It was the very plot on which he had wished to build a permanent home ever since his first encampment under The Black Walnut Tree, thirteen years previous, when he became a father—twice over—on a stormy night.

Specifically, the marker rested in a spot of honor once shaded by that glorious tree, beside two other gravestones, for *Aisha Rosza Beswick* and *Constance "Connie" Jamison.*

Instead of a home at this beatific site, a family cemetery had appeared.

Grandma Dika sobbed inconsolably throughout the private funeral, grieving for her son-in-law and weeping anew for her deceased daughter. Too, perhaps, Dika's tears rolled because she foresaw her own gravestone coming next.

Jamis and Lem, boys prematurely becoming men, bravely wore tearless faces as Doc delivered a poignant eulogy for their father.

"Tamás was more than my best friend, he was my brother," Doc began and a few minutes later, his voice having faltered more than once, concluded: "Köszönöm, Tamás, for the good man you were and for the very fine sons you fathered. Know that I will watch over Jamis and Lemuel—

"—know that they will watch over Dika and me, and over each other as well—

"—and know that we will all be thinking of you until we each see you again."

Doc whistle-hummed "Amazing Grace" and his two namesakes, his twin sons now, began to weep.

Rain For A Rose Bush

 In Greek mythology, a phoenix rises from the ashes.

In the aftermath of Doc's razed home, a new family rose.

The Butterfly Door, having miraculously survived the roaring flames still standing upright, disappeared two days afterwards. The theft saddened Doc, but his focus returned posthaste to something more important—he was intent on making sure the twins also stood tall after the fire, that from the figurative ashes of losing their parents they would gradually rise again into flights of happiness.

For Lemuel, Doc's loving attention was like rain for a parched rose bush.

"Lem," Doc said, finding the boy in the workshop. "Did I ever tell you I was bullied in school?"

"No, Pops," Lem mumbled, his concentration focused on the chair he was crafting.

"It's true," Doc resumed. "Kids made mean-spirited sport of me because of my missing finger. Called me *Nine.* Most hurtful of all was when they said I held my pencil like a retard. That's the ignorant word they used—*retard.*"

Lem stopped sanding, looked up, listened fully.

"My missing finger has actually been a blessing, Lem," Doc went on. "I turned that taunting nickname into a personal motto: *Nine is fine!* Part of the blessing, naturally, is that I didn't lose my finger in a traumatic childhood accident. Had that been the case, I would've needed to learn how to hold a pencil differently and figure out a new way to tie my shoelaces. Or, if I was already a doctor, relearn how to tie sutures—"

A short pause, a wry smile.

"—and, of course, tie fishing flies."

Doc ran the three fingertips and thumb of his right hand over the in-progress cherry wood chair seat, whistle-humming at its pleasing smoothness, before continuing: "The thing is, I was born without my right index finger so it was always just normal for me. You can't miss what you never had—and what I didn't have actually made me better in some ways."

Lem, his dark hair dusted lightly with sawdust, tilted his head slightly, skeptically.

"For instance, I'm right-handed but I compensated by using my left hand a great deal. That became an advantage. My goodness, delivering you would've been even more challenging if I wasn't basically ambidextrous.

"No, Lem, you can't miss what you never had," Doc reiterated. "That goes for a finger, or having a lot of money, or being an intellectual genius. Your dad said something the night you were born that's always stuck with me: *I play the clarinet because my arms are too short for the trombone.*

"That's pretty wise, Lem, don't you think? To me it simply means *do the very best you can with what God gave you.* We all have flaws, that's what makes us human and unique. Think about the burl wood you love—its beauty and hardness actually come from flawed growth. Yes, being different can be special.

"You're plenty smart, son. Don't let anyone make you feel otherwise. Maybe you learn from books more gradually than other kids, but that's kind of like me missing a finger—you compensate in other ways."

"How so?" Lem asked.

"Like how you relate to animals," Doc allowed. "You've got a sixth sense and a healing magic with 'em. They can *feel* your kindness—so do people. Not only are you kind to everyone, you have a rare ability to bring out kindness from others. Even bullies soften a little thanks to you because instead of getting mad and swinging at them, you set a powerful example by offering your hand as a brother.

"Yes, you bring out the warmth and good in people the same way you bring out the beauty in wood. And no one is smarter than you when it comes to carpentry—you can *see* a piece of furniture in a tree or board and then you have the skill and patience to make it a reality. That's genius, Lem, truly it is. One day you're going to be the finest cabinetmaker Belmont County has ever seen."

The boy grinned, fleetingly but proudly, as he returned to sanding the chair seat. Never again would Lem think of himself as being lesser.

House Raising, Housewarming

Jamis, as well, grew more comfortable with Lem's cerebral shortcomings.

He also became far less combative with others. This emotional evolution was chiefly due to Doc.

Just as a single medication very often can effectively treat more than one ailment, Doc used the example of his missing finger to teach different life lessons to both twins. As he had done with Lemuel, Doc privately told Jamis about being mockingly called "Nine" as a boy and about turning pain into persistence, disadvantages into advantages, hardships into triumphs.

The pretext for Jamis and Doc's shared walk in the woods had been to hunt rabbits, but neither the boy nor the man aimed his rifle's barrel. Instead of small game, Jamis found a large measure of solace. Under the canopy of birch, pine, buckeye, and black walnut trees, all worthy of a Joyce Kilmer poem, the poisonous juglone that burdened Jamis began to run dry.

Healing fully, of course, required more than one walk, one talk, one lesson. The most important ingredients in the potent salve, which was administered liberally and repeatedly, were Doc's unconditional love and bottomless forgiveness combined with Lem having selflessly—and falsely—confessed to arson to protect his brother.

These expressions, plus the catalyst of time, resulted in a metamorphosis as wondrous as a caterpillar turning into a butterfly. After a metaphorical long winter in a cocoon of cold rage and dark-eyed loneliness, Jamis emerged on the other side of the vernal equinox filled with sunny warmth and inner peace.

One more thing rose from the ashes at 210 Frederick Street, fondly known as Freddy Street by all in town. With the camaraderie of an Amish barn raising, the community built Doc a new home. It was a thing of beauty—not just the structure, but how it came to be.

Not once had Doc ever turned away a patient. Oftentimes this meant donating his medical care outright. It was also not uncommon for him to be paid with a chicken or basket of eggs or cut of beef. His mossy derby was payment once, as were his favored grey tweed sport coat and most-prized bamboo fly-fishing rod. When he was paid in cash, rarely was it in full.

While Doc never went hungry, his bank savings remained malnourished. Certainly he could not afford to rebuild his house without taking out a loan. Before he had a chance to discuss the prospect with Bank of Bellaire owner Marcus Murphy, neighbors near and far stepped forward.

Townsfolk who had received free care from Doc in the past now found ways to make good on their unwritten IOUs. Some did so with money, others with lumber or nails or bricks, more still with building skills and volunteering hands.

Even those without a debt on the unofficial ledger contributed. Some saw it as a down payment for future house calls; others because they knew it was what Doc would do if roles were reversed. Indeed, Doc's fidelity to honesty, honor, and goodness was so universally recognized that Bellaire locals, old and young alike, often asked themselves when faced with a test of character: "WWDD?"—*What Would Doc Do?*

And so it was, a mere six months after his house burned to the ground, Doc, Jamis, Lem and Grandma Dika moved into *their* new home. It was nearly identical to Doc's old house, down to black shutters and a white porch swing, with a bonus backyard shed ideal for tying flies—and woodworking.

The new home did have one doleful omission: the masterpiece Butterfly Door had not been recovered. Lem tried his best to remedy the loss by secretly making a replacement door as a housewarming gift. Fashioned similarly from black walnut, it lacked the unique butterfly-image knot and as well did not possess a stone-hard surface owing to a fantastical lightning strike. These absences proved as inconsequential as Doc's missing index finger, for the new door was a true work of art.

Displaying craftsmanship surpassing even Tamás's great skill, at the dark-wood door's center Lem used white oak inlays to form an elegant serpent entwined around a staff—the famous Greek "Rod of Asclepius," the symbol of medicine and healing.

Metamorphosis

The person who pirated The Butterfly Door from the charred house ruins was no coal-hearted thief.

It had been Lemuel.

With Jamis's help.

No sooner had Doc become the twins' guardian than a bolt of inspiration struck Lem—he would turn the beautiful door his father made as a wedding gift into an equally beautiful table for Doc as a housewarming present. The youngster's old-soul reasoning for the conversion was most beautiful of all.

"A front door keeps people apart," Lem told his brother in their shared bedroom, in their pushed-together beds, the second night following the house fire that Jamis started. "But a table—where people eat and talk and laugh and play cards and have birthday parties and holiday celebrations—well, that brings folks together."

"Never thought of it like that," Jamis whispered in reply, in agreement, in the quiet darkness. Moonlight shone through opened shutters, casting slit shadows on the opposite wall that looked like an illuminated ladder.

Lem's mind climbed the rungs, double-checking each step of his plan, then he rejoined in a volume as soft as their shared quilt: "So here's what I was thinking. Let's go get the door that Dad made for Doc—for *Pops*—and I'll remake it into a dining table."

"Think you can?"

"Don't see why not," Lem said with confidence. "I've never made a table before, that's true, but Pops says he never delivered twins before us. I betchya a table is easier to make than a chair—and a lot easier than delivering twin babies in a thunderstorm."

"The butterfly knot will sure look grand in the center of a table," said Jamis, who was undergoing his own transformation from a shut door to a welcoming table. "I reckon you'll turn it into the prettiest table ever."

"Thanks," Lem said, adding: "One more thing—"

"What?"

"—let's keep it a surprise."

"That's a bang-up idea, Lem!"

Next morning, so early every rooster in town was still slumbering, the thirteen-year-old twins snuck over to 210 Freddy Street. Hauling The Butterfly Door home undetected, and hiding it in Tamás's old woodshop, proved easy enough. More difficult was keeping their secret after seeing how downcast Doc was when he discovered the door had been looted. Lem wanted to fess up right away, but Jamis convinced him the big reveal would be worth a small deceit.

Lem envisioned a "Mission Style" table with simple, clean lines. The legs would taper gracefully—square, not spindle, for Lem did not have access to a foot-wheel lathe—and be attached from beneath the Shakers' way with hardwood pegs, not nails.

The first order of business was to remove the doorknob and fill in the resultant hole. Unable to perfectly match the singular surface of The Butterfly Door, Lem decided a contrasting light-colored wood would be more pleasing than having two slightly different hues of black walnut. He settled upon white oak—timber in kind he would later use for the "Rod of Asclepius" inlay in the replacement front door—imagining the round plug would look like a full moon in the night sky.

At Jamis's suggestion, Lem further selected a darker piece of maple and used the contrasting tones to create a yin-yang circle. Jamis said the two halves represented identical twins. The trinity of woods—black walnut, white oak, rich maple—would hold another metaphor in Doc's eyes: a surrogate father and his two sons.

Next, Lem enlarged The Butterfly Door, for it was a wee bit small for a dining table, adding a six-inch skirt of white oak that resulted in noble dimensions of four feet wide and seven and a half feet long.

The marriage of black walnut and white oak proved so handsome, Lem added further contrast by fashioning the legs from maple. At first look, the handcrafted legs appeared identical. On closer inspection, however—like Jamis, who had four freckles resembling the bowl of the Big Dipper on his right earlobe, while Lemuel completed the constellation with the handle of three freckles on his left lobe—each Table leg was unique.

As he labored on the masterpiece, Lem whistle-hummed faintly in concentration, in contentment, in his own world.

Homecoming

 Love asked Tavis to a Sadie Hawkins dance in middle school and as high school seniors they were voted "Class Sweethearts."

Off they went to different colleges—heated rivals, in fact; Love to The Ohio State University and Tavis to Michigan—and fell out of touch.

But never fell out of love.

Surprising and wondrous Fate's roulette wheel can prove to be. Were it not for his career-ending injury as an NFL rookie, Tavis would not have returned to the University of Michigan to pursue a Master's degree in Education precisely when Love was there studying for a postgraduate degree in Marriage and Family Therapy.

Within weeks of their reunion, according to Love's retelling ever after, the two were once again lovebirds. Tavis's version claimed it happened in the span of a skipped heartbeat. On one thing they agreed: together again, their love blossomed like a field of sunflowers in the French countryside. Three months to the day after coming back into each other's lives, they wed. Tav's longtime friend and high school football teammate, Rhett Kingston, served as Best Man; Love's sister, Patience, was Maid of Honor.

Upon earning their Master's diplomas, Tavis and Love both launched promising careers in Ann Arbor. When they decided to have a child, a heartbreaking miscarriage was followed closely by a second. Grief filled them to the marrow of their bones, yet the couple never lost faith. And so, fittingly, when Love gave birth to a healthy and beautiful double-rainbow baby, a daughter, they named her Fayth.

The young family's roots took strong hold in Michigan's loamy soil over the next decade and then Tavis received an offer from his high school alma mater in Ohio. His initial reaction was to turn down the opportunity on behalf of Love, who had built a flourishing family counseling practice, and Fayth, who enjoyed a circle of good friends.

Bless her little heart, when the ten-year-old overheard her parents discussing the situation, she said with heartfelt zeal: "Daddy, if you want to move, I want to move!"

Love, despite internal misgivings about leaving Ann Arbor, was outwardly supportive: "Marriages and families need help everywhere, so finding work isn't a problem. And Fayth will make friends at a new school in a day or two—if not a minute or two. If you want this, babe, you should grab it with both hands."

On the one hand, the homecoming was Tavis's dream; on the other, Cleveland Peak High's football program was a nightmare. The past four years, the Cougars had won only three games total with two winless seasons.

"Things aren't like they were when I played there," Tavis told Love. "I made a couple phone calls—they don't even have a booster club. Basically, the program's a disaster."

"Maybe so," Love admitted, well aware that her husband felt unfilled at his current job, "but where's the challenge in taking over a winning program anyway?"

Tavis grinned. It was yet another example of why he loved Love so deeply.

Truth was, Tavis had no shortage of confidence he could restore winning on the field. What weighed heavier on his mind, tipping the scales against accepting the offer, was that the school as a whole was in worse shape than the football program. Contacts warned him teachers were underpaid, understaffed, and their morale was underwhelming.

Furthermore, graffiti covered the school's walls; clogged toilets remained backed up for days; broken windows went unfixed for months. The janitor was doing triage.

Academically, as well, word was Cleveland Peak High had sunk to Grand Canyon-like depths.

Along with being head football coach, Tavis would teach four periods of History classes. In his heart of hearts, he derived greater satisfaction in the classroom than on the gridiron, so this was a giant checkmark on the "Pro" side of the ledger.

The "Con" side, meanwhile, had run out of room.

"You've never run from a challenge before," Love reiterated. "I don't think you should start now."

Buoyed by Love and Fayth, Tavis phoned Cleveland Peak High's newly hired principal: "I would be honored to be your new head football coach."

"That's wonderful news," replied Principal Rhett Kingston. "Welcome home, Tav, ol' buddy."

Four Gallons of Paint

The rest of the football team was already on the practice field, lined up in rows, chatting, waiting to begin warm-up exercises, when Lincoln *and* Keven jogged out together—

—two minutes late by "Tavis Time."

The assembled players froze in their cleats, the dead-silent dread palpable, as Coach Jordan theatrically looked at his watch.

As a high school quarterback, Tavis was wizardly with his play-action sleight of hand; now he feigned his emotions with an annoyed frown and furrowed brow. In truth, he was actually pleased to see these two stepping forward together as leaders—even if their means of doing so was by purposely breaking a team rule.

"Looks like Baxter's watch is also broken," Coach Jordan said acerbically.

"Coach," Linc asked in stride, "how many hundreds?"

"None," Coach Jordan said, surprisingly, adding ominously: "I've got something much better in mind for the pair of you than punishment running. My office. After practice. Understood?"

Linc and Keven stopped cold in tandem, looked at each other with wild-eyed worry, then nodded at Coach. The rest of the team collectively muttered hushed sympathies for their two comrades.

"That's enough!" Coach Jordan barked, instantly regaining iron-fisted control of practice. "Let's get to work!"

~~~

After practice, after showering and dressing, after all the other players had cleared out of the locker room, Linc and Keven felt like dead men walking as they headed to Coach Jordan's office.

Tentatively, Keven knocked on the door that had been left a knuckle's width ajar.

"Come in, men," Coach Jordan said, looking up from his battleship-grey steel desk.

"You wanted to see us, Coach?" Linc said, his voice tinged with foreboding.

"What I want is to see you both here tomorrow morning—at six."

"*S-i-i-i-x?*" echoed Keven, the syllable stretching like a rubber band.

"In the *morning?*" Linc added with disbelief.

"That's right. Six *aye em,*" Coach reiterated.

"Why so early?" groused Linc.

"You'll find out tomorrow," Coach Jordan replied, wearing a no-nonsense countenance. He was also wearing a black T-shirt trumpeting the Cougars' motto *WE PLAY HARD!* in gold, in bold, in all caps. He added wryly: "Get to bed early, you're gonna need your sleep."

The two players turned and departed, but before being out of earshot Coach shouted a final reminder: "Don't forget, men—six o'clock *Tavis Time* means ten-till."

"Yes, sir!" the two best friends hollered in unison without looking back over their shoulders. Had they done so, they would have seen their coach leaning back in his chair, contentedly, hands clasped behind his head, grinning like Wonderland's Cheshire cat.

"What was that about?" asked Principal Kingston, dropping by Tav's office from the opposite direction.

"Just two kids as hardheaded as you and I used to be," Tavis needled. Growing serious: "Rhett, this school looks like crap. It wasn't a dump when we went here."

"Things always seem more golden in the good 'ol days," Rhett countered. "It's not so bad now."

"Like hell it's not," Tavis scoffed. "Look around. There's trash everywhere. And the graffiti—damn it, I hate graffiti! I betchya if I stood still in the hallway for three minutes, I'd get tagged with spray paint."

"Let's not be overly dramatic, Tav."

"I'm just saying—it's hard for students to have pride in their studies, and their sports teams, if they don't have pride in their school."

Rhett, surrendering: "I'll see what I can do about beautifying the campus, amongst everything else on my Get-It-Done-Yesterday list. In return from you, a winning season would be beautiful."

Although he trusted Rhett's word unconditionally, Tavis distrusted red tape wholly. Drumming his fingers on the steering wheel in beat with Prince's "Way Back Home" on the radio, Tav took a detour on his way home to a home improvement store. Flinging the driver's door shut, he did a 180-degree counter-clockwise spin as if faking a handoff to the tailback, grabbed an empty shopping cart and, with a winner's bounce in his step and a hum on his lips, went inside.

In short order, Tavis came out with two paintbrushes, two paint rollers and rolling trays, a quart of paint thinner, and four one-gallon cans of white paint.

Hallway Showdown

For the first time, Linc had company in the desolate shed.

Keven slept over, making it easier to be at school at first light. Bleary-eyed, he and Linc were waiting when Coach Jordan drove up to the gym parking lot.

"You're early, even for *Tavis Time*," Coach praised, having glanced at the dashboard clock—5:47.

Linc and Keven unloaded the cans of paint and other supplies from the truck bed, lugged it all to an eyesore wall, and went to work covering over the graffiti.

"This sucks," Kev griped only minutes into the chore.

"I'd rather be running punishment laps," Linc grumbled in agreement.

~~~

"That's enough for today," Coach Jordan told the boys upon returning to campus after his customary six-mile morning run. "Nice work. Now clean up and be sure to get to your classes on time. No excuses, understand?"

"Don't worry, Coach," Keven answered. "We won't be late for class—or practice. We don't ever want to do *this* again."

"Oh, you guys aren't close to being done," Coach said, brimming with amusement. "Tomorrow morning, you start on the lockers by The Quad."

"That's not fair," Keven protested.

"Someone's gotta do it," Coach parried. "How can students have pride in our football team if the school looks like a homeless hangout?"

"There'll just be new graffiti faster than we can paint over it," Keven pointed out. "We'll never finish."

"I think you will," Coach reassured. "Everyone respects you two. That's why I'm having you paint on school days instead of the weekend—so they'll all see you being punished. I'm betting no one wants to make extra work for you guys."

The two remained mopish.

"Look at it this way, men," Coach rejoined, grasping each boy by the trapezius with a fatherly squeeze. "You have the opportunity to do something no one else in this school can pull off, myself included—create a culture of pride. I think that means you have a responsibility to do so, don't you?"

The challenge was the perfect play call.

"Bring it on!" Linc announced.

"That's the attitude," Coach said. "I'll leave the paint out for you tomorrow morning at six-thirty."

"We know—six-*twenty*," Linc said.

"You're learning," Coach Jordan said, pleased.

~~~

The third early morning, after unlocking his office for Linc and Keven to retrieve the painting supplies, Coach Jordan again went for a run.

Finishing his loop back to campus, Coach was greeted by the unexpected—heard before seen: rap music, blaring from a boom box. Jogging toward the source, he rounded a corner and pumped the brakes. Linc and Keven—and half the football team—were busy painting. With haste, and with a smile, Coach spun and headed to his office, his mood so buoyed he could have run another six miles.

Linc, meanwhile, was about to run head-on into confrontation.

During the transition from third to fourth periods, Quentin—a tough kid known by all simply as "Q"— stopped Linc in the hallway. The two greeted each other with a respectful handclasp and fist bump. Pleasantries out of the way, Q, with a handful of his friends loitering behind him, straightway got down to business.

"Listen up, brother," Q warned. "Don't be messin' up my artwork."

"Sorry, Q, really," Linc said amiably, yet assuredly, gaining height with sudden museum portrait-like posture. "But I've gotta paint over your stuff—Coach's orders."

Q glared, his eyes narrowing like a snake's, unmoved by this justification. The air temperature seemed to plummet. Tension mounted. Inside the classrooms, the second hands on the clocks made a full lap, but in the hallway time stood still.

At last, Linc ended the muted stalemate: "Q—can you do me a solid?"

Q cocked his head curiously.

Linc continued: "Your style is ballin' and I'm a big fan. But maybe you can take a break and not make more work for me, just until football season's over—cool?"

Q huddled with his crew and conversed out of earshot. The bell rang for fourth-period classes, but Linc knew he would have to be tardy. At this instant, Q's potential wrath outweighed Coach's certain ire.

He Needs You

The bell between periods stopped, its clanging echo faded, the hallways became a ghost town.

Except for Lincoln, Quentin, and Q's crew, who remained at a tense crossroads.

Eventually, Q offered his verdict: "You helped me in Algebra, so I owe you. I guess we can move our creations away from school for a while. And we'll spread the word—no more taggin' by *anybody* till football season's done."

Q took a step closer to Linc, now chest to chest, leaned his mouth an inch from Linc's ear and added for only him to hear, "I know about your shed."

The assertion jolted Linc like a seismic shock, but he managed a measure of Zen. Instead of revealing concern, he responded with heartfelt honesty, privy only to Q: "Mega thanks for the painting break—and for keeping my secret."

As the two teens headed tardily in opposite directions for classes, Linc called out an afterthought: "Hey, Q. You should come out. We could use you."

"To paint over *my own* artwork? Now you talkin' crazy."

"No, man, not to paint—to play on the football team."

Q waved a hand dismissively, as if swatting away a mosquito.

"Just think about it," Linc appealed.

Four early mornings later the football forces, varsity and JV, finished erasing the last of the graffiti—with one exception: a striking bold-stroked mural by Q of a red Phoenix rising from black flames. Linc had convinced Coach Jordan to let stay. The players celebrated the end of their long labors with a spirited game of paint tag that left them all splattered white as Halloween ghosts.

Walking the hallways later that day, Principal Rhett Kingston admired the school's fresh look. Even the trash had been cleaned up.

Never bet against Tav, Rhett thought. *He's still got the magic.*

~~~

Tav saw *the magic* in someone else.

"The team's really coming together," he told Love and ten-year-old Fayth at the dinner table. "Largely because of Linc. He's not the best player, by any means, but there's something special about him."

"How so?" asked Love.

"He's got this hard exterior, but on the inside his heart is unusually kind," Tavis answered. "He has a real gift for connecting with everyone—jocks and cool kids, outcasts, the musical and artsy kids, the brains, even with teachers. I think his teammates would jump off the roof for him."

"Sounds like you twenty years ago," Love said, knowingly.

Tavis grinned: "It's different with Linc. I was more outgoing—he's reserved. And being a quarterback lends itself to leadership—he's a receiver, which makes his leadership all the more unique. The most unique thing, though, is *how* he leads."

"What do you mean?"

"Two weeks ago, for example, he was late for practice every single day," Tavis recounted. "Just before I lowered the boom, I overheard him talking to Keven in the locker room—Linc told him he was being late on purpose to distract me in order to protect his teammates from being punished."

"That's selfless," Love observed. "And courageous. He must have terrific parents."

"That's the amazing part," Tavis intoned. "He comes from a troubled home. Rhett tells me the dad was never in the picture."

"Fayth, sweetheart," Love said, sensing the conversation taking an adult turn. "Why don't you go read for twenty minutes, please."

After she was out of earshot, Tavis picked up his thought: "Rhett says the only thing the dad ever gave Linc is his last name—Jamison. His mom has apparently battled substance abuse."

The couple cleared the dishes and moved their exchange to the kitchen sink. Love washed, Tavis dried while resuming: "In the face of his hardships, Linc has resiliently thrived. He's an excellent student—well, until recently. Something's changed. His grades have been slipping, A's to C's. He's even skipped a couple classes."

Love dried her sudsy hands and placed them on her husband's chiseled cheekbones, looked him in the eye, and asserted: "He needs you."

"I know," Tavis said, his voice wavering with rare uncertainty. "But honestly, babe, I'm not sure what to do for him."

"Be patient and trust in yourself," Love counseled. "The answer will come to you."

New Home, New Vision

One summer's day, Doc wore a winter's old wool scarf as a blindfold on his way to a new beginning.

Jamis and Lem, holding their Pops' hands on either side, guided him down Freddy Street. Waiting at address 210 were dozens of townsfolk who helped make this red-letter day a reality.

En route to the big reveal, Doc and the twins had made a short side trip to the courthouse. Under Judge Cullen Graham's authority, Dr. Lemuel Jamison legally adopted Jamis and Lemuel Beswick. The boys, at their suggestion and insistence, took Doc's surname. Now, following the brief juridical proceeding, the three *Jamisons* joined the celebratory gathering.

Grandma Dika was notably absent. Her only child, Aisha, was gone from the living and Dika need not be clairvoyant to foresee her two grandsons soon being grown and, in many ways, gone from her life as well. Her future, she realized, was now her past—in Hungary where she had left behind two younger sisters, a handful of cousins, and numerous dear friends.

So it was that a week before the house unveiling, Dika boarded a Pullman car on the B&O Railroad—which had connected to Bellaire nine years previous in 1857—and headed east to Baltimore to catch a sailing ship back to her homeland. Tamás's winnings from the grim poker game made this salmon-like natal homing journey possible.

Bidding her grandsons and Doc farewell at the train station, Grandma Dika dug her fingernails into her palms, unsuccessfully trying to forestall tears. With a handkerchief blue as a summer sky, she dabbed her eyes—then unfolded the linen square to reveal the Hungarian Opal ring.

"My wish," she said, addressing Jamis and Lem, "is that the first of you who weds gives this to your bride."

Worsening cataracts had not clouded Dika's *visions* and she now offered a farewell prophecy to her grandsons and Doc: "I see a railroad, a perilous railroad. But it is not this train I am soon to board, so for me do not worry. Also, I see a tiger's tail and the tail of a comet—these dangers I fear for you as well."

Dika took a deep breath, exhaled lengthily, as if trying to dispel into thin air her feelings of impending doom. Forcing a smile, she concluded: "I see also love—as much love as there are stars in the night sky. Yes, more than anything, I see love in all your futures."

She kissed Jamis and Lem, tearfully; hugged Doc, tightly; and then, like Aisha and Tamás, Grandma Dika was gone.

The coming Sunday, a cloud-dotted sunny afternoon worthy of Monet's brushstrokes, the Jamison trio received a new house. Standing in the front yard, Doc removed the plaid scarf covering his eyes. He had kept his promise—as he always kept his promises—to stay away during construction, so this was his very first glimpse.

He was overwhelmed.

The community's love and largesse left Doc speechless. Time suspended as he took it all in. Gradually, his wide-view gaze focused in on the serpent-and-staff front door and he knew instantly it was Lem's masterful handiwork. At length, Doc gave the highest of his compliments: a long, slow, lovely whistle-hum.

"Go on, Pops—go inside," urged Jamis, winking at Lem in shared giddy anticipation.

A second revelation was the first thing to greet Doc within. Opening the front door that serves to keep people apart, just beyond the entry foyer, he saw The Butterfly *Table*. For now, it would serve as the heart of this resurrected home; for the ensuing century and a half, spanning seven generations of family, it would serve the elevated purpose of bringing people together.

Doc approached the dining room with the unhurried, slightly hesitant steps of a bride walking down the aisle, his eyes transfixed on The Butterfly Table. Arriving, he ran his right thumb and three fingertips along the length of the familiar glassy surface. Making a second sweeping pass, he paused midway to caress the beautiful winged knot.

In time, Doc looked at Jamis and Lem, at his twin sons, at his future. For the first time since Connie's death, he wept with joy instead of grief.

God-Awful Bloody Mess

 One more gift awaited inside the new home at 210 Freddy Street.

This surprise was not for Doc; it was for Lem and Jamis.

Doc and Fire Chief Gus Harris, who was hiding in the kitchen, had a special present for the twins. It actually shared a number of similarities with The Butterfly Table: four legs, graceful lines, and a handsome union of dark and light.

When the moment was right, Gus cracked opened the kitchen door and into the dining room scampered a Dalmatian puppy. Jamis and Lem dropped to their knees and petted the wiggly tail-wagger.

Lem looked up at Doc and asked, "He's ours?"

Doc nodded and smiled.

"Really, Pops?" Jamis said, unable to believe this good fortune.

"Yes, sons, really," Doc confirmed, his smile widening further. "Gus's firehouse dog, Flame, had pups and he kindly saved the pick of the litter for you boys. I think you deserve it."

"Thanks!" the twins said in unison, twice—first to Doc, then turning to Gus.

"He'll be a lot of work," Doc rejoined. "So I'm counting on you both. A dog is a major responsibility—and your first responsibility is to give him a proper name."

The boys undertook this assigned duty with resolute seriousness. For the remainder of the day, and half through that night—after Doc read them a few more pages of *A Midsummer Night's Dream* before bedtime— they dealt suggestions back and forth like two card players trading gin discards.

After going through the entire alphabet from A (Ace) to Z (Zorro and Zeus) and backwards to A (Atlas) again, the boys settled on their agreed winner. With the puppy resting between their ankles at the foot of their pushed-together mattresses, they decided to sleep on the chosen name before making it official.

At breakfast, still pleased with their decision, Jamis and Lem shared the verdict with Doc.

"We're naming him Puck," Lem declared.

"From Shakespeare's story," added Jamis.

Doc beamed, pleased by the literary lineage: "Puck— the mischievous elf and merry wanderer of the night. That's a mighty fine name, boys. I do believe Puck suits our new friend well."

On the heels of the surprise house and surprise Table and surprise puppy, at this very moment came one more surprise—*bam!-Bam!-BAM!*—three rapid, make-you-flinch knocks, loud as gunshots, on the serpent-and-staff front door. Doc hurried to see who was making such a commotion.

"Oh thank goodness you're awake," outpoured Thaddeus Weller, butcher by trade. His words continued to rush out like air from an untied balloon: "Emmett done got run over by the trolley! It's bad, Doc—real bad!"

Bellaire's horse-drawn streetcar began operation less than a year earlier—on October 16, 1865, as proudly

commemorated on a bronze plaque in the town square—
to band-playing fanfare. This was the trolley's first serious
accident and it was as horrific as it was implausible.

The chain of events began with a harmless garter
snake slithering across the dirt road. One of the two draft
horses—Raven, a black steed on the tandem's right
side—got spooked and jerked hard to the right, pulling
the front wheels off the iron tracks. Partially derailed, the
trolley ground to a halt with the rumbling sound of
thunder. The violent deceleration sent the driver—
Emmett   Riley—flying   nose-over-toes   into   the
hindquarters of Hercules, hitched on the left.

Emmett's impact startled Hercules, causing the
powerful horse to bolt forth while simultaneously yanking
hard left. In doing so, the flaxen chestnut impossibly
pulled the front wheels back *onto* the rails in perfect
alignment. This, in turn, allowed the trolley to lurch
forward and resume rolling at top speed—

—over Emmett, who had bounced off Hercules and
tumbled to the ground.

"His leg! Oh, Jesus, his leg!" continued Thaddeus,
bug-eyed with panic. "It's a bloody mess, Doc, a god-
awful mess!"

*If Thaddeus, of all people, is this distraught, the injury must be
severe indeed,* Doc reasoned. Presently, Sheriff Clint
Garman and Nate Higgins, a local baker, arrived carrying
Emmett up the porch steps.

There was no time to take Emmett to Doc's medical
office in town. He would have to treat the gravely injured
patient at home.

Drunken Distraction

"Jamis, fetch my satchel please," Doc directed, his voice betraying no alarm. "It's in my bedroom, next to the nightstand."

"Lem, you clear off the Table. Be quick, but don't hurry—no need to risk breaking dishes."

"Jay-Jay," Doc called out in afterthought, using a nickname he coined while signing the papers to legally adopt *Jamis Jamison*. "Grab a blanket, too."

Both boys did as requested. Next, they spread a Hudson's Bay blanket, scarlet with wide black stripes, over The Butterfly Table. While Doc selected necessities from his medical bag, Clint, Nate, and Thaddeus with care placed Emmett, half-dead and three-quarters unconscious, supine atop the blanket.

Doc never wore cufflinks, even when dressed to the nines, and the genius behind this idiosyncrasy revealed itself now: he saved precious seconds rolling up his sleeves.

"Lem, fetch some towels," Doc summoned while cutting away a blood-soaked trouser leg. "Old ones would be best—just make sure they're clean."

Applying a tourniquet high on Emmett's left thigh, Doc continued his instructions: "Jay-Jay—my vial of ether's well-nigh empty. I should've refilled it right away after I last used it, but with all the housewarming excitement I flat-out forgot. That's no good excuse, but no matter about that now. Pull over a chair in the kitchen, you'll need it to climb up on. In the cupboard, on the top shelf, there's a full bottle of ether. As always, son, be quick, but don't hurry—I don't need you falling off a chair and giving me *two* people to stitch up."

Again, the twins did as asked; again, quickly without rushing.

"Thank you," Doc told Lem. "These towels 'll do just fine."

"Well done," he praised Jamis when the ether arrived.

With the six strong hands of Clint, Nate, and Thaddeus restraining Emmett, Doc went to his task. A few steps away, with Puck at their feet sensing this was no time for puppy play, the twins watched in wide-eyed wonder.

Thaddeus's layman diagnosis was dreadfully accurate: Emmett's left leg was indeed "a god-awful bloody mess." Flesh was torn and muscle was shredded; the tibia was crushed and the femur suffered a displaced fracture protruding through the skin; blood vessels were severed.

Saving the life would require sacrificing the limb.

As Doc readied to proceed with the amputation, Willie straggled through the one-of-a-kind front door left open during the recent commotion. Not yet ten o'clock in the morning, "Drunk Willie" was already living down to his nickname.

"Goo' mornin', fellers," Willie slurred.

Doc glanced up, his concentration broken and his patience soon to follow suit. The inebriated interloper stooped abruptly, dry heaving, the sound rough as 80-grit sandpaper. When the episode passed, Willie moaned: "Doc, I got hellfire in my appendix."

"I don't have time for your nonsense, William," Doc admonished, his usually dormant Irish temper flickering to flame. "I'm too busy trying to save Emmett to fuss around with you. Be gone."

"But—" Willie protested.

"Go on. Get going."

Willie did not move.

"Now!"

"But my belly's killin' me, Doc. You gotta help me."

Touching gently here, probing more firmly there, applying and releasing pressure elsewhere, Doc's hands were enchanted at diagnosing ailments from bone fractures to appendicitis to myriad other maladies. But he needed no medical training to identify this affliction. Willie, his boozy breath strong enough to make a bystander dizzy, simply had a hangover with a head start on another.

"I've told you before, William," Doc said, vinegar in his tone. "Don't come 'round here bothering my patients, or me, when you're drunk. I'd ask Clint to toss you in jail, but he's tied up helping me. So here's what I'm gonna do—take a seat and when I'm finished with Emmett, I'll put you out of your misery."

"Ya will?"

"Yes, William, I will," Doc promised, stabbing a finger at him. "I'll fix you up a shot glass with poison—that'll put an end to your bellyache once and for good."

Drunk Willie reeled and zoomed out the front door with laughter from everyone but Emmett chasing at his heels. Never again did Willie dare visit 210 Freddy Street, or Doc's office in town, unless he was sober.

Huck-le-ber-ry Finn

Ether is far more potent than whiskey or even Hungarian *pálinka*.

Doc poured the colorless medicinal liquid on a folded white handkerchief, monogrammed "LJ" in gold, and held it over Emmett's mouth and nose until consciousness faded, faded, faded fully away. Doc handed the moistened cloth to Lem and instructed him to repeat the process while saying "Huckleberry Finn" slowly—*Huck-le-ber-ry Finn*—three times whenever Emmett stirred in the slightest.

Next, Doc asked Jamis to retrieve a backsaw and a fine-cut file from the workshop shed.

"Nothing good comes from hurrying, boys, in anything we do," Doc reiterated when Jamis returned with the tools. It was the beginning of a monologue, interrupted occasionally when the operation required Doc's deepest concentration.

"My dad told me hurrying leads to worrying," Doc continued.

Lingering pause.

"And worrying clouds the mind."

A silence measuring *Huck-le-ber-ry Finn* ten times over.

"And a clouded mind doesn't make good decisions."

Elucidation yielded to whistle-humming while Doc made an incision with a scalpel, creating a palm-wide flap of skin on the lateral side of Emmett's left thigh.

"A clouded mind is like a rushed hand," Doc picked up where he had left off. "It doesn't allow us to perform our best."

Whistle-humming while using the backsaw to sever the distal femur, six inches above the knee, then: "As a doctor, I've got to be quick or else a patient—like Emmett, here—might bleed to death."

Whistle-humming while tying off an artery, and next: "Jay-Jay, please look in my black bag for more silk thread."

Whistle-humming while filing smooth the edges of the exposed thighbone so it would not pierce the skin flap, and resuming: "But if I hurry, well, I might just make things worse. So I've got to always remain calm. This isn't important only for doctors—take your woodworking for example, Lem. If you hurry, you're likely to make a mistake. You might measure wrong or make a crooked cut. Certainly, you won't create the best furniture you're capable of if you hurry. And yet, if you aren't a little bit quick about your work, you won't finish many pieces."

Lem nodded, all the while paying close attention to Emmett in case he stirred and needed another three *Huck-le-ber-ry Finns* of ether.

"This also applies to hunting, Jay-Jay," Doc went on. "You need to take aim quickly, but you can't hurry squeezing the trigger or you won't be accurate."

Whistle-humming while pulling the skin flap across and taut and suturing it closed, except for a small drainage hole, and now: "My dear Connie—she was a schoolteacher, as you know—she said it was the same with reading and writing. If you hurry, you won't understand what you're reading. And if you're in a rush, your handwriting will be sloppy. Yes, I think my dad's advice to *be quick, but don't hurry* wisely applies to just about everything we do."

Lastly, Doc fashioned a heavy bandage over the sutured stump. This was a simple task that allowed him to finish his impromptu seminar without further interlude.

"Jay-Jay, Lem, I'm proud of you. You both did exactly as I asked of you. Most people get woozy—quite a few even faint, in fact—the first time they see much blood, but you boys never wavered.

"Do you know why you didn't pass out or panic? Because you were focused on listening to me tell you all about *not hurrying*—that kept your minds clear instead of clouded with worry about Emmett.

"Let that be a lesson you can call upon whenever you're taking a school test or faced with some other difficult challenge. Remind yourself, *be quick, but don't hurry* and *be calm, carry on*, and it'll help you do your best.

"Now go on outside and have some fun with Puck."

On the battlefields of The Civil War, surviving a leg amputation similar to Emmett's was basically a coin toss with a mortality rate above forty percent. On The Butterfly Table, the coin came up heads: twenty-seven-year-old Emmett Riley resumed driving the trolley four months later and would live to age ninety-two.

At age fourteen, that very morning, Jamis decided to become a doctor.

Our Jester, Puck

 Like his Shakespearean namesake, Puck the Dalmatian proved to be quite a character.

As well, Puck was a superior hunting dog. This made sense because defying his stereotypical firehouse white-with-black-spots appearance, Puck was actually half-poodle—a breed long prized as "water dogs." George Washington, no less, had owned a black hunting poodle named Pilot.

Jamis diligently trained Puck to pilot him to small game. Puck, however, haughtily turned up his superior sniffing nose at retrieving shot animals and cleverly figured out a ploy to avoid this unappealing duty.

After successfully tracking the scent of a bird, rabbit, or squirrel, Puck would properly freeze at point. Then, with a sixth sense knowing exactly when Jamis was about to pull the trigger, the hound would preemptively bark to scare off the prey.

Each time Puck pulled this stunt Jamis responded by shooting more hurriedly the next time—but Puck intuitively kept barking sooner as well. Jamis's temper simmered hotter with each missed opportunity.

The fifth time Puck sabotaged Jamis's shot, the boy's anger exploded—

—into hearty laughter. He simply could not help but love Puck, shenanigans and all. It surely helped matters that Puck's affinity for prey reminded Jamis of Lem's inherent kindness to animals.

Doc likewise shared a soft spot for Puck's mischievousness for he had his own impish side. As example, like Grandma Dika, Doc was a seer of sorts. However, he reserved his predictions exclusively for telling expectant mothers whether they would give birth to a girl—or boy. Incredibly, Doc did so with unassailable 100-percent accuracy.

There was a method to his magic. While conducting an exam with a pregnant woman, usually late in the second trimester, Doc made a point of mentioning how high—or low—she was carrying the fetus. He furthermore asked about any food cravings. After theatrically considering this information, Doc confidently told the mother-to-be she was going to have a daughter—or else declared with certainty it was a son. The specific proclamation of gender did not matter because Doc secretly, and craftily, wrote in his red leather patients journal the *opposite* of what he predicted aloud.

When The Big Day arrived, the new mother would either remark with amazement about Doc's clairvoyance—or tease him for being wrong. If the latter happened, a coin-toss occurrence of course, Doc simply grinned and kindly insisted she must have misheard him. He would then display the journal page with—*Boy!* or *Girl!*—written beside her name. Every mom, without fail, fell for the playful trick.

Puck learned a new trick of his own one afternoon after loyally waiting, as was his custom, for the twins outside the schoolhouse. On their walk home, Jamis and Lem liked to stop at Nate's Bakery for two saucer-sized fat oatmeal raisin cookies at a nickel each. This day, the boys bought an extra one as a treat for Puck. He devoured it and a daily ritual was born.

Over summer, the twins had not visited the bakery for a few weeks when Doc took them for an unexpected snack. The bigger shock was when Nate announced the bill for the four cookies—one each for the twins, Doc, and Puck—was one dollar!

"Don't you mean twenty cents," Doc corrected, politely. "Your cookies are second-to-none, Nate, I'll grant you that, but a quarter apiece seems a bit overpriced."

"Oh, they're still a nickel," Nate confirmed. "The extra eighty cents is on account of Puck—he's been comin' 'round every afternoon like clockwork. Since Jamis and Lem always buy him a cookie, I figured they'd want me to give him one. So I started a credit account for Puck— hope that's okay."

Doc looked sternly at Puck, who was not at all fooled by the feigned curmudgeonliness. The dog smiled and, if you can believe it, winked at Doc.

"That certainly sounds like our little jester," Doc chuckled. "Yes, that's quite fine, Nate. And I'll thank you if you keep Puck's tab open. Naturally, only one cookie per day—we don't want our spotted friend getting too husky."

So it was that Puck became the first dog in Bellaire, perhaps the entire country, to have his own charge account.

Puck, Don't Give Up

 In July, instead of a friendly cookie, someone fiendishly fed Puck a piece of raw meat laced with strychnine—rat poison.

It was truly a midsummer's nightmare with seven other dogs in the neighborhood also falling victim to the heartless heinous act. All fingers pointed directly at Drunk Willie on account of Doc's threat to poison him, made in obvious jest, the morning Emmett Riley's leg was run over by a streetcar.

Jamis and Lem's spirits felt run over when Puck crawled onto the front porch, coughing up blood. Exacerbating the emergency, Doc was out making house calls.

Tearfully, helplessly, anxiously, Lem and Jamis kept sentry for Pops. The instant he rounded the corner into view, with daylight dying into evening, the twins hollered. Doc could not make out their words, but panic in their tone rang clear as a church bell and he broke into a dead sprint, holding his hat on with one hand, clutching his medical bag in the other.

The four-legged patient was panting rapidly, trembling violently. Doc suspected poisoning straightaway. The ensuing scene unfolded much as it had with Emmett: after Puck was placed on The Butterfly Table, padded by a quilt made by Connie, Doc went to work. Whistle-humming soothingly, he tenderly held an ether-soaked handkerchief over Puck's snout until the painless fog of anesthesia took hold.

The vapor-induced unconsciousness arrested the potentially deadly seizures, but only fleetingly; each time the sleeping potion began to wear off the fierce convulsions began anew. Because a continuous dose of ether would itself prove fatal, Doc needed to constantly monitor Puck and administer a careful *Huck-le-ber-ry Finn* whiff only as necessary. It was a medical high-wire act without a safety net below as Doc artfully kept Puck precariously balanced between slumber and seizure, between life and death, trying to buy time for the poison to safely dissipate.

It would be another eleven years, in 1879, before Iowa State University established the very first college of veterinary medicine in the United States. All the same, Puck could not have received better care from a trained veterinarian than he did from Doc.

All evening and throughout an unbearably long night, Doc kept vigil by Puck's side while Jamis and Lem kept vigil next to their Pops. Eventually, there were three sleeping heads resting on The Butterfly Table—although only one required ether's mollifying assistance.

Puck stopped breathing, twice, about a half hour on either side of midnight.

On both occasions, still detecting a faint heartbeat with his stethoscope, Doc did the opposite of what he had done when Connie was on her deathbed. Realizing she was suffering terribly, and knowing there could be no miracle cure, Doc had tenderly joined hands with his beloved wife and said a final goodbye before giving her permission to stop battling. Her eyes remaining closed, she had squeezed lightly, seemingly in symmetry to the length of their lingering wedding kiss twelve years before.

Then, peacefully, Connie's radiant spark of life flickered out.

"Puck, don't give up," Doc cooed now, lovingly stroking behind his patient's ears each time death's grip tightened. "Hold on a wee bit longer and let this dreadful poison wear off. You're a mighty good dog and I need you to be strong."

The mighty good dog faithfully obeyed.

When the sun rose, so did Puck, and the mortality rate on The Butterfly Table remained zero. Tragically, all seven of the other poisoned dogs died because Doc had not known about their shared assault and thus was unable to provide his expert care.

Sheriff Clint Garman expeditiously cleared Willie, whose drunkenness on this occasion actually proved beneficial because it gave him an airtight alibi—passed out in the barroom of The Hotel Bellaire—when the ruthless canine crimes were committed.

Whiskey not only absolved Willie, it helped capture the guilty miscreant. A deranged drifter who lost an arm—and half his mind—in The Great Rebellion was arrested three days later. He got drunk, ironically at the bar Tamás repaired, and boasted about shutting up a bunch of barking mutts for good.

The morning following Doc's all-night heroics, Lem decided he would one day become an animal doctor "just like Pops."

Benched

 Keeping his homelessness under wraps was no easy endeavor for Lincoln.

More than once, when classmates were partying on the practice field, Linc had to lie in wait well past midnight before he dared risk sneaking inside the shed. He had to be equally careful each and every time he departed his lonesome lair.

As further precaution, Linc stashed away all his things during the daytime just in case the groundskeeper ducked inside. The hollowed backs of the blocking sled's pads served as a clothes closet, food pantry, and bathroom cabinet. A paint-stained canvas tarp kept his sleeping area cloaked.

Keven remained a godsend, bringing Linc a sack lunch daily—always with a folded five-dollar bill tucked inside for a fast-food dinner—and laundered his friend's clothes each weekend.

Linc grew comfortable inside his hideaway.

But he got careless outside of it.

Friday night, with his helmet off during pregame stretches, the glare of the bright stadium lights flickered off Linc's diamond stud earring and for a second time the infraction caught Coach Tavis Jordan's attention.

"Jamison!" Coach growled, grimacing, exasperated. "Again? You know the rules."

Linc was puzzled, but when Coach stalked over and extended his upturned palm, the teen stiffened with cold realization of his unintentional transgression.

"I was in a hurry and forgot to—" Linc began in contrite explanation.

"Quentin! You're at slot receiver!" Coach cut in, in a bellow, not interested in an excuse. "Mikey Lynn, you move to wideout!"

As an exclamation point to Linc's benching, Coach clenched his fist around the diamond earring, cocked his right arm and snapped it forward in a blur like he was throwing a thirty-yard spiral to an open receiver at midfield.

Linc flinched as if Uncle Roy had just slapped him across the face for being late to dinner.

The diamond stud was Linc's insurance policy. If his situation became too dire, he figured he could pawn it to pay for a motel room or, worst case, bus fare back to Bellaire. Now his sole possession with any value was lost, a needle in a chalk-lined green haystack.

Linc's loss from the first-string lineup was felt immediately. Two Cougar drives stalled when Q failed to hold onto catchable passes for first downs, and he flat-out dropped a third ball in the end zone. A fourth spiral skipped off Q's fingertips into the hands of a defender, who returned the interception for a touchdown.

Following each miscue, Q jogged hangdog off the field. Each time, Linc was the first to greet him on the sidelines with words of encouragement: "No worries, Q"—"That was a tough one"—"Night lights take some gettin' used to"—"You'll catch the next one."

At halftime, the visiting Arlington Golden Bears led 14-0.

Coach Jordan knew his players were expecting to get chewed out for their sloppy and uninspired play.

Tempting as an iron-fisted outburst was, he decided the players—particularly Linc—needed a velvet glove instead.

"That opening half reminds me of when I took my driver's test the day I turned sixteen," Coach began, with quiet equanimity, addressing the team in the locker room. "First off, I forgot to buckle my seatbelt. Exiting the parking lot into the street, I made a rolling stop. Then I failed to put my turn signal on before changing lanes. When I made an illegal left turn, the instructor had finally had enough. *Jeeee-sus!* he bellowed. *Is this your first time behind the wheel? I should've failed you for the seatbelt. Take me back to the DMV—without getting us both killed, if you can manage it.*"

The metal lockers rattled from the players' raucous laughter.

"There's more," Coach went on. "In my rush to get the disaster over with, I went through a yellow light that turned red sooner than I anticipated—

"—I got a traffic ticket before I even got my license!"

Bedlam of laughter.

"Here's the serious point to the story," Coach concluded. "I rebounded from that epic fail by kicking ass the second time I took the test—with that same instructor. Men, we've got a whole 'nother half of football to play. Let's go kick some ass!"

Second Half, Second Chance

 The fired-up Cougars stormed out of the locker room for the second half.

On their way out, Coach Tavis Jordan intercepted Q and Linc at the doorway.

"Jamison—you're in," Coach said, adding: "Quentin—you'll get another chance, don't worry. Stay ready."

Q jogged off, actually relieved by his demotion.

Coach held Linc back for an abrupt private moment: "The ball's coming to you—don't let go of it."

Linc nodded, still resentful about the earring confrontation, but thrilled to be back in the lineup. He was not going to let go of his second chance.

Coach Jordan proved prescient: the ball came Linc's way, time and again and more. In just one half of playing time, No. 11 had nine catches—including all three of the Cougars' touchdowns—in a thrilling 21-14 come-from-behind victory.

"You guys passed your driver's test!" Coach proclaimed in the exuberant locker room. "You looked like a real football team. Defense—you guys made four sacks and shut them out the second half. O-line—you dominated the trenches like beasts. Special teams were outstanding. And Jamison—if you keep getting open and catching everything Baxter throws your way like you did tonight, I'll get *my* ear pierced before the league championship game."

Ear-ring! Ear-ring! chants echoed off the concrete walls and tiled showers.

Linc did not join the enthused chorus; he was too focused on holding back tears over the lost diamond stud.

As his teammates, almost all wearing pricey letterman jackets, headed off to the victory party, Linc, in Keven's *Fighting Irish* hoodie, one cuff fraying, strayed onto the deserted football field. The stadium lights were off, but dim illumination drifted over from the adjacent parking lot.

Alone in the shadowy darkness that mimicked his mood, Linc dropped to his knees at midfield and began combing his fingers through the gridiron grass. Square foot by square foot, he searched for his earring like a blind man reading Braille.

Coach Jordan, walking to his pickup truck, spotted the hunched solitary silhouette on the field and angled over.

"Jamison—whatchya doing?" Coach called out from the end zone.

Linc grumbled a profanity, not loud enough to be heard fifty yards away.

"Come here," Coach said.

Linc paid him no mind.

"*Linc-oln*," Coach said, his voice stern with concern rather than impatience. "Come here—please."

Linc rose to his feet, leaving his team duffle bag behind at the forty-five-yard-line to mark his searching point, and trudged over with heavy feet.

"Nice game," Coach greeted. "You really put on a pass-catching clinic in the second half."

"Thanks, sir," Linc answered, his voice chillier than autumn's late night air.

"Truth is," Coach rejoined, "I was actually more impressed with your performance in the *first* half."

Linc cocked his head, confused.

"If it wasn't for you, Linc, we'd have been down a lot more than fourteen-zip," Coach praised. "I saw you— how you kept bolstering your teammates' sagging spirits. When they made mistakes, you wouldn't let them stay disheartened. You're a helluva leader, son. Keep it up. Now go on and join the victory party—but be smart."

Linc managed a half-hearted smile.

"One more thing," Coach said, digging his fingers into his pants pocket. He pulled out a clenched hand, extended it towards Linc like a slow-motion fist bump, turned his palm up and opened it: "Is this what you're hunting for in the grass?"

Linc's brooding eyes lit up like July fireworks.

"My earring," he said with marvel. "How'd you find it?"

Coach laughed: "Nice fake, huh? In case you didn't know it, I wasn't a half-bad play-action quarterback in high school."

"You sure as hell fooled me," Linc said and started to insert the earring post into his left ear.

"No third chances, Linc," Coach warned, warmly. "Don't wear it on the field ever again—understand?"

Linc paused in thought before handing the earring back: "You keep it, sir."

Now it was Coach's turn to be puzzled.

"*You* can wear it for the league championship game," Linc explained.

Coach Jordan grinned, slipped the glittering earring in his pocket—then put his arm around Linc as they walked off the darkened field under a clear starlit sky.

Critical Crossroads

Monday morning, so early the faculty parking lot remained deserted, Lincoln sat, slouching, on the red no-parking curb nearest the gym.

He had something important to tell Coach Jordan.

Linc's homelessness had been discovered. Gone from the shed were the down sleeping bag, pillow, Pendleton blanket. Gone were the electric camping lantern, Walkman, cassette tapes.

Gone, too, was the possibility of staying in Cleveland Heights. Linc needed to return—*retreat in defeat*, in his mind—to Bellaire.

On the blacktop, at Linc's feet, was a black plastic lawn bag. Only half-full, it contained all his worldly possessions that had been left behind by the pitiless thief: four T-shirts and a long-sleeved flannel, pair of jeans, socks and underwear, navy blue watchman's cap, New Balance running shoes, and three paperbacks—*Catcher in the Rye, Uncle Tom's Cabin, The Old Man and the Sea*—all assigned for English Literature.

What the emotional toll of his father's abandonment and his mother's drug dependency had both failed to do, what Uncle Roy's physical punishment had also failed to cause, the burglary now accomplished: Linc broke down sobbing. He felt as vanquished as Santiago—Ernest Hemingway's elderly fisherman character—after losing his giant marlin to sharks.

Linc, feeling truly orphaned and rootless, surrendered to the realization he would have to go live with Aunt Veronica and Uncle Roy. After honorably telling Coach Jordan goodbye, he would walk to the Greyhound station and—thanks to Keven's saved birthday money—catch a bus to his dismal destiny awaiting in Bellaire.

Pulling into the parking lot, Tavis's pulse spiked with the caffeine kick of three espressos and a Red Bull chaser. He ignored the lined spaces and stopped directly in front of Linc.

"You're *really* on Tavis Time today, Jamison," Coach said, trying to lighten the mood despite his heavy apprehension. "There's no more graffiti to paint over—so what has you here so early?"

"I'm quitting the team," Linc blurted, skipping all pleasantries.

"Because of the first-half benching?"

"No, sir. I deserved that and appreciate how you gave me a second chance so soon."

"Then what is it?" Coach pressed.

Linc's words spilled out frantic as whitewater rapids: "I need to quit because I have no place to live and my stuff got stolen and everything I own in the world besides an antique table that's in the library in Bellaire is in this stupid trash bag and I'm broke except for some money Kev gave me and my family's opal ring is gone and my dad is gone and my mom is gone and—"

"Whoa, slow down, son," Coach said, his tone as reassuring as an unrushed hug.

"I don't want to move back to Bellaire with my aunt and uncle—especially Uncle Roy because he's a mean sonuvabitch," Linc resumed, slowing down only barely.

"But I have no choice, Coach. I've got no other damn choice."

Linc's heartbreaking monologue ended only because his tears began.

Coach had not digested half of what he heard, but one thing was fully clear: Love had been right—*The answer will come to you.*

"I'm sorry," Linc wheezed, embarrassed, wiping a waterfall of snot on his *Fighting Irish* hoodie sleeve.

Without another word, Coach Jordan hoisted the garbage bag and slung the meager belongings into pickup bed. With little ceremony, it was no small thing. Then he opened the passenger door, left it ajar, walked around to the driver's side and climbed in.

Linc remained seated curbside.

Coach waited wordlessly, waited patiently.

Linc, at length, stood up and got in.

The truck, its cab filled with disquieting silence, made a rolling stop out of the parking lot.

One left turn, followed by two rights, brought man and boy to a crossroads. The red traffic light at an empty four-way intersection turned green, but Coach kept his foot on the brake—kept it there, kept it there, kept it there, the watershed moment requiring resolution—and the green light turned yellow and then red again.

"Well, Linc—what do you want to do?"

"I want to go home with you, sir."

Coach Jordan slid his right foot to the gas pedal and turned left against the red light.

All In

Love was at the kitchen island cutting crust off a peanut butter-and-grape-jelly sandwich while Fayth sat at the table eating oatmeal topped with banana slices and honey.

"Fruit roll-up or baby carrots in your lunch?" Love asked.

"Roll-up, of course!" answered the fourth-grader.

"Okay, *both* it is," Love teased.

The front door pushed opened with a tired creak and shut with a resolute click and Tavis led Linc into the kitchen.

"Fayth, Love—this is Lincoln," he said, gesturing to each as he made introductions. "He's going to be staying with us."

"Hey, nice to meet you, Fayth," Linc said, adding formally: "Hello, ma'am."

"Call me Love, please. Have you had breakfast, Lincoln?"

"No, ma'am—" Linc began, but rightly corrected himself. "I mean, no, *Love*, I haven't. And you can call me Linc."

"Well, *Linc*, have a seat," Love said, warmly. "Are Cheerios and a banana okay? It's quick and I don't want y'all late for school. Tomorrow I'll make you a real breakfast."

"I'm a huge fan of cereal." Linc smiled. "Cereal or Pop-Tarts and I'm happy as a puppy."

"Mom won't let me have Pop-Tarts," Fayth said nonchalantly, not whining.

"That's probably smart," replied Linc, nodding across the table at Fayth. "Bananas are way healthier—lots of potassium, you know. I think I'll skip Frosted Pop-Tarts from now on. Maybe it'll make me faster on the football field."

Love smiled to herself at the friendly banter. Barely two minutes inside the front door and already she felt an affinity for this winsome kid.

Fayth and Linc's easy conversation extended between spoonfuls. Meanwhile, in regards to a conversation they had not had, Love shot a wifely telepathic glance at Tavis: *We need to talk later.*

Aloud Love said: "Tav, why don't you take Linc's things to the guest room. We can get him settled in this evening, but right now you two better shake a leg getting to school."

Already, Linc was feeling so comfortable in the Jordan household he wisecracked playfully: "Yeah, Coach, if you're tardy to first period you'll have to run punishment laps at practice."

"If I'm late, you'll be late too," Tavis retorted, grinning wryly. "And you wouldn't want an old man to leave you in the dust in front of your teammates, would you?"

~~~

Love and Tavis had their talk that evening.

After dinner, while at the kitchen table Fayth read her minimum twenty minutes and Linc did his homework, the adults slipped away to their bedroom. Tavis, speaking quietly, shared everything he knew about Linc's situation, especially the boy's fears of his uncle.

Love could be excused for having misgivings. This was not like bringing home a stray cat. Taking a high school student in under one's roof—for who knows how long—was something that should have been discussed beforehand. It was a big deal, big responsibility, big complication.

And Love's answer was a big "yes"—albeit with one stipulation: "If we do this, babe, we have to be *all in.*"

"Absolutely," Tavis said. "All in."

"I mean it, Tav," said Love, her eyes and words weighted with conviction. "This kid has been through too much to be let down again. If things get rocky and we fail him, it will destroy him. I've seen it happen."

"We won't fail him," Tavis assured.

"You know people are going to accuse you of doing this only because he's a standout football player," Love warned. "Linc being white—rather, us being Black—will also upset folks."

"To hell with 'em," Tavis derided. "The boy needs this. He's been dealt one bad break after another. We can give him a stable family."

"What if Rhett says he can't stay on the team if he lives with us?" Love said, playing devil's advocate. "You know, for eligibility reasons."

Tavis, without hesitation: "If Linc has to quit the team, so be it. He needs this—needs us."

Love considered all sides before offering her final verdict: "I think Linc also needs to keep playing football. Since no one knows where to find his mother, you need to have his aunt and uncle give us temporary guardianship."

"All in," Tavis said.

"All in," echoed Love.

Circus Comes To Bellaire

 The railway boom's connection of the Baltimore & Ohio Railroad to Bellaire provided the town with economical transportation of goods to the Eastern Seaboard.

In turn, the local populace grew threefold in one decade's span—from fewer than fourteen hundred residents in 1860 to more than four thousand citizens when the next census was taken in 1870. The small burg had become a city. Indeed, with access to major markets, glass-making facilities opened by the dozens and Bellaire earned the nickname "Glass City."

Transporting glass windows, glassware, and glass bottles daily to the East was important, but the arrival of the B&O also facilitated a special import: the circus came to town. Specifically, the famous Robinson & Howe's Champion Circus, which traveled in thirteen custom-built railcars, added Ohio to its annual summer tour.

When the circus came to Bellaire for the first time, in 1866, it was like Christmas in July for Jamis and Lemuel. As The Big Day approached when they would finally see the magic under The Big Top, their imaginations soared and spun like high-flying trapeze acrobats. Perhaps even more excited than the fourteen-year-old twins was Doc, a kid at heart of age forty.

By midweek, colorful Robinson & Howe's Champion Circus flyers popped up throughout town boasting:

JAMES ROBINSON—The Unquestioned Greatest
Bare-Back Rider And Acrobat Who Has Ever Lived!
~ ~ ~
An Exhibition Peerless And Matchless Over All Others!
A Glittering Galaxy Of Artists Performing Dazzling Acts!
Sven "Braveheart" Eriksson's Tremendous Menagerie
Of Rare Wild Beasts!
THE GREATEST SHOW ON EARTH!!!
~ ~ ~
Remember The Name:
Robinson & Howe's Champion Circus
Don't Forget The Date: Saturday At Two O'Clock

Friday morning bright and early, a long string of eye-catching mustard-and-ketchup-red boxcars rumbled into the Bellaire train station.

The remainder of the day saw the tent, equipment, and *Tremendous Menagerie Of Rare Wild Beasts!* unloaded from the train and transported by horse-drawn wagons to the fairgrounds—coincidentally, a mere stone's throw away, by a powerful arm, from the very spot Doc had delivered Jamis and Lem into the world.

On this day, Doc delivered the twins on site in time to watch the circus arrive.

Lem, especially, was mesmerized by the parade of animals—elephants, big cats, bears, zebras, horses, a rhinoceros and hippopotamus, camels, even alligators—that looked like Noah's Ark disembarking. Jamis, meanwhile, was most captivated by the impressive railroad train. Doc's favorite part, a crowning memory he would cherish into old age, was the glowing elation on Jamis and Lem's faces.

No ticket was required for this pre-performance spectacle and so a good hundred townspeople, an equal mix of children and young-at-heart adults, turned out. While everyone else watched in awe as the muscle power of two elephants and a handful of horses, plus a dozen men including the circus's Herculean Strong Man, erected the colossal canvas tent, Doc slyly ushered the twins away on a surreptitious quest.

Hidden from the crowd's view by the rising tent, the traveling zoo encamped under nearby shade trees. Exceeding Doc's hopes, he and the boys found the lion-tamer feeding his collection of big cats: three lions, two tigers, and one each panther and leopard, all in individual cages.

"You can't be here," the lion-tamer commanded.

"Don't mean to bother you," Doc said politely, extending a handshake. "I'm Dr. Jamison—everyone calls me Doc. I was just bringing my sons by to say hello to the tigers. This is Lem—and this is Jamis. I hope you don't mind if they have a quick look-see before we all get outta your way."

"Aw, you ain't bothering me none," the lion-tamer said, flashing a sudden smile so warm it threatened to melt the beeswax off his impressively curled handlebar mustache. "I'm Sven. Nice to meet y'all. The tigers are Pollux and Castor—named after the ancient Greek's Gemini twins. I'm just feeding 'em a late lunch. You're plenty welcome to watch—just make sure you keep them hands back from the cages. Don't want you boys getting the nicknames *One-Hand Lem* and *Nine-Fingers Jamis*."

Sven laughed at his own biting humor and then went back to feeding his feline troupe.

Cages And Chains

 Wishing to remain *Two-Hands* Lem and *Ten-Fingers* Jamis, the twins hastily withdrew a full step from Pollux's cage to safely watch lunch being served.

Big cats first joined an American circus in 1833 when the showman Isaac Van Amburgh strode into a giant iron cage jointly occupied by one each: lion, tiger, leopard, and panther. Costumed as a Roman gladiator in a knee-length white toga, shiny gold belt, and sandals with leather straps extending up his calves, Van Amburgh enhanced his act by wielding a crowbar—not a bullwhip—to beat, rather than scare, the wild cats into tamed compliance.

Having thus established his dominance with the brutality of a tobacco plantation slavemaster, Van Amburgh would then theatrically put one of his arms— he still retained both—into the mouth of each ferocious beast, in breathtaking succession, to prove his absolute bravery.

Merciful critics cried foul at the display of cruelty, but Van Amburgh responded with a Biblical defense: "Did not God say in Genesis 1:26 that men should have dominion over every animal on the Earth?"

Robinson & Howe's Champions Circus's less barbaric dominion over its seven big cats, each confined with barely room enough to pace a tight circle, still saddened Doc immeasurably. After bidding Sven goodbye, he shared these feelings with the boys.

"Those are beautiful animals," Doc began. "Especially the tigers—to me, they're the most striking. Their copper-colored coats remind me of a brand new penny's glint in the sunlight, with stripes black as coal. Gorgeous, absolutely gorgeous."

Doc whistle-hummed in admiration, then deadpan: "Did you know I have a tiger's stripe?"

"Really?" Jamis said with Lem's widening eyes echoing the query.

Doc pushed up his left shirtsleeve, high, revealing a six-inch-long birthmark on the inside of his bicep. It looked like an artist's single brushstroke of black paint— or a tiger's stripe—wider near Doc's shoulder and tapering as it flowed towards his elbow.

"Ginchy," admired Jamis. "But I like the lions best."

"I can't choose," Lem offered. "I love 'em all. Maybe the leopard is my favorite 'cause it has spots like Puck."

Doc, drifting contemplative, rejoined: "I think there's one thing we can agree on—it's heartbreaking to see magnificent animals locked in cages like criminals in jail. God's masterpiece creations should roam free."

The boys nodded their affirmation and Doc extended his sermon: "I've never seen a tiger or lion in the wild, but I can't imagine they're as skinny as these poor fellas. Did you see how their ribs showed? That's from not being fed enough—and also on account they're not getting enough exercise. Wild animals are meant to roam and run and hunt. I fear that being locked up has taken away their will to live—or, at the least, sapped their thrill for living. We all need a purpose in our lives or we grow ill."

"That's sad, Pops," said Lem.

"It certainly is," Doc agreed. "It's not just these beautiful big cats in their small cages that's sad. The circus's giant elephants are imprisoned with a leg shackled to a small post in the ground. Animals shouldn't be kept in cages or bound by leg chains or have their spirits broken by a whip.

"This is true also for men. That's why you should both be very proud of what your father did. Tamás fought so that men would not be kept in chains nor beaten into subservience. He fought so slaves could have their freedom. I cannot think of a higher purpose for one's life.

"Sons, we haven't talked about slavery before—partly because you're so young and partly because slavery is such an ugly thing to discuss. The short conversation is this: slavery is dead wrong. It's a dreadful sin of sins— and don't let anyone convince you otherwise. Your dad was a true hero to join the war and fight for the abolishment of slavery."

The surrogate father and two sons walked homeward, three abreast, lost in thought each. After a good long while Lem broke the silence: "Pops, can we still go to the circus tomorrow?"

"Oh, yes," Doc replied. "I hear they've got a knife-thrower I really want you see."

The Greatest Show In Bellaire

Circus Day arrived warm and sunny and dappled with cumulus clouds a child's imagination could turn into tigers and clowns and elephants.

A cooling breeze flowed off the Ohio River, carrying with it a troupe of circus performers aimed at heating up excitement for that afternoon's big show. Posters, flyers, and a story in *The Bellaire Bulletin* weekly newspaper had drummed up early interest, but the appearance of a tuxedoed barker, three clowns, two acrobats, and one juggler outside The Hotel Bellaire was promotional gold for guaranteeing robust attendance.

The clowns attracted a generous gathering with snappy jokes and choreographed pratfalls.

The juggler doubled the headcount by keeping three beer mugs airborne—then four, five, and eventually six—one always remaining filled with ale!

The acrobats raised the thrills, literally, by walking and dancing and somersaulting on a rope stretched taut five feet off the ground across Main Street.

"We'll perform at a death-defying height this afternoon," one of the tightrope artists boasted, loud and proud, "with no net to save our lives if we fall!"

Standing on an overturned fruit crate, the barker bellowed to the growing crowd: "Robinson and Howe's Champions Circus is the greatest show on Earth! Bring your families! Tell your friends! Come see James Robinson—the supreme bareback rider known to man!

Come see the lions and tigers and elephants! Come see the world's most accurate knife-thrower! Come one, come all to The Big Top today at two o'clock!"

At the breakfast table, and about every half hour thereafter, Lem and Jamis excitedly asked Doc if it was time yet to go. At high noon, he finally gave in to their impatience and off to the fairgrounds the trio headed, the twins half-skipping.

Still two hours before showtime, Doc took the boys on a circuitous route passing by Nate's Bakery. No sooner had they ordered three oatmeal raisin cookies than an unexpected guest entered.

"I guess you'll be wanting a fourth cookie," Nate said as Puck padded up to the front counter, performed a few head-chasing-tail spins, then obediently sat on his haunches waiting to receive his usual treat.

"How'd you get here?" Doc chortled, adding gently: "Lem, Jay-Jay—one of you must've left the door open."

"Wasn't me," they said in twinly synchronicity.

"No harm done," Doc said. "Yes, Nate, an extra cookie for our four-legged friend, please."

Outside the bakery, Lem pointed and commanded: "Home, Puck, go home! Circuses don't sell tickets to dogs."

Puck, knowing every scent between Nate's Bakery and 210 Freddy Street, trotted away while Jamis and Lem scampered off in the opposite direction towards the fairgrounds with Doc lagging behind.

In short time, the twins stopped and waited for their Pops and together they walked the rest of the way. Rounding the final turn, the colossal yellow-and-red-striped canvas tent came into view.

"Wow!" said Lem.

"Oh, boy!" Jamis exalted.

Doc whistle-hummed.

Admission tickets were a dime apiece for the boys, and a quarter for Doc, and a bargain by far. Billing it as "The Greatest Show on Earth" may have been hyperbolic, but without question it was the greatest show in Bellaire.

The clowns warmed up the sellout crowd and juggling acts followed.

The Strong Man bent an iron bar into a U and outdid that by lifting a farm wagon on his Herculean back.

Acrobats in sequined leotards of every color in the rainbow executed flying cartwheels and somersaulted like flipped coins in dizzying combinations. They followed with two- and three-person balancing stunts. For their high-risk finale, the acrobats performed their repertoire of amazing balancing feats on a tightrope thirty feet above the dirt floor with no safety net, as promised.

Next, the ringmaster, decked out in a scarlet tailcoat, black pants with matching boots and top hat, announced with exuberance through a megaphone: *"Laaa-dieee-sss and gen-tle-mennn! Girlsss and boysss! Please welcome—*

"the man whose impossible feats include a world-record—

"twenty-three consecutive backward somersault flips—

"while standing on a running horse!

"Put your hands together for the greatest!—

"bareback rider!—

"who has ever lived!

"The one! The only!—

"Jaaaamesss! Rob-in-sonnnn!"

In rode the living legend, greeted by a foot-stomping ovation so thunderous The Big Top flapped and fluttered as if by a cyclone.

Blindfolded Knife-Thrower

The Great James Robinson rode into the circus tent *standing* on a bareback horse, a magnificent white Arabian with jingle bells braided into its flowing mane.

Dressed in scarlet jockey silks and golden knickers tucked into tall black boots, the supreme showman dropped to his knees atop the hindquarters, then rose and balanced on a single foot, pirouetting once, twice, thrice.

Next, he hopped to the ground and, in one fluid motion, rebounded back to standing again on the trotting animal, repeating the trick on the starboard side. He followed this by leaping from the snow-white steed onto the back of a midnight-black beauty now striding alongside—and jumped back. In turn, he stood with one foot astride each horse's saddleless back as they cantered side-by-side.

Properly warmed up, Robinson performed his famous trademark. Eyes forward while standing on the croup of the Arabian's muscular hindquarters, he took two steps towards the withers and—*Whoosh!*—launched airborne into a back somersault, landing perfectly whence he sprang, with the horse never slowing step.

A log hurdle was raised and the white horse trotted *beneath* it and—*Whoosh!*—Robinson did a forward somersault *over* it.

A giant hanging hoop was set ablaze—*Whoosh!*—Robinson somersaulted through the ring of fire, again landing neatly.

For his grand finale, "The Greatest Bareback Rider Who Has Ever Lived!" strung together his famous backward aerial somersaults like shiny pearls on a necklace—*Whoosh! Whoosh! Whoosh! . . .* —twenty gems in a row by the ringmaster's bellowing count. The audience drained their vocal cords at the dizzying exploit.

As Robinson triumphantly rode out of the sawdust ring, a loose-limbed knife-thrower gallantly strode in.

A wooden wall featuring a human silhouette, arms out from the torso and legs spread slightly, was wheeled out. Facing the target from ten overly long paces, the knife-thrower practiced his flinging motion three times over. Aim zeroed in, he tied a black blindfold over his own eyes.

Doc, all the while, could hardly believe his eyes. The rumor was true—

Hanzi must be nearly thirty years old now, Doc thought, reflecting on the night the boy fetched him when Aisha was in labor and hours later hit a derby target twice in the knife-throwing contest. *My goodness, time passes in the blink of the eye.*

In a blink, the blindfolded performer threw his first knife—piercing the silhouette's head, nose-center. The crowd roared in communal laughter.

Peeking from beneath the blindfold with one eye, Hanzi sheepishly announced: "Maybe I best not wear this today!"

More guffaws, louder.

Blindfold removed, Hanzi let the second throw fly— *Thwack!*—and the crowd groaned for the knife blade was imbedded in the faux groin.

"That was a practice throw!" Hanzi proclaimed. "Now I am warmed up!"

An assistant, wearing a shimmering sequined leotard that nearly matched her waist-long golden waterfall of hair, took her place mimicking the silhouette target.

"I don't need this anymore—but you might," Hanzi announced and tied the discarded blindfold over the blonde beauty's eyes. Enhancing the theatrics, he balanced a ripe red apple atop her head.

Hanzi marched off ten exaggerated paces, pivoted, and took his mark facing the brave woman. Nudging the tension higher yet, he displayed six glistening knives to the hushed crowd, selected one, took pantomimed aim—

The first throw stuck between the woman's parted legs, thigh-high.

The second found its mark between her right hip and forearm; the third knife did likewise on her left side.

The next two flings pinned the wooden wall mere inches from each shoulder.

"Now the apple!" Hanzi bellowed boastfully, taking measure with the sixth-and-final knife. He hesitated, flamboyantly wiped sweat from his brow, retook aim—

—then, suddenly, strode forward and plucked the apple off his assistant's head; used his throwing knife to cut a slice from the fruit, which he fed into her mouth; removed her blindfold and used it like a napkin to dab the corners of her ruby-red lips; and bowed expressively to the adoring crowd.

Amid the swollen ovation, Doc leaned in close to Jamis and Lem: "Your dad could have hit that apple dead center—I saw him do as much the night you were born."

Fainting Spectator

 Under The Big Top, which smelled of popcorn and sawdust, came the menagerie parade.

A pair of elephants, long-tusked and lumbering and trumpeting loudly, each with a silver-sequined female acrobat seated upon its upturned trunk, led the grand procession, followed by bookend giraffes, a dancing bear, one rhinoceros in a caged wagon, five camels in single file, four chimpanzees riding two zebras, and—in a train of seven miniature boxcar cages—three lions, two tigers, and one each panther and leopard.

The elephant keeper began the animal acts by putting his pachyderms through their slow-motion paces—sitting down, raising a front foot to "shake hands," standing upright on hind legs—as if they were giant-eared dogs weighing four tons apiece.

Big size was followed by big danger.

Sven "Braveheart" Eriksson—costumed toe to head in knee-high black riding boots, khaki jodhpurs, golden waistcoat over a long-sleeved white safari shirt, tan pith helmet—entered the sawdust ring, now enclosed by fourteen-foot-high iron fencing with a net ceiling. One by one, he released his charges from their cages on wheels and led each to its own oversized wood stool.

Next, Braveheart escorted the big cats—again, individually—around the ring and back onto their stools. In turn, he directed all seven together, single file, for two laps before returning to their assigned stations.

Raising the bar of difficulty, and holding a cane chair aloft as a shield, Braveheart guided the two star Bengal tigers onto separate steel platforms set a staggering twenty feet apart. He raised his whip—*Crack!*—and Pollux leapt across to Castor.

Crack! Castor sailed to the now empty table-sized perch.

Crack! Both tigers bounded simultaneously, seemed to brush furry flanks in midflight, and landed nimbly on the opposite platforms.

Crack! Again both tigers vaulted in unison, but this time Castor traveled a lower arc while Pollux soared in a high rainbow *over* his striped twin!

The crowd buzzed in awe.

After directing the lower-jumping Castor back onto its wooden stool, Braveheart strutted to the unoccupied steel platform, positioned his prop chair directly behind it, sat down, and removed his helmet.

A breath-holding hush, impossibly quieter than a library, fell over The Big Top.

"Attack!" came the command and Pollux sprung airborne as if flung by catapult. With feline grace defying its six hundred pounds, the copper-and-black flash flew even higher than previously and landed safely on the opposite platform, sharp fangs glistening as it *ROARED* mere inches from his trainer's face.

Braveheart, true to his moniker, did not flinch; even his handlebar mustache did not twitch.

He raised an index finger to his lips—

—the ferocious *ROARING* shushed.

He stood and lifted his arms, slowly, skyward—

—Pollux sat on hind haunches.

He brought both hands down to his waist—

—the regal cat reposed like The Great Sphinx of Giza.

He raised his right hand shoulder high, palm out, and cooed loudly: "Good boy, good boy"—

—Pollux lowered its head, the lion-tamer rubbed its snout, and the savage beast closed its eyes like a house cat taking a nap.

The audience was mesmerized, but Braveheart was not yet finished. "Open sesame!" he instructed and Pollux roused as if with a giant yawn—

—and Braveheart stuck his *head* inside the perilous jaws!

With that, a woman spectator fainted, toppling forward from her seat.

Hearing the commotion in the bleachers, Braveheart withdrew his Scandinavian locks from guillotine-like jeopardy. Instead of guiding the seven jungle cats—one by one—into their individual wheeled cages inside the fenced-in ring, with haste he directed them en masse through a chute leading to a communal iron-barred training enclosure outside the main tent.

Meanwhile, the ringmaster impulsively announced the circus was over; clowns scrambled to hawk souvenirs to the departing spectators; and Doc rushed over to the unconscious woman. No sooner had he taken her pulse—slightly rapid, but strong—than she became alert. Still, the welt on her forehead made him concerned about a possible concussion.

"Boys, I'm gonna stay a little while to look after her," Doc told Lem and Jamis. "You head straight home and I'll be along shortly."

In all the hubbub, no one noticed Pollux slip through a missing slat in the chute en route to the outdoor cage.

Lem The Braveheart

 If only Puck had padded over to Nate's Bakery to beg for a second cookie.

Instead, lonely at home, he went in search of Lemuel and Jamis and wound up at the circus. The twins had already departed, but Puck found Doc inside the main tent administering first aid.

"Well, hello," Doc greeted with amused surprise. "I'm a bit occupied, but you can catch up to your boys if you're quick about it. Home, Puck. Go home."

Puck obediently trotted off, two blocks behind the twins—

—while Pollux stealthily followed the black-spotted dog by half that distance.

Jamis and Lem were just ascending the porch steps when Puck barked: *Wait up!* In a rush to dutifully fill a dog dish with kibble, they left the front door ajar for him.

As Puck chowed down in the kitchen, in the dining room Jamis and Lem opened their *Robinson & Howe's Champions Circus Official Souvenir Program.* Unnoticed as they intently studied the photographs within, the escaped tiger crept into the entry foyer.

Simultaneously, the twins felt a sudden shiver and looked up. Watching the big cats under The Big Top had been breathtaking, but what Lem and Jamis saw now was suffocating. Only The Butterfly Table, lengthwise, stood between them and the jungle man-eater.

Pollux crouched, frozen and taut, ready to pounce.

Jamis and Lem, tingling shoulders abreast, stood motionless as the dead.

For the second time in his young life, Lem was about to be attacked by a wildcat predator. This tiger, however, outweighed that Ohio bobcat by five hundred pounds. And Jamis did not have a hunting rifle at the ready.

Jamis this time tried to save his brother's life by becoming a human shield, sidestepping in front, sacrificing himself in hopes Lem could flee without harm.

At once, Pollux powerfully uncoiled into flight.

Jamis, mercifully, did not feel the tiger's swift and savage wrath, its dagger claws, the bite of its teeth—

—because in a slow-motion minute, Lem executed a lifetime's worth of heroics.

First, standing behind Jamis, Lem flung his brother sideways out of death's way, shoving with such force, thanks to an orgasm of adrenaline, that Jamis stumbled into the adjacent kitchen. Puck, startled, looked up from his feeding bowl, the fur on his back bristling with alarm. Before the dog could attack protectively, and suicidally, Jamis commanded—under his breath, but with authority—"Sit! Stay!"

Puck, thank goodness, obeyed.

Meanwhile, Lem steeled his spine tall and straight and, with as much alpha-male confidence he could muster, willed himself to not flinch as Pollux flew toward him like a carnivorous comet.

Landing atop The Butterfly Table, the tiger skidded as if on a frozen pond. Its four-inch-long sharp claws were useless as brakes, unable to scratch the granite-hard thunderbolt-polished surface, much less dig in for traction. Instinctively lowering its center of gravity by leaning back on its rump and tail, Pollux slid to a stop at the far edge—nearest Lem.

Regaining its balance, the striped brute rose into a four-legged stance and *ROARED* menacingly.

Lem did not recoil.

Coolly, the boy raised a finger to his lips—

—the *ROARING* shushed.

Lem raised his arms skyward, slowly, again just as Sven "Braveheart" Eriksson had—

—Pollux sat on hind haunches.

"*Goooood boyyyy*," Lem The Braveheart cooed, hands still high aloft. In the same soothing tone, he directed his words now to the kitchen: "Jay-Jay. Climb on a chair, don't make a peep, and get Pops's spare bottle of ether. Pour it on a dish towel, soak it real good, then wad it up into a ball. After you've done that, I'm gonna lower one hand and hopefully the tiger will lie down. But I'm gonna keep my other hand up.

"*Goooood boyyyy*," Lem repeated to Pollux. "When I tell you to, toss me the towel. You've gotta hit my raised hand dead-square. If I have to move to catch it, even an inch, it'll spook the tiger for sure. I know you can do it, Jay-Jay, 'cause I've seen you hit a squirrel high up in a tree with a rock.

"*Goooood boyyyy*—"

Jamis readied the towel, cocked his right arm behind his ear, and threw.

A Terrible Sin

Pollux sat on The Butterfly Table, mouth parted and panting, pearly fangs wet with drool.

Lem, so close as to be hit by hot pungent breath, lowered his left hand, cautiously—and slightly out to the side. The tiger's eyes, luminous and resembling the fiery gold in the Hungarian Opal, tracked the movement and, just as Lem had hoped, did not notice that his right hand remained raised.

As Pollux had done for Braveheart half an hour earlier, lowering himself onto his stomach, he now did for Lem.

"*Gooood boyyyy*," Lem said and continued in the same lullaby voice: "*Jaaaay-Jaaaay—nowww.*"

Jamis's throw would have made Tamás proud, a perfect center-of-a-derby-bull's-eye, the balled-up towel sticking to Lem's raised palm like a throwing knife into a tree trunk.

Coolly, Lem raised his left hand back up, palm out, shoulder high. Again, Pollux did for the brave boy as he had for Braveheart and rested his head.

Lem pulled in a deep breath, held it, held it, and with his trembling left hand—gently at first, then more firmly—petted the tiger between its ears. The beast's eyelids lowered, as did its tail—*this must be the tiger's tail Grandma fearfully foresaw,* Lem realized.

Still stroking the fury head, Lem held the ether-soaked towel over the tiger's nostrils. The fearsome feline's whiskers twitched—

—but its eyes remained shut. One *Huck-le-ber-ry Finn* anxiously passed into five, ten, a full thirty before the anesthesia turned the circus act's feigned nap into heavy slumber.

"He's out for now," Lem stage whispered assuredly. "Bring me the rest of the ether, then go get Pops and some circus people—I'll keep watch on the tiger."

"Leave him be and let's get outta here," Jamis countered, his heart racing, each beat as loud in his ears as Judge Graham's pounding gavel. "We can close the door and lock him inside while we *both* go for help."

"No," Lem insisted, quietly, wisely. "If he wakes up, he'll tear the house apart and they'll have to shoot him. The only way to save his life is for me to keep giving him ether. You go, Jay-Jay—and take Puck."

"Ain't worth risking your life if it wakes up," Jamis argued.

"I'm not leaving," Lem said, steadfast. "Even if we lock him inside he could break out through a window and hurt someone else. No, the safest thing is keep him asleep like I done with Mr. Riley."

Jamis and Puck were barely out the front door when two circus hands, along with Sheriff Clint Garman, showed up. All three men carried rifles.

"Step aside, Lem," Sheriff Garman commanded after entering the foyer, his voice steely, his gun aimed, his finger on the trigger. "That animal's dangerous."

Lem did not move.

"Step away," Sheriff Garman repeated.

"He ain't hurt no one," Lem pleaded, giving the tiger another five *Huck-le-ber-ry Finns* of ether. "You can't shoot a sleeping animal. That wouldn't be right."

"Lem-u-el, I told you—" Sheriff Garman said, darkly, loudly, the syllables sounding like rolling thunder.

"Clint," Doc interrupted, having just arrived. "My boy's right. You can't kill a sleeping tiger. That'd be a terrible sin."

"Doc—" Sheriff Garman began, but Doc cut him off, taking full control of matters without raising his voice: "Listen here, Clint. Give your rifle to Jamis—everyone knows he's the sharpest shot in town. He'll keep watch and shoot the tiger if need be. I'll take over administering the anesthetic and Lem can take Puck outside. In the meantime, you and these men go fetch a cage."

"But Doc—" Sheriff Garman protested.

"Put a sock in it!" Doc barked, his customary even-tempered manner overcome by impatience and intensity. "Get a cage—and hurry."

Sheriff Garman acquiesced.

"Pops," Jamis said after the three men departed. "Didn't you mean to tell the sheriff to *be quick*?"

"Jay-Jay," Doc answered, his good nature returning. "I think it might do him some good to *hurry*—and maybe trip because of it. Falling on his head might knock some ignorance out of him and make room for a little more common sense. My goodness, anyone who'd shoot a beautiful sleeping animal has rocks for brains."

World's Greatest Blueberry Muffins

 The circus tiger's life was spared and the following day Doc's life, at age forty, was resurrected.

Caring for patients, and raising Jamis and Lemuel, filled Doc with worthy purpose. Still, a chasm of emptiness had remained since Connie's death three years prior. He likened his enduring anguish to Emmett Riley's.

After his leg was amputated, Emmett suffered phantom limb pain; Doc's amputation was emotional—a piece of his heart, half his soul he felt, had been cleaved when Connie died. For both men, what was missing ached fiercely.

Physicians are warned not treat themselves. This wisdom Doc ignored. His prescription was to heal thyself by healing others; mend his broken heart by focusing on the twins; replenish his soul by being the father Connie would have wished her husband to be.

This analeptic proved chiefly effective. Doc's valleys of despair grew less deep with time's passage and further spaced, their pastures flatter and more flowered. Looking skyward from this pastoral contentment, Doc accepted the fact he would never again enjoy the view from a mountaintop half so beautiful as he had savored with Connie, nevermore feel a romantic happiness that made his molecules vibrate with music.

And then came a delicate *rap-rap-rap*.

Doc opened the front door adorned with the Rod of Asclepius inlay and in doing so the symbol of Medicine and Healing turned from metaphor into reality—a cure for his melancholy malady appeared.

"Good afternoon, Dr. Jamison," said Alycia Hall, her winsome smile as warm as the fresh-baked blueberry muffins in a handled basket she offered forward. "I wanted to thank you for yesterday."

"That's mighty kind," Doc said in greeting. "But there was no need to go to such trouble."

" 'twasn't any at all," the unexpected visitor said, demurely. "I'm embarrassed it's only muffins. After all, you saved my life."

Doc guessed Alycia to be safely in her early thirties. There was no question about her attractiveness, highlighted by Cupid's bow lips and emerald eyes that seemed to smile even when she did not—and cute dimples that appeared when she did.

"Save your life?" Doc said, whimsy in his tone. "I did no such thing. I merely kept a watchful eye in case you needed further medical attention. Happily, you didn't. How's your forehead, by the way—a little sore I imagine?"

"My pride's more bruised than my noggin," Alycia replied, her dairy skin blushing to the hue of pink azaleas, her favorite. "Who, besides me, faints at a circus? How embarrassing!"

"Not at all," soothed Doc. "You'd be surprised what can cause people to faint. A tiger is a whole lot more faint-worthy than a spider and I once sewed up a soldier—a manly sergeant, if you can believe it—who discovered a baby tarantula in his beard and keeled over, and in the process carved his ear half-off with his own bayonet."

"You're making that up!" Alycia said, almost singing. "All the same, I thank you for it."

"It's the truth," Doc assured, crossing his heart, then lifted a corner of the red-and-white gingham napkin that blanketed the goodies: "Blueberry muffins—always my top choice. *Mmmmm.* They smell and look delicious."

"They're actually *plain* muffins," Alycia corrected, grinning with a hint of mischief.

"Really?" Doc said, plucking a small round morsel. "This sure looks like a blueberry."

"Oh, it is," Alycia rejoined, adding a delicious lilting laugh. "I may not bake the world's greatest blueberry muffins, but—if I do say so myself—I make the tastiest *plain* muffins anywhere!"

Doc chuckled, helped himself to a whole muffin and took a bite, then allowed: "Miss Hall, these are by far the most delicious *plain* muffins I've ever tasted."

After savoring a second bite, he whistle-hummed before proclaiming: "In fact, I dare say these are also the world's greatest *blueberry* muffins."

The odds of life are dished out in lightning strikes and dangerous blind curves, in tuberculosis and fatal pneumonia, and also in blind luck and meet-cutes at a circus.

Following an eight-month courtship, blueberry muffins were stacked tall as a mountain in the center of The Butterfly Table at the wedding reception for Dr. Lemuel and Mrs. Alycia Jamison.

Road Trip

 "Linc, hurry up—" Tavis called out, the volume needing to carry from the kitchen table across the family room and up the stairs, "—food's gettin' cold."

Following the Cougars' victory the previous night, Love had promised to make any dinner of Linc's choice on Saturday.

"Sloppy spaghetti," he requested.

"Sloppy spaghetti?" Love parroted, bemused. "Isn't *all* spaghetti a little messy?"

"It's my mom's special recipe," Linc explained. "Sloppy Joes served on pasta instead of a bun."

Presently, Tavis, Love, and Fayth were already seated for Saturday's dinner, but Linc lingered in the guest room.

"Maybe his headphones are too loud," Love suggested.

"He's not listening to music, he's on the phone," Fayth interjected. Her tone now rising, "With a *girrrrlll.*"

"Might as well start without him," Tavis surrendered.

"No, Daddy, let's wait," Fayth insisted. "Dinner starts when *everyone's* here. You'd wait for me if I was on the phone—he'll be down soon."

"Fayth's right," agreed Love.

Outvoted two to one, Tavis still cast the deciding ballot: with two fingers parting his lips, he blew like a train whistle.

Linc at once flew down the stairs, two steps at a time, and expecting a stiff reprimand offered amends: "Sorry—I didn't mean to keep you waiting."

"The sauce needed to cool down anyway," reassured Fayth, an old soul at ten. Acting more her age, she teased: "You were talking to your *girrrlllfriend*, huh?"

"No, just Kev," Linc protested, blushing nonetheless at Fayth's assertion. "He had some questions about our essay assignment. I told him I'd come over after dinner to help him—and maybe spend the night, if that's okay?"

"Of course," Love said. "Tavis'll drive you."

In the cab of the pickup, in night's darkness that emboldens revealing vulnerability, in the same passenger seat he had been in when his life took a U-turn, Linc confided: "Sometimes I feel like an orphan, Coach—I miss my mom and don't have a dad."

"You do now, son," Tavis said, rare tenderness in his timbre.

Radio off, the two drove in comfortable wordlessness until they reached Keven's house.

"I'll pick you up in the morning at seven," Tavis directed.

"That means six-fifty," groused Linc. "Why so early on a weekend?"

"You and I are taking a road trip," Tavis answered. "Tell you what, let's make it ten after eight."

~~~

At the stroke of eight, Linc was waiting curbside when Tavis pulled up.

"So, where are we going?" Linc inquired after buckling his seatbelt.

"Bellaire."

"*Whhhhyyy?*" The single syllable trembled like a tambourine.

"We're paying your aunt and uncle a visit," Tavis disclosed. "We're going to make it on the up-and-up for you to live with us."

"So I'll stay eligible for the team?"

"More important than that—so you're legally enrolled in classes here. Even if you couldn't play football, we want you to live with us—understand?"

"Really?"

"Honest on my life," Tavis said.

Linc turned away, looking out the passenger window, embarrassed by the rising tide in his eyes.

Over breakfast at a twenty-four-hour diner, chicken and waffles for both, Tavis shared his plan: "I had a lawyer friend draw up papers for your aunt and uncle to sign, making me and Love your legal guardians—until your mom returns."

"You'd do that for me?" Linc said.

"Honest on my life," Tavis repeated. "But I need you to do something for me—actually, something for yourself."

Tentatively: "Sure—what?"

"I've learned we grow the most when we tap our demons on the shoulder and confront them," Tavis expounded. "I know you don't want to face Uncle Roy, and that's why you *need* to. So I'll drop you off and *you* are gonna ask him to sign the document."

"Without you?"

"It's best that way," Tavis assured.

"Because I'll grow more?"

"Partly," Tavis answered. "Also, honestly, because you'll have a better chance getting him to sign if you're alone."

Puzzlement washed over Linc's face.

"The world isn't colorblind," Tavis said. "From what you've told me about Uncle Roy, the sight of me might be a non-starter."

Nodding dolefully, the boy made a manly promise: "I'll take care of it, sir. I won't leave without his signature."

HowWhoWhy?

"No way in hell," Uncle Roy sneered, even though Aunt Veronica had agreeably signed the emancipation papers already.

"Why not?" Linc beseeched. "Why would you want me to come live with you when you don't even like me."

"Lets go outside and see this coach of yours—"

"—so you can see what's in it for you?" Linc interrupted acerbically.

"Ain't nothin' free, boy."

A ripple of fear shot down Linc's spine and back up; fear that Tavis would prove right if Uncle Roy saw he was Black.

"No, Uncle Roy," the nephew said firmly. "This is between you and me—"

Linc drew in a deep breath, drew in courage with it, then reached forward and literally tapped his demon on the shoulder: "—man to man."

"I said no," Uncle Roy persisted, not ready to fold his cards.

"Okay, here's what's in it for you," Linc said, going all in. "I'm too big and strong for you now—you definitely don't want me living here."

Bullies generally back down when confronted, and Uncle Roy was no exception. Having made good on his signature pledge to Tavis, Linc made a goodbye pledge to his uncle: "If I hear about Murray or Jimmy getting a single bruise, you'll find out this wide receiver's got a linebacker inside of him."

~~~

Tavis, concurrently, was tending to another important matter.

A week earlier, he had phoned The Matthew Murphy Memorial Public Library. Initially brusque, the head librarian did an about-face when Tavis mentioned—and summarized—the note a ten-year-old boy had taped to a handsome, and orphaned, antique table seven years prior.

"Can you hold for a quick moment?" Mrs. Kibrick asked, her voice instantly turning sweet as Ohio apple butter.

"I'm back," she rejoined, no more than thirty seconds later, and began reading: *My name is Lincoln Beswick Jamison and this cool table that belonged to my many-greats-grandfather is now mine. I, being of sound mind, wish to lend it to The Bellaire Library to use as a big homework desk until which time I can come back to reclaim it. Thank you, Linc Jamison, age 10. P.S. Please take good care of it for me!*

Mrs. Kibrick continued, her own words now: "We framed that precious note and it's been hanging in the private office ever since. I've always hoped we'd hear from Linc again. Please tell him we've taken very good care of his lovely table."

Tavis told Mrs. Kibrick his wish was to reunite Linc with the heirloom—and do so as a surprise. Arrangements were made to pick it up Sunday at noon when the library opened its doors.

Tavis arrived at 11:50, only to find Mrs. Kibrick already waiting outside the double-door front entrance. He smiled, thinking: *Librarians must set their watches on Tavis Time, too.* A young man on staff helped Tavis load The Butterfly Table, legs up, on a moving pad in the truck bed.

Tavis returned inside to give his gratitude to Mrs. Kibrick and received a most thoughtful surprise in return: a collector's edition of *The Adventures of Huckleberry Finn* produced the previous year in commemoration of the hundredth anniversary of the seminal novel's original 1885 publication.

"This is for Linc," Mrs. Kibrick said. "It's my all-time favorite book. Please tell him it's the library's interest payment to him for kindly loaning us his beloved table."

~~~

"They signed it!" Linc declared, clapping his hands once as punctuation.

"I'm proud of you," Tavis said with quiet earnestness, then leapt out of the pickup and wrapped Linc in a bear hug.

Next, as if turning down a made bed, Tavis peeled back the blue-jay-blue plastic tarp. Even upside-down, with the butterfly knot and resplendent sheen hidden from view, Linc instantly recognized his cherished Table. Thunderstruck, he looked at Tavis, back at The Butterfly Table, then again at Coach.

"*Howwhowhy?*" Linc managed at long last, asking three questions at once.

"You know Love—she's been on me about getting a new dining table," Tavis said, deadpan. "You don't mind if we borrow yours, do you?"

For the second time in one day, the tears escaping Linc's eyes were of joy instead of sorrow.

Mystical Oration

 Nearing midnight, on a school night, Linc was the only one awake.

He had a midterm in the morning and was studying at The Butterfly Table in the dining room, but the alchemy of weariness was transforming his eyelids from flesh to lead.

He closed his U.S. History textbook with sleepy satisfaction, slid it aside, turning his focus to studying the Table—*his* Table, *his* history. With his right index finger he traced the orange-and-black butterfly knot precisely, repeatedly. Next, he dragged his fingertips over The Butterfly Table's glassy wood grain, back and forth, lightly, slowly, more slowly still.

Juglone, a toxic chemical released by black walnut trees, strongly repels other plant life from growing nearby. Now the exact opposite effect took place: Linc's right hand was strongly attracted to the black walnut wood, drawn to it as metal to a powerful electromagnet, as love to a soul mate. His roaming fingertips made smaller and smaller sweeping passes until their caressing stopped and his palm pressed down—was pulled down—firmly on the butterfly knot.

Closing his eyes, an act that heightened his concentration, Linc was certain he could feel a heartbeat in the black walnut.

Through osmosis or mystical alchemy, or perhaps it was a vivid dream that seemed so very real, the wood—the heirloom—communicated with Linc.

I never imagined I would be a study table in a library, but does anyone ever know the path their future will traverse?

After all, I never imagined being a front door, either.

But what a special chapter for me it was to be in the library the past seven years. Your gift to the library, Linc, was indeed a gift to me as well.

"How so?" you might ask. Well, in my experience people are generally happy when they are in a library. I am reminded of something Holden Caulfield says in The Catcher in the Rye: *"What really knocks me out is a book that, when you're all done reading it, you wish the author that wrote it was a terrific friend of yours and you could call him up on the phone whenever you felt like it."*

People who sit in my company feel like my terrific friends, and when they enjoy a terrific book in my presence it really knocks me out. You are surely wondering, Linc, how can I possibly quote a line written by J.D. Salinger, and the answer is I have memorized every sentence of every book that has ever rested upon me. I think it's partly the words on the paper pages—a cousin of wood, of course—magically seeping into my cellulose fibers. As well, I have felt the ethereal vibrations of some people's lips moving while they read mutedly.

Sometimes, the best times really, I could actually hear people reading to themselves, unknowingly, in faint whispers. This especially happened with poetry, Linc, and oh how I loved it! Dickinson, Frost, Rumi, Shakespeare of course, Angelou—a hundred poets, and more, I know and love. As you can imagine, Joyce Kilmer's "Trees" is one of my dearest favorites—"I think that I shall never see, a poem lovely as a tree. Poems are made by fools like me, but only God can make a tree."

You should have seen me when I was a tree! I was not only lovely, I was majestic. I'm not boasting, mind you— "majestic" is how your four-times-great-grandfather Tamás described me before a lightning bolt split me in two more than a century ago. His tall praise made my sap tingle.

As you may know, Linc, I became a front door originally and thereafter this Table. I must tell you, a door does not get to know people as truly as does a table in a kitchen or dining room—or library. A kitchen table learns about people more intimately than even a four-poster bed does. People talk and laugh, argue and discuss, share their lives around a kitchen table. Chefs like to say "the table comes first" because fellowship and communion happens in breaking bread. It still knocks me out to be a conduit for such enchantments.

Mystical Oration, Part II

Metamorphosing from a door to dining table, I believe, raised me to a higher purpose.

And I think that's how it should be, Linc—we should not be limited to one purpose, but rather grow and evolve to higher and higher callings as our days pass into years and to decades. I dream of my maple legs becoming a concert violin one day—some of the finest violins are made of maple and spruce. Perhaps this desire comes from the ebullient fiddling I heard the night I was felled by the lightning bolt from the heavens that left my surface as hard as Moses' stone tablets.

As well, I dream of becoming a church pew—about the highest calling I can imagine. The most sorrowful destiny for a tree, on the other hand, is to be used for a lynching—even to become firewood is a far better fate.

Linc, you have probably noticed that one of my legs, near the bottom, is damaged. That's where Puck—the cutest Dalmatian, belonging to your three-times-great-grandpa Lemuel and his twin brother Jamis—chewed. It's funny, a big fierce tiger didn't scar me—now there's a story for another day!—but a cuddly puppy did.

Here is something else funny—I'm glad that Lemuel, who crafted me from a door into a table, nor any of your forefathers since, didn't repair my leg. I think there is great virtue in imperfection.

As an example, most people considered Lemuel to be imperfect because his mind worked at its own leisurely pace.

But my goodness, Linc, Lemuel was as near to a perfect person as seems possible. He truly loved thy neighbor as thyself, and you are blessed to have his genes and heavenly stardust within you.

From an encyclopedia a boy was reading upon me one rainy afternoon, I learned that the Shakers—renowned for their carpentry craftsmanship—deliberately introduced a "mistake" into each piece of furniture in order to show that man should not aspire to the perfection of God. Flawed, they believed, could be ideal.

This seems a wise lesson for everyone, Linc—instead of focusing on trying to be perfect, whatever that is, far better to take pride in making the effort to do our very best.

Similar to the Shakers, Native American Navajos purposely weave a single imperfection into their handmade blankets. To their eyes this makes the patterned blankets <u>more</u> handsome, not less so, and each truly unique. That's exactly how I feel about my chewed leg.

Instead of seeing physical blemishes and scars as ugly, I wish people would embrace them as beauty marks—as badges of having survived the difficulties life has thrown their way.

Speaking of appearances, I'm grateful not to be made solely of one type of wood. I feel my black walnut top is enhanced by the diversity of being married, if you will, to my white oak border and maple legs just as complementing woods in a violin make its music sweeter.

Oh, what sweetness I've been blessed with, Linc! I've seen your ancestors enjoy meals as newlyweds, and celebrate silver and golden anniversaries. I've experienced the miracle of childbirth on me; had lives saved on me; had love letters written on me. I've savored Thanksgiving and

Christmas dinner gatherings around me. I even fondly remember you hunched over me with coloring books and jigsaw puzzles and Legos.

All these experiences, and a million more, have been absorbed into my grain—and now you will enrich my patina further, Linc, during your life journey ahead.

~~~

In the morning, in the twilight between dreams and wakefulness, with his head resting on the history textbook as though it were a pillow, Linc again unconsciously caressed the butterfly knot.

Instead of hearing an apparitional voice speaking about the past, Linc—reminiscent of his five-times-great-Grandma Dika—had a prescient vision of the future. He *saw* The Butterfly Table covered with blankets, layered high and soft as a mattress, and a young couple atop the makeshift bed making love. Come sunrise, when the newlyweds roused, they were inexplicably a few years older. And they had a child. Actually, they were parents of two toddlers—

—twin boys.

Haiku: Masterpiece Man

 When you find yourself at the end of your rope, tie a knot and hang on for dear life like John Howland did after falling overboard off the famous Mayflower.

The abandoned athletic shed had served as Linc's rescue knot and just when his hands were cramping and his grip was slipping, just when he was about to let go and plummet into the deep cold rough sea, Coach Tavis Jordan hauled in the lifeline and lifted the forsaken boy to safety.

Thereafter, from that fateful left turn through a red stoplight at an empty intersection, Linc's life was filled with hope and faith and love—

—and with Love and Fayth and Tavis.

Almost overnight, Linc's despair became delight, his fears found comfort, his soul was nourished. He not only had a comfortable bed, he had his own bedroom. He had home-cooked meals, clean clothes, a sense of belonging.

He also had new chores, such as emptying the dishwasher and taking out the trash and mowing the lawn, which made him feel all the more like a member of the Jordan family. The thorns in his life were turning to rose petals, juglone to nectar, storm clouds to sunshine. Instead of hollow, he felt full. His emotional tempest calmed and his dulled eyes sparkled anew.

Linc's joy swelled on the football field as well, as chronicled by newspaper headlines the following four weeks:

Cougars Rally for 31-28 Victory
Cats Continue Aerial Show
Dynamic Duo Baxter & Jamison Shine Again
New High for C-Peak: Win Streak Hits 8

Through all of this winning, for Coach Jordan the most rarefied highlight did not happen on the gridiron under the bright glare of Friday night lights.

Rather, it came to pass beneath the dull-humming florescent tubes in the faculty lounge on a Tuesday noontime. Rhett and Tavis were eating lunch when Mr. Thompson, an English teacher, approached their table.

"Coach," Roger greeted. "Just the man I wanted to see." Nodding hello to Rhett, he added: "Mind if I join you two?"

"Please, Rog, have a seat," Rhett said.

"What's up?" Tavis followed, expecting congratulations on the team's winning streak—or, he dreaded, a discouraging heads-up regarding someone's sagging grades.

His worries metastasized when Roger, looking him in the eye, began: "You won't believe the in-class essay one of your players wrote yesterday."

Tavis braced for the other cleat to drop.

"The topic was, *Who do you think is the most important person in the world—and why?*" Roger continued. "I gave the kids the entire period and Lincoln Jamison wrote fifteen words. Fifteen. Total. In fifty minutes."

Tavis slumped at the news that Linc had failed the assignment. Worse, that the boy had failed to even try.

"As you might imagine, most of the students wrote about President Reagan or Pope John Paul II," Roger went on. "Pro athletes—sadly, in my opinion—were addressed by a few kids. Everyone, except Linc, filled page after page."

From an inside breast pocket of his sports coat, a cliché of camel corduroy with leather elbow patches, Roger retrieved a test blue book, neatly folded in half. Rhett, sitting nearest Rog, opened it and examined the exam. The grade at the top, in red ink, shocked him.

"An A?" Rhett challenged, mystified.

"It's by far the shortest essay I've ever given a passing grade to—much less a top mark," Roger remarked.

Knocked off balance with relief, Tavis asked: "How can that be?"

"It's a haiku," Roger explained. "The Japanese form of short poetry consisting of exactly seventeen *morae*—syllables—arranged in three lines of precisely five, seven, and five syllables. Like da Vinci said, *simplicity is the ultimate sophistication.*"

"Linc's simplicity here is the ultimate compliment," Rhett opined, smiling at Tavis. "It's titled, *Masterpiece Man.* I'll read it to you—

"The M-V-Person / in *my* world is Tav Jordan / I love Coach—he cares."

Rhett handed the exam back to Roger, who graciously slid it across the Formica tabletop.

"Keep it, Tav—I'll tell Linc I misplaced it," Roger said. "Just don't let him know I showed you. He might be embarrassed."

With care, and with eyes closed, Tavis closed and refolded the keepsake.

The Promise

 Tavis pulled a folded piece of paper from his pocket, opened it, read aloud.

"Five and five."

He crumpled the note into a ball and tossed it aside.

"Five and five, gentlemen," he repeated. "That's the prediction I wrote down before the season began for the win-loss record I believed you were capable of. Frankly, I think five wins was an optimistic goal considering this program's dismal seasons lately."

Coach Jordan audited the faces in the locker room, locking eyes briefly with each Cougar player, one after another after another, stars and starters and reserves alike, optically traveling bench to bench until every last one of them had personally felt his genuine devotion.

"I underestimated you boys—you fine young *men*—and greatly so," he eventually resumed. "Five wins? You're nine-and-one going for your tenth victory tonight. I apologize for underestimating your character and your valor—and your unwavering commitment to each other."

Forty-eight pairs of eyes looked on, too spellbound to blink, the players hanging on every sentence, every word, every syllable.

"I'm burstin' proud of y'all!" the coach-teacher-turned-momentary-preacher fairly sang as if it were a hymnal lyric. "Every single one of you. You proved me, and all your critics, wrong. Dead wrong. You have the hearts of champions—"

Another slow panoramic glance over the sea of faces.

"—one more win tonight and you'll have the trophy of champions."

Whoops and hollers rattled the metal lockers, echoed off the concrete walls.

We Play Hard! and *9 Wins, 1 Loss* was written on the chalkboard behind Coach Jordan. He crossed out the *9* and above it wrote *10* and reiterated: "One more win will make you league champs."

"One more!

"One! More!

"ONE! MORE!" the players crowed, each refrain louder than the previous.

Coach waited for quiet, then continued: "You're going up against the Hastings Eagles, our fiercest rival, on their home field, before their rowdy fans. None of that will matter. They also have a coaching legend—Coach Harry McFadden, my ol' coach—on their sideline. Again, it won't matter."

"Won't matter!

"Won't! Matter!

"WON'T! MATTER!" came the rising chant.

"Hastings' strengths are its pass rush and defensive secondary," Coach rejoined. "That doesn't matter either. We're going to pass—all!—night!—long! A great warrior once said, *You can beat a foe by defeating his weakness, but you destroy him by defeating his strength.* We're not going to just beat the Eagles, we're going to *destroy* them!"

"Dee-stroy!

"Dee!-Stroy!

"DEE!-STROY!" the team chorused, and one player stood up.

"Coach—you forgot one thing," Linc said, boldly.

"What?"

"Your promise."

"What're you talkin' about, Jamison?" Coach Jordan said.

"You promised that if we played for the league championship you'd get your ear pierced," Linc reminded him, grinning. "Remember?"

Another eruption from the choir: "Ear-ring!

"Ear!-Ring!

"EAR!-RING!"

"There's no time—" Coach said, then halted the excuse in midsentence. "No, you're right. A promise is a promise. If a man's word isn't good, he has nothing of value. Do you have what you need?"

"Yep," Linc beamed.

"Of course you do," Coach sighed. "Okay, can you do it quickly?"

"Yep."

Quentin punched a blue chemical icepack, activating its instant-cold reaction.

"Hold this on your earlobe to numb it," Q directed.

Linc sterilized the point of a safety pin in the flame of a disposable lighter, then warned: "Here goes—"

"No crying, Coach," Q teased.

In went the hot pin, out of Coach Jordan's lips came not a peep, nor did he flinch or grimace. Next, Linc ceremoniously raised a single tiny gold hoop earring high overhead for all the team to see before he inserted it.

"Wait—" Coach said. He stood up and, from inside his wallet, retrieved Linc's diamond stud. "—use this one."

In went Linc's earring, out came exultation: "Coach! J!

"Coach!! J!!

"COACH!!! J!!!"

Fingering his newly bejeweled ear, Coach Jordan smiled, then issued his final marching orders: "All right, men, I kept my promise. Now promise me you'll go out there and rise tall and give your full effort from the first play to the very last. If you do that, no matter the final score, to me you'll be champions."

If

 Racing onto the field the Cleveland Peak High football team burst through a huge paper banner painted in gold and black: *Go Cougars! We Play Hard!*

Play hard the Cougars did, as did the host Hastings Eagles.

At halftime, the league championship showdown was tied, 7-7. Bruises and injuries also seemed deadlocked.

In the locker room, Coach Tavis Jordan concluded his intermission remarks with a few stanzas from Rudyard Kipling's famous poem, "If."

"If you can meet with Triumph and Disaster and treat those two impostors just the same," he recited with passion. "If you can fill the unforgiving minute with sixty seconds' worth of distance run, yours is the Earth and everything that's in it. And—which is more—you'll be a Man, my son!"

Playing like men in the second half, the Cougars forged ahead in contusions dealt out. The Eagles, however, held the only lead that mattered—*Home: 14, Visitor: 7*—in the fourth quarter.

With three precious seconds remaining, time enough for only one play, the Cougars had the ball on the Eagles' two-yard line. Coach Jordan made the call: "Twenty-Eight Pitch, Sweep Left—and block like your lives depend on it!"

Keven took the snap under center, spun, pitched the football to Q. Three weeks earlier, Q had moved from backup receiver to starting tailback and was an immediate star. Now, Q swept left, patiently waiting, desperately hoping, for a hole to open, but the wall of defenders remained brick-solid. The play was doomed, the championship lost.

Suddenly, a sliver of daylight, Q-hit-the-gas-pedal-touchdown!

Home: 14, Visitor: 13.

A successful extra-point kick would force overtime.

Another Kipling stanza flashed through Coach Jordan's mind: *If you can make one heap of all your winnings / And risk it all on one turn of pitch-and-toss . . .*

Tavis locked eyes with Coach McFadden across the field, grinned cocksure at his mentor, and made a peace sign. The Cougars would risk it all on one turn of *pitch-and-toss* and a two-point conversion attempt.

"Fortune favors the bold," Coach Jordan told his huddled offense during a timeout. "To hell with overtime, we're goin' for the win right now. I want each of you to look at the teammate standing next to you on your left—"

The eleven offensive players swiveled their heads.

"—and your right."

Heads turned again.

"If you all come through for the two teammates beside you, the Eagles can't stop us. Okay, here's the winning play—Wideout Left, Reverse Right, on two!"

Coach Jordan grabbed Keven and Linc by their facemasks. He had special instructions for the two star juniors. The private exchange occupied mere seconds, but did not escape Coach McFadden's attention.

That sonuvabitch thinks he can pull his old trick pass again, Coach McFadden thought, recalling Tavis's heroic play with Rhett a generation before. *Like hell he will!*

"Wilson! Whalen!" he yelled to his defense. "Watch the quarterback! He's gonna be a receiver! Stay with him! Both of you!"

At that very instant, Keven took the snap, spun, faked a handoff to Q, then pitched the football to Linc, who was streaking back from his wideout spot. Keven proceeded to curl out of the backfield heading left—where Linc had just vacated—towards the end zone while Linc continued sweeping right.

"Cover the quarterback!" Coach McFadden screamed and Whalen and Wilson obeyed.

By simple math, double-teaming Keven meant the Cougars had a ten-to-nine player advantage on the remainder of the field—just as Coach Jordan had schemed. He had *wanted* Coach McFadden to see him hurriedly talking to Kev and Linc. He knew precisely what his old coach would deduce.

Keven acted his deception supremely; the offensive line blocked like bulldozers; Linc pump-faked convincingly, then tucked the ball away and accelerated in a blur following Q, who steamrolled the final defender remaining in the way as if his life depended on it.

"Jamison *scoooores!*" the announcer shouted over the PA system. "Cougars win, 15-14!"

Linc could not know it in that moment of Triumph, in a cocoon of joyous teammates, but he would soon meet with Disaster and be tested in discovering "If" he was Man enough to treat it as an imposter.

Unexpected Benefactor

Fall 1879, Doc and Alycia celebrated their twelfth wedding anniversary—it marked the same span Constance and he had been wife and husband.

As Doc's love for Alycia magnified, his enduring love for Connie did not diminish. Nor did Alycia, a Civil War widow, feel the love for her first husband, Zachary, wither as her love for Doc blossomed fuller year after year. Love, after all, is not a zero-sum game.

To the contrary, love is an infinite-sum blessing.

Alycia had been a librarian in Cincinnati, not far from Camp Dennison where Zachary—and, very likely, Tamás—enlisted with the Union. Zachary served in the 137th Regiment, Ohio Infantry, losing his life in June 1864 during the bloody defense of Baltimore.

After receiving a "Telegram of Tears" every soldier's loved ones most fear, Alycia bid goodbye to "The Queen City" for a fresh beginning. Fate, as if offering sincere apology, soon smiled kindly on the bereaving young widow—her second week in Bellaire, Robinson & Howe's Champions Circus rolled in.

In town on a shopping errand when the acrobats were drumming up excitement on a tightrope strung across Main Street, Alycia was enticed to attend the big show that afternoon.

Warm temperatures and heavy humidity, combined with poor ventilation inside the circus tent, took a toll on

Alycia. Dehydration, not the fright of seeing Braveheart put his head in a tiger's mouth, had caused her to faint. Of such serendipitous events, strung together in perfect order, at the perfect time, are lives sprinkled with golden fairy dust.

The magic rippled out out out far beyond the resulting courtship of Alycia and Doc.

Alycia—like Connie—was not destined to experience childbirth, but being a stepmother to the twins filled her heart, and theirs, to overflowing. Truth be told, she and Doc had a thousand children in addition to Lemuel and Jamis. Doc's extended family of kids were the babies he delivered and young patients he treated; Aly's were the youth who came through the frosted-glass front doors of the library she founded.

Upon her arrival in Bellaire, Alycia had been dismayed to learn it had no public library. Tirelessly, she worked to remedy this shortcoming, raising funds, seeking book donations, purchasing new volumes.

Finding a suitable site, all the while, proved as elusive as trying to grab a wisp of pipe smoke and hold onto it. Twice, empty lots were pledged on which to build a new library. Both times, profit prevailed over philanthropy when buyers stepped in with lucrative offers and development plans that did not include nurturing literacy. Similar disappointment happened—three times—when donations of existing buildings were selflessly promised, only to be greedily withdrawn.

Despite a decade of overtures and failures, Alycia remained as resolute as an ocean's tide. Out of the blue, in the red-gold-orange autumn of 1879, her persistence was finally rewarded: the deed to a prime parcel at the north end of Main Street was legally signed over to the library campaign. Moreover, the parcel came with a big check covering full construction costs for a grand two-story building of red brick.

The biggest stunner of all was the generous benefactor's identity: Marcus Murphy. The merciless man who had shot his own kid brother in the leg, in a duel, in cold blood; whose card cheating caused Tamás to abscond to the Civil War; who was the most-reviled person in Bellaire, if not all of Belmont County; that scoundrel had gone through a metamorphosis as wondrous as if he, too, had been dashed with pixie dust.

Bookend occurrences pushed Marcus from bad guy to Good Samaritan. Severe pneumonia, forcing him to face mortality before Doc rallied him to health, was the first. The second was seeing his brother Matthew's physical decline—limping with a cane, needing a wheelchair, bedridden the final years of life. During his invalidism, reading had been Matty's chief pleasure.

In Marcus's mind, surely as Cain killed Abel with a stone, his evilly aimed bullet in the long-ago duel had caused Matty's slow death. His satanic eyes lost their fire. He sought atonement by contributing the land, building, and bookshelves for The Matthew Murphy Memorial Public Library of Bellaire.

All Things Possible

 Lem handcrafted the front reception desk for The Matthew Murphy Memorial Public Library of Bellaire.

The long handsome desktop, at its center, featured an intricate inlay of the state seal of Ohio, complete with a sheaf of wheat, bundle of arrows, Scioto River, and glorious sunrise. Per Alycia's request, however, Lem altered the state's official motto "With God, All Things Are Possible" to "With *Books,* All Things Are Possible."

The arrival of the library coincided with a departure: Jamis boarded a passenger train to pursue his boyhood dream of studying medicine.

He had set his sights on high academic marks with the same deadeye accuracy he displayed hunting wild game. Actually, Jamis spent so much time with textbooks spread across The Butterfly Table during high school that area pheasant populations were said to be soaring on account of his rifle gathering dust.

Despite his brilliance in the classroom, Jamis graduated from Bellaire High School three years behind his original classmates. The setback had nothing to do with academics and all to do with loyalty and love: Jamis refused to accept his diploma until Lem received his. Thus, Jamis remained living at home and worked at the Bellaire Goblet Works Company to earn money for college while also tutoring Lem in his current studies.

On a dazzling May afternoon in 1873, with Alycia beaming and Doc fairly bursting every button off his waistcoat, the twins received their high school diplomas together.

Jamis planned to stay on at the glass factory in order to save enough money to attend Oberlin College for all four years. Not having to work part-time while enrolled would allow him to focus fully on earning the high grades required for acceptance to medical school.

Jamis figured he would reach his financial goal in another three years, but this proved a miscalculation. He neglected to factor in the value of family. The evening of the twins' high school graduation, Doc surprised Jamis by saying he would pay for half of the tuition, room and board, and books—to be spread out over the four years.

"Jay-Jay, I'd love nothing more than to give you *all* the money you need," Doc said. "I even looked into taking out a loan, but the bank turned me down—ol' Marcus hasn't completely changed his spots. So I guess you and I'll just have to be fifty-fifty partners, but at least you can start school next year instead of waiting longer."

"Wow! Thanks, Pops!" Jamis said, adding a tight embrace and, "I love you."

It is said that great minds think alike; so, too, do great hearts. The very night of the day that Doc privately promised Jamis half the needed funds, Lem, knowing nothing of this generous gift, whispered to his twin in their shared bedroom before falling asleep: "Jay-Jay—I wanna pay for half of your college education."

"Oh, Lem, that's mighty swell of you," Jamis replied, knowing the offer was impossible. "But college is really expensive."

"I know," Lem asserted, softly. "That's why on top of my usual orders for doors and tables, I've been making one extra chair every month or so for the past few years to earn money to help you out."

"I—um—wow!—but no," Jamis stammered.

"I insist," Lem countered. "I'm not college material, but if I can help you—well, that'll make me sort of feel like I'm goin', too. And my furniture business is goin' gangbusters, so when you graduate from college I'll have more saved up for your doctor schooling."

Jamis stood steadfast: "I can't accept your hard-earned money, Lem—I just can't."

Come morning, Doc again played the role of King Solomon: "Jay-Jay, you're looking at this from the wrong angle. Lem isn't just giving you a gift—*you* are giving him a gift in return. Being able to help you will warm his soul. But by declining Lem's offer, you'll be denying him that joy."

Jamis heeded this wisdom and gave Doc *and* Lem the gift of joyously helping him through college.

Four years later, the gifts were renewed as Pops *and* Lem joyously watched Jay-Jay board a train taking him away to study the art of healing.

Family Tree Grows

The train from Bellaire to Philadelphia, where the University of Pennsylvania School of Medicine is located, was running twenty minutes behind schedule and speeding like an iron comet to make up lost time.

The blind curve was sharper than the engineman, newly transferred to this route, anticipated.

Termites had feasted on a short stretch of oak crossties, allowing dozens of five-inch-long spikes to pull free from the weakened wood.

The derailment was horrific: twisted iron and broken bodies; billowing coal smoke, black as death, roaring flames the color of bright autumn leaves; bone-chilling screams, then ghostly silence.

By the time rescuers arrived, there were no survivors—just as Grandma Dika, a quarter-century before, had foretold.

As identical twins, the same endearment for animals Lemuel inherently displayed was also encoded in Jamis's DNA—it had just remained long dormant. Over time, however, this trait surfaced, he even stopped hunting, and Jamis realized that if he became a veterinarian instead of a physician, Lem could be his assistant—with no college degree required—and two life dreams would be fulfilled.

So it was that Jamis was *not* a passenger on the doomed eastbound train. He had boarded a railcar traveling toward sunset, to Iowa State University where he was enrolled in the 1879 inaugural class of the nation's very first public college of veterinarian medicine.

Men make plans and God shakes His head in bemusement. Jamis indeed became a veterinarian, displaying the same passion caring for animals that Doc did for humans. God's giggles were because Lem, by choice, did not become Jamis's assistant. Rather, as Doc had foreseen, Lem rose to prominence as the finest cabinetmaker in all of Belmont County and far beyond.

The pages of time turned. Doc healed townspeople. Alycia educated minds with books. Jamis treated sick and injured animals. Lem crafted masterpiece furniture.

Chapters passed. Lem married first, giving Marjorie the heirloom Hungarian Opal ring when they exchanged vows. Jamis wed Marianne, slipping onto his bride's finger Connie's ring—an early wedding gift from Doc, who had given Alycia a new gold band when they wed.

Ensuing chapters brought children. Lem became a father—a mere forty-five minutes ahead of Jamis—when Lemuel Tamás Jamison was born on December 31, 1881. Just across the New Year's threshold, on January 1, 1882, came the arrival of Alysha Constance Jamison—her first name a coalescence of grandmothers Alycia and Aisha.

Doc delivered both of his grandchildren. Naturally, he correctly "predicted" the gender of each—although Marianne initially teased her father-in-law for being wrong. Doc kindly said she must have misheard him and pulled out his patient book with *Baby Girl!* written beside her name. Jamis winked knowingly at Doc while Marianne was none the wiser.

More pages turned, more chapters unfolded.

In 1899, Jamis became a grandfather to Jamisha Marie Yewell. On the other side of the new century in 1901, just as he had been born on the other side of the vernal equinox from his twin, Lem too became a grandfather.

When Lemuel Tamás's wife, Karen, became pregnant, Doc had told her: "You're going to have a son, I'm certain of it." For the only time in his half-century as a physician, he wrote a matching prophecy in his patient book: *Baby Boy!*

Doc's first genuine prediction proved as accurate as Tamás's final knife thrown into the center of the green derby the night the twins were born. A baby boy it was— Samuel Beswick Jamison.

Doc's medical bag, the black leather spider-webbed with cracks, showed its years—as did he. Now a man of seventy-four winters, he decided delivering Samuel was the perfect bookend to his obstetrics career. His first two deliveries—Jamis and Lemuel—had been the most difficult he would ever face; this final birthing was so easy Doc said, "All I had to do was spread my nine fingers and catch little Sammy."

One last detail made Doc's swan song sweeter than wildflower honey. Karen's sudden labor advanced with such haste that when she was rushed to 210 Freddy Street there was not time enough to carry her upstairs to a bed.

Doc welcomed Samuel into the world on The Butterfly Table.

Made Of Oak

 On a clear autumn night in 1835, a boy of age nine stargazed heavenwards at Halley's Comet.

Now it was springtime 1910 and Halley's Comet returned and that boy was a man in his eighty-fourth year, his thick mop of bright Irish hair now dull pewter and wispy, and the celestial flyby once again enraptured him.

The night air still carried a dose of winter's chill and Doc, a quilt draped over his bony shoulders, warmed himself with thoughts of Alycia, who "got her wings" only two years before, and Connie.

"Not everyone sees Halley's Comet once in their lifetime—much less twice," Doc said, twisting his wedding band, Jamis and Lem snuggly flanking him. "And not every man is blessed with one true love of his life—much less two, like I was given."

Doc had battled fierce pneumonia at Christmastime, his survival testament to hardy stock. His father Darragh—Gaelic meaning "oak"—made the arduous journey from Ireland to America, back in 1813, in the rotted timber bowels of a merchant ship, never seeing the color of the sky. "Coffin boats" such vessels were called because so many emigrants routinely died en route. Only fourteen, yet knotty muscled with steely fortitude, Darragh lied to being eighteen to get onboard.

Midway across the Atlantic Ocean, a savage storm struck and the rickety ship took on water. Below deck of this hellish escapee's haven to a new life, a drowned rat, belly-up, tail straight and stiff as an ice pick, floated past Darragh's lower bunk as he endured brutal cold—and cold brutality.

When two ruffians tried to steal Darragh's precious food, he broke his right hand fighting them off. A second assault came the following night, but he was ready. He knew he must vanquish his assailants, decisively, or be victimized the remainder of the crossing; that *one* poleax punch was demanded, not fifty defensive jabs. Gritting his teeth in anticipation of white-hot pain, Darragh threw the mightiest haymaker he could muster—with his dominant, already broken, hand—and shattered the attacker's orbital socket. Thereafter, Darragh was left alone. He had boarded the ship as a boy and disembarked a man.

Doc, contrary to his gentle bedside manner, inherited Darragh's gristly toughness. He needed it now because pneumonia—"The Old Man's Friend" Doc called the disease because it afforded a pain-free death to infirm elderly—was making its own second assault.

Other than his midnight viewing of Halley's Comet, Doc was bedridden. Actually, *Table*-ridden. To accommodate the steady stream of visitors, his mattress was moved downstairs atop The Butterfly Table. He rallied his strength for most callers, but feigned sleep in the presence of some.

"Pops, I know you're awake," Jamis said after one such performance.

"You're rude even to some of your best friends," Lem added.

"Boys, I'd love to visit with everyone," Doc allowed. "But sometimes the truer kindness is to *not* do so."

"How so?" asked Lem.

"Saying goodbyes are always difficult, but a final goodbye—as this may well be—can be overwhelming," Doc explained. "It's easier for some people if they can talk *to* me instead of *with* me. If I'm asleep, they needn't fret about cheering me up or saying the wrong thing. They can unburden their emotions more freely."

The twins nodded, each taking one of Doc's gnarl-knuckled hands—the gifted baby-catcher hands that long ago delivered them—in theirs.

"Life's an adventure, and mine has been truly grand, but the road's nearing its end. I'm not sure which is the better way to pass, with warning or without. I suppose a sudden death is a blessing if no *I love yous* have been left unsaid—although there's always a million more still to say. So maybe this way, with a chance to say *goodbye* and *I love you*, is a gift."

"I love you," two sons said as one.

Doc smiled, wan but soulful, and purred: "You fill my heart with birdsong. Never forget how proud of you both I am—and always remember that I love you boys beyond measure."

He closed his eyes, whistle-hummed so very tenderly, and squeezed his namesakes' hands like he would never let go.

Old Man's Friend

Jonny Gold knocked on the Rod of Asclepius and Jamis showed him in.

With pneumonia gaining a stronghold, Doc requested the barber come by after dinnertime—with his straight razor and strop, lather cup, soap and brush.

"Jonny, I wanna look my best when I see Aly and Connie again," Doc instructed. "So shave me real close in case tonight's the night."

Doc feigned falling asleep mid-shave when his dear neighbor, Kimberly, and her daughter and granddaughter—all three generations delivered by Doc—came calling. After Jonny's steady hands finished their task, and the room emptied of visitors, Jamis said: "Pops, please don't ever fake being asleep to me and Lem."

"Promise us," echoed Lem.

"I promise," Doc said. "And I have a promise to ask of you both."

"Of course," Lem said with Jamis adding, "Anything."

"Jay-Jay, because you shot that bobcat you are forever responsible for Lem's life," Doc began. "That responsibility now includes Lem's beautiful family." Jamis nodded solemnly.

"And Lem, because of your heroism with the circus tiger, you are likewise responsible for Jay-Jay's life and his previous family. Always take care of them."

"I will," Lem said. "I promise."

"Good, but that's not the promise I'm asking for," Doc continued, pausing to breathe. "I was just reminding you of those responsibilities to each other. *Breathe.* What I want you to promise me"—*breathe*—"is that you'll grieve only one day for me." *Breathe.* "After one day, dry your eyes and focus on always remembering our good times together"—*breathe*—"and never forgetting how much I love you."

Tears bathed the twins' cheeks.

"There's something I never told you"—*breathe*—"and probably should have," Doc continued, weakly. With growing effort he proceeded to share the depths of his bereavement and suicide attempt, including the exploding ether bottle that awakened him the night his house burned down. "So you see"—*breathe*—"you boys saved my life."

"We had no idea," said Lem.

"We'll still never say who really started that fire," Jamis said, playfully.

"I have my suspicion," Doc retorted, winking intimately at Jay-Jay.

Turning serious again: "As I've often told you, try to make each day your masterpiece. *Breathe.* If you're successful doing that most days, day after day and week after month after year"—*breathe*—"when you get to the end of your adventure you'll have lived a masterpiece life. *Breathe.* I've made some flawed brush strokes, certainly, but all in all, I'm pleased"—*breathe*—"with my life's painting. Yes, I feel happy and fulfilled. My only real regret"—*breathe*—"is that it's all passed by so swiftly, in a blink it seems. *Breathe.* I feel like I did when I was a kid on the pony ride at the fair"—*breathe*—"I want to go around one more time."

Jamis leaned over The Butterfly Table and hugged Doc, embracing his Pops longer than he ever had, and still it was far too brief. Lem, lightly stroking Doc's left arm, suddenly realized the brushstroke-like birthmark resembled Halley's Comet—*The tail of a comet that Grandma warned us would bring tears*, he thought.

Doc slept for most of the next two days, awaking only for short spells—including evening shaves from Jonny. Breathing became more labored as his weakening lungs slowly filled with drowning fluid. During Connie's illness long before, and again with Alycia not so long ago, Doc lovingly told them it was okay to "let go" rather than suffer. But he found it impossible to grant himself similar merciful permission.

Jamis and Lem gave it instead.

"Keep fighting if it's for you, Pops," Jamis said, his tone tender as a requiem. "But if you're doing it for Lem and me, we'll be okay—go be with Aly and Connie. We love you beyond all measure."

"We'll never forget your love," Lem whispered, his lips brushing his namesake's ear.

Doc opened his eyes, blue-grey like the ocean on a cloudy day, and with clear recognition grinned fragilely at Jamis, then at Lem, letting them know he heard their lovely words. His eyelids lowered shut and he squeezed his sons' hands and whistle-hummed, almost inaudibly, before being gently spirited away by "The Old Man's Friend."

Disaster

Love wanted to give Linc something special for Christmas, his first as part of their family, and she had the perfect gift in mind.

The Hungarian Opal ring.

Unfortunately, neither Love nor Tavis, despite Linc having told them about the heirloom, knew exactly what the ring looked like. Tracking it down, even aided by a photograph, would be difficult; doing so blindly seemed needle-in-a-hay-silo impossible.

Weighing necessity over secrecy, the couple enlisted Linc's help. The weekend before Christmas, Love suggested her husband take Linc to every pawnshop in the area with the mission of finding—and buying back, cost be damned—the antique ring.

At their first four stops, the search party of two was shown more than a dozen rings that the shop owners suggested might be what they were looking for. Linc shook his head each time, his countenance growing more hangdog, the proprietors determinedly trying to make a sale anyway.

"Better than your mom's ring!" one owner callously insisted about *six* different rings, all of them second-rate baubles. Linc's posture deflated like an inflatable Santa Claus decoration when the air pump is turned off.

Down to the final pawnshop on their list, Linc once again described the ring and its opal stone of midnight blue and translucent swirling fire.

"Yes, yes! I *know* that ring," came the answer with animated assurance and seeming sincerity. "I *have* that ring. A *beautiful* ring it is!"

Linc's heart leapt and his chin lifted and he smiled hopefully at Tavis.

"Let me go find it," the shop owner said. "I'll be back in two shakes of a cow's tail."

The promised brief retreat to retrieve the jewel anxiously extended long enough to harass an entire herd of cattle before he returned—

—empty-handed and full of bad news.

"It's no longer here," the shop owner said, apologetically. "My son tells me he sold it."

Linc's shoulders slumped again, his revived hope went into freefall.

Politely, Tavis asked if he could speak to the son.

"Yes, yes, of course," the shop owner said and summoned the boy from the back room to the front counter.

"Can you tell me who bought the ring?" Tavis asked the teenager. "Was it, by any chance, the woman who pawned it?"

"Don't remember," the son mumbled, punctuating his curt reply with a question-mark shrug.

"You sold a ring worth thousands of dollars," Tavis pressed, unsatisfied, "surely you remember something about the buyer. Please, it's really important."

"It was a month ago," the son offered, wearing a smiley face T-shirt but rudely keeping his Walkman headphones on. "Maybe longer. The ticket had expired, I remember that much, so it probably wasn't the same person who pawned it."

"Not to worry," the pawnshop owner cheerfully interjected. "I have another ring that I think—"

Tavis and Linc were halfway to the door before the proprietor finished: "—you will like even better!"

"I'm sorry," Tavis said, resting his hand on the nape of Linc's neck and massaging gently with his fingers and words: "Truly, truly sorry. I know how much the ring means to you. At least, I think I have an idea how important it is."

"*Was*," Linc corrected, dully, before falling silent as a muted TV. He felt like he had lost the ring all over again, been punched in the gut once more with lung-emptying force. The two walked wordlessly to the pickup, climbed in the cab and buckled their seatbelts, and only then did Linc speak again.

"That ring and The Butterfly Table are the only things my dad ever gave me—besides a ton of sadness," Linc said, buried resentment rising like a zombie. "My mom pawning the ring—*my* ring—that totally sucked, but having it resold and gone forever hurts way worse."

Linc absently cracked his knuckles, then his tone quickly softened: "But you wanna know what matters more than the ring?"

"Tell me," Tavis said, eyes on the road ahead but his attention focused squarely on the teenage boy sitting to his right.

"You and Love and Fayth matter way more to me."

Linc had treated this Disaster like a Man, but a bolder Disaster loomed unseen just over the horizon.

Fight Night

The first game of his senior season, in the first quarter, Linc broke his right hand.

Fractures in the proximal phalanx of the index finger and middle metacarpophalangeal knuckle joint healed fully by the seventh game, but Linc's high school football career was over nonetheless. He had already been permanently suspended from interscholastic athletics because of *how* he was injured—throwing a linebacker to the ground, pouncing on him, then balling up his fist, tight and hard, before ramming a sledgehammer blow through the opening above the facemask, shattering his antagonist's cheekbone.

Two assistant coaches escorted Linc to the locker room; calm was restored on the field; and the game resumed. Meanwhile, the pummeled player's parents summoned the cops who took Linc to the police station to be charged with battery.

At halftime, upon receiving an update on Linc's arrest, Tavis did something he had never before done as a coach—he put an individual player above the team. After placing his top assistant in charge for the remainder of the game, Tavis rushed to the precinct house, paid bail, and when Linc was released into his custody—and into his safe embrace—whispered chin-to-cheek to the shaken boy: "Are you okay, son?"

Linc's reply poured out lacking all commas and periods: "I'm sorry I got ejected my hand's killing me thanks for coming did we win?"

"Let me see your hand," Tavis said, worry eclipsing anger. "Wow—it's really swollen. Sure looks broken to me."

"Probably is I'm sorry I got arrested it's really throbbing he deserved it."

"Let's get you to the E.R. for X-rays," Tavis said with soft concern, then turned stern: "Why did he deserve to get the crap beat out of him?"

"He taunted me."

"*Linnnnnc*," Tavis admonished.

"Called me the N-word," Linc revealed, his own words again rushing forth in a sprint. "N-lover actually I ignored him tried to anyway even reading that word in *Huckleberry Finn* punches me in the heart especially now so hearing it felt like being stabbed."

"Slow down," Tavis soothed. "*Bre-e-e-eathe.*"

"Like I said, I tried to ignore him," Linc resumed at a slower pace. "But on the very next play, he said it again—except this time he called you that."

Weighing various responses, Tavis decided to bare his scars: "You think I've never been called that nuclear word of hate before? Hell, the first time was when I was buying a comic book—*Batman*, I still remember—by the store clerk. I literally flinched and my eyes burned hot with tears. Part of my childhood died right then and there, at age eight, in a comic book store that's supposed to be filled with happiness and fun."

Linc listened raptly as Tavis continued, composure quelling his indignation: "At every level of football—Pop Warner, high school, college, even the NFL—vile, bigoted opponents baited me with racial taunts. Hell, yes, I was tempted to punch their lights out. But if the mailman stopped to kick every dog that barks at him, he wouldn't get many letters delivered. Instead, I gave the racist vermin an ass whuppin' between the snap and whistle.

"That's not the half of it, Linc. Remember my failed driver's test? What I didn't tell you guys was that the instructor told me beforehand he'd never pass a Black kid on the first try. That put me in a blind rage and I drove like it. Nowadays, I get pulled over for Driving While Black—in stores, security guards shadow me. I appreciate you sticking up for me, really I do. But, son, I don't need you fighting my wars."

In the passenger seat on their way to the E.R., Linc straightened up and spoke up: "Coach, I didn't do it for you. I did because he also called little Fayth that poisonous word."

Tavis pulled into the hospital lot and parked, sat, sat, sat in thought, and at last pivoted to look Linc in the eye: "What I'm about to tell you is between us. You and me only, understand?"

Linc nodded.

"You did the wrong thing—for the right reason, and I'm damned proud of you. Now let's go get that hand of yours X-rayed."

Candy Bar

"My granddaddy liked to say," Tavis told Linc, "when life hands you sour lemons—"

"—make lemonade," Linc interjected, tartly, crestfallen by the school district's heavy-handed suspension for the entire football season.

"No, that's what other people say," Tavis rejoined. "If something disappointing happened to me, Granddaddy Eli would say: *Tav, my little man, when life hands you sour lemons—have a sweet candy bar.*"

The homespun maxim failed to lighten the anvil-heavy chip on Linc's shoulder.

"Then he'd take me to the drugstore," Tavis continued spinning the homily. "Usually I got a Milky Way, sometimes a Hershey bar. When I finished my treat, Granddaddy would clap his hands—"

CLAP!

"—and say it was time to rise up tall from my troubles."

Tavis savored the sugary trip down memory lane, briefly, then forged ahead: "Linc, the one who gets knocked down and rises up tall becomes stronger than the one who's never knocked down. That's a cliché, but there's truth behind most clichés. You've got to rise and move forward. The suspension is a tough knockdown, damned sure. It's a very bitter lemon. What you need to do is find a candy bar, metaphorically, to replace football."

His mood curdling, Linc objected: "Football means everything to me. You, of all people, should understand. Football was going to be my ticket to college—"

"Hold on there," Tavis cut in. "I'm going to be brutally honest, son. You weren't going to get a football scholarship. You're a good high school receiver, very good even, and I mean it. But you're not fast enough for Saturdays. That's just the cold hard truth."

Linc's face flushed hot, his pride as hurt as his right hand encased in a plaster cast.

"Before you start pouting all woebegone, let me say something else," Tavis ventured. "I hate it when I hear coaches talk about a player who gives *110 percent* or *exceeds his potential.* Those things are impossible. You can't eat 110 percent of an apple pie, can you? A seagull can't exceed its potential and become an eagle. The best one can do is work hard to maximize their God-given talents."

Linc remained disconsolate, his face like a rainy weekend.

"Here's the thing, Linc—you've made me reconsider. I've come to believe you really do *exceed your potential* as a football player because you're a human ladder who lifts each of your teammates, and your coaches as well, up higher towards reaching their potentials.

Linc stubbornly tried to maintain his sulking expression, but the compliment had begun its medicinal work. Gradually, like summer's sun peeking through morning clouds, his lips parted to reveal a sliver of a smile.

"What we need to do," Tavis opined, "is find a new challenge for you to explore your potential. Any ideas?"

Silence.

"What else interests you?" Tavis nudged.

"The suspension isn't fair!" Linc whined, still dwelling on the past instead of looking to the future.

"No, son, it isn't," Tavis agreed. "Life often is unfair—this is one of those times.

Extended silence.

"Granddaddy Eli had another saying, related to his candy bar wisdom with Kipling's *If* mixed in," Tavis tried anew. "*Things turn out best for those who make the best of the way things turn out.* If you choose to, you can make this turn out for the best. Honestly, you can. Football wasn't going to get you a college education—Lord knows football kept me from getting one."

"But you were a Michigan Wolverine," Linc contested.

"I played football there—but I didn't study," Tavis confessed. "I was so focused on being a star athlete, as a student I totally dropped the ball. It wasn't until after football was taken from me that I realized what I'd thrown away. Linc, *my little man*, you've been given a big gift—if only you're willing to look at it that way."

When no response came, Tavis pressed on: "How about joining the school's Speech Club? You're smart and an excellent writer, and you have confidence and charisma. You'd be terrific. Success in oratory contests might even open some college doors."

"That sounds good," Linc said—

CLAP!

"—and so does a Snickers."

Abe And Lincoln

The assignment of selecting a renowned orator to focus on in Speech Club was not at all difficult for Linc: Abraham Lincoln, with whom he shared a February 12th birthday and, in turn, his name.

Choosing a specific speech also seemed straightforward: The famous Gettysburg Address for it is as brief as it is eloquent. The conciseness—a mere 272 words—made memorization less painful and furthermore eliminated the need for editing to fit within the speech competition's maximum six-minute time limit.

Tavis, to the contrary, was of a strong mind the Gettysburg Address was too short, too obvious, too often done.

"If you want to earn the right to be proud, in any endeavor, it's necessary to take on something challenging," Tavis counseled Linc. "I'd encourage you to read other speeches by Mr. Lincoln and choose one you don't think any other contestant could effectively pull off—then pull it off with excellence and grace. That's what will truly impress the judges. More importantly, by doing a difficult thing well, you will impress yourself and thoroughly earn the right to be proud."

It was, as usual coming from Tavis, sage advice.

Linc, as usual, took it to heart.

After school let out each day, when he would have been at football practice prior to his suspension, Linc now went to the public library and studied up on "The Great Emancipator." He read Lincoln's brilliant "House Divided Speech" from 1858 that kicked off his campaign for the U.S. Senate. He considered using Lincoln's "Farewell Address" made as president-elect to his hometown of Springfield, Illinois in 1861. He perused Lincoln's 1861 "Address in Independence Hall" that focused on the Declaration of Independence. And, of course, he savored Lincoln's first and second Inaugural Addresses of 1861 and 1865.

In the end, Linc settled on Lincoln's landmark "Cooper Union Address" delivered on February 27, 1860, on a snowy night in New York City. The origins of the speech dated back four months when Lincoln accepted an invitation from prominent abolitionist clergyman Henry Ward Beecher, brother of famed author Harriet Beecher Stowe, to lecture at his New York church.

At Cooper Union, Lincoln elaborated his views on slavery and claimed the Founding Fathers would not have wanted it to expand into the Western Territories. Historians ever since have contended this speech landed Lincoln in the White House.

More than seven thousand words in length, the address took Lincoln the candidate well over an hour to deliver; Lincoln the student faced the daunting task of culling a mere 360 seconds to deliver in competition.

Beginning with the opening greeting, "Mr. President and fellow citizens of New York—" student Lincoln seamlessly weaved together three independent passages, before concluding with candidate Lincoln's dynamic closing: "Neither let us be slandered from our duty by false accusations against us, nor frightened from it by menaces of destruction to the Government nor of dungeons to ourselves. Let us have faith that *right* makes *might*, and in that faith, let us, to the end, dare to do our duty as we understand it."

Linc was faithful to further guidance from Tavis: "Practice, practice, practice until you are twice as good as everyone else." It was a creed Tavis preached to his football players; a creed he tried to practice in his own life; a creed instilled in him as a boy by his father, who saw the tenet as a racial necessity.

"My daddy always told me," Tavis told Linc, "that Blacks have to be twice as good if we want a level chance. I've seen firsthand some truth to it. You aren't Black, of course, so what does this have to do with you? Just this, Linc—if you strive to be twice as good as all the rest, you'll be running with a stiff tailwind and nothing can stop you."

Nothing, specifically no one, could stop the doubly well-rehearsed Lincoln in the school district's annual citywide speech tournament. Nor in the regional competition that Linc also won decidedly to advance to the statewide championships to be held in Columbus.

Before embarking on a three-hour drive southwest to Ohio's capital, Linc made a much shorter life-altering road trip.

Fateful Appraisal

 The story in *The Cleveland Plain Dealer* was a mere six paragraphs, on an inside page, near the bottom, easy to miss.

Auspiciously, the small-point headline caught Tavis's eye: *Antiques Appraisers' Fair To Visit C-Town.*

Tavis knew next to nothing about antiques and owned only one—an Elgin railroad pocket watch, the gold case worn smooth by use on the outside and "Jordan" engraved inside the front cover, a family heirloom passed down four generations. Still, his interest was piqued. Reading that an assemblage of "world-renowned experts from Sotheby's in New York and regional authorities specializing in the Midwest" would be at The Convention Center, less than a dozen miles from Cleveland Heights, he had a revelation: *I must take Linc.*

"You might discover more about your roots," Tavis said as they loaded The Butterfly Table into the pickup, surface down, legs up, on a thick padding of blankets. "Who knows—maybe Tamás was a famous furniture maker?"

"I doubt he was famous," Linc said. "But he made a beauty here."

"Sure did," Tavis agreed. "Even if we don't learn anything, we'll have a fun adventure."

Fayth joined the expedition party of three and following a twenty-minute drive, two hours waiting to enter The Convention Center and another full hour in the "Furniture" line, they at last had their turn with an antiques expert. He looked the part: Van Dyke goatee, pewter in color and neatly trimmed to a point, professorial round tortoise shell glasses, three-piece suit of grey wool.

The scholarly gentleman trailed his fingers across the burnished black walnut surface, an appreciative hum rising as he did so. He leaned down, close, to examine the butterfly-shaped knot, then admired the workmanship of the yin-yang symbol—where the doorknob had originally been—and white oak border. Thereupon, he genuflected to inspect the maple legs and underside.

Concluding his perusal, "Mr. Highbrow"—as Linc privately nicknamed him—rose from his knees and asked: "What do you know about this handsome Table?"

"My four-times-great-grandfather, Tamás Beswick, made it around 1850—1852, actually, according to family lore," Linc shared. "He had twin sons, Jamis and Lemuel, and the night they were born a lightning bolt supposedly split a tree in two—that's where the Tabletop's wood came from. Tamás later died in the Civil War fighting for the Union. I don't know if he made any other furniture—we were hoping you could tell us."

Mr. Highbrow nodded, stroked his chin hair while digesting Linc's narrative, and politely excused himself to consult with a colleague. Upon returning, he asserted: "I think you're half-right. Indeed, this probably was made in 1852—"

He grinned.

"—and also around 1870."

Linc's eyebrows became question marks.

"The black walnut portion of the Table's surface was, I believe, originally a *door* made by Tamás Beswick," Mr.

Highbrow expounded. "He was a Hungarian immigrant and became quite renowned in eastern Ohio for carpentry—exquisite doors, chiefly. His son Lemuel, who lived to be ninety-six, became *the* preeminent cabinetmaker in the Tri-State area."

Tavis and Linc, with considerable care, turned The Butterfly Table on its side. Using a wooden pointer that resembled a magic wand, Mr. Highbrow drew their attention to three capital block letters—*LEM*—branded up near the top on the inside of one of the legs; then, in the adjoining corner on the underside, to *Tamás* scratched in cursive, the "signature" shallow yet legible.

"I'm confident this is a hybrid piece created by *two* nineteenth-century craftsmen of consummate skill—a stunning door made by Tamás Beswick that his son, Lemuel Jamison, later transformed into an enchanting Table. As to value, it's difficult to say."

"I'll never sell it," Linc blurted.

"No, no, of course not," Mr. Highbrow acknowledged, his erudite goatee framing a pleased smile. "For insurance purposes, however, I'd place the value at twenty to twenty-five thousand."

"Dollars?" Linc asked in disbelief.

"Yes."

"Wow!"

"One additional thought," Mr. Highbrow intoned. "Two weekends ago, we were in Detroit and my colleague, whom you saw me consulting with in Books & Manuscripts, examined a Civil War-era journal. Here's the owner's phone number. His name is Luther Douglass—

"—tell him you're related to Tamás Beswick."

The Pando Tree

 Linc phoned the number he received at the Antiques Appraisers' Fair.

He was curious and, his shaky voice revealed, as nervous as if asking a girl out on date.

"Hi, um, hello, ah—Mr. Douglass?"

"*Reverend* Douglass, yes," greeted a voice deep as a cello, warm as sunshine.

Linc introduced himself, explained that an antiques expert urged him to call about a Civil War journal, and further noted his relationship to Tamás Beswick.

Intrigued, Reverend Luther Douglass shared how he found the century-old diary while cleaning out the church basement after the hot-water heater burst. Boxes and boxes of old photographs and bibles and hymnals were ruined in the flooding.

"But this little diary miraculously didn't drown," Reverend Douglass sermonized. "It survived dry as Death Valley in August. I started reading it right there, standing shin-deep in water, and I couldn't put it down—except to dab away tears now and again.

"When the Antiques Appraisers' Fair came to Detroit shortly thereafter, I thought it was simply a pleasant coincidence—not a sign from high above. However, with what you've just told me young man, I'm beginning to think it was indeed a Godwink of divinity, not serendipity. One thing's certain—Tamás Beswick's diary rightly belongs in your hands, not mine."

"Really?" Linc said.

"Absolutely."

"Will you send it to me?"

"I'd be much glad to, Linc, except I think it's too priceless—not monetarily, but emotionally and historically—to trust to the mail. I know Detroit's a lengthy drive from Cleveland, but perhaps you could pay me a visit sometime and accept it in person?"

"Hold on while I ask—"

Plans were made without delay for Linc and Tavis to make the pilgrimage that coming Sunday at one o'clock.

~~~

Even by *Tavis Time*, the two arrived notably early.

Reverend Douglass, a mountain of a man with an apostles-esque beard, a bit untamed, was delivering his eleven o'clock sermon so Linc and Tavis quietly sat down in an empty rearmost pew. Catching their eyes from afar at the altar, where he stood in a spotlight of stained-glass sunlight, The Reverend nodded and flashed a welcoming smile before resuming his closing homily.

"What do you think is the largest living organism on our planet?" Reverend Douglass rhetorically asked the assemblage of Baptist brethren, although Linc felt like he was speaking directly to him. "An African elephant, perhaps, weighing six tons? No, the blue whale is much larger—at one hundred fifty tons, and one hundred feet in length, it's grander in size than the largest dinosaurs. Yet the leviathan blue whale is also surpassed.

"What about the Giant Redwoods of California? A better guess, but even these three-hundred-foot-tall colossuses are not the largest living things on our planet. That distinction belongs to a different tree—a tree in Utah's Fishlake National Forest.

"This tree, called *Pando*—that's Latin for *I spread*—is actually a clonal colony of a single Quaking Aspen. Estimated to be forty-seven thousand separate trunks above ground, below terra firma they share one labyrinthine root system. In fact, they share identical DNA because they began as *one* tree that sprouted new stems from its roots. These stems became trees that in turn sprouted new stems, and on and on since long before Jesus, for eighty millennium.

"While I'm no scientist, I believe there's one living thing even larger than the Pando—much, much larger. Forty-seven *thousand* connected trees is prodigious, but it is dwarfed by five *billion* humans all connected.

"And believe me, we are all connected. We share common roots back to Neanderthal man—

"—back to the original single-cell form of life—

"—back even further to stardust. No matter where we hail from on this blue-and-green globe, whatever our gender, regardless of ethnicity, all humans share DNA that is 99.9 percent identical.

"Sadly, we are far too often blind to this Pando-like connection," The Reverend preached on, clasping his hands in prayer, fingers symbolically laced together. "But when we embrace our connection, it's a beautiful thing—

"—a mighty thing—

"—a life-changing thing."

He bowed his head.

"Amen," sang the congregants, including two visitors in the back pew.

Diary

"Welcome, welcome," Reverend Luther Douglass greeted Tavis and Linc after the last of the parishioners had filed out of Second Baptist Church in Detroit's Greektown neighborhood.

"Please, follow me. We can chat in my office."

On a mahogany desktop, tidy and worthily proportional to its current keeper, Tamás's journal rested center stage. It was much smaller—only four inches by six—than Linc had imagined. Thinner, too, fifty pages at most. The leather cover, mud brown and crackled in full with a fist-sized black splotch, added to an unremarkable first impression.

"Doesn't look like much, I know," said Reverend Douglass, the back of his sexagenarian hands matching the diary's chapped texture. "But if ever there was a book not to be judged by its cover, this is the one. The story inside is beautiful. Heart-wrenching, too. Above all, glorious."

The Reverend shared an overview of what was recorded within, in dull pencil, the cramped but neat printing running to the very edge of each yellowed page. He enriched his retelling by adding other relevant history with which he was familiar. The result was the long-missing final chapter of Tamás Beswick's life story.

~~~

They had all been wrong, Doc and Aisha and Grandma Dika and the twins, and everyone else in town.

After hightailing it out of Bellaire in autumn 1863 to escape retribution for flinging a steak knife square into Marcus Murphy's forehead, Tamás had second thoughts about enlisting in the Union army. Emotionally devastated at causing one death, he realized he did not have the stomach for war and abandoned his plan of enlisting in the Ohio Volunteer Infantry.

And so, instead of joining the biggest and bloodiest gunfight America had ever witnessed, Tamás stepped forth for a different battle. It was a grisly and perilous battle all the same. And a sacred one. He hoped that if he fulfilled this duty, and survived, Bellaire would be so proud as to welcome him home, his debt to society considered paid in full.

Rather than heading due west to Camp Chase in Columbus; or fleeing southwest to Camp Dennison near Cincinnati; Tamás traveled directly north towards Camp Taylor in Cleveland, then turned west and followed Lake Erie's shoreline. In all, in eleven days, he traveled more than two hundred miles by foot from Bellaire to Oberlin College, Doc's alma mater and a place Tamás had heard him speak of often and fondly. But Tamás did not go there to pursue an education.

Oberlin Institute, as Oberlin College was originally christened, was of historic importance by being the first college in America to admit women, doing so when it opened its classrooms in December 1833 with twenty-nine male students and fifteen females. Two years later, it was a pioneer again as the first college to enroll Black students.

Thereafter, Oberlin became a center for abolitionist activities. Its undertakings included being a key stop along the Underground Railroad—the vast network of secret routes and safe houses used to harbor escaped slaves seeking freedom in Northern states and Canada.

Oberlin famously championed the abolition cause in 1858 when local residents rescued a fugitive slave—John Price—from U.S. marshals and helped him cross the north border. The liberators were jailed in Cleveland for violating the 1850 Fugitive Slave Act, an event that attracted national attention and subsequently was credited with playing an important role in lighting the fuse for The Civil War—at the time commonly called The Great War.

In the abolitionists' own great war, Tamás became a "conductor" on the Underground Railroad. He would be guided on this journey not only by the stars and a magnetic compass, and once by a "map" braided in the cornrows of a woman slave, but also by his north-pointing moral compass.

Tamás had never forgotten his dept to the elderly pawnshop owner in New York City. By kindly not charging interest on the loan for the Hungarian Opal ring, Laszlo rescued Tamás and Aisha's dreams for a better life in America. In that bygone pawnshop, Tamás privately vowed to one day repay the currency he owed—a responsibility to help someone else who had fallen into dire straits.

That day had arrived.

Midnight And Dawn

 Tamás's involvement with the perilous Underground undertaking seemed written in the stars.

The night his twin sons Jamis and Lemuel were born—March 20, 1852—was the very day abolitionist Harriet Beecher Stowe's seminal novel *Uncle Tom's Cabin; or, Life Among the Lowly* was originally published. The book proved to be an historical lightning bolt, its readership spreading like prairie fire in howling winds. By year's end, an unprecedented three hundred thousand copies had been sold and the anti-slavery narrative was headed to becoming the best-selling novel of the nineteenth century.

Astrology alone was not at play. During encampment along the Ohio River, at the site of The Black Walnut Tree, Tamás and his fellow Roma migrants had harbored a runaway slave named Jack, who escaped from a tobacco plantation down in Virginia.

One afternoon, while mending a tear in his coarse "Negro cloth" shirt, Jack's bare back was exposed. The grisly quilt of raised scars caused by savage lashings made Tamás wince. Horrifying, too, was the soot-black "RR"—either a master's initials of ownership; or signifying Jack had twice been caught trying to escape, one "R" for each failed Run—on his neck, left of his Adam's apple, branded there as though he were a steer.

Testament to even worse barbarism, Jack was missing his entire right pinkie and ring finger, and the first joint of his middle finger. As punishment for failing to harvest speedily enough, one finger joint—on five different occasions—had been chopped off with a tobacco knife. Each atrocious amputation diabolically increased the chances of another dismemberment by further slowing down Jack's dexterity.

The emotional tortures Jack described were no less inhumane: broken hearts wrapped in misery with slave families severed through the sale of the father to one place, the mother to another; children sold here, their siblings sold there; being fed calories in shortfall and humiliation in abundance.

Brimming with empathetic rage, Tamás decided to accompany Jack north on the life-risking journey to Canada. Aisha beseeched her husband not to go, and he capitulated, but a Samaritan seed had been planted.

"Godspeed, my brother—peace be with you," Tamás said in bidding Jack farewell. As precaution, should the prayer fail, he gifted the runaway his most-prized throwing knife.

Ever after, when life knocked Tamás down as it did time and again, he would recall Jack's unimaginable hardships and realize his own situation was not at all dire by comparison.

Always, when he thought of Jack, Tamás liked to believe he had reached freedom.

~~~

In Oberlin, in due time, Tamás earned the trust of prominent abolitionists and became a conductor on the Underground Railroad.

A conductor's mission was to lead "passengers"—also called "cargo," although Tamás eschewed this term for he felt it was dehumanizing—from one safe "station" to the next; from spare room to empty barn, to church, to hiding place deep in the woods; through rain, sweltering heat, snow.

Most conductors traveled only between two stations. Tamás, uncommonly, volunteered to guide passengers along the entire artery to freedom from Oberlin to Detroit, circumventing the eastern end of Lake Erie en route, the total odyssey approaching two hundred miles with each step forward weighted with danger.

"If you hear the dogs, keep going," a fellow conductor, quoting heroine Harriet Tubman, told Tamás. "If you see the torches in the woods, keep going. If there's shouting after you, keep going. Don't ever stop. Keep going."

Detroit's code name was "Midnight." The Detroit River was "Jordan." And across was "Dawn"—the beginning of a new life.

Even as Dawn drew near, however, freedom remained distant for Detroit was rife with bounty hunters. Bold slave catchers even ventured into Canada to kidnap their profitable prey.

When he first joined the Underground Railroad, Tamás resolved to make five trips from Oberlin to Dawn as penance for killing Marcus Murphy. After achieving that goal in less than a year's span, in the process safely delivering twelve passengers without once running his train off the track, Tamás made a fateful decision.

He had not heard the Lord's voice, as Harriet Tubman claimed to have, yet Tamás felt a divine calling in his heart: *I must save one more soul.*

Answered Prayer

 "I see doubt in your eyes, Linc," Reverend Luther Douglass said, his own eyes meeting the teen's. "You're not a believer?"

"I believe the Underground Railroad story you're telling us," Linc answered in a jaded monotone.

"That's not what I meant," Reverend Douglass volleyed back, gently. "You don't believe in God and His guidance—or miracles, do you?"

Linc's reply of intense stillness spoke volumes. The Reverend remained pensive and patient, as did Tavis, as both men sensed Linc was carrying a burden that threatened to crumple him if they were not able to find a way to help shoulder the Atlas-like load.

The silence lingered, and stretched, and hung uncomfortably, until at last Linc released a sigh so deep it could fully inflate a child's balloon, breathed in deeply, and decried: "Am I believer? Of course not! God's never given me a reason to believe in Him."

Blinking back tears, hot and rising and filled with hurt, Linc raged on: "Let me tell you about *your* God, sir. He took my mom away, just like He took away my dad. He took football away from me, too. God doesn't listen to me. *Your* God has never answered *my* prayers."

Reverend Douglass absorbed this outpouring, felt Linc's heartache as though it were his very own, then did something curious—he smiled at Linc, broadly with love, glanced knowingly at Tavis, and returned his warm gaze to the sufferer.

"Time absorbs grief, Linc, but never completely," The Reverend offered, his low-registered voice sounding like rich musical notes played softly. "Your feelings of having been forsaken by *my* God are natural."

Reverend Douglass loitered momentarily in thought in the underlit room, cozily so, stroking his grizzled beard, grey whiskers out-populating black ones, and resumed: "So you think God doesn't listens to you."

Linc nodded.

"And that He has never answered your prayers."

Another downhearted nod.

"Tell me, Lincoln," Reverend Douglass said, formally, posing the first in a series of clarifying questions. "Who drove you here today?"

Before Linc could answer, The Reverend continued, his words taking on the inflections and rhythm of a soaring sermon: "Tell me, son, who took you to pick up your beloved heirloom Table at the out-of-town library? Tell me, son, who took you to the Antiques Fair to learn more about your heritage? And tell me, son, who took you into his home—into *their* home—and made it *your* home when you had nowhere to turn?

"Let me tell you about banyan trees," Reverend Douglass rolled on, drawing upon his sermon's preparation researching the Pando tree. "Buddha is said to have sat beneath a banyan's canopy, but its mythological significance extends much deeper for these trees are believed to have magical powers. Banyans, you see, produce aerial roots that hang down and take hold wherever they touch the ground.

"According to ancient legend, a father told his son to cut open a fig from a fruitful banyan tree and examine the seeds within. The boy did so and next was instructed to slice one of the seeds in half, then tell what he saw.

"*Father, I see nothing,* the boy reported, to which the father explained: *That's the miracle of the banyan tree, son, for it can spring forth from nothing.*"

Confusion washed over Linc's face.

Reverend Douglass leaned forward in his chair, so far forward that the sizeable desktop between the holy man and dispirited boy seemed to dissolve until they were nearly touching foreheads, and explained: "To spring forth from homelessness seems not dissimilar to me. If Tavis and Love and Fayth have not been your prayer answered, and most wonderfully so, then I am no longer a believer myself."

Linc's sagging head and chin lifted—

"And if the story chronicled inside this old diary, the story of your ancestors and your lineage, is not miraculous, then again I am no longer a believer."

—and his eyes locked with The Reverend's.

"But I am a believer, Lincoln. With all my heart, I am. And after I finish telling you about the miracle of Tamás and Sawney, I believe you'll stop feeling so forsaken by *my* God and see *yourself* as blessed by Him.

Devil On Their Heels

 Tamás Beswick was an extraordinary conductor on the Underground Railway.

He charted course by map and by constellations, also by a sixth sense that warned him when a devilish bounty hunter was on his—*their*—heels. When jeopardy closed in, Tamás made his passengers and himself disappear as if into thin air; silent as smoke they vanished deeper into the woods.

In one heart-pounding narrow escape, Tamás and two runaways turned invisible, lying supine amidst cattails in a pond, barely below the water's surface, breathing through hollow reeds until a posse of slave catchers passed. This was on Tamás's third passage; he had become too confident—too careless—and traveled during daylight.

Thereafter, Tamás redoubled his caution, trekking only at night. His darting eyes constantly read moonlight shadows just as a steamboat pilot reads a river. If delay might prove treacherous, he sped up. When swiftness seemed risky, he laid low. Between a straight easy road or difficult winding path, he chose the latter. He and his passengers fortified their courage with potent moonshine sometimes, more often with sober prayer.

So it was that Tamás successfully completed, without a single capture or casualty, his five vowed missions of mercy and penance.

The bonus sixth passage to *save one more soul* in pursuit of absolution had been the smoothest of all, all the way to

"Midnight" without a hitch. The weather was oddly warm for early December, starlit nights giving blessing and guidance, and the most important prayer was answered with no trace of fugitive slave catchers anywhere between Oberlin and Detroit.

In Greektown, an old Detroit neighborhood with Romanesque architecture, Tamás escorted his last passenger to the final station—Second Baptist Church. Before feeling one's way by hand along a brick wall, moist and slimy with mildew, down a lightless stairway into the basement, runaways fleeing hell's bondage passed beneath this sign: *Entrance to Escapees' Haven.*

Haven, however, remained two long miles from Canada's heaven.

Always in the past, Tamás handed off his passengers for the journey's ending leg. This time, no other conductor was present. He would have to cross The Jordan himself. Unable to scrounge up an abandoned dinghy for a stealthy night crossing, Tamás bought two ferryboat tickets. For the first time since the cattails scare, he would move cargo in daylight.

~~~

The wind-lashed afternoon was grey and biting.

But it was the command that froze Tamás: "Won't give you no trouble if let me have 'im peaceably."

A ferry passenger, burly and bearded and clutching the runaway in a one-armed headlock, flashed his overcoat open to reveal an ivory-handled pistol.

As he had done two decades prior when a deckhand accosted Aisha, Tamás measured this foe, measured the situation, and measured tall with fearless action.

"You're too late," Tamás said evenly. "He's a free man now. Best you leave that gun be."

The slave catcher erred in not heeding the warning.

Tamás made a grim mistake as well.

In a blur of commotion, the runaway, too near Dawn to have freedom denied, broke loose and dove into the angry frigid water; the slave catcher drew his revolver, took hurried aim; all while Tamás pulled a hunting knife from his boot top and threw a steel-bladed thunderbolt that split flesh and penetrated bone, just as the brawny bushwhacker squeezed the trigger—

Ka-pow! Piercing howl! Thud.

—the human grizzly crumpled.

Tamás bolted to the side railing just as his Underground passenger disappeared below the surface, dead or drowning.

Harriet Beecher Stowe wrote, "Friendships are discovered rather than made." During their two weeks together on the run, Tamás had discovered a kindred spirit. With bulletproof bravery, he leapt overboard into the swift currents in rescue.

Tamás's grim mistake, with Marcus Murphy flashing to mind, was apprehension about possibly killing the slave catcher. Thus, he had not aimed for head or heart. Thus, with a knife buried deep in his thigh, the ruthless predator rose in agony, lifted his six-shooter, and fired all five remaining shots.

Two bullets found flesh, squarely—

—one body went slack in the bloody water.

Journal In The Jordan

 The first bullet ripped into the left upper shoulder from behind, burned like hellfire, but levied no grave damage.

The second lead slug was more merciless, striking six inches lower, boring deep into the lung. Peril in the biting-cold morning air had already seemed thick as blood; now the water, white with choppy wave crests and axe-head ice chunks, turned crimson also.

The escaped slave gasped for breath, desperately, his chest raging with searing pain—

—but not because of a bullet wound.

The runaway was fighting for air because he had been submerged for an eternity, until being on the razor's edge of passing out, dodging gunfire. Finally resurfacing, his vision blurred from a dizzying lack of oxygen and by water in his eyes, he made out Tamás floating facedown ten yards off.

It might as well have been ten miles.

Panting panting panting for survival, the runaway started swimming towards his hero, a hero who had fearlessly dived into the icy water—and into a hail of bullets. A rogue current had the unconscious Tamás in its cruel clutches and the short gap swiftly widened to thirty yards.

The escaped slave was not a strong swimmer, although he had harrowingly conquered "The Deep River," as the Ohio River was nicknamed, earlier on this journey. But this river was angrier, frothing and tossing and splashing like soapy water in a washerwoman's steel tub. Fueled suddenly by fear's adrenaline, and also by friendship, the runaway with great effort slowly cut the distance in half.

Bone-tired and in the early grips of hypothermia, the runaway's hopes began to sink, his resolve drowning. At this do-or-die moment, Tamás rolled onto his side trying to tread water with his unwounded arm.

The sight revitalized the runaway. Sprinting, with arms flailing frantically, he reached Tamás and grabbed his coat collar. Their roles now reversed, the passenger guided and towed the conductor towards Canada's distant shore.

Dunked by a violent whitecap, the new conductor swallowed water and choked and feared his own death unless he abandoned Tamás. Instead, he tightened his hold and impossibly swam beyond the limits of his strength and endurance.

Bad turned worse.

Then worse became worst.

By the time they reached northern landfall, Tamás was again unconscious, his pulse thready and erratic. As the runaway used his palms trying to dam the river of blood, Tamás's breathing grew ragged—

—slowed—

—slower—

—until his chest fell still.

Like sand slipping through the fingers of a fist, Tamás's great life had slipped through and away.

Unlettered even to read his own name, the escaped slave nonetheless rescued the small journal from Tamás's coat pocket. He had seen his Underground guardian write in it daily when they holed up, waiting again for night's cover of darkness on freedom's path. He felt an obligation to somehow forward the keepsake to Tamás's kinfolk.

The runaway resolutely safeguarded the diary—its entries in English, not Tamás's native Hungarian; intended for his sons' eyes one day, by God's grace— until his return to America at Civil War's end. After crossing back over The Jordan, this time uneventfully in a ferryboat the whole way, the former escaped slave revisited the haven of Second Baptist Church of Detroit and gave the diary to Reverend William Monroe. Asking that his verbal account be added to its water-damaged pages, he shared the story of Tamás's heroic death.

So it was that when Reverend Luther Douglass— reading aloud from the rescued diary to his two visitors— finished Tamás's final entry, the pencil printing as faded as an old childhood dream, a new writing hand in larger black-ink cursive began: *As told to me on the 26th of May 1866 by Sawney Jordan, a free man* . . .

"Sawney Jordan?" Tavis echoed, in hushed wonderment, after being momentarily hypnotized by the unimaginable revelation.

Reverend Douglass nodded.

"He was my great-great-great-grandfather," Tavis related.

The Reverend smiled, not the least bit wonderstruck by the impossibility of the reality. Pensively stroking his silver-and-wisdom-streaked beard, so thick it could nest a small bird, he professed: "Like the wondrous Pando tree, we really are all connected to one another. Not just in the present, but through the ages."

To Thine Own Self Be True

Tavis read the venerable water-damaged diary in one sitting upon returning home from Second Baptist Church of Detroit.

Three more times the following night he reread Tamás's account of his fateful—and final—sixth trip as a conductor on the Underground Railroad, along with the heroic epilogue, as dictated by Sawney, that concluded with eleven heartfelt words worthy of an epitaph: *My brother Thomas is the greatest man I shall ever know.*

Waves of reverence and gratitude washed over Tavis, Hawaiian-sized surfing waves, each rising swell surpassing the previous one. Had Tamás not guided Sawney to freedom, Tavis realized, in a reversal of lineages he would not be alive to be Lincoln's present-day "conductor."

Nor would Fayth have been born.

And Love would not be carrying a second child.

Marveling at Tamás's bygone selflessness, Tavis felt likewise about Love's now. When he brought Linc home that desperate morning, Love only the day before had learned she was again pregnant. In deference to the busyness of football season, she decided to wait until the coming Sunday—the Jordans' weekly "Family Day"—to share the unplanned-but-wonderful news with Tavis and Fayth.

In her mind, Love had already excitedly turned the guest bedroom/study into a nursery. But she also fretted over how shrunken their modest home would feel with the addition of a baby. Living space alone, much less a hundred more reasons, made Tavis's fostering proposal unreasonable.

And yet without a nanosecond's pause, Love opened her home—and heart, fully—to Linc.

As with Tavis, the antique diary made Linc's soul sing. The resentment he had always harbored for the genetic tree branch springing from his deadbeat dad was now replaced by pride as he imagined the fierce courage and unyielding character encoded in Tamás DNA also being infused in the blood that pulsed through his related veins.

And so it was that Linc made an audacious decision. A scant three weeks before the Ohio State High School Speech Championships in Columbus, he abandoned his twice-triumphant Abraham Lincoln oration and began anew. Inspired by having learned from Reverend Luther Douglass that Frederick Douglass—"No authenticated kinship to *The Lion of Anacostia*, but I like to believe we have shared roots"—once spoke at Detroit's Second Baptist Church, in 1859, Linc selected his roaring "The Hypocrisy of American Slavery" address delivered on July 4, 1852, in the Corinthian Hall at Rochester, New York.

English teacher and speech club advisor Roger Thompson insisted an eleventh-hour change was downright foolish and tried to forbid the switch, but Linc held steadfast.

"Linc has a legitimate chance to win State," Roger told Tavis, attempting to recruit an ally. "Doing so would not only stand out on his college applications, it carries twenty thousand dollars scholarship money. You need to talk some sense into that boy."

Tavis indeed sat Linc down, but did not try to steer him away from the Frederick Douglass selection. To the contrary, he sprinkled Linc with motivational stardust.

"Mastering a brand-new speech in such a short timeframe is a daunting challenge," Tavis conceded. "But as my Granddaddy liked to say, *Worthwhile things should be hard. If they were done easily, everyone would do them and they'd no longer be worthwhile.*"

"So you don't think I'm making a huge mistake, like Mr. Thompson says?" Linc asked.

"To thine own self be true," Tavis answered, quoting Shakespeare's *Hamlet.* He squeezed Linc's shoulder, firmly, and added: "Methinks after our road trip to Detroit, *not* changing your speech would be the mistake. The great poet Robert Frost once said, *No tears in the writer, no tears in the reader*—I believe that holds equally true with giving a speech."

His decision validated, Linc enthusiastically and deftly distilled the lengthy Douglass speech to six elegant minutes. He memorized the words, sentence by paragraph by page, then stayed up late, night after night, rehearsing his cadence, rehearsing his inflections, rehearsing his gestures with exacting detail. Even in his dreams, Linc rehearsed.

As a high school senior, Linc's personal championship football game would instead take place on an auditorium stage. But one thing remained unchanged: he was determined to be at his best when his best was needed.

Gross Injustice

 Linc arrived at The Ohio State University's Weigel Hall Auditorium prepared to be at his best.

In the white glare of the spotlight, he drew from the yellowed pages of Tamás's diary and his newly discovered lineage, and from Sawney, and channeled these marrow-deep emotions into his performance.

"Fellow citizens, pardon me, and allow me to ask, why am I called upon to speak here today?" Lincoln began, just as Frederick Douglass had opened his remarks a century and thirty-six years before. "What have I or those I represent to do with your national independence? . . ."

Linc's cadence picked up steam: "I am not included within the pale of this glorious anniversary! . . . This Fourth of July is yours, not mine. You may rejoice, I must mourn. . . . Fellow citizens, above your national, tumultuous joy, I hear the mournful wail of millions, whose chains, heavy and grievous yesterday, are today rendered more intolerable by the jubilant shouts that reach them. . . ."

As the timing clock tick-tick-ticked down, Linc concluded in a rousing crescendo: "What to the American slave is your Fourth of July? I answer, a day that reveals to him more than all other days of the year, the gross injustice and cruelty to which he is the constant victim. To him your celebration is a sham; your boasted liberty an unholy license; your national greatness, swelling vanity; your sounds of rejoicing are empty and heartless; your shouts of liberty and equality, hollow mock; your prayers and hymns, your sermons and thanksgivings, with all your religious parade and solemnity, are to him mere bombast, fraud, deception, impiety, and hypocrisy."

Linc had been nothing less than flawless. He had not missed a word nor misplaced a comma, had enunciated every syllable clearly, had displayed poise and passion and charisma. And yet, shockingly, at soliloquy's end the audience withheld all applause other than Love's and Fayth's lonely handclapping in the third row.

The chilly reception landed with the clout of Uncle Roy's fist. Staggered and breathless, Linc's eyes sought Tavis—standing in the rear corner of the auditorium—for reassurance, for oxygen. Tavis tapped his right fist on his heart, the family's private sign meaning varyingly: *Well done—Be tough—I'm proud of you—I love you.* In this instance, the gesture was all-inclusive.

As Linc took his first steps of escape, Disaster suddenly, startling, proved to be an imposter. Triumph, loud as touchdown cheers, applause reverberant as the ocean's roar, shook dust off the valance of the stage curtains. Even the five judges, stoic all day, failed in their efforts to restrain nods of smiling appreciation. Linc departed the stage as if floating inside a giant soap bubble.

The next competitor promptly popped it.

Quilting together excerpts from Dr. Martin Luther King, Jr.'s historic "I Have A Dream" speech, the competitor transported the audience to The National Mall while transforming the stage into the hallowed marble steps of the Lincoln Memorial. Moreover, the Black student *became* Dr. King in a way Linc could not *be* Frederick Douglass.

Midway through the rival's pitch-perfect performance, Linc knew he no longer had any chance at first place. He also knew he would not have fared any better by sticking with his original Abraham Lincoln presentation.

When the winner was announced, Linc knew a third thing: the judges' decision was, in Frederick Douglass's words, *intolerable*, a *sham*, a *gross injustice*.

"How can they say I won?" he asked Tavis. "He was twice as good as me."

"No, he wasn't," Tavis soothed, sincerely. "You were truly masterful, Linc—he was only ten percent better. But since you're white and he's Black, he *needed* to be *twice* as good."

"It's not fair," Linc muttered, eyeing his victory as counterfeit. "He was better—he deserves to be the champion."

"You of all people know life can be unjust," Tavis said.

"It should be less unfair," Linc demanded and, guided by the inherited moral compass Tamás followed north to Detroit six times, the four-times-great-grandson squared his shoulders tall and strode to the judges' long table and forfeited the first-place trophy—along with the twenty-thousand-dollar college scholarship prize—to the runner-up.

Valiant Man

 Linc rested his head on crossed arms on The Butterfly Table.

Past midnight, his mind swirled like troubled waters in the Jordan. He was not upset over the State Speech Championships. To the contrary, he felt proud for relinquishing a crown he did not merit.

"Winning would've been a great achievement," Tavis had praised, "but what you did was supreme. It's something to one day tell your grandchildren about."

In the other direction on his ancestral line, Linc liked to think he had lived up to Tamás's legacy. And therein lay the headwaters of his despair. He wished his father, Flynn, had been like Tamás—and Tavis.

A salty droplet of heartache dripped onto the black walnut surface, and for the second time Linc heard The Butterfly Table orate.

This leaden pain that burdens you, Linc, I have experienced before. Your father's forlorn tears as well fell upon me, seeping into my grain, telling me his story.

It is a story you need to know.

Linc, you are wrong about your father.

He did not desert you. Nor was he fearful and weak of character. He was, in truth, a valiant man.

Before marrying your mother, your father was in the Vietnam War. Unlike most, he was not drafted. No, just as Tamás voluntarily joined the Underground Railroad, Flynn enlisted for hazardous duty.

War changes a man and your father was no exception.

The first time Flynn was awakened by a bamboo rat, beady-black-eyed with razor teeth, creeping across his legs, he was so petrified he did not sleep the rest of the night.

The next night, he was ready and waiting and speared the rodent with his combat knife.

The sixth time a rat awakened him, its claws inching upward on his chest towards his chin, he nonchalantly swatted it away and quickly went back to sleep.

The tenth time, when four rats trespassed on him at once, your father did not even care.

War numbed your father in darker ways, too.

Flynn wept the first time he killed a man. He cried a little less the second time. After the fourth, he felt only a twinge of remorse. By the sixth, or eighth, his heart was so calloused it was as if he had merely killed a bamboo rat. War brainwashes a man into believing the enemy is subhuman.

Once, on a routine patrol, your father and a Viet Cong soldier did not see each other until they were only ten yards apart. In that life-and-death split second, with their up-close gazes locked, your father realized the other man's eyes were as young as his; as scared as his; as focused on self-survival as his. A searing realization ravaged Flynn after he pulled the trigger first: If our eyes are the same and he is subhuman, then so am I.

Another incident haunted him even more.

Flynn's infantry unit was in Phouc Binh, in the jungle, in 1969—the carefree Summer of Woodstock back in the States. Although there was no pressing need to hurry back to camp, Lieutenant Frank Saunders chose a shortcut down a narrow dirt path. The detour, flanked on either side by trees and thick foliage, was at risk for ambush.

"Could be a trap," Flynn cautioned.

"I didn't ask you," barked Lieutenant Saunders.

"But sir—"

"That's an order!"

Twenty yards forward, a bird flushed from the vegetation—

Hold-your-breath silence.

—and a pair more took flight.

"It's nothing," Lieutenant Saunders exhaled. "Keep going."

Not ten paces later, the soldier leading the single-file unit stopped dead in his tracks. He raised a warning fist, then knelt, examined the ground a footstep ahead, and announced: "Landmine, Lieutenant."

Flynn shot a look of alarm at Lieutenant Saunders: "Now can we turn back?"

"Mark it. We'll go around," growled the lieutenant.

"No," came a defiant voice from the ranks. "This is a suicide mission."

"It's an ambush!"—"You're gonna get us all killed!"—whisper-shouted two others.

His leadership questioned, Lieutenant Saunders stubbornly doubled down. He fired his M-16, once, straight up in the air, and bellowed: "I swear I'll shoot any coward who doesn't follow orders! Now march, motherfu—"

A second shot rang out.

Unspeakable Thing

A second shot rang out.

The final two syllables of Lieutenant Frank Saunders's angry command died on his lips. The bullet pierced his heart—the left atrium, precisely—cleanly and fatally. He was a corpse before he hit the ground.

The rest of the platoon, peculiarly, did not dive for cover. There was no need. The killshot had not come from a Viet Cong sniper.

Survival instinct can make a man do unspeakable things. One of the Americans decided a single death was necessary to save the other twenty-six lives in their band of brothers.

Linc, your father was not guilty of the murder, but he was complicit nonetheless. All those G.I. soldiers were. By not bringing the shooter—the assassin, to be truthful—to justice, it was as if every one of them pulled the trigger.

To a man, they swore allegiance to a cover-up story. This was easy to rationalize: Lieutenant Saunders was already a "dead man walking" when he insisted on heading into an ambush situation. Perhaps the hells of war made him suicidal, but he had no right to take them all to eternity with him—that was their believed justification.

Ergo, Lieutenant Franklin Johnston Saunders was flown home in a vulture-black rubber body bag and the official report read: "Bravely Killed In Action by Viet Cong sniper using captured American M-16."

Linc, your father deeply grieved Lieutenant Saunders's death. He blamed himself for not being able to talk sense into him. But what really poisoned your father's soul, what led to Post Traumatic Stress Disorder, was that if someone else had not shot the crazed lieutenant, Flynn believed in his heart he would have.

And yet, upon his homecoming Flynn seemed to have left his dragons behind, slain in the jungle. Against all odds, he resumed a happy life. He met Vanessa, fell head-over-heels in love, got married.

In reality, he had returned from war a broken man—but the fissures were hidden.

On their honeymoon in Niagara Falls, during a spectacular electrical storm, the nightmares began. Sometimes, Flynn dreamed he shot Lieutenant Saunders. Other times, he was choking the life out of a Viet Cong combatant. Repeatedly, your father woke up with his hands squeezing Vanessa's throat.

During Vanessa's pregnancy, Flynn's PTSD worsened. His jungle exposure to Agent Orange, a "tactical use" chemical defoliant a million times more potent than juglone, further repelled all peacefulness. Even awake, Flynn's inner rage could boil over. He tried to tame his dragons with alcohol, with drugs, with no success.

Fearful he might hurt Vanessa when his night terrors struck, your father began sleeping on the couch. He sleepwalked and choked her anyway. A deadbolt lock on their bedroom door lessened his nighttime anxieties, yet he knew daylight didn't provide your mom guaranteed safety from his violent episodes.

His greatest horror, Linc, was that he might harm you. This stranglehold on his conscience is why he decided he <u>must</u> leave. It was an act not of desertion, but of love. Ironic, isn't it—sacrifice one man to save two lives.

Your father sat where you do now, Linc, writing a letter trying to explain all of these things I have told you. He started and stopped, over and again, a number of times. Each try, he felt his words failed. Every letter that he threw away shared one promise to you: when he got well, he would come home.

Linc, perhaps your father has not yet healed.

~~~

In the morning, in the mental twilight between slumber and wakefulness with his head using Tamás's diary as a pillow, Lincoln unknowingly caressed the Butterfly knot.

Once more, he had a vision:

A giant raindrop fell fell fell from the heavens, striking the peak of the Continental Divide and splitting in two. One of the halves rolled downhill eastward into watersheds that eventually drain into the Atlantic Ocean. Reaching this destination, the sea was grey and cold and angry.

Gravity pulled the twin half of the split raindrop downward west, ultimately arriving at the Pacific Ocean, its waters calm beneath a sky blue as stonewashed jeans.

Linc's eyes fluttered open with an epiphany—

—he was the half headed for sunshine.

Hope

 Vintners believe the finest and heartiest grapevines grow in soil that has struggled.

This forces roots to grow deep, and branch out wide, to survive. When the rains at last arrive, these hard-tested grapevines thrive.

So, as well, it was with Linc. His childhood had been one of heat and hurt, drought and doubt, tears shed and hope foreclosed. Being taken in by the Jordan family was the warm sunshine and gentle rainfall—and loving attention—inducing him to bloom.

For each valley of sorrow Linc had traversed, he soon experienced a corresponding peak. One peak was a letter from the Dean of the English Department at Kenyon College, a small but highly respected liberal arts institution a hundred miles southwest of Cleveland.

"Over the course of my three decades as an educator," Dr. Ruby Tuttle wrote in part, "I have never before witnessed an example of higher character from a student than you displayed at the Ohio Speech Championships at which I was a judge. Without doubt, you would enrich our student body at Kenyon College. I have spoken with your principal, Mr. Rhett Kingston, who sang your praises far beyond your excellent grades. Indeed, even the circumstances behind your football suspension speak volumes about your morality. I have discussed this issue with our President, Trustees, and

Admissions Board, and we are in consensus agreement—we wish to offer you a four-year scholarship covering full tuition and housing."

Another lofty peak: Cleveland Peak High School's Class of 1987 selected Linc to be its student speaker at graduation. By good fortune, an off-duty reporter for *The Cleveland Plain Dealer* was in attendance for a niece and was so impressed by his inspirational address she told her editor about it. Two days later, the newspaper ran Linc's speech in its entirety as a guest column.

A peak rising tall as Denali had occurred a month before the commencement ceremony, in the hospital, on April 29, after Love gave birth to another daughter. Tavis, Fayth, and Linc were peering through the maternity's nursery window at the newest Jordan when another new father sidled up.

"Looks like you're a proud dad for the second time," the man told Tavis while smiling at Fayth—and ignoring Linc. It was an honest mistake to assume the white teenager was not with the Black pair. All the same, the comment stung Linc like an angry wasp.

"My second *girl*," Tavis corrected, politely yet sharply, and rested a hand on Fayth's shoulder. "I also have a boy—"

With his other hand, Tavis pulled Linc close.

"—this is *my son*, Linc."

The words and gesture wrapped themselves tightly around Linc's heart, yet Love—and Fayth—would surpass this unconditional expression that very evening.

"Sweetheart, have you settled on her name?" Tavis asked his wife as she nursed their newborn daughter in the hospital bed.

"Neither seems quite perfect," Love answered, referring to the two names they had narrowed the final choice down to. Having secretly received Fayth's blessing for her new proposal, Love proceeded: "I've been giving it a lot of thought and I think Linc should choose the name—something different through fresh eyes."

"That's a great idea!" Fayth said. "I was actually never all that crazy about Sawney or Tamara."

"Okay," Tavis confirmed. "The honor is all yours, Linc."

"You're kidding, right?" the honoree asked, feeling more nervous than he had in Weigel Hall Auditorium.

"I'm totally serious," Love said, conspiratorially squeezing Fayth's hand with a dose of tenderness.

"Give it some thought," Tavis offered. "Take a day or two—"

"I don't need more time," Linc interjected.

"Really?" Love and Tavis replied as one.

"Tell us! Tell us!" Fayth animatedly pleaded.

"It's pretty obvious," Linc began. "Y'all changed my life, saved my life really, when you took me in. You've given me so many things, not least of all a roof over my head. But honestly, your most important gifts have been love, faith and—

"—Hope."

"*H-ooohhh-pe*," Fayth sang in a test run. "I love it!"

"So do I," said Tavis.

"It's perfect," Love agreed. "Hope it is."

Opening her eyes at the sound of her mother's voice, baby Hope smiled.

Riding A Tiger

"In your dream life, what would you do for a living?" Tavis inquired shortly before Linc departed for his freshman year at Kenyon College.

"I wanna be a writer," Lincoln answered, without pause and with certitude, then added with specificity: "A novelist, actually."

"That's a mighty tall order, Abraham," allowed Tavis, using an affectionate nickname he sometimes called Linc in private.

"Worthwhile things *should* be difficult," replied Linc, his gold-flecked brown eyes twinkling with mirth, the student posturing as the teacher.

"Touché," said Tavis and, having accurately anticipated these lettered ambitions, began a prepared monologue:

"With its proud literary history, I think Kenyon is the ideal place for you. I looked it up—illustrious alumni include Robert Lowell, a two-time Pulitzer Prize-winning poet, and novelist Flannery O'Connor was a Fellow. Most famous of all—although he didn't actually study or teach there—Robert Frost made several visits to Kenyon, including his final public appearance shortly before his death in 1963 when he dedicated the school's new library."

"Cool," Linc said.

"Your dreams won't work if you don't," Tavis orated further, employing one of his many *Tav-isms.* "Don't be someone who talks about the grand castle they dream of living in someday—show me the stone blocks you laid *today*, show me the manuscript pages you wrote *today*. Remember, before being *great* you need to be *very good*, but first you must be *good*. As the philosopher Nietzsche said, *He who would learn to fly one day must first learn to stand and walk and run and climb and dance; one cannot fly into flying.* It's surely the same with writing novels—there can be no shortcuts."

Linc nodded.

"Actually, there is one shortcut," Tavis went on. "Not a shortcut so much as a proven path *less traveled by*, as Mr. Frost would say, *that makes all the difference.*"

Linc's attention was riveted.

"Some truly legendary authors learned their craft first as journalists," Tavis sermonized. "Twain and Hemingway and Steinbeck—a lot of people know they were newspaper writers. But so were Dickens, Kipling, Stephen Crane, Alex Haley, and Kurt Vonnegut to name a famous handful more.

"It makes perfect sense that journalism is an ideal apprenticeship for a novelist. By necessity, newspaper writers write *a lot*. The more you do something—anything—the better you become and the more discipline you develop. Newspaper reporters must also write *fast*. This serves as an inoculation against Writer's Block because staring at a blank page or computer screen isn't an option when you're facing a short deadline. And, vitally, journalists learn *how* to tell stories. So, words to the wise, Abraham—join Kenyon's campus newspaper."

Linc followed Tavis's guidance and distinguished himself as a staff writer for *The Kenyon Collegiate*. He also had two lengthy fiction pieces published in the prestigious *Kenyon Review* literary magazine.

As a college graduation gift, Tavis gave Linc a leather-bound edition of *The Poetry of Robert Frost* with a blue-ink inscription within:

Congratulations, Son—
Wishing you Triumphs on life's road less traveled by.
—With unconditional love and boundless pride, Tav

~~~

Linc's career road traveled to three newspapers in five years before a homecoming at *The Cleveland Plain Dealer* as a general-interest columnist.

"Writing four columns a week is like riding a tiger," Linc told Tavis, Love, Fayth and Hope around The Butterfly Table during Christmas dinner. "It's a wild thrill, but sometimes you wanna jump off—"

He took a forkful of mashed potatoes.

"—except you're afraid to let go!"

After penning the column for three years, more than six hundred wild thrill rides, Linc bravely let go of the tiger's neck fur. He had been working on a novel—three different novels, in fact, the first two losing momentum in the muddy middles before being abandoned—since graduating from Kenyon, but his newspaper job was a Sisyphean millstone affording too little time, with too much distraction, for his creative writing.

To achieve his novelist dream, Linc realized, he must pursue it with full commitment. Emulating Tamás's boldness when setting sail for America, Linc left his columnist position on the shore behind, accepted Tavis and Love's invitation to move back home, and climbed onto the back of a new tiger.

Lovebirds

 Sixteen months—and seven drafts—forward, Linc completed his polished manuscript.

Two months more, he signed with a young go-getter literary agent at a big firm in Manhattan. After rejections from nineteen publishing houses, Christmas came in July: a book deal with Random House.

Skipping one autumn to the next, The Bookworm in Cleveland Heights filled its entire front window display with Lincoln Jamison's newly released autobiographical novel: *Homeless No More: My Journey of Hope, Faith & Love.*

That very same week, on Saturday October 27, Linc began a new journey—as a husband.

Second Baptist Church of Cleveland Heights was abundantly decorated with sunflowers and jack-o'-lanterns, and featured a costume theme for the wedding party and guests alike. The bride, thanks to her October 30 birth date, always loved Halloween more than any other holiday and wished to combine its magic with this special occasion.

Three days shy of twenty-four, yet still age five at heart, the bride fairly skipped down the aisle dressed as a royal princess complete with a faux bejeweled tiara. She was more beautiful than a Frost poem, than an ocean sunset, than a child's birthday smile.

By the pipe organ's third note of "Wedding March," and the first sight of his princess bride walking towards him, Linc's vision blurred between blinks. He simply could not believe the glad fairytale his once-troubled life had been rewritten into.

"I promise to love you beyond the measure of time," the groom vowed at the altar, his heart pulsating disco-fast.

Keven, serving as Best Man and wearing a circus lion tamer's red tuxedo tails and black breeches, handed Linc the bride's ring—

—the Hungarian Opal ring.

The midnight blue-and-sunset-colored heirloom had been an early wedding gift from Aunt Veronica, she being the unidentified woman buyer in the pawnshop so many years before precisely in hopes of this blissful day.

The bride, her face in full bloom, eyes glistening like dew drops in morning sunlight, recited her handwritten vows: "My love for you extends beyond the moon, beyond the sun, beyond the stars—"

Fayth smiled gloriously at her groom.

"—and forever will."

Reverend Luther Douglass, having traveled from Detroit to perform the sacred ceremony, with great pleasure pronounced the couple "husband and wife" and they happily, and lengthily, kissed as family members and friends in the pews applauded their blessings.

The Maid of Honor, thirteen-year-old Hope—wearing a tiger-striped dress and a headband adorned with kitten ears to complement Keven's costume—handed the bridal bouquet back to her big sister. The newlyweds then danced on air down the aisle to an eclectic marbling of fiddles and African hand drums. Outside, everyone gathered as 101 butterflies were released to symbolically carry joyous wishes heavenward so as to be granted to the couple.

At the reception dinner, at the conclusion of Fayth and Linc's first dance as wife and husband—to Savage Garden's "Truly Madly Deeply"—Tavis gently clinked his wine glass with a spoon to get everyone's attention.

"From the day Fayth was born," the father of the bride toasted, "I had a wish—well, many wishes, of course. One wish was that she would grow up into a strong and beautiful, kind and generous, intelligent and lovely woman. As everyone whose life has been blessed to cross paths with Fayth knows, this all came true.

"I also wished that she would one day find a man who was *half* worthy of her. Honestly, I didn't think someone half-good-enough was possible, but our dreams should sometimes surpass our reach. Anyway, about ten years ago, my thinking changed and I *raised* my hopes. I began wishing Fayth, and Hope, too, would each one day marry men who halfway measure up to Linc."

Tavis winked at his new son-in-law, beamed at Fayth while tapping a fist on his heart, then turned to Love, holding her gaze intimately in the crowded ballroom.

"If you'll raise your glasses with me," Tavis at length rejoined, and all present obliged. "To the happy couple—

"—to the young lovebirds—

"—to Fayth and Lincoln! May your love be grounded with roots like the wondrous Pando tree and soar higher than the Giant Sequoias."

Fireworks

Their love story had surprised Fayth and Linc as much as anyone.

After all, when Linc moved into the Jordans' home he was seventeen and Fayth only ten. He was a junior in high school, she in fourth grade. The age gap between them was the Grand Canyon.

The canyon gradually shrank into a valley, then a barranca, and eventually became narrow as a trickling creek—*crick* in local parlance. By the time Fayth graduated from Ohio University in Athens, their seven-year age difference seemed insignificant. Indeed, both were in their twenties: Fayth, a 1976 bicentennial baby, was twenty-two, and Linc, a first-man-on-the-moon 1969 arrival to Earth, was twenty-nine.

But Linc had been blind all along in recognizing this contracting landscape as the seasons turned and a decade peeled away. When he moved off to college, then embarked on a newspaper career, she always remained "Little Fayth" in his eyes.

It was not until Linc moved back home, at Love and Tavis's rent-saving invitation, to focus on writing a novel that he saw Fayth in a new light. Precisely, it happened on the Sunday following her college graduation when she invited a suitor to a family dinner and Linc found himself spilling over with jealousy—

—just as Fayth had hoped, and schemed.

Indeed, she coyly orchestrated the evening in an effort to make Linc realize what she already felt certain of: they belonged together.

Linc's heart thereafter readily agreed. After a week of feeling like a schoolboy with a mad crush, he at last ignored the Monarchs flitting about in his stomach and asked Fayth if she wanted to attend a local book signing by Maya Angelou, her favorite poet and author.

"Linc-y, are you asking me on a *date*?" Fayth said, adopting a serious expression.

Fearing suddenly he had crossed a forbidden line, Linc urgently backpedaled: "A date? Um, no, of course not."

"Well, if that's the case," Fayth said, pouting theatrically with playful indignation, "then I don't think I want to go."

It was the soft nudge Linc needed.

With no need for the usual get-to-know-each-other questions of a first date, they felt like they had been sweethearts for years. Their first kiss—stolen by Linc in the back row of folding chairs set up in Waldenbooks— as Maya Angelou read from *Even the Stars Look Lonesome,* suggested a contradictory night sky.

"Fireworks," is how Fayth always described the kiss in her retellings.

"No," Linc would forever disagree, his eyes sparkling. "It was a Fourth of July grand finale."

Knowing his heart would be forever lonesome without Fayth, Linc proposed before their first official date ended.

"Yes!" she answered, "once you ask my dad for his blessing."

~~~

On the bridal night, before departing come morning for a Canadian honeymoon across the "Jordan" river in Windsor, the newlyweds stayed in their newly rented apartment in Cleveland Heights.

While their first night as wife and husband had finally arrived, their mattress and bed frame had not. In fact, none of the furniture they bought weeks earlier was delivered as scheduled on account of the store's truck being involved in a minor accident.

One piece of old furniture, however, was waiting within when Linc ceremoniously carried Fayth across the threshold. Tavis and Love had surreptitiously brought The Butterfly Table over, believing the young lovebirds should have it from the very start to ensure providence and good fortune in their shared lives together.

"We might as well spend the night at your—*our*—parents' house," Linc told Fayth, disappointed over the missing mattress. "We'll truly start our honeymoon tomorrow night—alone—in a hotel room."

Fayth, with nary a word of reply, retrieved an armful of blankets from a moving box marked BEDDING/TOWELS and layered four of them, thick and plush, atop The Butterfly Table. With a woman's seducing touch she smoothed the wrinkles and added two pillows.

Linc watched, mesmerized into immobility, for he suddenly remembered *seeing* this exact vision more than a dozen years prior. He grinned to himself, certain how the rest of this dreamy night would unfold.

At sunrise, three weeks before a urine test would show a bold plus sign, Linc knew Fayth was pregnant.

Ooooh! Ahhhh!

The obstetric technician, whose bedside manner was as chilly as the aqua-blue gel she failed to warm before squirting liberally on Fayth's expanding belly, maneuvered the ultrasound wand—circularly, upward, downward, sideways.

Before the tech zeroed in on a clear image, Linc already knew with crystal clear clairvoyance what her surprising pronouncement would be.

"Twins," he stated as fact, not a guess. "We're having twins."

The medical magic wand continued its exploration, its movements ranging smaller and smaller, then paused. The technician studied the monitor, its black-and-white image as grainy as historic footage of Neil Armstrong's first step on the lunar surface, and repositioned the wand ever so slightly. Her eyebrows arched, her lips tightened, her head turned towards the father-to-be.

"How in the world did you know your wife is carrying twins?"

"Lucky guess," Linc fibbed.

"Actually, he had a premonition," Fayth professed. "He was certain I was pregnant *with twins* before I even knew I was pregnant."

The tech, having heard her share of cockamamie prediction stories, rolled her eyes and returned to task.

"Hear that? That's the heartbeat of one of your babies," the technician reported, her frosty voice warming as the ultrasound wand focused on the first twin. "Nice and strong."

A moment later: "The other twin's heartbeat—"

The tech smiled.

"—also very strong."

Fayth and Linc's hearts danced as they listened to the amplified drumming.

"Next time you come in, I'll be able tell you their sexes," the technician offered. "If you want to know, that is—most couples do."

Fayth linked looks with Linc, making sure they remained in agreement. He shook his head, slightly, wrinkled his nose slighter still.

"We're old-fashioned," Fayth answered. "We want to be surprised."

A surprise that could not be seen by ultrasound, and that Linc had not presciently *seen* as a teen while resting his head on The Butterfly Table, was around the corner.

~~~

Fayth and Linc were lying on a navy blanket embroidered in gold with a crescent moon, sun, and galaxy of stars, a favored motif of Fayth's.

The blanket was spread on the high school football field where Linc once starred; in fact, in the same corner of the end zone where he scored a two-point conversion to win the league championship his junior year. The newlyweds gazed heavenwards as the town's Fourth of July fireworks show sparkled in all its starburst pyrotechnic glory.

The storage shed where Linc had briefly lived, homeless and lonesome before the Jordans changed everything, was gone. Its absence added to the enchantment of this sultry summer night, as did having Tavis, Love, and Hope, now fourteen, reclining on their backs on an adjacent blanket.

"*Oooh! Ahhhh! Oooooh!*" Hope murmured as three rapid-fire kaleidoscopic explosions quilted the night sky with a galaxy of shooting stars and colored comets.

"*Ooooh!*" echoed Love after another spectacular flower of rainbow-hued embers bloomed.

The Fort Sumter-like salvos continued, now without pause, illuminating the sky like a Jason Pollock painting in neon.

"*Ooooh,*" Fayth exhaled, softer. A deep breath, another exhalation, longer and louder: "*Oooooooh!*"

She was not admiring the grand finale overhead. Her water had broken. Two weeks before her due date, Fayth was in early labor.

Tavis, the former star quarterback, instantly became a blocking guard and cleared a path through the exiting throng of fireworks revelers. Love, Hope, and Linc followed closely, all helping Fayth amble half-bent-over to the car.

So quickly did Fayth's *oooohs!* and *ahhhhs!* intensify, their frequency increasing as well, that Linc insisted they rush her to the hospital without detouring home to pick up her small packed suitcase. At 11:57 p.m., less than two hours after the fireworks show ended, a new beginning: the first twin was born.

A boy.

Without delay, and likewise without difficulty, the second twin made *his* grand entrance.

Except for different birth dates—July 4 and July 5—bookended around midnight by mere minutes, the newborns shared everything, down to their DNA spirals. Indeed, the brothers were as genetically matched as two Pando tree shoots. This was a mild surprise because identical twins are about ten times more rare than fraternal twins.

Another revelation would prove far more extraordinary.

Moswen And Lemuel

 The newborn twins were like a single raindrop alighting on the peak of the Continental Divide and splitting in two, one half rolling downhill eastward and the other half traveling westward, both to sea.

One had Fayth's Black complexion, the other Linc's light Irish skin. Together, wondrously, they resembled The Butterfly Table's yin-yang symbol of white oak and deep maple where the doorknob long ago had been.

When a mixed-race couple has fraternal twins—*dizygotic* being the scientific term—where each life starts out as a separate egg fertilized by a different sperm, the odds of the two biracial babies being born with markedly different skin tones is approximately one-in-five-hundred.

With identical twins—*monozygotic*, where a single egg is fertilized by one sperm and then splits forming two identical embryos—disparate tones are almost impossible. *Almost.* Despite perfectly matching DNA, the phenomenon occurs in astronomically rare instances because skin color is determined, in varying degrees, by seven different genes working together. Sometimes this array aligns diametrically against all odds, like a thousand consecutive coin tosses coming up heads for one twin and a thousand coming up all tails for the other.

Remarkably, or perhaps not so at all, the new parents did not initially notice the striking difference in skin colors until their obstetrician mentioned the anomaly—

Fayth and Linc had been too focused counting the combined twenty tiny fingers and twenty toes.

Cradling her twin sons for the first time, one swaddled newborn in each arm, the image of a wedding present flashed to Fayth's mind—a painting by a Basquiat-influenced "graffiti" artist who, to critical acclaim, recently held his first big solo exhibition in a downtown Manhattan gallery.

The four-foot-square oil-on-canvas gift featured two large hearts, one blue and one pink, half overlapping each other like a Venn diagram with the shared intersection purple. Above the curved left top of the blue heart rested a five-pointed gold crown, as of a king. A four-pointed crown, as of a queen, adorned the top right side of the pink heart. And inside the merged purple section was a smaller three-pointed crown, optimistically signifying a young prince or princess in the couple's future one day.

"Linc-y," Fayth said from her hospital bed. "Wouldn't it be wonderful if Quentin could add a second little crown to the beautiful painting he made for us?"

Because he was born on July 4, Lemuel "Doc" Jamison's shared birth date, the firstborn was given the name Lemuel Sawney Jamison. The middle name honored Tavis and Fayth's distant relative, Sawney Jordan, the escaped slave.

The second twin was christened Moswen Thomas Jamison. Moswen is Botswanan meaning "light in color" and celebrated the fair-skinned infant's distant African roots. The middle name Thomas honored Tamás Beswick, who six generations earlier had helped Sawney reach freedom, and also means "twin" in Greek.

Linc, owing to his own racial enlightenment from living with the Jordans and most especially Tavis's fatherly influence, had further reasoning behind the boys' name selections. Specifically, for the apparent contradictory first name of each son that most people would expect to go with the opposite twin. That is to say, the Anglo-Saxon Lemuel seemed like it should have been given to the "white" son, and Moswen to the "Black" son. Purposefully as well, each twin had a contrasting middle name—African heritage *Sawney* for Lemuel and Anglo-Saxon *Thomas* for Moswen—that did stereotypically reflect their outward appearance.

Knowing full well his "Black" son would perpetually face racism due to his skin color, Linc's hope was that a "white" first name would in some small way lessen this hurdle as far as first impressions when giving his name over the phone or by résumé.

No less importantly, Linc and Fayth wanted their light-skinned "white" son to experience—even if only when giving his Black-sounding first name on the phone or on a resume—what his darker-complexioned brother went through daily in in-person interactions. The parents hoped this would further braid the boys together, tight as a twisted-ladder DNA double helix.

There was one other visible difference between the twins, a disparity that would prove imperceptible to everyone except immediate family—Lemuel had Linc's smile, Moswen had Fayth's.

One Bike, Two Boys

As youngsters, Lemuel and Moswen remained innocently colorblind to the conspicuous difference in their appearances.

In first grade, the twins had different teachers. One afternoon, Moswen's class was to have a spelling test for which he forgot to study. Lemuel, having scored nineteen out of twenty on the very same list of words earlier that morning, had an idea.

"Mos, let's switch classes and I'll take the spelling test for you," Lem said on the playground before the bell clanged marking the end of lunch recess. "I'll even get *yellow* right this time with *two* L's."

"But what if we get caught?"

"We won't if we swap sweatshirts," replied Lem, wearing blue to Mos's green.

"Okay, let's do it," Mos said, both boys laughing, truly believing that since they were identical twins their teachers would be unable to tell them apart.

Naturally, Miss Mac and Ms. Y—as the students more easily called Ms. Yasukochi and Miss McCart—were not fooled. They marched the twins out of their respective classrooms and across the hallway to make a one-for-one Prisoners-Of-War-like exchange. Moswen and Lemuel were dumbfounded.

"How'd you know?" the POWs asked in twinly unison.

"That's top secret," Miss Mac said, feigning sternness.

"Teachers have special superpowers," Ms. Y added, suppressing a laugh. "So don't ever try another switcheroo."

The incident was no joking matter to Linc and Fayth. While the twins' tomfoolery indeed made them smile, their own naivety in believing they could shield the boys from the realities of their contrasting skin tones gave them serious pause.

Fayth and Linc had long grown calloused to society's monochrome vision and ignorant, chilly, even downright racist remarks regarding their interracial marriage. But acrid comments about the twins from strangers, even worse from people they knew, always struck raw nerves:

"Are you blind? Look at them—they aren't twins."

"Obviously there was a mix-up at the hospital and they sent you home with one wrong baby."

"Wake up, Linc—Fayth had an affair."

"Mos must be Linc's favorite and you must love Lem more, right Fayth?"

And so on and on.

While seething internally, Fayth and Linc tried to maintain their composure outwardly in reply—albeit often with half-veiled causticity.

"We love them both equally and unconditionally," became Fayth's stock response, while sardonically confessing: "Sometimes I wonder how they can be identical twins since their *personalities* are so different."

"Mysteriously wonderful things happen and this is one of them," Linc routinely responded, adding wryly: "Honestly, the only way I can only tell them apart is that Mos is right-handed and Lem is a lefty."

One innocent remark surprisingly stung Linc so sharply it made him recoil and retort venomously.

It was a summer weekend shortly after the twins turned nine. Lemuel's new birthday bike got a flat tire, thanks to an exposed nail on a wooden jumping ramp the boys had built. After repairing their ramp, Linc sat in the driveway patching the punctured inner tube. Meanwhile, the twins were riding together double on Moswen's new matching stingray—Mos pedaling while standing, Lem on the banana seat clutching his brother's hips for balance.

As the twins rode off down the street, a young mother pushing a stroller passed them coming towards the Jamisons' house. Although Linc had never seen her in the neighborhood before, he offered a friendly hello.

"Hi," she replied, smiling. "I just saw something that warmed my heart."

"What was it?" Linc asked.

"I saw a white boy riding double on the same bike with a Black boy," she noted. "They were having such fun together—it was wonderful."

Perhaps it was the aggregation of a thousand past insensitive comments about the twins; perhaps it was a flashback to his racially charged fight and suspension from the football team in high school; or perhaps it was a flashing vision of the future and the heavy crosses to bear that awaited his sons, especially Lem, as they grew into men. Most likely, it was all this and more that made Linc bristle.

"What would be wonderful," he said, his tone as caustic as chlorine, "would be if you had simply seen *two boys* riding double and having fun together."

Stonecatchers

"Where're we going, Grandpa?"

"It's a surprise," Tavis told his nine-old twin grandsons riding in the backseat.

"Give us a hint," Moswen pleaded.

"What're we gonna do when we get there?" Lemuel joined in.

"Catch stones," Tavis said, sunshine in his voice. "You're gonna be Stonecatchers."

"That sounds dangerous," Lem said warily.

"And fun!" Mos animatedly added.

Tavis glanced in the rearview mirror at the boys; their smiles contagiously jumped to his lips.

"Grandpa, are *you* a Stonecatcher?"

"I try to be," Tavis said.

"Do you catch the stones with a baseball mitt?"

"We didn't bring our mitts."

"You won't need your baseball gloves," Tavis assured.

"Who throws the stones?"

"Do they throw 'em hard?"

"Are the rocks big?"

The questions came like pitches in an automated batting cage with too little time between for answers.

"Time out, time out!" Tavis interrupted. "Listen up and I'll tell you all about the mysteries of being a Stonecatcher."

Mos and Lem leaned forward against the restraint of seatbelts, eager to hear a magical tale.

"Stonecatchers don't actually catch stones," their grandpa began. "Well, I suppose a long, long time ago they did and that's where the name comes from. When someone hurled a stone at a person who was unable to defend him or herself, the Stonecatcher jumped in and caught the flying rock.

"But nowadays a Stonecatcher is someone who helps another person who is defenseless or in need—like protecting them from a bully, or buying a homeless person a meal, or donating blood to save someone who's ill. You can think of a Stonecatcher as a Good Samaritan.

"Lem—Mos—you boys come from a long proud heritage of Stonecatchers."

"We do?" they said in stereo.

"Oh, yes," Tavis resumed. "Your many *greats*-great-grandfather, Dr. Lemuel Jamison, was a Stonecatcher who adopted identical twins when they lost their mother *and* father. He had actually saved the twins' lives when they were born and thus they were named Jamis and Lemuel—your namesake, Lem—in his honor.

"Those twins' real father, Tamás—that's where your middle name comes from, Mos—was a Stonecatcher by helping your five-times-great-grandfather, Sawney Jordan, escape from slavery on the Underground Railroad. In truth, Tamás was the ultimate Stonecatcher because he gave his life safeguarding Sawney.

"Sawney, in turn, was a fearless Stonecatcher because he swam into bullet fire trying to rescue Tamás who had been shot. While he couldn't save his friend, Sawney did save Tamás's diary, which is how we know about their shared bravery—and about how our family roots are entwined reaching back to those two heroic men.

"Yes, the Jamisons and Jordans have been filled with Stonecatchers. Your Grandpa Flynn was a Stonecatcher for America in the Vietnam War. And Grandma Love was a Stonecatcher for your daddy when he was young and lost and needed a roof over his head—and, most of all, needed some love.

"I'm definitely proud of the Stonecatchers your parents are. They're always helping others in big ways and little ways—sometimes it's the small acts that turn out to be the biggest ones.

"For example, it's hard to imagine a simple *Hello, how're you doing today?* being important. But to someone who's having a bad day, that small gesture can mean the world.

"I read a story about a boy who was planning to commit suicide because he had no friends. That very day at school, during lunch, a classmate saw him sitting off by himself and went over and ate with him. They had a nice conversation and the dejected boy changed his mind because he no longer felt so lonesome. You see, being a Stonecatcher doesn't always require bravery—sometimes kindness is all that's needed.

"Mos—Lem—I expect you boys to be Stonecatchers. I want you to go sit with the person who's all alone. I want you to cheer for the teammate who rarely gets off the bench. I want you to stand up to the bully who picks on others.

"And right now, I want you to help me paint the kitchen for a lovely elderly lady. Her name is Jewell. That's how we'll be Stonecatchers today."

Back Bending

"I'm proud of you," Tavis told his grandsons on the drive home. "You were both good Stonecatchers today."

In chorus: "Thanks, Grandpa."

"Did you notice Miss Jewell stooping a little?" Tavis continued, picking up the thread from his earlier lesson. "That tells me she's been a champion Stonecatcher herself."

"Maybe she's just old and frail," said Lem.

"Yes, Miss Jewel has lived a long life," Tavis agreed. "But the reason she's bent slightly is because she carries a heavy weight around her neck. You see, each time you act as a Stonecatcher you earn a small stone bead. These beads are invisible and go on an invisible Stonecatcher necklace."

The twins listened, raptly, as if their grandpa were reading a Harry Potter tale aloud.

"When you're young, the necklace is so light you don't even notice it. But as you grow older, if you collect enough stone beads, you feel the weight grow. Miss Jewell, I'm guessing, has been such a selfless Stonecatcher that she wears three, maybe even four, necklaces, all filled and heavy, and that's why she's stooped over.

"I hope when I'm Miss Jewell's age," Tavis concluded, "and when you boys are old, a long, long time from now, our backs will be proudly bent like hers."

~~~

On the drive home from Miss Jewell's, red-and-blue lights flashed in the rearview mirror. Tavis, as he had done untold times since turning sixteen, pulled over promptly, rolled down his window, held his hands at ten-and-two on the steering wheel.

"License and registration," the police officer commanded robotically.

Tavis did as told—not only as told by the cop, but as told when he was young by his father: *Always be extra polite to the police; always say "Yes, sir—no, sir"; and never ever make a sudden move.*

"Taillight's out," the officer said, sparsely, tersely.

"I didn't know my blinker was broken, sir," Tavis, with dinner-party politeness, replied. "I'll get it fixed right away."

"I said your *taillight's* broken—don't you listen?" the cop snapped, seemingly taking perverse pleasure in humiliating Tavis in front of the two boys. He walked back toward his squad car, stopped en route, drew a baton from his belt—

—THWACK!

Crackle.

The cop returned with a trumped-up speeding ticket, and a final dose of hate.

"Best not forget to get that busted light fixed real quick now—

"*—tiger.*"

Tiger is not what the cop snarled under his breath, it is what Tavis made himself hear so as not to take the racist bait, lose his temper in defiance, and wind up in jail—or worse.

Arriving home, before they got out of the car, Grandpa Tavis addressed the disquieting incident.

"Lem, because you look more like me—that is to say, *Black*—while Mos looks like your daddy, this is most important for you to hear. No matter how wrongly a policeman treats you, no matter how angry you get or how humiliated you might feel, you must always, *always,* remain polite and calm. With ninety-nine percent of the police you've got nothing to fear—but the other one percent, well, your life's at risk. Martin Luther King, Jr. said, *A man can't ride your back unless it's bent.* Dr. King was as great and wise a man who's ever lived, but I'm telling you that during an encounter with the police—bend your back. I'm sure Sawney bent his back when he was ridden ruthlessly by his slavemaster—"

Tavis turned, fixing his eyes on Lem.

"—but he never let anyone *break* his back. When the time was right, Sawney stood tall and brave and escaped—that was the bravest victory of all."

That night, in their shared bedroom before falling asleep, Mos made a hushed request: "Lem, promise me you'll always be as brave as Grandpa is if a policeman stops you."

The room seemed to grow as pitch dark and muted and cold as outer space.

"Lem—" Mos said anew.

A reply at last came, Lem's voice weighted with ache: "You think Grandpa was brave today?"

"Super brave," Mos asserted. "He didn't bend for himself—he was worried about us in the backseat. Grandpa was *our* Stonecatcher."

LeMos

In the hospital's nursery, Lemuel and Moswen had cried without pause until a wise and kindly nurse finally placed them in the same bassinet. Simple as that, they went straight to sleep.

Upon their homecoming, the twins spent all of ten minutes in separate cribs before Fayth gave in to their wailing complaints—into the garage went the second crib.

Graduating to beds, the boys would begin each night in separate *bedrooms* only to wind up sharing one or the other's *bed* come morning. After months of thinking they would outgrow this routine, Linc relented and moved both beds into one room. He figured the arrangement was temporary—

—but misjudged the twins' ironclad bond. Lem and Mos—"LeMos" as Fayth and Linc often singularly referred to them—shared a bedroom all the way through high school.

LeMos stubbornly shared one more very important thing. Despite being born straddling midnight on July 4 and July 5, since age four the twins insisted on celebrating their birthdays together with one joint party on Independence Day. The choice between dates was easy— they happily opted for a parade and hotdogs and fireworks.

Fooling friends and classmates about their unified birthday was no problem, but there was no deceiving the Ohio Bureau of Motor Vehicles when the twins turned sixteen. Lemuel's driver's license listed his date of birth as 7-4-2002 and Moswen's DOB read 7-5-2002.

Junior year at Cleveland Peak High, the twins were driving home from school following a cross-country meet. Lem had finished second overall in the varsity race, and Mos third, while placing one-two for the Cougars. By edging Mos, per their private ongoing bet, Lem won the right to drive home.

Exiting the school parking lot, Lem flicked his left blinker on and waited until traffic was clear both ways. At the end of the block he obeyed the stop sign fully, cautiously scanned for cars and pedestrians, and was accelerating appropriately when a police cruiser flashed its blue-and-red twirling lights. It marked the fourth time the twins had been pulled over, together, in the fourteen months since getting their licenses—*all* when Lem was driving, *never* with Mos behind the steering wheel.

Lem dutifully handed his driver's license to the police officer and when asked who the passenger was respectfully told the truth: "My twin brother, sir."

Knowing he had been lied to, the cop demanded Mos's driver's license as well. Seeing the discrepancy in the dates of birth, he grew visibly agitated.

"Twins, huh? You don't much look like twins. "You're *Black*—"

He eyeballed Lem through mirrored sunglasses, then gestured with a head tilt at Mos.

"—and he's *white*."

A smirk.

"And you have *different* birthdays."

Lem had promised Mos he would always courageously bend his back, like Grandpa Tavis had, if need be to a cop. Instead of biting his tongue, however, he sat up ramrod straight and spoke up.

"I was born a few minutes before midnight, sir," Lem explained evenly. "And Mos was born eleven minutes later, just past midnight. We really are twins with different birth dates—just barely."

The cop removed his sunglasses to better reexamine the two licenses, studied the anxious faces in the front seat, both boys wearing T-shirts emblazoned with a giant *C* and *ougars oss ountry*, then said: "That's a pretty cool birth story. You actually do look a lot alike. Anyway, the reason I stopped you is your brake lights are out."

"It's our mom's car, sir," Lem offered, respectfully. "I'm sure she didn't know."

"Pop open the trunk," said the officer, before walking around the rear of the car. He bent down out of sight, poked around inside, then commanded: "Press your foot on the brake."

Lem, glancing quizzically at Mos, one eyebrow hovering, did as told.

"That's good," came the officer's voice, muffled. He reappeared at the driver's window: "They're working now—just a loose connection. I've seen it before. By the way, how'd your cross-country meet go?"

"Our team won, sir," Lem answered, buoyed with relief. "Individually, we were second and third overall."

"Congratulations," the cop said, adding with a mirthful grin: "But please drive home slower than you ran in your race."

Be Like Kenny

 Senior year, Lemuel and Moswen's high school cross-country season rolled on like a hero's parade.

The twins established themselves not only as the two best distance runners in Cuyahoga County, but among the top handful in the entire Buckeye State. The swiftest runner in their shared bedroom, meanwhile, seemed to change race by race by only a stride or three.

Led by LeMos, the Cleveland Peak High Cougars clinched the league title before the final regular-season meet. After practice, the twin co-captains knocked on Coach Jimmy Hart's gym office door.

"Coach, we've got a proposal," Mos said, straight to the point.

"I'm listening."

"It's actually a favor," Lem interjected conspiratorially. "Not for us—for Kenny."

~~~

Kenny Alpine was a fellow senior who spent four seasons on the junior varsity.

All that time he never missed a practice, never missed a meet, and never finished a single spot ahead of dead last.

Kenny had mild cerebral palsy.

With his right foot twisted slightly outward, resulting in a permanent limp, and because his left hand was frozen in a semi-claw, people often assumed Kenny also had an intellectual disability. To the contrary, he was a valedictorian contender. When Mos and Lem struggled with Precalculus as juniors, Kenny's patient tutoring helped them both earn B-pluses.

Mos and Lem had befriended Kenny long before Precalculus. First day as freshmen, the twin Stonecatchers saw Kenny sitting alone in the cafeteria and asked if they could join him. The three were lunch companions, and fast friends, ever since.

LeMos encouraged, cajoled, and finally flat-out insisted that Kenny join the cross-country squad. Unlike every other sport on campus, it had no roster cuts. If you came daily to practice, and gave an honest effort, you made the team.

Kenny did not just make the team—he made the team better. Skinny as an old man's arthritic finger, he was a role model of grit and perseverance. Even though Coach Hart allowed him to do less, Kenny steadfastly completed every speed interval, every long run, every single mile his more physically blessed teammates did. Often, Kenny belatedly finished his workout in falling darkness.

Early on, Coach Hart would dismiss the rest of the team to go home, but Mos and Lem—exclusively—without fail stuck around until Kenny determinedly finished. It was one of the reasons the twins became the first freshmen varsity captains in the program's history.

More than by words, leadership is done by deed and by example. As the moon waned, then waxed full again, a couple other runners began joining LeMos in waiting for Kenny; a few more stayed; eventually the entire team collectively lingered. Kenny's fortitude was so inspiring that instead of complaining about tough workouts, the Cougar runners dug down deeper and asked Coach to work them even harder.

Be Like Kenny became the cross-country team's mantra.

Senior season, *Be Like Kenny* was printed on the Cougars' team T-shirts and sweatshirts.

Being like Kenny required more than running hard in practice and giving your last ounce of mettle in races. Being like Kenny also meant hollering yourself hoarse while urging on teammates. Although he brought up the rear in every JV race, Kenny was always the blue-ribbon teammate at cheering for the varsity. For all this, and more, LeMos felt a calling to catch a stone.

~~~

"Coach, I want to sit out Saturday's race and let Kenny take my place," Lem proposed.

"He's never run varsity and it's his final chance," Mos added. "He deserves it. We've already clinched the championship so it won't affect the league standings."

"That's a generous gesture," Coach Hart said. "But I don't feel it's right to rest a runner from a race except for medical reasons."

"What if we say Lem has a sore foot?" Mos offered.

"No," Coach Hart asserted. "When he runs faster than ever in the postseason, everyone'll know it was a lie."

"Come on, Coach—" Lem pleaded.

"—for Kenny," Mos underscored earnestly.

"I said no lying about an *injury*," Coach Hart reiterated, lacking sternness. "But I'd surely believe you Saturday morning, Lem, if you told me you had a sick stomach."

Forty-Eight Stonecatchers

 "To your marks—" the race director directed.

Forty-nine varsity runners, in as perfect choreographed synchronicity as the Radio City Rockettes performing high leg kicks, each took one step forward, shoulders rubbing, and toed the chalk starting line for the season's final seven-team cross-country league race.

Lemuel wriggled his right shoe, his push-off foot, securely into the dew-dampened grass while Moswen—in a change of plan—watched from the sidelines.

"Get set—"

The runners crouched as one, ninety-eight legs locked and loaded, all ears alert, every face focused.

BLARE!

Kenny bolted to the front like a spooked jackrabbit.

"*Whoa!*" warned Lem, a stride behind Kenny's right shoulder. "Pace yourself, buddy. We've got a *long* way to go."

Surging adrenaline overpowered the cautionary advice and Kenny, his limp lubricated by excitement, continued sprinting as if it were a hundred-meter dash instead of the 3.1-mile varsity distance.

Due to ongoing construction of new restrooms, the cross-country course had been altered. Instead of an opening half-mile loop around the grassy area in full view of spectators, the route veered into the woods after only two hundred meters. The runners would remain out of sight until reemerging for the same two hundred meters coming back to the starting line. They would then retrace the circuit.

Kenny disappeared into the woods on the first lap with a twenty-meter lead over everyone except Lem. None of the coaches batted an eye for they had all seen overly enthused novice runners enjoy a brief moment in the limelight before slowing to a defeated shuffle.

"Look at Kenny go," Coach Jimmy Hart marveled, to no one in particular. "Good for him. I just hope he doesn't get lapped on account of his happy foolishness."

When the lead runner finally—*Was the course miss-measured?* everyone had begun to wonder—emerged from the woods, jaws dropped. Kenny's cerebral palsy-related limp had returned, he was sucking desperately for each breath, and yet no one—not even Lem, still on his heels—had passed him.

Coaches and spectators eyed one another, all thinking the same thing: *What in the world is going on?*

Answer: the true league final had been an underground event Friday morning at six o'clock before school.

LeMos hatched the plan a week earlier and surreptitiously shared it with the other schools' team captains: *Let's hold a secret race the day before the league final and then we'll all finish in the exact same order—except with Kenny replacing the Cougars' top Friday morning finisher—at Saturday's official meet.*

So wholly respected were Mos and Lem, and so widely admired was Kenny, the other captains all jumped onboard.

Mos edged Lem to win the clandestine race and thus secured a first-place finish for Kenny the next day—and secured his own feigned food poisoning.

~~~

Kenny exited the woods on the second loop still in the lead, still limping, still huffing—and smiling like a kid at a county fair.

As he hobbled the closing two hundred meters, the cheering was so thunderous that birds flushed out of the treetops. Despite complete exhaustion that caused his posture to become nearly as contorted as his claw-like left hand, Kenny managed to flash a "thumbs-up" sign with his right hand.

Crossing the finish line, the winner, having set a Personal Record by more than two minutes, collapsed to the grass and promptly vomited. Forty-eight Stonecatchers followed in the same order they had finished the previous day—although each about fifteen minutes slower this time—and enveloped the victor in a vortex of joy.

That his win was fixed did not lessen the thrill for Kenny. If anything, the grand orchestration made his "victory" all the more meaningful. And not just for Kenny.

Lemuel was the individual champion in the state meet that season and ran competitively all four years in college. He would go on to run in the U.S. Olympic Team Trials Marathon and later win a coveted sub-twenty-four-hour finisher's silver belt buckle at the legendary Western States 100-Mile Endurance Run.

Yet when asked to name his most memorable race, Lem forever replied: "League finals my senior season in high school when I finished second behind Kenny Alpine."

Art Nite

Mos had zero desire to enter the high school talent show his senior year.

After all, he had not participated as a freshman, sophomore, or junior—and for good reason: he did not play the piano or guitar, or even the cowbell or kazoo. Nor could he sing or juggle.

A stand-up comedy routine was a possibility because Mos's joke telling was legendary among his friends. Unfortunately, he was the king of corny dad jokes. Among his favorites:

What's the best kind of music to listen to when fishing? . . . Something catchy.

Groan.

Another fish quip: *Where do fish keep their money? . . . In a riverbank.*

Gr-o-o-an.

What did the T-Rex use to cut wood? . . . A dino-saw.

Gr-o-o-o-an.

What's the best bird to work for a construction company? . . . A crane.

Gr-o-o-o-o-an.

Birds again: *Why don't seagulls fly over the bay? . . . Because then they'd be bagels.*

"Bay gulls, get it?" Mos explained when greeted by his friends' pained silence.

While both twins were enormously popular, Lemuel was the one who had the aura of a movie star. When he walked across campus, or entered a classroom or the cafeteria, *Hey, Lem!* and *Lem!-u!-el!* and similar greetings of adoration rained down upon him like tossed rice on newlyweds leaving the church after their wedding.

Moswen, on the other hand, was constantly showering his classmates with rice, so to speak, always saying *hi* to them first, usually by name, and asking how they were doing. It was no act. He was not like a phony politician glad-handing for votes; Mos was genuinely interested in others. He knew which birds had broken tail feathers and went out of his way to offer them thoughtful, even healing, words. Lem was friendly and kind to a high degree, but Mos was the patron saint of inclusion. Empathy was woven into the cloth of his being. In his soul, Moswen was a stonecatcher.

It was this virtue that made Mos sign up for the talent show, the motivational seed having been planted a month earlier at "Art Nite."

Mos loved making art because it afforded the same meditative escape running did, albeit painting was easier on the lungs, and he felt honored and thrilled to have one of his pieces from class—a pair of running shoes, the soles worn ragged from hundreds of miles and a hole emerging by the pinky toe, laying haphazard on the floor below a locker room bench—selected for the show.

Jeffrey Spencer, meanwhile, without question the most gifted artist in Mos's class, had a series of three pieces on display in the show. Each painting was bigger than the previous one, like Russian nesting dolls, with the largest, in acrylic on a four-by-eight-foot plywood panel, depicting a heart, anatomical not emoji-like, engulfed by flames; the burning heart was inside a knife-stabbed body;

all of which was inside a barbed-wire brain within a skull. Jeffrey's two smaller images, oils on canvas, were no closer to rainbows and sunshine.

Pamela Post—"Ms. P.P." she was affectionately, and humorously, called—encouraged Jeffrey, as she did each and every one of her students, to express themselves without constraint. She thought his pieces were dark, yes, but also powerful and brilliant.

Unfortunately, Principal Maxine Sowerwood was as dour as a Dickens character, and sometimes as malevolent. In private, students callously called her "Blinky" on account of a chronic dry-eye condition, or "Ol' Sourface." As both judge and jury, she deemed Jeffrey's exhibited works to be "disturbing," "frightening," and "unsuitable" for a high school art show.

Ms. Post passionately stood up for Jeffrey, but she was new to the school, relatively young and greatly overmatched, and lost the battle. Less than five minutes into "Art Nite," under Ol' Sourface's fiat, Jeffrey's paintings were covered—censored—with old dry-splattered drop cloths and he was told to meet with the school counselor the next morning.

Moments after Jeffrey stormed out of the art show, Mos, with his running shoes on canvas tucked under his arm, also made an early exit from the cafeteria and raced through the hallways after him.

Poetry

"That was brutal," Moswen called out to Jeffrey in the hallway on "Art Nite."

The artist of the banned paintings ignored him and kept walking away, head hanging, feet dragging.

"Totally unfair," Mos tried again, his double-time steps closing the gap in half.

Again no response.

"Come on, Jeffrey—wait up."

Mos caught up and pumped Jeffrey's breaks with a tug on his backpack.

"Stop for a sec."

Jeffrey acquiesced, but did not turn around.

"Dude, what just happened was total bullshit," Mos said, still from behind, then stepped around in front to be face to face with his classmate. "You're crazy talented. Everyone in class knows it—Ms. P.P. certainly does. She's *soooo* pissed at Blinky. You should've seen her. For such a chill lady who's always quoting Rumi, she's got one helluva potty mouth."

Jeffrey, noticing the painting of the running shoes, cocked his head.

"If your stuff can't be in the show," Mos said in answer to the nonverbal question, "there's no way in hell mine belongs."

Jeffrey said nothing. Silence descended and lingered and lengthened until Mos, at last, addressed the uncomfortable thing he felt he must: "Be honest with me, J-Man—should I be worried about you? You know, like are your paintings a cry for help? Are you thinking of hurting yourself?"

"You wouldn't understand," Jeffrey muttered.

"Try me."

"Look, Mos, you're a cool guy and I like you, but you've never felt invisible. Everyone knows you and likes you. Me, on the other hand, if I didn't come to school tomorrow no one would miss me—"

He scuffed at the tile floor with the toe of his hiking boot, a boot that by appearances had endured countless rocky trails, muddy streams, mountain miles.

"—if I didn't come home tonight, no one would miss me either."

"If you didn't come to school I'd miss you," Mos interjected. "I mean it."

"Yeah, that's probably true—you've always been cool to me," Jeffrey conceded. His expression remained icy, but his voice warmed a few degrees: "Hey, if Ol' Sourface thinks my paintings are dark, she should get a load of my poems."

"You write poetry?"

"I dabble."

"Can I read some?"

"Nah." Jeffrey shook his head. "I write just for me."

"Come on," Mos nudged. "I won't tell anyone—not even Lem."

Jeffrey appeared unmoved, yet did not move. After a stretch of consideration, he shrugged off his backpack, unzipped it, dug around, withdrew a composition book. The cover, marbled black and white, was as battered as his boots and stained with paint splatters, or spilled salsa, or both. A hundred pages thick, most were already filled.

"Give it back in class tomorrow," Jeffrey said, handing it over.

Tomorrow? Mos smiled at this. It meant he would not have to worry about Jeffrey tonight.

~~~

"You weren't kidding—your stuff's pretty damn dark."

Mos lingered a beat at Jeffrey's easel, then added: "Can I ask you a favor?"

Jeffrey's forehead creased.

Mos forged forward.

"I want to sing an original song in the talent show. The problem is, I have no idea how to write lyrics. But one of your poems would be perfect—"

Mos grinned slyly.

"—except I don't want Blinky yanking me off the stage for too much gloom and doom. So I was thinking, maybe you could flip-flop a poem, maybe the one *This Is How It Is*, by changing all the hate and darkness into love and lightness."

Jeffrey, without comment, flipped through the pages of his notebook until he found it:

This Is How It Is

This is how it is—
invisibleness and self-loathing grow
sometimes they fade, but you just know
they will reappear, oftentimes even stronger.

This is how it is—
forlornness flows and ebbs
just when we think we know
someone will stay, is when they go.

This is how it is—
we can only live lonely
love will never fit us snug as a glove
glowing in our heart like stars above.

This is how it is—
your broken heart begins to heal
when her whisper tells you "our love is real"
but for me that will never be how it is.

Talent Show

Moswen loved Jeffrey's revised poem and strode ahead with his plan.

Even though he usually ate lunch outside, in The Quad, with his running teammates, this day Mos ventured into the cafeteria in search of Lisle.

Lisle, pronounced *Lyle*, was short for *Little Island* which contracted to *Li'l Isle*, which shortened further to *Li'sle*, and finally to *Lisle*. Her dad, she explained, was creatively inspired by her being born on tiny Chappaquiddick Island near Cape Cod.

A year earlier, Lisle would have been eating at The Band Table. But after her father died over the summer, she quit band and quit going to church and basically quit on herself. Her flip-flops gave way to Army boots; her blonde hair was now Goth black, the ends dipped in fuchsia; coal-dust grey lipstick matched her general mood.

It was cancer that took Lisle's dad's life. Mos learned this painful truth when their Biology class was studying Charles Darwin; that during his famous expedition on the *HMS Beagle* he had discovered a parasitic wasp that laid eggs inside a live caterpillar, and the hatched grubs would then eat the host caterpillar, alive, from the inside. This event, Darwin wrote, caused him to challenge his belief in God; this caused Lisle to break into tears in class. When Mos tried to comfort her, she sobbingly said malignant tumor had eaten her dad's body alive from the inside and that even God didn't love her.

~~~

"Hi, Lisle. I've got a favor to ask," Mos began now. "I've never been in the school talent show, so I figure it's now or never. Anyway, I was wondering—if I gave you some lyrics could you write the music, a melody or whatever you call it, to go with them?"

"I *could*," Lisle said, sarcastically.

Mos smiled: "*Would* you?"—a beat—"Please."

She took a bite of pizza, pepperoni, the best meal the cafeteria served, chewed, considered the request, swallowed, then answered: "Okay. But only so I can watch you make a fool of yourself."

Mos laughed and handed over Jeffrey's poem: "Mega thanks. I owe you."

One final puzzle piece still needed to fit in place.

Mos asked Mimi, a girl every bit as shy as she was gifted as a vocalist, to be his singing coach so he might not totally humiliate himself onstage. If Mimi were to enter the talent show, which she never had, she would be the brightest star of the night. Alas, she sang only in choir—and maybe the shower, a thought that momentarily jump-started Mos's teen hormones.

Every school day thereafter, after cross-country practice and before dinnertime, Mos met Mimi in her garage for lessons. On the eve of the talent show, she joked: "I must be the world's worst vocals coach because honestly, Mos, you still can't hold a tune to save your life."

"I'm totally gonna get booed," he agreed, lightheartedly. "But you'll be there giving me moral support, right?"

"I wouldn't miss it."

~~~

By chance, not by merit, Mos was the closing act.

"It's not too late to change your mind," Lemuel cajoled when Moswen's on-stage at-bat arrived. "Otherwise, this may turn out worse than when we swapped sweatshirts for the spelling test."

Mos smiled, showing nary a trace of nervousness, and the Master of Ceremonies—Lem—went back out to the mic and announced: "Looks like we've saved the *worst* for last."

Following the playful wisecrack, Lem's timbre carried unmistakable pride: "Give it up for my brother, Mos, performing an original song titled *This Is How It Is.*"

Generous applause, applause that surely would not return after his performance, greeted Mos as he strode confidently onstage. He carried a guitar—"Mos plays guitar?" everyone on the track team seemed to whisper in sync—and upon reaching center stage adjusted the height of the microphone, making it a little too low, but perhaps out of self-preservation he did not want his voice fully amplified.

There was no turning back now. Standing in the spotlight in the packed auditorium, Mos looked out at the sea of familiar people, many of them inching forward in their seats with each passing second, took a deep breath, and began—

This Is How It Is

 "This song—"

Mos was cut off by the piercing *screeeech!* of microphone feedback.

"This song," he began anew in the packed auditorium, "was written by the very talented artist, *and poet*, Jeffrey Spencer. J-Man, please come join me for moral support."

Heads turned, a scattering of hands clapped politely, and Jeffrey, visibly reticent, made his way onstage. Principal Sowerwood, seated in the front row, dead center, stiffened in posture, her blinking eyes narrowing to make her taut face seem even more Dickensian.

"Lisle Barney deserves recognition for writing music for Jeffrey's lyrics," Mos said next. "Get up here, Lisle."

As Lisle walked down a side aisle, then up five narrow steps, Mos continued: "And lastly, Mimi Sherman, my very patient vocals coach, come on up!"

Mos spotted Mimi, saw her shake her head *no, no, no* to which he nodded *yes, yes, yes*, smiled, and pleaded: "Please, Mimi. I'm not going to start without you by my side."

Mimi relented and stood with Lisle and Jeffrey. Gentle applause dissipated like frozen breath in a breeze and Mos, as poised and confident as if he were standing at the starting line of a cross-country race, strummed his guitar—twice, sourly—then confessed: "I can't play this worth a lick, and my singing is even worse."

He stepped away from the microphone stand, huddled with his three classmates, whispered, then unshouldered the guitar strap and handed the instrument to Lisle—

—guided Mimi to the mic—

—gave Jeffrey a bear hug—

—and walked to the wings, stage left.

Mimi, rooted in place in the squeezing grip of anxiety, closed her eyes and kept them closed for a long while as more than a thousand people empathetically held their collective breath. What they did not know was that Mimi was imagining herself in church, in choir, in full song at the altar.

Opening her eyes, Mimi winked at Lisle, who took it as her cue to play the opening chord; Jeffrey and Mos exchanged smiles; and Mimi's voice took flight:

> *This is how it is—*
> *love, once invisible, can appear*
> *sometimes it decides to stay*
> *other times just fades away.*
>
> *This is how it is—*
> *love will ebb and it will flow*
> *at times it hurts, but this just know*
> *love tested can stronger grow.*
>
> *This is how it is—*
> *love's flame can burn fickle*
> *just when we think we know*
> *they'll stay, is when they go.*
>
> *This is how it is—*
> *we can live lonely thinking*
> *love will never fit us like a glove*
> *nor twinkle like the stars above.*

This is how it is—
your broken heart begins to heal
when she whispers to you "our love is real"
yes, yes, this is how it will be.

After the final note was played and last lyric emoted, even Ol' Sourface stood and applauded her palms red.

Can one small deed by a stonecatcher have a big impact? Here are three answers: Mimi, suddenly inoculated against stage fright, would go on to become a grandly successful folk-pop indie recording artist. Lisle would run her own youth music academy. As for Jeffrey, the letter he sent Fayth and Linc a year later avowed to how wholly Moswen affected him. In green India ink, in the steady hand of an artist, it read:

Dear Mr. & Mrs. Jamison,

You raised two amazing sons, but I know Mos better and I'd just like to tell you he is the nicest ("young man" is scratched out) *person I've ever met. I was spiraling down to a very dark and scary place until Mos reversed the powerful riptide. He was a beacon in my storm, a lighthouse guiding me out of danger. He helped me transform from a gloomy mess of a poet and artist who hated himself into someone who finally has self-worth. You see, a lot of my poetry and paintings were about my own self-loathing—until your son suggested I change the words and themes from "hate" to "love." He saved my life that day. Mos isn't just a golden human being, he's pure platinum.*

Warmly,
Jeffrey Spencer

Special Gift

All who knew Lemuel and Moswen knew they planned to attend the same college.

The only suspense: *Where?*

"Cincinnati," LeMos disclosed at dinner, at The Butterfly Table, with Linc and Fayth joined for the big reveal by Tavis, Love, Hope, her husband Albert, and the couple's six-year-old daughter Grace. "We're gonna be Bearcats!"

While the twins would be realizing their goal of running intercollegiate track and cross-country, their ultimate decision rested primarily on academics not athletics: The University of Cincinnati had a proud reputation for preparing Pre-Med students for acceptance to medical schools, including its own. This dovetailed perfectly with Mos's aspirations of becoming a doctor.

Additionally, UC, located in the same city famed author Harriet Beecher Stowe once called home, offered an undergraduate degree in Creative Writing—as well as postgraduate Master of Fine Arts and PhD programs in the craft—ideal for Lem, who wanted to follow in his father's novelist footsteps as a storycatcher and storyteller.

One final factor clinched the deal—with the campus being less than a four-hour drive away, visits home would not be limited to Thanksgiving, Christmas, and Spring Break.

"You can bring your laundry as often as you like," Fayth teasingly enticed, then turned more serious: "You'll be close enough for us to come see some of your races."

"*All* of your races," Linc corrected. "Even another kidney stone won't keep me away."

For going away gifts Linc planned to write each twin a letter filled with cherished memories and thoughts of wisdom for this next exciting chapter on their life adventures. After beginning, and abandoning, several drafts, he realized there was really nothing new to tell his sons that he had not consistently imparted over the previous eighteen years. This awareness caused a deep warmth to surge through him for it meant he had succeeded as a father—Lem and Mos already knew his values, knew his immeasurable pride in them, and, above all, knew his unconditional love for them.

Linc came upon a second idea for a special gift. Shortly before Mos and Lem were to leave for their freshman year, he went to the bank and made a retrieval from a safety deposit box.

"I've told you the story a hundred times," Linc said that evening. "Now I think it's time you read it for yourselves. It's far more powerful to hold the pages of our family's history—yellowed pages damaged by water and stained by blood, pages infused with tears and sweat, pages filled with hopes and prayers—in your own hands as you relive it and revere it.

"I was going to scan the diary so you'd each have a PDF copy," Linc went on. "But that would be like looking at a photo of the Mona Lisa—it can't compare to seeing the masterpiece in person. It's the same with letters and diaries and books. In my opinion, that's why eBooks will never fully replace old-fashioned printed ones. When you hold a real book, your senses of touch and smell get involved. Turning the pages also reminds you of the passage of time—as the pages remaining to be read gets thinner and thinner, you feel the drama growing thicker because you know the story is nearing its end.

"Another thing, especially with older books that have been long forgotten on a back shelf in a library or second-hand bookstore, is that when you turn their pages you inhale a bibliophilic potpourri—olfactory whispers of dust and mustiness and nostalgia. It's a wonderful perfume that simply can't be duplicated. I think you'll find all of these magical elements in this little book."

His eloquent preamble finished, Linc handed LeMos their shared gift, on loan: Tamás's timeworn leather journal that had been saved from the waters of the "Jordan" river between Detroit and Canada, between slavery and freedom, between one life and one death.

Linc allowed a week's cushion for both boys to have time to read the diary cover to cover before departing for Cincinnati, but Lem and Mos began right then and stayed up into the wee morning hours taking turns reading it aloud to each other across The Butterfly Table in one sitting.

Final Mission

Tamás Beswick's diary contained magic beyond the words written within.

Even before being opened, the water-stained leather cover testified to its long-ago drenching in the Detroit River—known on the Underground Railroad as the "Jordan"—at freedom's edge. The edges of the pages, wavy from the soaking, added to this palpable narrative. The penciled printing, blanched almost to invisibility in some places, indelibly connected Lemuel and Moswen backward through the generations to Tamás for they could imagine him writing the entries during hiding breaks.

In the same manner caressing the patina grain of The Butterfly Table, eyes closed in a fusion of concentration and imagination and faith, could create a connection to forebearers who once sat around it, so did the journal possess a mystical nature. When LeMos tenderly drew their fingertips across the pages, yellowed and wrinkled and brittle, it was as though DNA traces left behind in Tamás's skin oils conveyed echoes of his spirit to the twins.

The delicate aromas drifting off different pages added to the ethereal experience. Turning to an entry where Tamás chronicled a stormy night on the trail, a whiff of the very rain that had seeped into the pencil's graphite *then* was released anew *now*. Turning to the page where Tamás wrote about a treacherous stretch traveling through dense woodland to shake off a slave catcher, pine tree scent and hints of musty fallen leaves were reawakened.

And on the back cover, a fist-sized bloodstain underscored the deathly fate of Tamás's final mission, about which Lem now read aloud:

This Railroad trip is my last one as a Conductor. I truly mean it this time. I feel a special bond with Sawney that I cannot explain fully. Society sees me as a man and him as a beast of burden but I see us as brothers. We are both dangerously seeking freedom. I am running from a murderous mistake and Sawney is escaping slavery's shackles. Does this not make us alike men? Would Sawney not be my Conductor if our skins were reversed? I know in my heart this is so! I wish to be a faithful brother to Sawney like Doc has been to me.

Pages later it was Mos's turn: *Harriet Stowe's great book Uncle Tom's Cabin has been my constant companion on the Underground RR. Today I read these powerful words—"Of course, in a novel, people's hearts break, and they die, and that is the end of it; and in a story this is very convenient. But in real life we do not die when all that makes life bright dies to us." Should I die guiding Sawney, I hope life's lights will continue to shine brightly on Aisha and Jamis and Lemuel.*

And this entry, the last in Tamás's hand, in Lem's voice: *I have never crossed The Jordan but tomorrow I shall. Tomorrow I must! The solemn duty to escort Sawney the final leg to Dawn's freedom falls on my shoulders and I pray they are broad enough and strong enough for the task. Facing this peril I draw courage from Isaiah 43:2—"When you go through deep waters, I will be with you. When you go through rivers of difficulty, you will not drown."*

Two blank pages followed those cryptic words before the next entry, in black ink, in cursive, began: *As told on 26 of May 1866 by Sawney Jordan a free man . . .*

Mos read the epilogue's closing sentences aloud, with Tamás's name misspelled: *Thomas was the best friend I ever did have. He was my brother. In my heart he's the greatest man I shall ever know.*

"That's exactly how I feel about you, Lem," Mos said, in an unguarded whisper, as he closed the journal with loving care.

"Me too, Mos—me too."

Barely had these heartfelt sentiments left their lips when the brothers each rested his weary head on The Butterfly Table, on arms folded, and drifted to sleep.

As the sins of the father can visit upon the son, so too can the blessings. As it had ages ago with the first Lemuel twin, and twice more with Lincoln, The Butterfly Table spoke now to LeMos.

Soulful Soliloquy

You two boys—no, fine young men—are about to set sail on a new journey.

College promises to be filled with fun and excitement, and also challenges. I am confident you will conquer all hardships ahead like brave knights slaying fire-breathing dragons.

Moswen and Lemuel, you come from a lengthy line of fearless knights and pathfinders—stonecatchers. Genes remember what minds forget; through your veins pulse their stony courage and bedrock integrity, their hopes and poise, faith and fight, goodness and love. These traits are your richest inheritances.

Darragh Jamison, father of the original Lemuel, fled famine and poverty in Ireland's County Cork at age fourteen. Alone, and still but a boy, he lied about his age—claiming to be a man of eighteen—in order to gain passage on a tall-masted merchant ship. While Darragh's genetic coding is not woven into your fibers, he passed along his last name and an example of fortitude as unbending as the trunk of my mighty ancestral Black Walnut Tree.

Tamás and Aisha's ocean crossing was similarly bold, yet their biggest challenges awaited in New York City. As Hungarian immigrants they were greeted by abundant bigotry—a malignancy still uncured by mankind.

As you both know, Moswen's light-colored skin is no shield from racism. Indeed, his "whiteness" oftentimes makes him an outsider in both Black and white communities.

Of course, Lemuel's visible "Blackness" makes racism a daily travail he must face. Press on, and stay strong, together.

Your parents were sagacious in selecting the names Moswen and Sawney to honor your African heritage. What proud roots these are! Sawney's daring escape from the chains of slavery on the Underground Railroad rivals the boundless perils of any ocean crossing I can imagine—with one exception.

That would be the ghastly voyage from West Africa endured by Sawney's father—or grandfather or great-grandfather, for only the Lord knows how many generations ago the wicked bondage of your family began. This much is certain: "The Door of No Return" on Senegal's Goree Island was the antithesis of the "Entrance to Escapees' Haven" that Sawney passed through—the latter held hope, the former only hopelessness.

American schoolbooks celebrate the Pilgrims' jeopardous journey to Plymouth, yet it paled to sailing—and surviving—the seas in a slave ship, in manacles, in evil inhuman conditions. Sinful as it was, you should be as supremely proud of this harrowing heritage as are Mayflower descendants of their ancestry.

Lemuel and Moswen, you are the seventh generation of your family I have known—and, yes, spoken to. While you should be proud of your forebearers, keep in mind we do not choose our lineage. Fate, or perhaps merely chance, fortuitously gave you exemplars to emulate and admire, not scoundrels to surmount and be ashamed of. With this gift comes the solemn obligation to honor your progenitors by lifting ensuing generations upon your sturdy shoulders.

During your life odysseys, I pray you will continually seek to ascend to a higher and higher purpose. This has been my golden blessing—I began as a tree providing a home and food to wildlife, shade and oxygen and beauty to humans; became a door, again part of a home; and am now this Table you cherish, bringing people together. Perhaps, come some future sunset, my calling shall soar higher still as the "canvas" for a masterpiece painting—the Mona Lisa is on a poplar panel, I'm proud to say—or as a concert violin or church pew.

~~~

In the morning, in the twilight between the dream world and wakefulness, their heads resting on The Butterfly Table with Tamás's diary lying between them, Moswen and Lemuel had similar unsettling visions.

Mos saw himself riding double on a bicycle with Lem as passenger. Suddenly, magically, they were each riding separate stingrays and veering away from one another down divergent sidewalks. As he pedaled out of earshot, Lem turned his head and shouted—

—but Mos could not make out the words.

Lem, meanwhile, saw himself and Mos running hip-to-hip in a cross-country race. Suddenly, inexplicably, Mos took a trail that split off. As the distance between them grew, Mos similarly hollered over his shoulder—

—but Lem's ears had fallen deaf.

Twins-Giving

As it had for seven generations, The Butterfly Table continued bringing people together.

Along with family, including grandparents Love and Tavis, Thanksgiving at the Jamison home was graced by a baker's dozen of Lemuel and Moswen's fellow students from the University of Cincinnati.

Two of the guests, Wayne and Bryan, were Mos and Lem's college roommates. Although the twins began freshman year sharing a dorm room, they interpreted their visions of cycling and running divergently when The Butterfly Table had spoken to them as signs to nurture a degree of independence from one another. As a first step, Lem swapped rooms and joined Bryan across the hallway while Wayne moved in with Mos. Elsewise, LeMos remained as inseparable as two sides of a running shoe after a tight tug on the laces.

Other guests were cross-country teammates, more dorm friends, and four classmates living too distant to travel home for the short holiday break. Lem and Mos did not bother asking Fayth for approval before extending invitations to everyone they knew, or simply learned of, who did not have a place to go for Thanksgiving. They were certain their mother's answer would be an enthusiastic, "Yes, of course! The more, the merrier!"

Fayth, after all, was never one to worry about too few chairs or fret over mismatched dishes and hodgepodge back-of-the-drawer silverware. Nor did she mind preparing a second menu—tofu turkey roll, cauliflower stuffing, vegetable gravy, dairy-free mashed potatoes—for attending vegans.

Hers was not faux kindness. Fayth genuinely saw a growing guest list not as added stress, but rather an opportunity for expanded joy. It was a trait she grew up seeing modeled by Love—including, of course, to a homeless teenage boy named Lincoln.

Love's innate big-hearted capacity for inclusivity was reinforced and magnified by the small-minded mother of her sophomore college roommate. Petra had invited Love home for Thanksgiving, but when she told her mother her mother told her to rescind the invitation. There simply would not be enough food for another guest or enough room, the mother asserted without empathy, as the dining room table was already a tight squeeze accommodating extended family members.

Dining on cold leftover pizza in solitude in her off-campus apartment that Thanksgiving evening, Love made a private oath to always *always* make room for one more guest—or three more, five more, even a dozen more. This gospel, through deed, was passed down to Fayth.

With an eleventh-hour supplemental shopping list in hand, Fayth cheerfully navigated the grocery aisles while Linc rushed out to buy eight folding chairs and two card tables. Four air mattresses were also borrowed. Where others might focus on the crowded chaos and additional work required, Fayth saw only the blessings of communal happiness and louder laughter and amplified love.

"This will be the best Thanksgiving ever," Fayth, almost in song, told Linc.

When "Twins-Giving" arrived, which is what LeMos's schoolmates nicknamed the holiday gathering, so did three carloads of company. All were welcomed with effusive hugs as tight as a Tupperware seal.

Two classmates were international students who had never celebrated Thanksgiving, so the holiday—Pilgrims and Indigenous Americans and their shared feast in 1621—was explained. In turn, the long-distance students shared rituals and meal traditions of their own homelands.

Despite shoehorned seating around The Butterfly Table, and bumping elbows, Fayth kept one chair next to her empty. When Linc asked why one of the college kids at a card table could not join them here, Fayth replied breezily: "Oh, it's just a silly superstition of mine to always have a seat ready for an unexpected guest."

Linc and the twins had never before heard Fayth say this—nor could any of them recall her ever purposely keeping an extra chair empty. All the same, all smiled, all knowing such a thoughtful gesture was true to her nature.

No sooner had young Grace finished leading the gathering in saying grace than a tentative *rap-rap-rap* came on the front door.

"Everyone, start eating," Fayth said. "I'll get it."

Out of view, the assemblage heard the front door open followed by Fayth's warm greeting: "Welcome, welcome. Of course we have room for one more!"

Mending Hug, Broken Glass

 "This is Vanessa," Fayth said in polite introduction of the late arrival.

Lincoln had not seen his mother in three decades and long ago assumed she was surely dead, likely from substance abuse. Otherwise, why had she never returned or at least phoned or written?

Feeling abandoned anew, old scars torn freshly open, Linc's reflexive reaction was seething anger. He lurched from his chair to storm out of the dining room. Just as abruptly, he halted. From his black hole of pain, light impossibly emerged; from bottled-up hate, came love; to Vanessa's great wonderment—and even more so, his own—Linc went to his mother and embraced her, tightly, warmly, longly.

Fayth, and Fayth alone, was not surprised by this sublime act of grace and forgiveness. When she invited Vanessa to Thanksgiving dinner, Fayth was certain her husband's better angels would prove more powerful than his demons.

Ever since Vanessa, out of the blue—and fresh out of another rehab center—first contacted Fayth eleven years prior to ask how Linc was doing, Fayth had been trying to orchestrate a mother-son reunion, without success. Thereafter, during clean and sober stretches, Vanessa periodically contacted her for updates that were happily given. Despite Fayth's heartfelt pleas, Vanessa always insisted on maintaining secrecy.

"It's better to let his memories of me fade and die," Vanessa reasoned to Fayth, "than risk breaking his heart over and over and over."

Having maintained a nun's sobriety for five years, by far her lengthiest span, Vanessa finally yielded to Fayth's entreaties. Rebelling against her worries, she agreed to see Linc—and, at long last, meet her twin grandsons.

Fayth explained none of this at the "Twins-Giving" gathering. Instead, she said nonchalantly: "Moswen, Lemuel—this is your grandmother. She's been doing poorly for a very long time, but now she's gotten well. I think this is a blessing worthy of giving extra thanks."

~~~

Thanksgiving yielded to a Friday of putting up Christmas decorations and then a Saturday night of spirited board games.

LeMos and three classmates were playing *Monopoly* on The Butterfly Table. The rest of the Cincy students had departed earlier in the day; these five would drive back to campus on Sunday.

After his roll of the dice, resulting in bankruptcy for landing on Boardwalk—with a hotel—and owing Bryan two thousand dollars, Mos went to get a soda from the refrigerator. Suddenly, the sound of breaking glass made all heads swivel.

Mos had not dropped a drinking glass back in the kitchen—

—a window had shattered at the front of the house.

Glass crackled again and this time everyone heard the sharp *Pop!* of a firecracker.

"Get down!" Mos demanded with urgency. "That's gunfire!"

Instinctively, Mos reacted like the hero in Kipling's "If" by *forcing his heart and nerve and sinew* into action. In three *Huck-le-ber-ry Finns* time, he dashed from the kitchen into the dining room and shoved The Butterfly Table forward, sliding it over and past his twin brother and their three friends all crouching on the floor, and in the same continuous motion flipped The Butterfly Table onto its side to create a rampart. Next, his heart racing a metric-mile a minute, Mos pushed everyone down lower and blanketed his body atop them as a human shield.

The odds in life are dished out in lightning strikes and cancer cells, in blind dates and blind curves, in a human embryo splitting identically in two—and also in a domestic altercation across the street escalating violently.

The first two 9mm bullets sailed into the house at high trajectories, both impacting the far wall of the kitchen near the ceiling. A spray of three shots followed, all striking The Butterfly Table-turned-bulwark. These slugs bounced off the supernaturally hardened black walnut surface as if it were inch-thick steel plating, harmlessly leaving behind three impression scars arranged in a perfect triangle.

A sixth and final bullet hit The Butterfly Table's Achilles' heel—the yin-yang symbol of white oak and dark maple filling the hole where a doorknob had originally been. It struck the circle inlay at the six o'clock mark, knocking it free.

As it passed through the opening, the bullet ricocheted sharply.

Rare Bloom

"There's a flowering plant named Agave Americana," Reverend Luther Douglass told a grey sea of tearful mourners, the high tide overflowing beyond the pews into standing room only at the sides and rear of Second Baptist Church of Cleveland Heights.

"It is a desert plant native to Mexico and found throughout most of California and Florida, as well as southern Texas and Louisiana," The Reverend explained. "Indigenous Americans once used it for soap and weaving, food and liquors, even medicine.

"Today, Agave Americana is more commonly called the Century Plant because its flowers are so extremely patient in blooming. The name is actually hyperbolic, for each plant blooms once in a human generation's time rather than only every hundred years. Indeed, it typically grows for about two decades before finally flowering—just once—and soon thereafter dies.

"Imagine a plant that normally blooms annually, but instead saves up all of its flowers over a span of twenty years before revealing them in a single appearance—that is what the Century Plant does. Monet and Renoir and O'Keeffe, all together, could not do this spectacle justice.

"To give you a mental painting, the Century Plant's long spiked leaves fountain out at the end of a stalk reaching fifteen feet skyward—this on top of the plant's eight-foot-high base—before exploding in a bloom of opal-gem-like golden radiance spreading a breadth of a dozen feet. Because the flowers are so rare, and so short-lived, they are all the more amazing to behold.

"Our beloved Moswen was very much like the Century Plant. He did not live long enough, not even closely so—only an Agave Americana-like nineteen years—before being taken from us. But what a spectacularly beautiful flower Moswen was! Indeed, each of us blessed to have seen Moswen bloom, to have known him and loved him—which is truly one and the same thing, for to *know* Moswen was to *love* him—will forever remember his radiant flower."

Reverend Douglass, now past eighty, his waterfall beard now froth white, had traveled from Detroit to Cleveland Heights to give the eulogy for Moswen Thomas Jamison. It was the third time he had been a voice of value to Lincoln. Their first meeting, in Detroit's Second Baptist Church when Linc received Tamás's Underground Railroad diary, had been about questioned faith; the second time, in this very church, was about marriage and love; now it was about love and heartache.

Reverend Douglass met Linc's red-rimmed eyes in the family's front pew, gave a doleful tight-lipped smile, then turned his solemn gaze to Lem and spoke directly to him: "All of us here today are grieving, but none more deeply than you, Lemuel, for you have lost a brother, a twin, an identical piece of yourself.

"I had a dream last night, Lemuel," The Reverend continued, "in which I saw you stargazing—and weeping. You were peering at Gemini, the zodiacal constellation comprising the mythological Greek twins Castor and Pollux. You were inconsolable because half of the twinkling stars in Gemini, the Castor half, had gone dark, their heavenly light having died, just as Moswen's earthly light has gone out."

Reverend Douglass's eyes glistened with mourning's salty dew and he fell silent, removed his glasses and breathed humidly on one of lenses, wiped it clean with a handkerchief, then repeated the process with the other lens. His composure regained, The Reverend replaced his glasses and resumed his oration.

"When I awakened, I was weeping and continued to do so for a good long while. Suddenly, a lovely understanding came to me and dried my tears. I realized I'd been looking at my dream all wrong—that you, Lemuel, in my dream were looking at the constellation all wrong.

"The darkened stars of Castor do not represent Moswen—it is Pollux's stars shimmering with light that are Moswen! Our beloved Moswen is likewise now shining brightly in heaven. No, the unlighted half of Gemini is you, Lemuel, awaiting your arrival to join your twin brother before lighting up.

"As beautiful as this reunion will be," Reverend Douglass concluded, his head now bowed, "let us pray it is a very long, long time away."

Selfless Love

 Lem stood atop The Butterfly Table, barefoot, bare of will.

Earlier that day Moswen was buried in Bellaire, in Lemuel "Doc" Jamison Memorial Park, in the small private family plot where the leviathan Black Walnut Tree once majestically overlooked the Ohio River below.

Now nearing midnight, back in Cleveland Heights, Fayth and Linc were upstairs in bed, failing at falling asleep. The parents' grief was unspeakable; Lem's unbearable. He was but half of a pair of broken scissors, a flightless one-winged eagle, yin without yang. Having come from the same embryo as his identical twin, he felt that half of his own soul perished when a thirty-nine-cent bullet stole Mos's priceless young life.

Lem resolved to finish the half-done tragedy.

After securing an extension cord used for the Christmas lights to an overhead beam, solid and sturdy, he began fashioning a noose. As he did so, The Butterfly Table tried to speak to Lem, talk sense into him, save him. But as in a nightmare, no matter how loudly The Butterfly Table screamed, its voice remained muted.

This was the second time The Butterfly Table had been in a suicidal situation. Decades earlier, while on loan to the Matthew Murphy Memorial Library in Bellaire, a high school girl used to do homework on and read—Jane Austen novels being her dearest—at The Butterfly Table daily after school.

With autumn's cornucopia of warm colors giving way to winter's cold greys, the girl's world became sunless. Constant bullying made her shrink, withdraw, spiral. She developed an eating disorder. Misery, and Miss Austen, were her only companions. Oftentimes her buckeye-brown eyes were so blurred by tears she merely pretended to read.

The Butterfly Table tried to speak to the chestnut-haired girl, tried to warn the librarian and others, but its urgent pleas went unheard. One fateful day, the girl wrote a suicide note—her "i's" ironically dotted with tiny happy hearts—while sitting at The Butterfly Table. She never returned. The Butterfly Table hoped against hope the girl transferred schools, and received professional help, and found healing.

Now it was Lem who needed rescue. Standing on The Butterfly Table, he took a final moment to relive cherished memories of his parents and friends and, of course, twin brother.

The Butterfly Table, as well, reminisced. It thought about the seven generations of this family it had known and loved. It recollected experiencing the birth of a baby, the conception of another life, also Doc riding to heaven on Halley's Comet and a full rainbow of events between these spectrums. People had sewn quilts on The Butterfly Table; studied for college and medical school exams upon it; talked and laughed and shared their lives while sitting around it. The Butterfly Table could not bear to add a sorrowful suicide to this memoir.

Love is infinite things, but perhaps above all it is putting another person's life ahead of one's own.

Examination afterward would reveal one of The Butterfly Table's legs gave out under the weight of Lem's 158 pounds. That is not what truly happened. A six-hundred-pound circus tiger had once pounced upon The Butterfly Table and it held solid. That stony sturdiness had not measurably diminished with age.

Here is the truth. Focusing all of its love on a single wooden peg that helped secure the leg nearest where Lem stood, The Butterfly Table, with absolute selflessness, indomitably *willed* the peg to wiggle loose; *willed* it to weaken; finally *willed* it to snap in two as though cleaved by a thunderbolt.

With that, every moment to follow was forever changed.

The Butterfly Table trembled and teetered, then divorced lengthwise between the wedded halves of the lovely butterfly knot and Lem plunged as if a gallows trapdoor had swung open—

—*before* putting the makeshift noose around his neck.

Lying on the woodpile, squarely on his back, Lem saw the string of unlit Christmas lights swaying overhead and had an epiphany, a resurrection of purpose: *I have an obligation to carry on Mos's life through how I live mine.*

Lacking the aptitude to fulfill Moswen's dream of becoming a doctor, Lemuel would honor Mos's memory by achieving his own dream of being an author.

Epilogue: A Good Life

On the first anniversary of Moswen's death, Lemuel visited his brother's grave, alone.

Lem's experience that afternoon, as autumn battled to hold off winter's arrival, became the closing scene in his debut novel, a work of historical/autobiographical fiction that would be published four years thereafter by BarkingBoxer Press. Opening with the dedication, "For Mos—my twin, my best friend, my stonecatcher," the final pages of *The Butterfly Tree: An Extraordinary Saga of Seven Generations* read thusly:

It was three days following Thanksgiving and the season's first dusting of snow, from yesterday, had melted. The sun was shining, and warmly so, briefly cloaking November's end as being the beginning of Spring.

On this strawberries-in-wintertime-like afternoon, Lem strode across the Ohio landscape, the same grounds Iroquois and Shawnee First Peoples far back made their home, the same smiling countryside later surveyed by a young George Washington, the same pastoral parcel Lemuel's ancestors trod for nearly two centuries.

Near the crest of Doc Jamison Memorial Park, where the landmark black walnut Butterfly Tree once touched the sky, now a noble family tree of modest headstones rose within a small rectangular plot, immaculately manicured, and bordered by a hip-high black wrought-iron fence.

Lem considered how his family tree, like fruit trees, had prospered from grafting. Instead of the upper "scion" of a plant being combined with the lower "rootstock" of a different variety, different families were joined for the better. First, Beswick was grafted to Jamison when Doc assumed guardianship of twins Jamis and Lemuel. Future forth, Jamison was grafted to Jordan when Tavis and Love took in the rootless Lincoln.

Lem carried this lovely thought of diversity further, to how The Butterfly Table had been richer and more beautiful for having maple legs and a white oak skirt wedded to its black walnut surface; lovelier blending still, Linc's interracial marriage to Fayth; loveliest of all, how his and Mos's differences, despite being identical twins, enriched them as individuals.

As he made his winding way to Mos's grave, Lem paused and stooped, with repetition, picking up wayward small stones. Arriving, he arranged these tokens—selected for their smoothness as being good for throwing, and thus worthy of catching—in a neat row atop his twin's headstone, knee-high and granite and one-year new.

He saved a single stone, very flat and round, perfect for skipping on a pond, and solemnly balanced it on another headstone, this one patinaed by time and weather and lichen and moss.

Dr. Lemuel Darragh Jamison
July 4, 1826 – May 19, 1910

Lemuel did so not just to honor his namesake from the distant past, but also to pay homage to Moswen's dream for a future career. Lem reflected on the engraved poem:

A Good Life

The worker dies, but the work lives on
Whether a picture, a book, or a clock
Ticking the minutes of life away
For another worker in metal or rock
My work was with children and women and men—
Not iron, not brass, not wood
And I hope as I lay my stethoscope down
That my Chief will call it "good"
                              —"Doc"

Lem took an extended moment to mentally rewrite the ending stanza about A Good Life he desired:
My work is with words and plots and themes—
Not sutures, X-rays, nor stethoscope
And when I lay my keyboard to rest
That Mos will call it "Good" I do hope

Thinking further of A Good Life, Lemuel recalled something Grandpa Tavis once told him and Moswen—

"One must wait until evening to see how splendid the day has been. In the meantime, make each day your masterpiece. If you do so, evening promises to be splendid indeed."

After Mos died—LeMos perishing, too—Lem thought he would never again have a masterpiece day. Doc similarly had felt fully broken the first times he visited the graves of Constance and Alycia, graves that now bookended his own.

"Be patient, son," Linc had told Lem after finding him sobbing atop the collapsed ruins of The Butterfly Table. "Love requires patience. We grieve at the depth we love, Lem—so you will grieve the most for Mos, the longest, the deepest. Be patient with yourself."

Epilogue Part II: *Pretty Thoughts*

 Lem's debut novel concluded:

On the first anniversary of Moswen's death, Lemuel settled himself on one of two identical Benches positioned together, forming a V, near the ridge of Doc Jamison Memorial Park.

The Benches featured handsome stonework bases of dark grey flint, the state rock of Ohio, with each seat of burnished black walnut measuring nearly seven feet long. Lemuel whistle-hummed faintly as he admired with familiarity, and with his fingertips, one of the mirror image knots resembling butterfly—or, perhaps, angel—wings.

"One day, my grave will be here too, Mos," Lem avowed in hushed reverence. "In the meanwhile—a long, long meanwhile, I hope—I'll try to make each day a masterpiece, like you always did."

Still mourning deeply, Lem smiled genuinely. He realized The Butterfly Table had been granted its wish, for surely being a pair of Benches here—at this outdoor cathedral viewing a beloved family plot, at this beautiful public park overlooking the river—was a higher calling than as a kitchen table, concert violin, even church pew.

Lemuel's smile lingered. He felt blessed that so many of his forebearers had pursued their own higher callings, had not pawned their dreams for security—had, in truth, often done the exact opposite. He vowed to likewise pursue his writing dreams, doggedly and undaunted by any roadblocks the odyssey ahead held.

Despite the springtime feel in the air, the trees were bare of leaves and muted of birdsong symphony; all feathers had flown south. Lemuel's only company was a fox squirrel, buxom with winter's thick fur, ten yards nearby. Shortly, the bushy-tailed companion scampered off, quick as a lightning bolt, carrying a black walnut—a snack soon perhaps, or maybe dinner during the coming long cold months.

It was at this precise spot the magnificent Butterfly Tree had sprouted exactly four hundred springs earlier. Now, a new black walnut sapling took its place beside the two new Benches, a stone's throw—by a strong and able arm—from the western bank of the Ohio River.

"The Butterfly Tree's ancient decayed roots are nourishing the young living shoots reaching down," Lem thought, then: "As Hemingway wrote, 'Isn't it pretty to think so?'"

Someday, with rain and sunshine from above and nutrients and minerals from below, and a nod from the gods, this sapling would become a Herculean tree in its own right, providing shade to those who sit on these twin Benches—but that day remained distant in the future.

Wider still became Lemuel's smile as he recalled his father Lincoln's words five months past, when together they had planted this black walnut sapling: "It's a mighty fine thing, son, to plant a tree whose shade you shall never enjoy."

Lem closed his eyes and imagined seven ensuing generations of descendents, sitting here, enjoying the cooling shade that his aging parents never would. Whistle-humming anew, he became immersed deeper in thought.

Eyes still shut, Lem had a vision, a familiar vision from eight years previous. He saw himself and Moswen running side by side in a cross-country race. Suddenly, inexplicably, Mos veered off down a divergent trail. As the distance between them widened, Mos turned and shouted over his shoulder—

—but this time, unlike when he originally saw it play out, Lem was not deaf to his identical twin's words, hearing clearly: "I'll be thinking of you until we're together again."

Lemuel, in a velvety whisper, now replied: "Me too, Mos—me too."

Although the annual great migration of Monarch butterflies to Mexico took place two months prior, suddenly, inexplicably, a lone ebony-and-apricot jewel appeared in flight. The afternoon sun reflected off its silken wings, turning them luminous as a magnificent opal.

In Native American culture, butterflies serve as the archetype of metamorphosis and a symbol of resurrection. This belief enveloped Lem as he watched the lone Monarch float float float toward him and land on his knee. He sat, breath held, daring not move so as to enjoy its company as long as possible.

After a spell, the butterfly lifted airborne, leisurely, like a dandelion seed carried on an angel's breath of a breeze, orbited Lemuel once, then a second time, followed by a third, and flitted away.

Dear Reader,

The philosophical question, "If a tree falls in a forest and no one is around to hear it, does it make a sound?" has never resonated truly with me. After all, a fox squirrel or raccoon, blue jay or brown bear, or some other nearby wildlife resident, would surely hear the toppled tree crash to the ground, to say nothing of the thunderous air vibrations—sound—caressing the neighboring trees and grass and ponds and streams.

A better question, it seems to me, is this: "If a book is written and no one reads it, does that make it merely a bound-and-covered pile of paper?"

To be read, however, a book must first be found—on a bookstore shelf or library stacks or online site. For authors who have not previously attained Bestseller List status, this is a needle-in-a-haystack challenge.

And so, with hat in hand—metaphorically, Doc's favorite green felt derby—I ask you a favor: If you enjoyed *The Butterfly Tree*, please write a review on Amazon, Goodreads or the likes. Your review, even a single sentence, makes a surprisingly huge difference!

Too, please recommend *The Butterfly Tree* to your friends and also share on social media. Perhaps, even, consider doing as Coach John Wooden once encouraged me with one of his books: "Woody, why don't you buy one as a gift for a friend for no special occasion other than to make friendship a fine art."

For reading *The Butterfly Tree*, I consider you my friend and thank you sincerely,

Woody
March 2024

Acknowledgements

Let me begin, taking a roundabout path, with a wheat field in early autumn, in Ohio, in a common farm town, perhaps not far from where The Butterfly Tree in these pages once majestically rose. The story goes like this . . .

A small girl wandered away from home and became lost in the family's wheat crop that had grown taller than she. Upon discovering their daughter missing, her parents called out her name—loud, Loud, LOUDER, and repeatedly—but no answer came.

The little girl's three older brothers urgently spread out searching, and neighbors and townsfolk soon joined in. But as daylight dimmed, then disappeared, the little girl had not been found. The wheat field was simply too big, a vast ocean of golden grain, she a tiny dinghy lost at sea.

Night fell and rapidly the temperature followed. If the little girl were not found, very soon, she would surely perish from hypothermia on this eerie moonlit night.

At long last, her father called everyone in from the wheat field. No, he had not given up on finding his dear daughter. Rather, he had an idea. He instructed the volunteers to join hands and form a long human chain—more accurately, a human comb. Walking together, side by side by side, they combed through the amber waves without missing any areas, as had happened when searching separately, frantically, haphazardly.

Within minutes, the search party of more than one hundred individuals, now united as one, found the little girl curled up on the ground in the fetal position, eyes closed as if fast asleep—

—but shivering and still alive!

Bringing a book to life similarly requires many, many linked hands, and I would like to acknowledge a few here.

Thanks out of the gate to Geoffrey Simpson, publisher of BarkingBoxer Press and now my friend, for believing in my tale—and to you, dear reader, for believing in the magic of books, specifically this one.

Speaking of boxers, thanks to Murray who, before passing away, was a constant furry companion at my feet while I wrote the first draft of this manuscript.

Thanks, posthumously, to binate exemplars John Wooden—for being one of my cornerstone role models and mentors who still heartens me to *Make each day my masterpiece*—and Jim Murray—for inspiring me to become a writer and later, to my great fortune, befriending me.

Wholehearted thanks to Tavis Smiley, a Hoosier like Coach Wooden and likewise a human lighthouse always guiding the way, for inspiring me more than he can know.

Thank you to Bianca Blasquez for her absolutely beautiful tree and butterfly artwork on the front cover.

I remain grateful to Dave Stancliff, my first newspaper editor way back in the time machine, for more than once telling this fresh-out-of-college greenhorn that he liked my columns even better Jim Murray's—that sweet lie, and his continued friendship, have buoyed me ever since.

There are too many newspaper colleagues and writer friends to thank individually—I trust they know who they are—but special mention must go to the "Deadwoods" who most assuredly know who they are; and also to Rhiannon Potkey, Jeffrey Dransfeldt, and Barry Kibrick.

It is a fool's errand to try to single out every friend who merits mention, but nonetheless I would be foolish in failing to thank Connie Halpern and Alicia Stratton, bookend readers of early *TBT* drafts, for the sustenance they add to my life, and Mikey Weinberg-Lynn similarly.

With the words of E. B. White in mind—"It is not often that someone comes along who is a true friend and a good writer"— I raise a Guinness—"sláinte!"—to Ken McAlpine, a *great* writer who is the *truest* of true friends.

Great gratitude is insufficient for Wayne Bryan, possibly the most uplifting person on earth, who has been a cornerstone mentor since I was twelve and remains so.

A big hug to my Li'l Sis, Kym, a blessing in my life for a million reasons; and no small thanks as well are forever owed my two big brothers, Jim and Doug, and Pop.

Enduring thanks to Mom, unbelievably gone for half my lifetime now, for taking me to get a library card before I could read and later, in a family tree tall and leafed with physicians, encouraging me to follow my writing dreams.

Posthumous gratitude to Grandpa Ansel, my abiding North Star—and a role model for Doc in these pages, including his poem "A Good Life" borrowed verbatim.

Loving thanks to my son, Greg, for infinite reasons, not least for being well worthy of his middle name Ansel, and also for his own original poems that inspired some of Jeffrey's poetry in this novel.

Loving thanks, also for infinite reasons, to my daughter (and favorite author), Dallas, whose wise writing counsel and eagle editing eye helped me wax, buff, and polish *The Butterfly Tree* to the glossiest sheen possible.

Loving thanks, too, to my growing family tree's newest branches: Allyn, Maya, and Auden; and Jess and Amara.

Lastly, passionate thankfulness to the lovely brunette standing under the mistletoe at a college party—Lisa, you still make my heart flutter with butterflies.

About the Author

Woody Woodburn was born in Columbus, Ohio, in 1960; spent his adolescence in the '70s on the sweet-and-salty-aired coast of Southern California, and graduated from UC Santa Barbara; and for the past four decades has been a national award-winning newspaper columnist—sports originally and general interest for the past fifteen years.

Now writing for *The Ventura County Star*, his honors include Columnist of the Year by the Associated Press News Executive Council, Copley News Service, and E. W. Scripps Newspapers; and induction into The Jim Murray Memorial Foundation's Journalists Hall of Fame and Ventura County Sports Hall of Fame as a journalist.

Woody's work has also appeared in *The Best American Sports Writing* anthology and more than a dozen *Chicken Soup For The Soul* titles, and he is the author of two nonfiction books—the memoir *Wooden & Me: Life Lessons from My Two-Decade Friendship with the Legendary Coach and Humanitarian to Help "Make Each Day Your Masterpiece"* and *Strawberries in Wintertime: Essays on Life, Love, and Laughter.*

When he is not tapping away on a QWERTY keyboard, Woody can be found padding the pavement, park grass or local beaches as a "Streaker" who has run a minimum of three miles (and averaged 11.4 miles) every day without fail since July 7, 2003, for one of the longest officially recognized running streaks in the world.

"Woody's Holiday Ball Drive" has enjoyed an even longer streak while donating nearly one million dollars of new sports balls to underprivileged youth.

Longer still, Woody has a marriage streak of forty-one years with his college sweetheart Lisa.

Woody's Contact Information:

woodywriter@gmail.com
www.woodywoodburn.com
Instagram @woodywoodburn

Printed in Great Britain
by Amazon

40454189R00215